# DEAD VALLEY

Anthony Giangregorio

OTHER BOOKS BY ANTHONY GIANGREGORIO

**THE DEAD WATER SERIES**

DEADWATER
DEADWATER: Expanded Edition
DEADRAIN
DEADCITY
DEADWAVE
DEAD HARVEST
DEAD UNION
DEAD VALLEY

**ALSO BY THE AUTHOR**

REVOLUTION OF THE DEAD
DEAD RECKONING: DAWNING OF THE DEAD
THE MONSTER UNDER THE BED
DEAD END: A ZOMBIE NOVEL
DEAD TALES: SHORT STORIES TO DIE FOR
DEAD MOURNING: A ZOMBIE HORROR STORY
ROAD KILL: A ZOMBIE TALE
DEADFREEZE
DEADFALL
DEADRAGE
SOUL-EATER
THE DARK
RISE OF THE DEAD
DARK PLACES

VISIONS OF THE DEAD
(by Joseph Giangregorio and Anthony Giangregorio)

DEAD WORLDS: Undead Tales (Contributing story and editor)

## Acknowledgments

Thanks to my wife, Jody, and my son, Joseph, for all their help on this and every other book I have written. Without their tireless efforts, none of these books would have been possible. And to all those who have reached out to me over the past year, I owe each of you a debt of gratitude.
Thank you.

## Author's Note

This book was self-edited, and though I tried my absolute best to correct all grammar mistakes; there may be a few here and there.
Please accept my sincerest apology for any errors you may find.

Visit my web site at undeadpress.com

# DEAD VALLEY

For more info on obtaining additional copies of this book, contact:

www.livingdeadpress.com

# WHAT HAS COME BEFORE

One year ago, a deadly bacterial outbreak escaped a lab to infect the lower atmosphere across America, unleashing an undead plague on the world.

With rain clouds now filled with a killer virus, to venture outside in the rain was tantamount to suicide.

To get caught in the rain and exposed to the bacteria would be an instant death. But that wasn't the end. Once dead, the host body would rise again, becoming an undead ghoul, wanting nothing more than to feed on the flesh of the living.

The United States was torn asunder, civilization collapsing like a house of cards in weeks.

But mankind survived, eking out a dreary existence, always keeping one eye on the sky for the next rainstorm.

Only two years after the zombie apocalypse, the world has become a very different place from what it once was. Gone are cell phones, the internet, restaurants and shopping malls; now all lost relics of a culture slowly fading into history.

In this new world, the dead walk and a man follows the rules of the gun, where the strong are always right and the weak are usually dead. Major cities are nothing but blackened husks, nothing but giant tombs filled with walking corpses. Across America, though, smaller towns have become small municipalities with makeshift walls protecting them from both living and dead attackers. Strangers are not welcome and are either shot on sight or made to move on, that is, if they are not exploited by the rulers of the towns.

Through the destruction of what once was walks a man, crushing death beneath his steel-tipped boots. Before, he was an ordinary man, living a quiet life with a wife and a career, but the rules have changed and so to, has he adapted, becoming a warrior of death who wields a gun with an iron hand, but shows mercy and wisdom when it is needed.

His name is Henry Watson, and with his fellow companions, Mary, Jimmy, Cindy, Sue and Raven by his side, he travels across a blighted landscape searching for someplace where the undead haven't corrupted everything they touch; where he can lay his head down in safety.

Though life is fleeting, each breath means the possibility of one more day of life, and a better future for all.

# Chapter 1

"Get in a circle and watch your backs, don't let any of them get behind you!" Henry Watson screamed at the top of his lungs, his voice hoarse from spouting countless orders.

"There's too many of them, Henry, we can't hold them all off!" Jimmy Cooper snapped back, shooting a dead man in the head with the full brunt of his pump-action shotgun. The head disappeared in a glorious spray of blood and gore, the undead mob behind the now headless body becoming splattered with brown and black ichor.

"I know there's too many of them, dammit, but we don't have any choice!" Henry screamed back over the cacophony of gunfire.

"What do we do?" A woman's voice asked.

Henry glanced to his right to see Mary Roberts, her long brown hair blowing in the wind, her eyes hard as she fired round after round at the undead crowd. On her shoulder was the M-16 she had used only minutes ago, but now the weapon was empty, as was the ammunition bag on her hip.

"I'm out!" Another woman's voice called.

Henry glanced to his other side to see Cindy Jansen, her golden blonde hair and attractive features now warped into something feral. The woman pulled a .45 from her hip and began blasting the undead crowd, but for every one she took down, there were five more to take its place.

Slightly to his side, was a teenage girl named Raven. She was a dervish; her razor-sharp finger nails slicing into eyes and severing jugulars. Her feet were blurs as she kicked ghouls away from her, snapping spines and cracking skulls like a machine, her ink-black hair dancing around her like a living entity.

"Henry, help me!" Another woman's voice called, and the instant Henry heard it, he knew who it was.

Sue Anders was being surrounded and Henry knew he had to act or she was done for. One bite of those fetid teeth and she would become one of them either by infection or death, only to return later as one of the walking dead.

"Get down!" He ordered her and she obeyed immediately.

Swinging his 9mm Glock around, Henry double-tapped the trigger twice, sending four lead slugs into the two ghouls closest to her. Raven spotted the problem Sue was in and she lunged towards the last two ghouls, kicking one so hard it hit the railing of the bridge they were trapped on to tumble away into space and the churning water below.

"You okay?" Henry asked quickly.

Sue nodded and moved closer to Jimmy so he could protect her.

This new world of death and violence wasn't her way, and though it sometimes made her a burden, it was also what made Henry love her. Her innocence even in the face of so much destruction and hopelessness kept him going and he thanked God for the thousandth time that he'd found her.

Henry shot another ghoul in the face and scowled deeply.

How had they got into this situation? And worse, how the hell were they going to get out of it?

The wind cooled his sweaty brow and he shot a look to his front and back, seeing the open air all around him. The six companions were on a bridge in the middle of Colorado, and below them, the choppy waves of the Colorado River snapped at one another, as if they were clapping in thanks for the show being played above.

The moaning of the dead floated across the wind to caress his ears and it sent a chill down his spine.

They were trapped like mice in a cage. Both sides of the bridge, once called the North Colorado River Bridge, was filled with the animated corpses. There was nowhere to go and they were quickly running out of ammunition.

Jimmy expelled his spent shells and loaded new ones on the fly. A ghoul got too close and he swung the butt of the shotgun around, cracking the dead woman in the mouth with it. The dead woman began spitting teeth, bloody drool joining the mix, and Jimmy pumped the weapon and jammed it under her chin.

"Eat this if you're so damn hungry," he snarled and then fired, blowing her head clean off her shoulders. The body stumbled around for almost a minute before the feet tripped up and the corpse dropped to the asphalt of the bridge.

Henry fired again and then cursed when the gun cycled dry. With smooth precision, he popped out the spent clip and slammed another in, shoving the old clip into a pocket for later. They were becoming rarer than gold and he knew he couldn't toss them away like before, back when ammunition and weapons had been plentiful.

But with the dead walking for almost two years now, the gun shops and factories were closed and the way the world had existed was no more.

Henry fired four more times, taking three ghouls down with the shots, the fourth going wide and only striking a pale and bloated neck. Blood geysered from the wound, followed by a hissing sound, as the ghoul expelled air through its new air hole.

"Jesus Christ, Henry, this shit is bad, what the hell are we gonna do?" Jimmy yelled as he shot another ghoul in the chest. The torso exploded outward, ribs sticking out like daggers to impale another ghoul, the two dancing together as they tried to become extricated.

Henry was thinking that very same thing and he realized there was only one way they could go.

"We have to jump!"

"Jump? Jump where?" Mary called out, firing three times at a pair of dead teenagers.

"We have to jump off the bridge!" Henry told her.

"That's crazy," Cindy added. "We're too high up; it's got to be at least eighty feet to the water! We'll never survive the fall."

"Do you have any better ideas? Huh, anyone?" Henry inquired and shot a dead housewife in the left eye, the head snapping back as the ghoul dropped to the ground.

They had less than a minute before the main crowd was on them, both sides seeming to be moving as one unit.

When that happened, there would be so many bodies there would be no way they could survive the attack.

"The old man's right, we got no choice," Raven spit. She didn't speak much so when she did, the others usually listened.

Mary wanted to add her two cents to the mix, but realized there was no point.

She too could see their predicament and realized the only choice was to wait to be overrun or take their chances in the icy cold water below.

"So when do we go?" Jimmy asked, glancing to Cindy for confirmation. The two lovers were inseparable and had been since they had met.

"We go now!" Henry screamed. "Right now, no more talking, just go!"

Shooting three more ghouls, he grabbed Sue's hand and dragged her with him, the others following.

As they lined up along the railing, the bridge appeared even higher than before. The height wasn't so imposing they wouldn't survive, but it was borderline.

Still, better a quick death in the frigid water below than to be torn apart only to come back as one of the walking dead.

"So we're really gonna do this, huh?" Jimmy asked.

"Yeah, we are. Just remember to keep your legs together when you hit the water and make sure your weapons are secured.

"Who's first?" Mary asked, swallowing the knot in her throat as she gazed down to the water below. She had never liked heights and now was no different, especially when she was about to leap into space.

"I'll go," Raven said, and before anyone could stop her, she climbed onto the railing and leaped off, her body arcing like she was cliff diving.

Jimmy spun and took out three ghouls that were too close and realized it was now or never.

"You ready, babe?" Jimmy asked Cindy, the woman nodding quickly, the trepidation on her features apparent.

"Go, dammit, there's no time!" Henry shouted, shooting three more zombies and knowing he was about to run out of ammo any second.

Jimmy and Cindy climbed onto the railing, and hand in hand, they kissed once and stepped out into space, their bodies plummeting to the water below.

"Go, Mary, it's your turn!" Henry yelled at her, then shot two more walking corpses who were at his back. They had seconds now before there wouldn't be enough bullets in all of America to stop the undead moving towards them.

She nodded, secured her weapons, made sure her backpack was secured, and then climbed the railing.

"You better be right behind me," she said to Henry.

He flashed her a tight grin. "You know it, honey, just try and stop me."

She nodded, knowing to put it off any longer was meaningless, so she stepped into the void and dropped from view.

"Now you, Sue, get up there!" Henry screamed.

"But what about you?"

"I'm right behind you, now hurry up, damn you!"

She did as she was told though she was shaking in terror. When she was on the railing, she hesitated.

"I can't do this, Henry, I'm sorry, but I can't!"

Henry shot another zombie in the forehead and then backed up so he was standing right next to her, her feet even with his chest.

"Yeah, you can," he said abruptly, and then reached up and pushed her on the butt. She lost her balance and screamed, falling.

"Sorry," he said as he watched her drop away from the railing.

Now it was his turn and he climbed up onto the thin railing, holstering the Glock so he wouldn't lose it. His sixteen inch panga was riding his hip and the sheath was secured, so he was confident it would survive the fall, but as he did this, he didn't see the three ghouls sneaking up on him, their arms reaching out to tackle him while they climbed onto the railing like a suicide club ready to go through with their pact.

Henry punched one, his fist sinking deep into the putrid flesh, the blow doing nothing; but then he felt himself lose his balance. The three ghouls were still secured to him, growling and fetid breath filling his senses with death and decay.

The four bodies tumbled from the bridge, the ghouls ignoring their predicament, and Henry found himself battling for his life as he plummeted to the water below.

While he fell, the wind whipping his hair and slapping him in the face, he had visions of brown and yellow teeth trying to bite him.

He punched and pushed at the bodies as he fell towards the water like a lead weight and realized in the back of his mind he was all mixed up.

He knew in an instant he wasn't going to be able to strike the water the correct way, and if he did it wrong, it was possible he would shatter every bone in his body.

He jammed a hand under a jaw as teeth tried to snap at his face, the teeth clicking on nothing.

And then, like he had been bitch slapped by God Himself, he struck the water with the three ghouls still attached to him.

The impact knocked every ounce of oxygen from his lungs and he saw white stars flood his vision. Cold water surrounded him and seeped into every open orifice.

And as he sank into the watery depths of darkness, he lost consciousness.

# Chapter 2

Slowly, consciousness seeped back to Henry's befuddled mind.

Opening his eyes a hair, he instantly closed them when bright sunlight blasted his retinas.

His head was killing him and it felt like someone had sucked his brains from his head, leaving his empty cranium full of rocks which rattled around when he tried to move. Or better yet, maybe he had crushed his brains to mush, leaving nothing but gray slurry that now swished around inside his head like half-melted jell-o.

He decided to try and open his eyes again, and when he did, he glanced down his body, and immediately jumped up, rolling away from the zombie lying at his feet. His vision swam in circles and he felt like he was going to faint, but only his iron will kept him conscious. Reaching down, he pulled his Glock, hoping the weapon had survived the dip in the water intact. It was possible it would fire if he needed it to, but it was also very likely it wouldn't.

As he leveled the gun at the prone body, he quickly realized the body was motionless.

Slowly, he moved closer, and when he was standing over it, he nudged the corpse with his boot. The corpse rolled over, but did not show signs of life...or death, as the case may be.

That was when Henry saw half its face had been caved in, the brains even now leaking onto the beach. A few crabs were feeding on the gray mush and insects were a plenty.

Swallowing heavily, realizing the zombie's condition could easily have been his own, he tried to remember what had happened.

The fall from the bridge, tumbling through the air, and then he had managed to get the other bodies between him and the water. He remembered the corpses hitting hard, their skin breaking open like water balloons, but the cushion had been enough for Henry to survive striking the surface of the water.

He remembered the stench as he dropped into the miasma of slurry that was the exploded bodies, but then he was sinking deeper and the water washed him clean, like a Baptism.

Though he didn't remember swimming for the surface, obviously he must have as he was here now, alive.

Gazing down the beach, he realized calling it a beach would have been a compliment.

It was more just a place where the water touched land. There was no sand, only a muddy silt filled with the detritus of a fractured and broken civilization.

He spotted a small form a few hundred feet away from his position, and though it could have been nothing but another corpse, in a world that was full of them, he knew he needed to investigate.

His companions were somewhere and he could only pray they had managed to make it to shore like he had.

So, after checking to make sure his panga was still with him, and dry firing the Glock, satisfied that for now it was working properly, though knowing it would need a thorough cleaning very soon, he set off down the shore to check out the motionless form, and hoped he wouldn't find the corpse of one of his friends.

*   *   *

Mary snapped awake as if she'd been pinched.

Then she felt a small nip to her leg and realized she had been pinched.

Making a disgusted sound and pulling her face in revulsion, she shooed off the five crabs on top of her.

"Get out of here, get away from me," she snapped. She wasn't dead yet and the little bastards would have to wait for their next meal.

Reaching down, she felt the secure grip of her .38, and then saw her backpack a few feet down the mud-covered beach to her left. Shaking her head to blow away the cobwebs, she sat up, studying her surroundings.

Across the water, the bridge she had jumped off of was nowhere in sight, the current having carried her deeper into the channel. She saw no one on the beach with her and for a moment she felt the horror of realizing she could be alone now, that everyone she had cared about for over two years was gone, drowned in the watery depths of the river.

"Hey, Mary, Mary! Over here!" A muffled voice called out from further down the shore. Squinting to avoid the hot sun, she realized it was Jimmy, and alongside him were others.

Standing up, feeling woozy, she waved back, but Jimmy was still waving. He was yelling to her still, but she couldn't make out what he was saying as he was too far away. Only a few words reached her, the rest blowing away on the wind.

She couldn't figure out what was making him so animated. After all, she had waved back; she had seen him and the others.

Then she glanced down in front of her and realized where there was once only her shadow, there was now another.

Her battle instincts went into action immediately, realizing there was someone behind her, but she was too slow, her responses deadened by her time in the water.

She spun about so hard her head hurt, and she gazed up into the face of pure death. She had time for one gasp of shock and then the yellow and brown teeth began to descend, blocking out the sun as she let out a scream of anger and frustration at being caught so easily unawares.

*   *   *

Henry slowed in trepidation when he was only a few yards from the body lying prone on the beach when he realized who it was.

It was Sue, and she wasn't moving.

"Sue! Sue, honey!" He cried out as he quickly covered the remaining distance.

Reaching her, he dropped to the silt and cradled her in his arms. Her eyes were closed, but he still didn't know if she was alive or dead.

Turning her over, he cleared her mouth and began pushing on her chest. He cursed himself for not knowing CPR, something he had always wanted to learn but had never taken the time. He only knew what he'd seen on television.

Back when there was television.

"Come on, honey, don't you die on me," he pleaded as he pumped her chest, hoping he was doing things right.

Then her body spasmed and she spit up a lungful of dirty water, followed by vomit. Henry held her head to the side, letting her expunge whatever she had swallowed. She dry heaved a few times and then began to breathe more easily.

Henry rolled her onto her back as he gazed down at the woman he loved, the only woman to ever take his beloved Emily's place.

"Henry?" She gasped, blinking up at him. "What happened?"

"We had to jump in the water, remember?"

She looked down for a few seconds, contemplating his words, then she glanced back up at him and her eyes creased in anger.

"You pushed me. You actually pushed me off a bridge," she whispered, her throat now sore from vomiting.

He smiled wanly at her.

"Sorry, I had to do it." He smiled wider, the most sincere one he could manage.

"Forgive me?"

"Help me up," she ordered him, and he did as he was told. She was a little lightheaded, but in a few minutes it passed.

"Better?" He asked. "Just give it a sec', I felt the same way a little while ago."

"Yes, I do feel better, thanks." She scanned the beach. "Where's Mary, and Raven, and the others?"

Henry shrugged. "Don't know, you're the first one I found. Maybe they got washed further down the shore."

Sue was about to reply when a gunshot echoed across the beach. It came from the same piece of beach Henry had just vacated.

"What was that?" Sue asked, looking around.

"Gunfire, and I recognize the caliber. That's Cindy's M-16." He looked her straight in the eyes. "You up for a run?"

She nodded. "I think so, but if I slow down you go on without me, I'll catch up."

Another gunshot rolled across the beach and Henry knew something was happening.

"Okay, let's go, she may need help."

Sue took his hand, and like a couple on a date, they dashed down the beach hand in hand, only the weapons on Henry's body shattering the image of tranquility.

*   *   *

Mary was caught in that fragile split second between life and death.

That moment just before you are about to die when time stands still.

In the blink of an eye, everything that had happened to her for the past two years came flooding back like an avalanche.

She remembered leaving Pineridge Labs after a normal day only to be attacked by a city worker who had been a zombie. She remembered Jimmy appearing like a white night, running down the ghoul and saving her. Then they had met Henry on the highway and he had filled them in a little more on what had been happening in town. They had gone to his house to see to his wife, only she had turned into a ghoul, too, and Henry had to put her down.

After driving through a town filled with walking corpses they ended up back where they had begun, and after narrowly evading escaped convicts, had headed off into the woods to escape the quarantine. But then the contaminated rains had come, raining death down on all who were exposed.

When they all realized what was happening was far larger than their small town, they had waited for most of the storms to pass, and had then set out, only for Mary to become hurt by an accidental discharge of her weapon a few months later.

Henry and Jimmy had taken her to Pittsfield, a small town in Virginia, where Cindy had worked in one of the local bars. She had joined their group and they had all escaped with their lives when the walking dead had enveloped the town.

Images of the shopping mall, the winter spent there with her friends, and of the evil boss Barry holding her hostage on the roof. But she had saved herself that time.

Memories of the Groton Naval Base and the crime lord, Raddack, flooded her mind, and how she and Cindy had managed to escape his clutches, while thinking Henry and Jimmy had been killed, and then months later they had been washed ashore after a vicious storm had separated the companions yet again.

In California, they had found each other once more and had escaped while the town crumbled behind them.

Visions of the cannibals who had captured her and were going to carve her up like a Christmas goose flooded her mind, but Henry, Jimmy and Cindy had saved her.

And when Colonel Miller had conscripted them to join his army, it had been Henry and Jimmy who had foiled his mad plans; then freeing the people he had enslaved.

And all those victories and so many more adventures, as she struggled to survive this new, harsh world, were going to be for naught simply because she didn't check what was behind her.

The zombie snarled like an animal and began leaning forward, its dead eyes only for her exposed neck.

Mary braced herself, knowing the pain would be unbelievable, when a gunshot cracked across the beach and the zombie's head disappeared in a blinding spray of gore and bone matter, mixed with gray and white brains.

Mary rolled to the side on instinct, taking her chance to escape. When she came back up in a crouch, she was holding her .38, prepared to fire at anything that moved.

And it was well she was ready, because no sooner did she look behind the falling corpse, then more than a score of zombies were climbing over the small stone wall along the shore and trudging and stumbling towards her.

She looked left and right, wondering which way she should run, when another gunshot cracked and one of the lead ghouls toppled to the mud like a shot soldier storming the beach at Normandy.

"Mary, you all right?" Jimmy called out. Beside him was Raven and Cindy.

Cindy held her M-16 at head level and she fired again, taking down another ghoul.

When she was closer, Mary pointed to the weapon.

"Thought you said you were out?"

"Yeah, me too. Got lucky and found another full mag at the bottom of my backpack. Be glad I did, too."

She nodded, and raised her gun, firing at two ghouls that were even now coming for her.

One, two, the echo of the shots rebounded off one another and the two bodies were dropped, large holes in their heads. But there were more coming from behind and they needed to get moving.

Jimmy moved next to her, and she noticed he was missing something.

"Yeah, lost my shotgun in the water. Sucks," he said as he waved his own .38 in the air. Over the past two years they had acquired and lost weapons like they once would cell phones. He had owned the shotgun for a while and was going to miss it. Though he wasn't attached to it as much as Henry was to his Glock.

Henry had found the 9mm Glock on a dead policeman when the outbreak had first began and the man had taken care not to lose the weapon ever since. It was a piece of his past, Jimmy supposed, and he could relate.

"Let's get going people," Cindy said and fired at four more zombies as they slugged through the mud. The bullets were sloppily fired and all missed heads, only spraying necks and shoulders. Cindy muttered a curse, but fired again, talking down two of the ones she had missed with kill shots.

Raven wasn't idle either. When one of the ghouls, a teenager like herself, tried to go for her, she spun low, knocking the legs out from under the dead girl. Like a lion she hopped on top of the body, and with both hands on the dead girls' head, she twisted hard and fast, snapping the girl's neck and severing the spine. The body dropped to the ground, the brain no longer able to communicate with its lower half, though the dead girl's face did continue moving, eyes blinking and teeth snapping.

But it was out of action and that was Raven's plan. She knew not all ghouls had to be killed, merely put out of action.

Cindy was about to fire again, while the companions began backing up, knowing it was time to leave, when another gunshot echoed across the beach and Cindy saw the head she was lining up snap back with a neat, black hole in its forehead.

Turning, she was relieved to see Henry and Sue running towards them. Sue was a few feet behind, Henry pumping his arms as he dashed to aid his friends.

"Hey, old man, I knew you'd make it," Jimmy called out as he smiled from ear to ear.

Reaching him, Henry only nodded, his eyes taking in the situation in an instant.

"What the hell are you people doing here? You're wasting ammunition for nothing." He turned to head up the beach, away from the zombies.

"Come on, let's just go, they won't be able to catch us in all this mud." He turned to Cindy. "Cindy, don't you waste another shot, now let's go!"

She wavered for a moment, considering ignoring his orders, but in the end she lowered her rifle, nodding. She knew he was right, but she just wanted a little payback. The zombies weren't people anymore, they were now everything she hated in this new world and she took every opportunity to destroy them when possible.

Henry ran to Mary and grabbed her arm.

"Come on, Mary, fun time's over, let's go," he said. "And it's good to see you're all right, I was worried."

She smiled in reply. "Me too, Henry, for a little while there I thought I was the only one who'd made it."

They all turned and began moving down the beach, leaving the ghouls to flounder in the surf. At a steady jog, in ten minutes the ghouls were only small forms and another ten minutes later they were so small if the companions didn't know what they were, they never would have figured it out.

"Okay, let's rest for a while," Henry said. He gazed about the beach to see they had now made it back to what would once be called civilization. A few buildings could be seen on the edge of the mud-encrusted beach and a mile further in were houses, the roofs looking domestic.

"We need to hole up somewhere and recover and take stock of what we have left. Plus, all our weapons need a good cleaning." He held up his backpack, water still dripping from the bottom. "Everything we need is still wrapped up safe and dry in here," he said, referring to the gun oil and rags sealed tight in Ziploc bags. He had learned from their other adventures not to assume anything. Though he would have assumed it would have been rain that threatened the cleaning gear not a dunking in the river.

"Those buildings look pretty good," Jimmy suggested, gesturing to the closest one. It was a one-story brick building, similar to what city workers would use to store supplies in.

"Well then, let's go check it out," Henry said and headed for the building, Sue by his side.

Jimmy was on his left and Henry gestured to his missing shotgun.

"What happened?"

Jimmy shrugged. "Don't know, lost it, though. Sucks, Henry, I liked that shotgun."

"Yeah, well, better the gun than you, Jimmy," Henry said, slapping his younger friend on the shoulder. "We can replace the gun, we can't replace you."

"Thanks, old man, that's nice of you to say."

Cindy moved up and nudged Jimmy playfully.

"Cut it out, Henry, he's got a big enough ego as it is," she told him as she reached over and kissed Jimmy on the cheek. He spun his head and kissed her on the mouth instead, so she playfully slapped him for his move.

The rest of the walk was carried out with the companions chatting amongst one another, each glad the others were still with them. They all knew how lucky they had been, the fall from the bridge had been tenuous at best.

But once again they had survived to keep fighting for another day.

Approaching the building, Henry was in the lead, and his eyes scanned all the windows and the one chipped-paint door in front. It was wide, about double the size of an ordinary door and there was another small rollup door to the left.

To the right of the door, bolted to the bricks, was a faded No Trespassing sign.

When he had reached the door, he turned the doorknob, pleased when it turned easily.

As he opened it, the door swinging in on rusty hinges, he turned to the others to give them the usual reminder about taking all possible precautions when entering an unknown building.

As he spoke, he was aware of the gap in the door widening and his peripheral vision caught the shape of someone standing there, as if they were waiting for him.

He swung around, his Glock already coming out of its holster, but he already knew he was going to be too slow, too late.

He began to say "Shit," realizing his last words wouldn't have been much in the history of last words, when a deafening boom sounded near his head and a heavy blow spun him off his feet.

He heard a shrill snarl, like a scream, fill his ears and he wondered if that was him, his death rattle, when a heavy blow knocked him against the wall and his head cracked the door frame.

As he fell once more into the blissful arms of darkness, a small part of him actually embraced it.

# Chapter 3

Henry crawled back to reality, out of unconsciousness once again.

"Hey, there, you okay?" Jimmy asked as he leaned over him.

Henry blinked twice, and nodded. As he stood up, he winced, a sharp pain searing down the back of his scalp. Reaching behind him, he felt a small knot where he'd whacked his head.

"How long?" He asked.

"No more than five minutes," Mary replied from behind Jimmy.

The companions were all still gathered by the open door to the building, waiting for Henry to revive.

"What happened? I heard a gun shot, felt like I was hit," Henry said as he was helped to his feet.

"That gunshot was from Cindy," Jimmy told him, "and it was Raven who hit you." He gestured to Raven who was standing quietly on watch of the surrounding area. So far, with the exception of a few birds, the area was silent.

"Really, Raven laid me out? It felt like a truck had struck me," Henry added as he eyed the wisp of a girl, her long black hair blowing gently in the wind. Even now, after almost six months, the girl was an enigma.

"Yeah, when she saw that deader in there she kicked you out of the way so Cindy could take it out," Jimmy finished. "That was close. You gettin' lazy, old man?"

Henry shook his head, clearing the cob webs.

"Maybe, so has anyone gone inside to make sure it's clear?" Henry asked the others.

"Yeah, Henry," Mary replied. "Jimmy and Cindy did a recce, it's empty," she told him and he nodded.

"Okay then, let's get inside and see what's what." He took a step forward and seemed like he was going to fall and Sue reached out to help him, but he waved her away.

"I got it, I'm fine, just give me a second, dammit," he snapped at her, then realized his temper had taken over and he lowered his voice. "Sorry, Sue, that was uncalled for."

"It's all right, Henry, I understand," Sue said and turned to Raven. "You coming too?"

The teenage girl nodded, spun on her heels and then jogged to the building, slowing when she reached Henry.

"Thanks for saving my ass," Henry said to her. She may have been young, but she had proved more than once she was his equal in ferocity.

"It's okay, I saw that big one and I knew you were in trouble. Did what I had to do," she said and then entered the building, leaving Henry and Jimmy standing alone.

Henry blinked at Jimmy; surprised Raven had spoken for so long. For her that was a speech of epic proportions.

Jimmy moved forward and slapped Henry gently on the shoulder.

"So, how's it feel being saved by a little girl?" He asked snidely, never ignoring a chance to tease Henry when it came along.

Henry shrugged, rubbed the back of his head again as he moved into the building.

"Feels pretty, good, Jimmy, I'm still alive," he said.

Jimmy stood alone for a few seconds, taking in Henry's words, then, with one last glance around the area to make sure it was clear, he entered the building, closing the door behind him.

*   *   *

No sooner did Jimmy close the door then a filthy face appeared from around a rusted-out hulk of a car fifty feet away. The man's beady eyes flashed in the bright sun, and his bent nose gave him the look of a hawk.

The man was wearing rags, which had once been a thousand dollar suit, and his shoes would once have run him more than he could have made in a week as a financial broker on Wall Street.

After watching the companions enter the building and close the door, he stood up, not worried about being spotted, then dashed back down the street.

As he ran, he grinned widely, and his teeth, filed to points, glistened in the sun around the black and yellow spots.

While he ran, a necklace bounced on his chest, and anyone close enough to be able to see said necklace would have realized it was made of human ears.

Then the man disappeared around the bend in the road and was gone.

*     *     *

Stepping inside the building, Henry scrunched up his nose when the redolence of death and decay struck him. Glancing down to the dirty floor, he saw where the body of the zombie Cindy had taken out had fallen. Bits of brain matter were now covered with dirt and he pulled his gaze away from it.

He had seen far too much in the past two years to worry about some spent brain matter.

Inside the building, he saw it was one large room, with odds and ends piled in the corners. A lot of it looked to be old junk, such as plow scoops with peeling paint and a bobcat with no tires, plus a lawnmower with no engine.

There was a small card table to the left and the companions all moved towards it instinctively, not wanting to set their weapons on the dirty ground. With a large sigh, they all began removing their wet clothing, knowing they needed to dry it out before they moved on.

There was a window near the back and Cindy and Mary went to it, dragging an old oil barrel next to it. After picking up some old newspaper from a corner of the floor, she set the kindling into the barrel. When night came, the plan would be to start a fire, as the smoke would be hidden in the darkness. As for light seeping out of the building through cracks, that couldn't be helped, they would just have to try their best to cover them all. Drying their supplies and footwear was the most important thing right now. If their feet stayed wet for too long they could get trench foot, and in a world where cabs were far and between, that could prove fatal.

Unpacking his bag, Henry laid out the supplies he would need to clean his Glock, also taking his panga and setting it next to him.

The large, sixteen inch blade was razor sharp, and was about as wide as a machete.

If the angle was right, and he swung with all he could muster, he could take the head off a ghoul with one swipe.

As he began disassembling his Glock, lost in the ablutions of the simple task, Jimmy went to the door and peeked through the crack so he could check the area in front of the building.

"Anything?" Mary asked as she shook her jacket and took out anything of value so it could dry.

"Nah, so far so good, not a deader in sight," he said softly.

"That's good then, maybe we can get a few minutes rest for a while," Cindy added from across the room. She had her shirt off, her bra the only thing covering her breasts which were perfectly formed. She caught Jimmy eyeing her and she pointed a finger at him, then wiggled the finger back and forth in a, *nah-ah, none for you gesture.*

He frowned slightly, but then turned it into a grin when she winked at him.

He knew she wouldn't mind a roll in the hay either, but now was not the time. Truth was, the time had been few and far between at the moment and his balls were bluer than a deep blue clear sky.

Mary walked over to him and she flashed him a grin. She had her shirt off as well, having draped it over a metal rack, and Jimmy couldn't help but let his gaze drop to her chest. Mary was a woman who he now thought of as a sister, but there had been a time when they had almost become more, but that time was long past and though she was beautiful and sexy, he didn't see her that way anymore, though he still knew a great set of tits when he saw them.

Mary reached out and placed her hand under his chin, lifting his gaze.

"My eyes are up here, Jimmy," she said with a sneer.

"Sorry, Mar'," Jimmy said bashfully, "but they're right in front of me, I'm only human, for Christ's sake."

"Whatever, just go get cleaned up. I'll watch the street for a while."

He nodded and padded away while she took up watch. They had learned some hard lessons over the past few months, knowing one of them needed to be on guard at all times.

In the beginning, there had only been the undead to worry about, but over the past year a new threat had arose.

Cannibals.

The cannies were ruthless and had reverted back to the most basic animal imaginable, or unimaginable. Instead of trying to raise crops or salvage through the wreckage of a fallen society, they had decided to adapt to their new world by preying on the one food that was relatively still plentiful.

Man.

To a cannie, Long Pig was the perfect meal after a hard day of hunting, and as Mary stared out on the street, she remembered her last encounter with cannies.

Only her ingenuity had saved her that day and she didn't wish to be placed in that position again anytime soon. If it came to capture ever again, she would consider taking her own life before it could happen.

A chill went down her spin, causing her to wrap her arms around herself. It was in the low fifties and if she hadn't had a good dunking today, she would have been fairly comfortable. Her hands were only now becoming less wrinkled and pruned from the dip in the river, and her skin was slightly less moist to the touch.

Behind her, Sue and Henry were chatting softly while he cleaned his gun. Mary smiled at them. She was glad Henry had finally found someone. She thought of Henry as a father figure and knew he thought of her as the daughter he'd never had.

The two were closer than most families and both knew they would die for the other if it came down to it.

She scanned the room to see Raven sitting alone by the window with the oil barrel. She was a wisp of a girl, with the curvature of bone peeking through her lithe frame. As Mary watched her, the young girl reminded her of a runway model, back when such frivolous things mattered. But though the girl looked thin and weak, Mary knew Raven was an excellent fighter. One reason was her inch long fingernails that had been sharpened to a keen edge.

With those nails Raven could open a jugular before the victim knew they were sucking in their last breath.

Henry snapped the Glock together and dry fired it, then went to work taking out the bullets from the clips, drying any that needed it. Next to him was Cindy's M-16, which would need a thorough cleaning along with Mary and Jimmy's .38's. Cindy's .45 was lost, swallowed by her fall into the river.

Mary glanced back outside and spotted movement, and as she waited patiently, she saw one lone ghoul wander into her field of sight.

It was a pathetic piece of detritus. Its hair was all but gone with only a few tufts left to blow in the wind. One eye was missing, maggots squirming in the cavity, and its nose was gone, probably rotted off months ago. Its right arm was hanging by a few tatters of tendons and stitches of its shirt and one leg was bent at an unnatural angle. The deader shambled along like a drunk after last call and Mary felt her heart going out to the pathetic creature that had once had a family, hopes and dreams, and a life.

But now it was a shell, a meat shell that would kill her if it had a chance.

Jimmy moved closer to her and he shoved his head in her way so he could see outside.

"Anything?" He asked

She shook her head from side to side. "Nah, just one lone deader. It looks harmless," she said as she stepped back. "If you're so curious, you can take over again," she told him.

Jimmy looked like he didn't want to, but then he nodded, his eyes dropping to her breasts once again.

Mary sighed, thinking: *men, what are you gonna do with 'em?* Then she moved away to see if she could help Henry with their weapons.

# Chapter 4

The sun was just peeking over the horizon as the six companions set off from the building they had spent the night in.

All their clothes were now dry and their weapons had all been cleaned and oiled.

"So where do you think we are?" Jimmy asked Henry as they made their way down the silent street.

A few ghouls were around the area, but by the time they turned and began to shamble after the companions, they were quickly left behind.

A few buildings lined the street, mostly commercial. Every building had thick clumps of ivy growing on their facades as well as moss in between the mortar of the bricks. More than one window was shattered and most of the doors hung open, swaying back and forth in the wind, with the exception of where refuse had piled up to the point the door was made immobile.

As they walked, they had to side step the massive clumps of crabgrass and kudzu growing from every crack in the pavement. With man no longer maintaining the area, the weeds were slowly taking over. Henry gauged that in another year the entire street would be lost under a carpet of green.

Henry and Jimmy were in the lead, with Cindy, Sue and Raven in the middle. Mary took up the rear, her eyes constantly searching for trouble.

A ghoul shambled out to her right, heading directly for the group, and there was no question it would reach them easily. She raised her .38, prepared to blast it back to Hell, when Henry called out to her.

"I got it," he called as casually as if he was getting her a cup of coffee.

Leaving Jimmy for a moment, he peeled off from the group and moved directly towards the ghoul. When he was no more than three feet away, he slid his panga out of its sheath, and with a massive swipe, took the head off the ghoul, followed by both arms, and then legs, like he had carved a tree of its dead branches.

Stepping back to avoid the dark blood spray, maggots spilling from the corpse like rain, he moved back to the others.

Jimmy was standing with hands on hips and he nodded approvingly.

"Nice, old man, took that deader down in just five slashes."

"Glad you approve," he said with a slight grin. The two men had grown closer over the past year and a grudging respect was now given by Henry to Jimmy.

When Henry had first met Jimmy, he had been a wisecracking teenager, just past his nineteenth birthday.

Now, two years later, Jimmy was a hardened warrior, a man Henry was proud to guard his life if necessary. Now, even with that said, Jimmy was still a wiseass, but he had learned to temper his mouth with wisdom, if only slightly.

Henry wiped his blade clean on a clump of weeds, making sure to get it all off. He had just oiled and polished the blade, then had taken an hour to hone the edge, and he'd be damned if he would treat the weapon incorrectly now.

"Doesn't seem such a big deal when there's only a few of them, huh?" Jimmy said to Henry as he began walking again, the others following. Sue and Raven were chatting quietly, though Sue was doing most of the talking. Cindy had fallen back with Mary and the two were chatting about something as well.

"Yeah, well, as far as I'm concerned, they can all drop over and stay dead forever," Henry told him while he moved to point position as they approached a railroad bridge.

The street they were on shrunk down to only one lane as it went under the bridge, so that when there had been traffic only one side could have gone under at a time. When it had been busy here, Henry assumed it must have been a headache when two vehicles went at the same time and ended up bumper to bumper, then one would have had to back up to let the other through.

To go under the bridge they basically had to go into a small tunnel, no more than five car lengths long. But such was the angle of the sun that inside the tunnel it was only shadows and shapes.

Henry slowed as he approached the edge of the tunnel, his eyes scanning the railroad bridge above him.

He was considering climbing up to the bridge and then walking over the tunnel, his battle hardened instincts telling him something wasn't right.

For one thing, he heard no birds, which was odd. In the world of the dead, birds were plentiful, feeding on the corpses, of either the truly dead or the walking kind. The birds had truly become the dominant species as without man they had free reign of the sky.

The others slowed until all were standing near him, though not so close they would be considered one target if someone watching attempted to shoot at them.

More than three feet separated one from the other, the instinct to do this now ingrained into them.

"What's up, old man, why'd you stop?" Jimmy inquired as he wiped sweat from his brow. If he was right, then it was late June, though without a standard calendar to keep track of time he could have been off by more than two months. Now time was gauged by the seasons. Summer was summer, fall was fall, ect.

"No reason, I was just thinking maybe we should go over instead of under, that's all," Henry told Jimmy as he eyed the bridge.

There didn't seem to be an easy way to go up, he realized, as he studied the stone facade of the bridge.

"What? That's crazy. Why the hell would we do that? Come on, I think you're gettin' senile in your old age," Jimmy joked.

"What's the matter, Henry, you see something?" Mary asked, Cindy adding her same question to the mix.

"No, not really, it's just a feeling, that's all. Just look at that tunnel and tell me that's not the perfect place for an ambush. 'Sides, when was the last time we went into a tunnel and everything worked out. Remember Boston?"

"Boston was different, Henry," Jimmy said. "We had Jeffrey with us then."

"Oh, wow, Jeffrey," Mary said and she glanced to Cindy, remembering the man. The small, whiny man had been with them for a short time, but had been slaughtered in front of Mary and Cindy's eyes by the boss, Barry, at the shopping mall. Mary and

Cindy had also been destined to go into the cooking pots, but Henry had stopped that plan cold.

"I haven't thought about him in a long time," Cindy said.

"Yeah, poor little guy, no one should go out like he did," Jimmy said. "I mean, shit, I didn't like him, but I didn't want him dead, at least not like that. Hell, I thought I was gonna be the one to do it sooner or later."

"Jimmy, that's terrible," Cindy scolded him.

"Sorry, babe. I know the guy's dead, but come on, he was a pain in the ass, admit it."

"No, I will not admit it, now stop it, please. Respect the dead," Cindy replied with a touch of anger to her tone.

Jimmy looked at Cindy like she was his mother, then he rolled his eyes and shook his head. Well, she was close, after all. She was his girlfriend. Sometimes the two would get mixed up.

"Are you two finished or what?" Henry asked, annoyed that they would pick now to argue about something petty. They were in unknown territory and distractions could get them killed.

"Yeah, Henry, it's cool, I'm done," Jimmy said. Henry glanced to Mary and Cindy and both merely shrugged.

Sue moved a few feet so she was standing near Henry. "So, you were saying?"

"Oh, yeah, thanks, Sue." Then he waved his hand in the air, dismissing his hunch. After all, when he scanned the area, there was no sign of life. He was just being over cautious, if that was possible in the world he now lived in.

"Listen, let's forget I said anything and get going. You're probably right, Jimmy, I'm just being too careful."

Jimmy grinned from ear to ear, pleased Henry was agreeing with him.

"Good, okay, then let's go," Jimmy said, waving Henry forward.

Henry said nothing, but turned and continued on, Sue by his side. Jimmy, Mary and Cindy were walking together and Raven took up the rear, her eyes watching the bridge as they entered it.

Henry slowed when he entered the tunnel, the cooler air caressing his face and arms. He glanced up to the ceiling, but it was lost in the shadows, only the dimmest blur of the steel bars and I-beams that were used to construct and support the railroad tracks overhead.

With one last glance behind them to make sure it was clear, he moved into the tunnel, knowing in less than a minute they would all be on the other side and back in the sunlight once again.

At first his back itched, his sixth sense telling him he was right in the first place and the tunnel was all wrong, but by the time they had reached the middle and nothing had happened, he began to relax his guard, feeling foolish for saying anything in the first place.

It was when he was crossing the exact middle of the tunnel, the place where the shadows were the heaviest, that something heavy landed on his shoulders, crushing him to the ground as the breath left his chest.

He heard the anguished cries of Jimmy and the others, and for a second he thought the ceiling had collapsed just as the group had made it to the point of no escape, but then he smelled the foul odor of human waste and body odor and realized it was a man that had attacked him, not stone and steel.

All this flashed through his mind in an instant as he was forced to the ground. Before he could manage to try and reach for a weapon, white-hot fire lanced down his left side and dirty fingers wrapped themselves around his windpipe.

With oxygen unable to suffuse his system, he could already feel his heart beating faster and yellow spots appeared in his vision.

As he struggled to maintain consciousness, he could hear his fellow companions yelling out and screaming as, they too, were attacked by the dark shadows that had fallen from the ceiling like creatures of the night.

And as he fought with no result to free himself, he had to wonder if this was going to be when his luck finally ran out and he was sent on a one way trip to Hell.

# Chapter 5

Henry pulled his Glock from its holster as he was forced to the ground, but it was knocked from his hand to clatter across the tunnel floor.

Feeling hard muscle under clothing, he knew his assailant was human, and he struggled to breathe when a filthy, dirt covered sleeve was jammed over his mouth while fingers squeezed the life from his throat.

Henry's only edged weapon was his panga and it was much too large to use in a close fight like the one he was now in, so he reached down with his right hand and jammed it between his assailants legs, squeezing the testicles he found in the baggy pants of his foe.

There was a long yelp of pain and the hands around his throat lessened for a second.

He got his legs under his foe and pushed off, sending the attacker across the tunnel to rebound off the wall. But no sooner did the man strike the wall then he was charging back, face screwed up in a snarl of anger and hate.

In the shadows of the tunnel, Henry saw the flash of pointed teeth and knew instantly he was dealing with cannies.

The evil bastards had been everywhere as of late and it had been long overdue that the companions would come across more of them.

To his left and right his friends were fighting their own battles, and for the moment, Henry could do nothing to help them, as he was in a fight for his own life.

The cannie came at Henry hard and fast, and before Henry could get to his feet, the man was on top of him again, teeth going for his throat.

Well, two could play at that game, Henry thought as he blocked a swipe from a short spear the cannie was using as a weapon. The cannie was smaller than him and Henry figured the best thing to do was to go in charging, hoping to use his superior height and weight against the man.

His side pained him, but not too much, and he was confident he had picked up a superficial wound, but he knew that could change in an instant. He could feel a sticky warmth on his ribs where the lance had scraped him, and when the lance darted out again, he received a slight cut to the back of his left hand.

Beyond the cannie's shoulder, he spotted a flash of ebony hair as Raven dealt with her attacker, then Henry had to focus on his private battle as the man reached down with a hand and tried to repay him by crushing his genitals. Henry shifted his hip so the man only struck his thigh, then he reached down and grabbed the wrist, squeezing so hard he felt the brittle bones crack.

There was another howl and the cannie rolled off him, Henry rolling the opposite way as he came to his feet.

"Come on, you little bastard," Henry hissed, his jaw tight, his eyes creased. Adrenalin flooded his system and he was lost in blind rage.

The cannie obliged and charged at him again, the lance out in front of him. Henry sidestepped the shaft and grabbed it with both hands, yanking the cannie towards him. When the man lost his balance, Henry was there, and he wrapped his hands around the man's throat. But he knew he needed a weapon to finish the job so he used what he had at his disposal.

Leaning in, a snarl mimicking his attacker, Henry sunk his teeth into the side of the man's neck, directly over the artery.

Warm, salty blood shot into his mouth as he worried at the flesh, growling like a dog as the cannie tried to escape.

But the prey had become the hunter and Henry wouldn't let up.

On top of the blood he tasted dirt, sweat and grease, but his teeth dug deeper into the neck muscles, tearing like a starving wolf would a deer carcass.

Though smaller than him, the cannie was a cunning and ruthless fighter and he wasn't about to just lie down and die. Desperately, the cannie reached out and tried to pluck out Henry's right eye, but Henry sank his teeth deeper, spitting out the foul-tasting blood. His teeth clamped tighter, working their way through the beating wall of muscle protecting the carotid artery, and when he finally severed the flesh, he was rewarded with an explosion of plasma that flooded into his mouth, causing him to choke.

The cannie screamed, and as Henry released his clamped teeth, the man pushed off him, his hands going to his neck to staunch the flow of blood escaping his body. As the cannie did this, he dropped the lance, and scooping it up, Henry jabbed it into the man's chest, piercing his heart and ceasing any more chance of further attack.

The cannie's eyes rolled up into his head as he toppled to the shadowed, ensconced ground, but Henry was already moving to aid his friends. Pulling the panga free of its sheath, he took a step to his right and brought it down like a cleaver, taking off half the cannie's neck that had been on top of Sue. The man screamed in pain and popped up as he tried to reach the source of his qualms, but Henry yanked back like the blade had been trapped in a log and then brought it down again on top of the man's skull. There was a meaty *thwack* and the cannie dropped on top of Sue, who whimpered as she tried to extricate herself.

Henry left her where she was. She was fine for the moment.

Spinning on his heels, he saw Mary and Cindy fending off three cannies as a team. Deciding he needed to get them faster than it would take to cross the divide separating him from them, he called out to the middle cannie.

"Hey, shithead, over here!"

The cannie spun at the sound of Henry's voice and felt something slam into his chest.

Looking down, the man saw the handle of the panga sticking out of his abdomen, the sixteen inches penetrating his torso so that a few bloody inches stuck out his back. The cannie wrapped his hands around the hilt of the panga, but then he toppled to the side, dead before he hit the ground.

The distraction was all the others needed and Cindy lunged at the one on her right, slashing at the man's neck with her hunting knife. The jugular was split like warm butter and blood shot out to coat the tunnel floor. That instant gave Mary the time to draw her .38 and she shot her attacker in the chest, the body knocked off its feet to land in a heap of arms and legs.

Another shot from behind Henry caused him to spin, hands out as he prepared to fight hand to hand, but it was Jimmy's gun, silencing his attacker, the female cannie now curled up like a newborn babe on the tunnel floor.

Raven was the last and she spun in the air, her left foot connecting with the cannie's chin. When the man was knocked away, she cartwheeled towards him and then landed on his chest, forcing him to the ground. With the man's chin in her groin, she stood up, then slashed her fingernails across the man's jugular, severing it in an instant.

She jumped away as blood geysered up into the air like a water fountain, but in seconds the flow had slowed to only a trickle.

Henry kicked something in the shadows and glanced down to see it was his Glock. Picking up his fallen weapon, he flicked off the safety, prepared to take out the next attacker with hot lead.

But there was no one left to shoot.

The smell of offal and blood suffused the inside of the small tunnel as the companions gathered their wits and took stock of themselves.

"Henry, help me, please, get him off of me!" Sue called out as she struggled with the dead body on her. The man's shattered head and sliced neck seeped blood which flowed into her shirt and neck, making her feel beyond gross.

Moving to her, Jimmy next to him, the two warriors lifted the corpse off her, then Henry helped her to her feet.

He saw the blood on her chest, arms and neck and his eyes went wide with concern.

"It's okay, none of it's mine," she said as she tried to wipe her face clear of the already congealing plasma.

"Everybody all right? Anyone hurt?" Henry asked as he studied each dim shape and then the bodies on the ground. He received positive replies as each of the group surveyed their bodies to insure they were unhurt.

One of the cannies moaned and Henry went to him, glancing down at the man. He was a bedraggled piece of humanity with odd clothing which was no more than rags and a stink that made a zombie seem like a fresh flower.

There was a sucking sound when Mary pulled Henry's panga free of the corpse it was in, and then she walked the few feet and handed it to him.

"Thanks," he said curtly.

The cannie groaned again, and before any of the companions could say a thing to stop him, Henry raised the steel blade and brought it down on the cannie's neck, cutting the head off in one chop.

The arms and legs spasmed, dancing a jig of death as the blood seeped out of the jagged hole, Henry sidestepping the blood so as not to get his boots coated any more than they already were.

He caught movement above him and he glanced up to see another form hiding in the girders above. Without hesitating, he raised the Glock and shot the shape, a body tumbling out of the darkness to land head first on the tunnel floor.

"Christ, they're fucking everywhere!" Jimmy snapped as he raised his .38 overhead to make sure that was the last of them.

"Come on, let's get the hell out of here, it's too damn tight in here," Henry said as he helped Sue over the corpse of a dead cannie.

"Mary and Cindy, watch our backs," Henry called out, the two women nodding as they each began to walk sideways so they could study their back trail.

In less than a half minute they were back out in the sun, the feeling of claustrophobia drifting away like smoke on the wind.

Scanning the surrounding area, they saw nothing that appeared to be dangerous, though a few undead moans wafted on the wind, signifying the dead had heard the gunshots and were even now coming to investigate.

"Let's keep moving and as soon as it looks clear we'll rest and get cleaned up, okay?" Henry asked them, his eyes gleaming around a blood-coated face.

"Fine with me," Jimmy said. "I've had enough for one morning. Thanks."

As they walked, Jimmy noticed Henry was limping very slightly.

"You sure you're okay?"

"It's nothing, Jimmy," Henry told him. "The little bastard tried to rip my balls off, that's all. I returned the favor though, and then some," he grinned, his face still covered in blood. He looked like a demon from Hell who had come to Earth to see what mayhem he could cause.

"That's good, Henry, 'cause I know someone who would have missed them," he joked as he nodded to Sue who was walking behind them with Raven next to her.

Henry didn't respond, and with the sun rising into the sky, the group made their way deeper into the Colorado Mountains.

# Chapter 6

"Is he still behind us?" Henry asked out of the side of his mouth as he walked down the silent street.

The small town they had wandered into was completely deserted, neither living humans nor undead ghouls to confront the companions.

Henry had seen this before.

When the dead began to walk, many communities evacuated for rescue stations, abandoning their homes and towns. So while other towns had battened down the hatches and made fences and walls to keep out the potential undead attacks, others had become ghost towns where only the ghosts of the past now remained.

The once manicured homes were now rundown, a few scorched by fires months if not years old. Almost every structure had shattered windows, doors hanging open with small animals now living where man had once called home.

"Yeah, he's still there," Jimmy said as he cautiously glanced over his shoulder by pretending he was slapping at an annoying fly.

It had been almost thirty minutes since the attack at the tunnel and the group had yet to rest. Flakes of blood were falling away from Henry's face and neck and his shirt was sticky with dried blood. The others were no better. All wanted to rest, but they were still in danger and weren't prepared to stop, not knowing how many were still following them.

But as the minutes had passed since first discovering that they were being trailed, the assumption amongst the companions was there was only one person shadowing them.

"What do you think he wants?" Mary asked, trudging along in the middle of the group.

Henry shrugged. "Don't know for sure, but if I had to guess, I'd say he's gonna wait till we stop for the day and then get back to his fellow cannies to tell them where we are."

"So you mean that shit at the tunnel is only the beginning?" Jimmy inquired.

Henry nodded, but his brow creased, the lines on the skin making more blood flakes fall away.

"Oh, shit, I know that look," Jimmy said. "You're thinking about something that I don't want to know about, aren't you."

"Yeah, probably," Henry said and then glanced at each of them. Sue looked concerned so he flashed her a reassuring smile.

"Don't worry, we've done this before," he told her.

"Done what?" Mary asked, only catching part of the conversation between Jimmy and Henry.

"One thing at a time, Mary," he told her as he moved closer to Jimmy.

"Okay, you keep going forward, and when I peel off from the rest of you, just keep going, like I'm still with you, got it?"

"Yeah, Henry I got it, just watch your ass," Jimmy said as he lowered his hand to his .38.

"You know it, buddy," he grinned back and then shifted to the right so he was walking near the homes lining the street. Jimmy dropped back a little and filled the others in on what was going to happen while Henry waited for the right moment to move.

He waited until the group rounded a bend in the road, and the instant he knew he was out of sight from their shadow, he ducked to the right and dove into ten foot high shrubs that had once been only four feet.

Spinning around, he maneuvered so he was facing the street, and then waited while the others continued on. Sue flashed him a concerned look, but then she turned around, and Henry could only hope the shadow hadn't seen her do this.

Mary, Jimmy and the others had closed ranks a little, so from behind it wouldn't be obvious he was missing from the group.

Now all he could do was wait for the right time.


That time came a few minutes later when Henry spotted the figure leapfrogging from bush to shrub to rusted-out wrecks as he followed the companions. Henry waited for the figure to pass him and then lunged out of the shrubs.

The figure was completely caught off guard and Henry tackled him, not wanting to kill him yet as he was hoping for information.

Both he and the figure rolled in the tall grass as each tried to get the upper hand on the other.

But it didn't take long for Henry to overpower the figure and he quickly figured out why. With his knees on the figures chest, he found himself gazing down at the face of a boy, no more than thirteen if he was a day.

"Let me up, you old prick," the boy hissed as he tried to bite Henry's arm.

"I'll let you up if you calm down," Henry replied as he put more pressure on the boy's arms, pushing them into the moist earth. The boy cried out and tried to raise his hips, but Henry was twice his size and he quickly realized he was going nowhere fast.

At the sound of footsteps, Henry glanced up to see Jimmy and the others returning. They had waited around the bend and when they had heard the short fight had returned.

"Well, well, will you look at this, a runt," Jimmy said as he eyed the small boy.

"Let me up, old man, or so help me I'll kill you!" The boy snarled, trying to free himself again.

"Hey, how 'bout that, he knows your name!" Jimmy laughed as he moved to the side of Henry so he could get a better view of the boy. His eyes especially went to the boy's teeth, wanting to see if they were sharpened into points. The cannies had taken to making their people file their teeth as a badge of honor, so they could recognize one another immediately.

But those same pointed teeth would also alert others they now had a cannie hidden in their midst. It was now much harder for a cannie to go undetected in a town that had been targeted for future attack.

"Teeth look okay," Jimmy said to Henry as he knelt down and grabbed the boy's chin.

"Oww, get the fuck off me, you asshole," the boy snapped.

"Nice language, kid, you kiss your mother with that mouth?" Jimmy said back.

"Hah, reminds me a little of you back when you used to cut my grass, Jimmy," Henry chuckled as he shifted position on the boy's chest.

"Henry, are you going to let him up? It's obvious he's not a cannie," Mary said.

The boy spit and made a disgusted face. "I hate those fucks, they're always trying to catch me so they can eat me, but I'm too fast for 'em."

"Then why don't you leave this area? Why do you stay?" Sue inquired as she knelt down next to the boy. Her motherly instincts were taking over and her heart was going out to this tough but frightened child.

"Cause this is my home, bitch, that's why," the boy snapped at her.

Henry slapped the boy hard, but not too hard, on the face.

"Hey, be nice, or I'll bend you over my knee and slap your ass till its red."

Cindy and Jimmy began to chuckle and the boy glared at both of them.

"Both of you, knock it off. This ain't funny," Henry said. He turned to look at Jimmy. "So, what are we gonna do with him? He's not a cannie so..." He trailed off.

"You thought I was a cannie? That's a good one," the boy said. "Why'd you think that?"

"'Cause you were trailing us, that's why," Mary said. "We got ambushed in a railroad tunnel and figured you were one of them. Figured you were going to find out where we're making camp for the night and report back," she finished.

"Ha, you got caught in the railroad tunnel? Man, that's the lamest place to get ambushed, that why the cannies hide in there and wait for people to go through it. How the hell have you guys managed to survive for as long as you have out here?"

Henry frowned, not liking being ridiculed by a boy.

"We get by, thanks. Now listen, if I let you up are you gonna behave?"

"Depends," the boy replied.

"On what?" Cindy asked.

"On whether you got any food. I'm starving, that's why I was following you. I thought I'd see what I could take from you when you guys took a break, but this old fart jumped me instead."

Jimmy chuckled and Henry shot him a glare that said to stop it. Jimmy held his tongue, but he still had a wide grin on.

"We can give you something, dear, but we don't have much," Sue said. She looked to Henry. "Let him up, please, he's just a boy for God's sake."

With a sigh, Henry leaned back and rose to his feet, the boy lying prone on the grass. He lay there, not moving, staring up at the six faces gazing down on him, and then, before any of the group could act, the boy rolled to his side and tried to sprint off.

He would have made it, too, but Raven was quicker. As the boy darted past her, she stuck her left foot out and the boy tripped, his face going head first into the dirt. Spitting mud and grass, Henry nodded thanks to Raven and then leaned over and picked him up by the scruff of his filthy shirt.

"Look, son, you don't have to run away. We won't hurt you," Henry said and then he reached into his backpack and pulled out a power bar salvaged from one of their finds over the past few weeks.

The boy said nothing, but ripped the bar from Henry's hand and tore at it with his teeth. He then devoured it whole, barely chewing.

"Got another one?" The boy asked with a mouth full of food.

"No, that's all I have," Henry said annoyed.

"Henry, give him another one, please, for me," Sue pleaded.

With an annoyed look at her, he relented, wanting to please her. He reached into his pack and handed the boy another bar, which was promptly consumed in a second.

Like a wild dog that warmed up to you after you had fed it, the boy seemed less inclined to leave now. Henry doubted if the reason was anything other than selfish. By the look of the boy's thin frame, he hadn't had much to eat and he realized if he stayed with the companions more food would be obtainable.

"Well, at least we don't have to worry about the cannies now," Cindy said as she watched the boy warily. "We can just keep moving until we're out of their territory."

Raven said nothing, watching the entire tableaux in silence.

A low moan followed by footsteps carried to the ears of the group and they all turned to look behind them in time to see a dozen ghouls approaching, each coming from a different direction.

At the rate they were moving, it would only be a minute before they reached the companions.

"Shit, deaders!" Jimmy spit. "I knew it was too good to be true that we hadn't seen any for a while."

Henry counted the number of walkers and decided they would have no choice but to take them out. If they didn't, they would find themselves waking up in the middle of the night with pale and bloated faces gazing down on them.

No, they needed to take these dozen out before they could move on and hope no more arrived before they could set out again.

"Okay, gang, skirmish line. We need to take them out silently or we'll alert everything in the area we're here. Plus, we're really low on ammo," Henry told, the others.

"I know where you can get some more bullets," the boy said as he watched the ghouls, his eyes now full of fear. His brave facade was slipping now that he was staring at the walking dead. Henry didn't hear him, his attention focused on the ghouls.

They were a motley bunch, with bloated bodies and faces that were rotting off their skulls. Maggots squirmed in every orifice and a few were missing arms, hands or just fingers. Their skin was tight against their skulls and one was missing a lower jaw, the tongue hanging down like a slug necktie. It glistened in the sun and saliva dripped down on its chest, the decayed and torn shirt soaked through.

Henry always wondered about oddities like that. If the walking ghouls were truly dead, then how could they bleed or make saliva? He had always assumed the bodies worked despite not needing to, like an appendix or a tumor that grew, but was useless to the body.

Then such biological curiosities were redundant as the first of the dead reached the companions.

Cindy was the first to be attacked and she swung up her M-16 like a club and cracked the ghoul on the side of the head. The body toppled over, black ichor mixed with brain matter oozing out of its fractured cranium like gray pudding. Jimmy was right beside her and he decided to take the action to the enemy. With a yell, and a lunge, he jumped into the air, kicking the ghoul with the sole of his boot.

The zombie was thrown to the street, Jimmy hopping over the body to land in a crouch. As the ghoul struggled to right itself, Jimmy picked himself up, ran the few feet to it, and slammed his right heel down on the rotting face, not once, but three times until the porridge-like brains squirted out the sides.

Raven was like a ghost as she ran between the ghouls, kicking one in the knee and then breaking another's arm. In less than ten seconds three ghouls were wallowing on the ground, their knee caps shattered.

Sue took a step back when a large ghoul almost twice her height turned and came for her. She gazed up at the putrid maw and maggot-filled eyes and her mouth opened in a silent scream. She wasn't a warrior like the others and perhaps she never would be, and she stared up at the bloated face in abject horror.

The ghoul took three steps towards her and stopped cold, a meaty sound coming from behind it.

The head of the zombie swiveled to the left, and then *slid* off the neck like it had been shabbily glued there and the glue wasn't holding anymore. Black blood shot out of the wound and danced in the air to rain back down, and Sue's mouth opened and closed as she stared at the headless corpse. Then, like a tree falling to earth after being cut, the body toppled forward, Sue jumping out of the way with a screech.

As the body fell away, Sue gazed at Henry's grinning face. Though he smiled, his eyes were hard, his battle mode kicked in.

"You okay?" He asked her brusquely.

She only nodded, too shocked to speak.

"Good, just stay in the back of us and you'll be fine. Call out if you get into trouble," he told her and then spun on his heels and charged at a pair of zombies who were coming at Mary from the rear flank.

With his panga raised high, he called out so he could get their attention, and then brought the panga down in a chopping motion. Hands fell from wrists to flop in the warm sun as Henry spun and swiped a head clear off its shoulders. From a distance, he was like a dancer, the blade flashing in the sun as he traipsed around the ghouls. Each time he passed them however, another piece fell off, until the ghouls were nothing but legs, torsos and heads.

With his right boot, he kicked them one at a time to the ground and then stomped on their ankles, making sure they couldn't get back to their feet. When he was finished, he turned away, seeing who else needed help.

But he wasn't watching his own back while he guarded his friends and the zombie with no lower jaw snuck up on him before he realized it.

Dr. Tongue, as Henry dubbed the ghoul, reached out and wrapped its arms around him, the two of them falling to the ground with Henry on the bottom.

Henry's panga clattered away a few feet and he found his arms were trapped between himself and the ghoul. Dr. Tongue was hungry and only the fact he had no lower jaw saved Henry from being bit.

But the ghoul still tried, and as the mouth came down, the tongue slathered him with bloody drool, making his stomach churn inside him. Though he had seen scenes of carnage that would make a grown man weep, every now and then something would happen to him that would make the other tableaus inconsequential. This was one of those times, the tongue slathering him like a large dog, the miasma of decay and purification making his stomach roll over in his gut.

Acting fast, he head-butted the ghoul in the nose, the decayed cartilage cracking like an egg, the bone and cartilage going up into the ghoul's brain. That slowed it down and Henry bucked his hips, the body sliding off him slightly.

Henry used that advantage and kicked up with his knee right between the ghoul's thighs, not thinking clearly that a dead man had no need of testicles. Something popped when his knee connected and yellow pus began to drip out of the holes in Dr. Tongue's pants, right where the zipper was.

Testicle juice dripped onto Henry's clothing, adding to his already gore-covered wardrobe, and with a yell he tossed the body away from him. Like a crab he moved across the ground, reached out for his panga and then swiped it overhead, the blade coming down hard onto the ghoul's head.

Trying to pull it out, the blade was wedged into the skull and he was having a tough time of it. It was only when another shadow fell over him that he realized he was about to be caught unawares yet again.

But then the body was shoulder checked like a hockey player and it was knocked to the ground, Henry looking up at the grinning face of the boy.

"What's the matter, old man, break a hip or something?"

"Not funny, son, get out of here before you get hurt," Henry snapped at him.

"Hmmph, saved your ass, didn't I?" But then he yelped when an old woman with only one eye tried to grab him.

Henry kicked out his foot and swept the legs of the old ghoul out from under her, the body dropping onto the ground so hard this one did break a hip. With the ghoul next to him, Henry spun on his butt and cracked his other boot into her face, flattening what was left of her features as she was slammed back so hard to the ground the back of her skull cracked.

Then Henry was on his feet again and looking for what he could do to help the others.

The battle was about over, only Mary dealing with two ghouls which had her cornered.

Mary looked like she was going to try and fight it out but then he saw her frown, pull her .38 and shoot each one in the head, the bodies dropping away like sacks of cement.

"Mary, what the hell? We were supposed to do this quietly," Henry yelled at her.

"Yeah, well I wasn't about to take chances on getting bit for a little stealth, thank you very much," she replied, holstering her weapon. "There were two of them and only one of me, the answer was obvious. Sorry if you don't agree."

Henry was about to reply when more footsteps and wails of the dead floated on the wind. All heads swiveled to the north, where the voices were emanating from.

"Shit, looks like we're gonna get more company," Jimmy said as he stepped away from a gore-soaked patch of grass.

"Well, we're not sticking around to greet them. Everyone, get your stuff and let's move out. If we're lucky, we can be gone before we're spotted."

As everyone retrieved their backpacks, Henry walked over the boy.

"You got a name, son?" He was sliding his arms through his backpack while he asked.

"Jack," the boy said curtly.

"Just Jack?" Henry asked with a grin. "No last name?"

"Purcell, if you need to know so goddamn bad," Jack snapped back.

"No, not really, just thought it would be nice. "So, Jack, you want to come with us?"

"Why would I want to do that? I've been doing fine on my own," he said though his bluster wasn't as bad as before.

Henry shrugged as he began walking away from the boy.

"Suit yourself, but we could use a guide, you know, someone who knows the area. Could pay you in food if you want."

Jack's eyes lit up, but then he wiped the emotion from his face."

"Yeah, I guess I could help you guys out for a while," he said. "Seems like without me you'll end up dead inside of a day."

Henry chuckled slightly.

"Well, then, you should want to help us, you know, save us from ourselves and all that."

"Yeah, guess so," Jack replied and moved up so he was almost next to Henry.

Jimmy glanced over his shoulder when he saw Jack was walking near Henry.

"Hey, what the hell's this? What's the runt doing coming with us?"

"Fuck you, asshole," Jack spit to Jimmy, flipping him off at the same time. "I was invited by the old fart here."

Henry frowned deeply. "Look, son, if you're gonna stay with us, you're gonna need to curb that mouth, all right? Cursing has its place, but not as much as you seem to enjoy it."

"Fuck you," Jack replied back.

Henry slowed his stride and turned to glare at the boy.

"Look, son, you're welcome to come with us, but if you do, you follow my rules or you can get the *fuck* out of here right now, you hear me?" Henry growled in a rough tone, his intention clear.

Jack blinked at Henry, realizing he'd pushed it too far.

"Yeah, I get it," he mumbled softly.

"What's that? I didn't hear you," Henry said, his tone still hard.

"I said, yeah, I get it."

"Good, now that that's settled, go see Sue, she should have another candy bar for you, but that's it till we make camp."

Jack nodded and ran off to the front of the line where he tugged on Sue's sleeve. He pointed to Henry and he figured Jack was telling her what he'd told the lad.

Sue glanced to Henry and he nodded, she nodding in reply. Then she dug out a bar for him and Jack took it, eating it greedily. Sue reached out and wrapped an arm around the boy's shoulder and Henry was mildly surprised when Jack didn't pull away.

Jimmy moved next to Henry, a disproving look on his features.

"I don't like that little shit, Henry, he's trouble."

Chuckling, Henry looked askance to Jimmy. "Oh, yeah? Seems like there was a time when I thought the same thing 'bout you. He's a good kid. I think he's just scared. Being out here all alone, he's had to become hard. He'll get with the program sooner or later."

"And what if he doesn't?" Jimmy asked.

"Then he's out on his ass, simple as that. Look, I don't care how old he is, I don't need a liability that could end up getting us killed. That good enough for you?"

"Yeah," Jimmy replied. "Guess so."

"Relax, Jimmy, you just wait and see. Before long you two will be the best of friends."

Jimmy glanced ahead to Jack who was walking sideways so he could watch Jimmy and Henry talking. When Jimmy and Jack's eyes made contact, the boy flipped him off again.

Jimmy frowned deeply.

"Somehow, Henry, I highly doubt that's gonna happen."

Henry didn't reply, but only picked up his pace, leaving Jimmy to be last in line.

The wails of the dead floated on the breeze from behind him and with a quick look over his shoulder to make sure it was clear, Jimmy too, picked up his pace, not wanting to get caught all alone with a mob of ghouls popping up to bite him in the ass.

# Chapter 7

The lone road wound its way through the mountains like a meandering snake, the seven humans trudging across its back like fleas.

More than half an hour had passed since they had found young Jack and after the long morning all were ready for a respite.

The Colorado Mountains rose high in the east, west and south, only the north still open. High grass waved back and force and a red fox sat warily on an outcropping of boulders, watching the group pass. That bode well for the companions. The area was devoid of human life, living or dead, if the animals showed no fear of humans, and Henry raised his head high to see a solitary raven riding the thermals over the valley they were in.

Both sides of the highway were lined with the golden, cream colored butter flowers while wild plants worked their way in between them. In other spots, magenta flowers nodded and danced in the subtle air currents, a feeling of tranquility encompassing all of the companions.

They had become so relaxed Jimmy was taken off guard when a sinuous garter snake weaved across the highway directly in his path. He jumped up and backed away, aiming his .38 at the snake warily.

"Pussy. It wouldn't have hurt you," Jack chuckled

"Screw you, kid, I wasn't gonna take any chances," Jimmy retorted and continued walking, the snake now having disappeared on the other side, its tail flicking once before it was lost in the flowers and grass.

Henry chuckled at the two of them but held his peace. Jimmy would learn to accept Jack sooner or later, just as Henry had learned to accept Jimmy.


"I think it's an old gas station," Cindy, who was now in the lead, called out as the group slowed in the middle of the road.

Ten minutes had passed since the incident with the garter snake and all were hot and sweaty.

Henry's side was bothering him and he knew he needed to get it cleaned and bandaged. At least his wrist wasn't bad, only a few spots of blood still seeping from the wound. He could only hope the lance that had cut him wasn't so filthy he had to worry about infection. They had antibiotics salvaged from a drugstore in their bags and he was looking forward to popping a few aspirin for the pain in his ribs.

But first they needed to find a place to rest.

"No signs of fire damage?" Henry asked as he moved up next to her." More than half the buildings they came across were either burned up wrecks or filled with the remains of corpses.

All the windows on the small structure were shattered and a part of the roof had fallen in when a nearby tree had collapsed on it, and the one solitary gas pump stood silently watching over the land like a sentinel.

"Should we check it out or keep going?" Mary asked while shifting from foot to foot.

"Let's see what's what," Henry said. "It'll be night in a few hours and we might as well take this if it's safe. For all we know, there's nothing down this road but more road."

They all agreed with his assumption and set off to the right, moving as a team towards the gas station.

"Stay sharp till we know it's clear," Henry whispered as he pulled his Glock free of its holster, the others leveling their weapons.

For all they knew, there could be other survivors just waiting to ambush them. Once in a day to get caught in an ambush was enough for Henry. He would make sure to be ultra cautious after this morning.

Henry and Jimmy took the lead, with the others fanning out to the sides. With hand signals, Henry made Sue and Raven hang back. Raven didn't like it, but as she wouldn't carry a gun she knew she was vulnerable. Plus, she could protect Sue if needed.

Jack began to follow Henry and the older man slowed, then stopped, turning to stare at the boy.

"Just what the hell do you think you're doing?" Henry asked abruptly.

"Coming with you," Jack replied as if they were going for a walk in the park.

"No, you're not, stay with the girls until we say it's safe," Henry told him.

"I'm not staying with the girls," Jack spat back, insulted, his defiance clear.

Before Jack realized what was happening, Henry's left hand streaked out and slapped him across the face, the crack audible to everyone. Jack was almost knocked off his feet, but he maintained his balance.

The boy stood shell-shocked, staring at Henry, and his eyes began to tear up from either pain or humiliation.

"Listen, to me, Jack, when I give you a goddamn order, you'll fucking listen to it or you can hit the road now, you hear me?" He hissed each word carefully, his eyes hard.

Jack said nothing, only stared at Henry. He wanted to cry, but he was doing his damndest not to.

"Well, answer me for Christ's sake," Henry hissed back. This was careless, he thought. No sooner did he say he was going to be more wary, than he was arguing with a boy in the middle of a potential situation that could get one of them killed.

"Yeah, I got it," Jack replied, his voice shaky.

"Good, then get back with the girls and don't move till I tell you to," Henry said. Then, the matter settled, as if he knew the boy would obey, Henry spun around and continued onward.

Jack watched Henry's back, daggers in his eyes, but he did what he was told. When he reached Sue, she tried to console him, but he shrugged away from her, pouting behind the two of them. Raven only stared at him, her face impassive.

Jimmy had reached the door leading into the gas station and he peeked inside, seeing no movement and no signs of life.

He glanced to Henry and gave him the all clear signal, who nodded for him to go for it. While Jimmy opened the sagging screen door, Henry moved to the side, wanting to peek in one of the broken windows. Meanwhile, Mary and Cindy had worked their way around to the back, to see if it was clear.

Jimmy stepped into the gloom and shadows of the structure, his .38 leading the way. A chill went down his spine. He expected to hear a gunshot at any moment and feel a punch to his chest, but after a few seconds and nothing happened, he breathed a sigh of relief.

The one-story building was sectioned off into three parts. The office, the workshop, with a still intact glass sliding door, and the waiting room with two doors marked **Men** and **Women**.

A clump of windblown leaves from the aspens surrounding the building rustled in a corner now that the outside door was open, and there were a few old bird nests scattered near the ceiling rafters. Hundreds of shards of broken glass crunched underfoot, sounding loud in the abandoned building. A carcass of some furry animal, the size of a small dog, was in another corner, the petrified corpse long dried to the point there was no odor of death.

Jimmy moved to the bathroom doors, and without preamble, kicked each one in as he ducked back to the frame, hoping to avoid stray gunshots if someone was inside.

It was empty, luckily, and there was nothing inside but a dirty toilet and a few porn magazines on the men's side.

"Shouldn't you have knocked first in case someone was using the can?" Henry joked.

Jimmy chuckled slightly. "If someone had been in there this long, they would have had the biggest case of the runs in history," he quipped back, then closed each door.

"Looks safe enough," Henry said. "The shop's empty, though," he said sadly. "Not even a screwdriver's left."

"Oh, yeah? And what did you expect? Maybe a mint condition car with a full tank of gas and a charged battery?" Jimmy asked.

Henry sighed. "It could happen."

"Yeah," Jimmy joked, "maybe in your dreams." He turned to move to the door. "I'll go get the girls and tell them it's safe to come inside."

Henry nodded, and with Jimmy leaving, he surveyed the room a little more. There were a few small windows set high near the ceiling and he figured if they took out the glass, they could start a fire, the smoke then going out the high windows.

Henry wandered back to the glass sliding door, staring at the empty shop again. With the exception of a few dirty red rags the place was picked clean, only the remnants of lube oil staining the floor telling someone what the place had been used for in the first place.

He turned as the others entered and he gestured to the waiting room.

"Come on in and make yourselves at home," he said jovially.

Mary and Cindy were first, followed by Raven, Jack and Sue. Jack flashed Henry an angry glare, but he said nothing, just moved to the waiting room, picked a chair and sat down, his hands crossed and his head held low.

Sue moved next to Henry and took him aside while the others began to set up camp.

"Did you really have to hit him like that, Henry? He's just a boy for God's sake," Sue whispered, not wanting the others to hear.

"I know that, Sue, but if he's gonna stay with us he needs to take orders and not argue every time someone tells him what to do."

He sighed. "Look, I get it, all right? The kid's been on his own, but if he's gonna stay with us he follows my rules or he's out." He stared at her hard. "So what's it gonna be?"

She looked into his eyes and saw he wasn't going to waver and eventually she nodded. "Okay, you're right, I know you are, it's just, he's just a boy, no matter how old he thinks he is."

"Well, he's old enough to get us all killed if we're not careful." He took a step away from her. "Look, I'm done talking about this, okay? Please, let's drop it for now."

She nodded, then stepped closer to him and kissed him softly on the cheek, careful to avoid any of the remaining blood flakes on his face.

"It's been a heck of a day, hasn't it," she said while nuzzling her nose against his cheek.

He wrapped an arm around her and nodded. "Yeah, that's an understatement."

"Hey, you two love birds," Jimmy called out. "Are you gonna help us out or what?"

"Yeah, yeah, hold your horses," Henry said, and with Sue by his side, they moved to join the group.

Fifteen minutes later, a fire crackled in an old barrel, courtesy of some dry-sealed matches Mary had on her person. The fire had been tough to start at first as there was very little kindling. There were a few branches scattered around the building they could use once the fire was going well, but first they needed to get it hot enough.

Jimmy had opted they use the porn mags, and while Mrs. September, who liked long walks in the park and disliked people who were too opinionated, melted and burst into flames, they added the wood until they had a roaring fire that dried any of their cloths not fully dried out from the night before and warmed their tired bones.

Sue dressed Henry's wounds, cleaning the one on his ribs and then bandaging it was some clean rags they had saved in a Ziploc bag for just such a purpose. He had been lucky, the cut little more than a scrape, and once it was clean and wrapped, he felt better. His wrist was even easier, and once she poured hydrogen peroxide on it, the wound bubbling like an Alka Seltzer, she wiped it away and wrapped it in another cloth.

"There, all your boo-boos are clean," she joked as she leaned down and kissed his wrist over the bandage.

Henry said nothing, but felt his love for this woman grow twofold. Since losing his wife two years ago he'd been so alone inside. Now, after finding Sue, it was like there was a reason to live again, not just surviving for the sake of surviving. He'd never realized before that though he fought tooth and nail to live each day, he did it like he was on autopilot.

But now there was hope.

For an uncertain future, yes, but now there were possibilities he'd never considered before.

He glanced around the room, his gaze falling on each of his fellow travelers while they rested. Mary, Raven and Jack were talking softly while Cindy and Jimmy were on watch near a window in the front corner of the building, both cuddled up together. She giggled at whatever he was saying to her.

Knowing Jimmy, Henry thought, it was probably sexual, the man a horndog of epic proportions.

So, with everyone safe and sound, and a decent place to hole up for the night, Henry and Sue joined the others, planning on eating from their sparse supplies and getting some much needed sleep.

While outside, in the late afternoon sun, a lone wolf howled in the distance for its mate, and the gentle wind caressed the flowers, as if the world was still the same before the dead walked and man was still the dominant species.

# Chapter 8

The sun was just beginning to force its way into the overcast sky, banishing the darkness back to the netherealm when the fire began to dwindle.

Jimmy had decided to get up and take a leak, and when he was finished, he began looking around for more kindling.

At the door to the building, Mary was on watch.

"What're you doing," she whispered to him when she saw him moving around. She knew his watch had been earlier so he should've been sleeping.

"Had to use the bathroom and I thought I'd toss some more wood onto the fire, it's about to go out."

Mary shrugged in the dim glow of the dying flames.

"I think that's all we brought inside. Want to go out and get some more?"

"No," he replied, "that's why I'm tryin' to see if there's anything in here we can use." He went around the counter and inspected it. The cash register was open, the drawer empty, and he glanced down to see if there was anything worth taking. He thought maybe he could pull off a few of the shelves. His foot kicked a piece of molding and he realized it was loose. Bending over, he was easily able to wrap his fingers around the tip and pry it off. With a slight groaning of stressed wood, the molding came free.

But it was when Jimmy pulled the piece of wood up he spotted something behind it.

"Hey, Mar', toss me your flashlight, will ya?"

She did as he asked, the small penlight gliding through the air. Jimmy plucked it out of the air and flicked it on, aiming the tight beam where the molding had been.

"Hey, there's somethin' down here," he said as he leaned over, his voice becoming muffled behind the counter.

Mary waited; Jimmy's head was gone for what seemed like forever. She heard a scraping of metal on wood and then Jimmy reappeared, setting something down on the counter, waving for her to come over.

Mary glanced one more time out the window to see nothing but emptiness, then she padded across the room to the sounds of the others sleeping, Henry's snores the worst.

"What'd you find?"

"Don't know," Jimmy said, "but it was hidden in a hole in the wall so it must be valuable."

"So open it," she whispered, not wanting to wake the others. The square, metal container was a little bigger than a cigar box.

Jimmy tried but it was stuck. Then he looked closer with the light and realized there was a lock on it.

"Shit, it's locked," he said annoyance in his tone.

"So what? Break it open?" Mary said like she was talking to a child.

"No kidding," he replied and pulled his nine inch Bowie hunting knife from behind his back. Shoving the tip in between the thin line separating the top and bottom of the tin, he began to worry at it, hoping the tip of his blade didn't give out first and snap off.

While he worked, Mary returned to the door, wanting to make sure it was still clear outside. It was, and she leaned against the door and watched Jimmy work. She had to admit she was curious. What could be inside the box that would have had the owner hiding it inside the wall like that? Jewels maybe, gold?

It took him more than a minute, but finally with a tiny snap, the tin popped open.

Jimmy's eyes were wide as his imagination thought of what could be in the tin, but his excitement quickly faded when he saw what was truly hidden therein.

"Shit, that was a waste of time," he sighed as he spun the tin towards Mary so she could see what he'd found from across the room.

She chuckled softly.

"Oh, well, Jimmy, maybe there'll be gold in the next one," she consoled him.

"Yeah, oh well, indeed. But at least I found some more shit to burn," he said as he scratched his butt and carried the tin over to the dying flames.

So he would have something to use as toilet paper later, he shoved some of the contents of the tin into his back pocket, then dumped the rest into the fire without preamble.

With that done, he set the empty tin aside on the floor and returned to bed with a wave to Mary who returned it with one of her own.

Mary walked the few feet to the barrel as Jimmy stretched out and curled up next to Cindy in his bedroll.

She warmed her hands on the growing fire, enjoying the heat on her face. Then she turned and walked back to the door to watch over her friends while they slept.

As she did this, she barely glanced back to the seven thousand dollars worth of twenties, fifties and hundred dollar bills that fed the flames anew.

\*　\*　\*

Soft voices and movement caused Henry to open his eyes and glance around the dilapidated gas station interior. Even as he did this, his hand creeped down to his Glock lying next to him.

When he saw it was only the group moving about as they got ready to move on, he relaxed his grip on the gun, sitting up and dry washing his face.

"Well, good morning," Sue said as she moved over to him and handed him a cup of instant coffee. It had been a find they had stumbled upon in a kitchen cabinet of a burned out wreck of a house more than a week ago. The vacuum packed bag had made it through the fire intact and the companions now had hot coffee to drink for the next few days until it was exhausted.

The aroma coming off the paper cup caused his stomach to rumble and Sue chuckled.

"Someone's hungry," she said and then handed him an unwrapped bar.

"Christ, I'm sick of these things," he said as he took it from her and repositioned himself so he was leaning against the wall.

All around him the group was chatting and talking, the dying embers of the barrel fire still filling the room with warmth.

"Maybe so, but it's better than nothing, so eat it," she told him like a stern mother.

He frowned, but did as she said, chewing slowly, the coffee helping to soften the bar.

Suddenly, the sound of hollow metal, like a trash barrel, came from outside and everyone's eyes went to the front door as weapons were raised and safety's flicked off.

Cindy was on watch and she raised her left hand to calm the others down.

"Relax, guys, it's just a couple of roamers."

"Really, way out here?" Jimmy ruminated. "Shit, where the hell did they come from?"

"Maybe they followed us from town," Mary suggested as she chewed on a power bar. Her long hair was tied back into a ponytail and it made her look five years younger.

"Doesn't matter where they came from," Henry said as he shrugged out of his bedroll and slid on his boots. "They're here now and they need to go before they attract others."

The group nodded, knowing what he meant. Whenever there were more than three ghouls in a particular area, more would flock to them, and before anyone knew it there would be a crowd. No one understood why this happened, but just assumed the ghouls were attracted to movement and sound, especially of each other as they moaned and wailed.

So if they didn't take the zombies down now, in an hour there would be five, and another hour after that there would be ten, even way out here in the mountains. The dead were everywhere, roaming across the deadlands in search of food. They never tired and so could cover hundreds of miles easily, and it wasn't uncommon to find a victim that had died and returned in Boston to now be roaming the Midwest with footwear that was nothing but ribbons and the soles of its feet nothing but bone and gristle from wear.

Jimmy strode towards the door, his chest held out.

"I'll take care of 'em," he said like a proud warrior going into battle.

"Okay, Jimmy," Henry said. "But no messing around if you don't have to, and take Cindy with you, too."

"Fine," Jimmy said and waved for her to come with him.

Cindy stopped at the door and glanced to Henry.

"Are we just gonna shoot 'em or what?"

Henry shook his head.

"Not if you don't have to. Look, don't take chances to save a bullet, but if you can take them down with just your hands then do it. We're at the point where every round counts."

Cindy nodded, and with Jimmy in front of her, they headed out to deal with the ghouls.

"Think they'll be all right?" Mary asked as she watched Jimmy and Cindy leave.

"Sure, Mary, they'll be fine," Henry told her. "'Sides, if they get into trouble they can just shoot them and be done with it."

"Maybe they should just do that to begin with," she added.

"Maybe, but look what happened when you didn't listen to me, Mary. We had a shitload more coming for our asses." He leaned forward and his face grew hard. "I'd think after two years of this crap you'd have learned to trust me by now."

"Henry, how could you say that?" Sue asked.

"No, Sue," Mary said. "He's right. But I still stand behind what I did. If we're so worried about firing a shot that we risk getting bit, then what's the point?"

Henry said nothing, just sipped his coffee, and Sue considered Mary's words.

Raven and Jack had been sitting in the corner, talking. While Raven was a quiet girl, she seemed to have found a kindred spirit in Jack.

Jack now walked over to Henry, Raven next to him.

"Hey, Henry," Raven said. "Jack says he knows where we can get more ammo for your guns."

Henry glanced to Raven and then Jack.

"Oh, yeah? And how would he know something as valuable as that?" Henry was speaking directly to Raven, though Jack was right there.

"Why don't you ask me then?" Jack said as he crossed his arms over his chest.

Mary and Sue moved next to Henry and they all stared at the disheveled boy.

"So go on, we're listening," Henry said.

Jack looked at each of the companions, his eyes finally settling on Raven.

"Go 'head and tell him what you just told me," she said.

"Fine. The cannies have a shitload of ammo, but they don't have a lot of guns. I overheard the cannie leader saying how they needed to get more guns 'cause the bullets were almost worthless without 'em."

"That would explain why they only came at us with knives and spears at the tunnel ambush," Henry said.

"And how did you get into a position to hear all this, dear?" Sue inquired, moving next to him and placing an arm over his shoulder.

Jack's gaze went to the floor and he shuffled his feet as he remembered images he would rather not.

"Because I was there, that's why. They caught me and the gang I was living with. A bunch of kids like me. Three boys, a girl and their mother."

"And where are they all now?" Henry asked softly, realizing this was some troubled territory he was treading on.

"Dead I suppose, probably cut up and dropped into the stew pot the cannie's use. It's this old steam kettle they got from a nursing home. They got it propped in the middle of this warehouse about two miles from here."

Sue reached out and hugged Jack and this time the boy let her, distraught about what had happened to his friends.

Henry listened to Jack and then his brow began to crease as he formulated a plan.

Mary saw this and she frowned. "Oh, gees, there's that look again, Henry. What're you thinking about doing now?"

"I'm thinking we could get into their camp, take the bastards out so they can't hurt anyone else, and then grab as much ammo as we can carry. It's two birds with one stone, it can't fail."

"Are you crazy? That's suicide," Sue said, trying to make Henry see reason.

He nodded, agreeing with her. "Maybe, you might be right if we didn't have an inside man. You know, someone who's been inside the camp and knows the layout." His eyes drifted back to Jack who now realized he was the center of attention again.

Raven had wandered away to the front window to see how Jimmy and Cindy were doing and she turned suddenly, waving casually to get Henry's attention.

"Ah, Henry, I think Jimmy's in trouble out there," she said calmly.

Henry sighed. "Oh, great, what now? All he had to do is take down a couple of roamers, it shouldn't be that big of a deal," he said as he climbed to his feet to see what Raven was talking about.

"Wait a second, Henry. What about what we were talking about?" Mary asked as she called after him.

"In a minute, Mary, let me see what Jimmy's gone and done now and then we can figure out our next move."

Because Raven was so calm, he didn't move very fast, but when he reached the window and gazed out at the open area of the gas station, he realized Raven should have been a little more forthcoming.

Jimmy was prone on the ground, his gun a few feet away from him in the dirt, and there was a zombie in a filthy tuxedo standing over him. Cindy was occupied and didn't see her man was in trouble, and as Henry watched in horror, his hand already reaching down for his Glock, he saw the ghoul fall on top of Jimmy's surprised face before his features became buried under the stained and torn black suit covering the rotting body inside it.

The ghoul's brown teeth flashed in the morning sun as it leaned down, mouth open wide, and prepared to take a bite out of Jimmy's neck.

# Chapter 9

Five minutes ago.

Jimmy strolled out of the gas station with Cindy next to him.

Neither spoke as they stared at the three ghouls approaching them.

Two were female and the first wore what was obviously a wedding dress, the front and sides now covered with brown and maroon stains of dried blood and the long train of the dress dragging on the ground like a dead animal; bits of twigs, leaves and grass stuck to it. She still wore one shoe, the once white, five hundred dollar Manolo Blahnik now covered in dirt and grime. She hobbled as one foot was raised and then set down, her body off kilter.

The other female of the dead trio was the bridesmaid. She wore a purple dress that Jimmy bet the woman wouldn't have been caught dead in, though now she would be dead in it forever.

The last ghoul in the wedding party was a man, the groom probably, by the look of the filthy tuxedo. He wore a purple sash that went great with the bridesmaid's dress and it was easy to imagine the off color theme of this wedding. His pale and rotting face was frozen in a rictus grin and one of his eyes was nothing but a jagged hole, a few insects, and larvae squirming within the dark pit.

"You get the deader in the white dress, I got the other two," Jimmy told Cindy as he stepped onto the gravel lining the gas station. Off to his right and to the side was the gas pump, still standing watch over the empty building like a lone sentry overdue to be relieved from his duty.

"Okay, but watch yourself," she warned as she moved away, her M-16 cradled in her arms like a baby.

"Hey, babe, it's me you're talkin' to," he said in the overly suave manner she'd grown to dislike.

"Yeah, that's what I'm worried about," Cindy replied with concern and then she had to concentrate on the dead bride when the ghoul lunged for her throat with a dry hiss of decayed lungs.

But Cindy was ready, and she raised the M-16 and spun it around, slamming the plastic stock into the dead woman's face. Cartilage collapsed and the bride staggered back, maggots and other choice insects escaping from her now open sinus cavity to dribble onto the ground like rancid rain.

A pocket of purification surrounded her and more yellow pus and black ichor seeped out of her shattered visage to fall onto her dress and splatter between her feet.

But in a moment the bride was shambling back to Cindy, mouth sagging open as brown teeth gleamed in the morning sun, bloody drool slipping from cracked and blackened lips.

Cindy took a step back so she had more room to maneuver and then swung the rifle like a bat, the solid plastic stock cracking against the bride's left cheek. Withered skin split in two, and this time the bride went down hard, arms flailing outward like a fallen toddler.

Spitting to clear the foul taste in her mouth from the redolence of decay, Cindy stepped over the bride and raised the butt of the rifle one final time.

The ghoul reached up with withered hands, as if it wanted help to get up.

Slamming it straight down, the face seemed to implode as the stock sank straight through the middle of the face, breaking skull and compressing the brain to mush. The arms of the bride reached upward again, like she was asking God why this was happening. Then the limbs dropped down to the earth to remain still.

Breathing heavily from the morning's exertion, Cindy wiped sweat from her brow and turned to see how Jimmy was doing.

"Oh, shit," she gasped upon seeing Jimmy falling under the rotting groom. She raised her rifle to her shoulders, wanting to take a shot, but already knew she would be too late to help as the dead groom fell on top of him and prepared to tear his throat out.


Two minutes ago.

With Cindy moving to his right to take care of the bride, Jimmy moved to deal with the other two.

A few dead branches about the thickness of his arms were lying across the driveway, so he picked one up, hefting it quickly to gauge its weight.

"This'll do nicely," he grinned as he swung the branch like a bat, cracking the bridesmaid on the side of the head.

Splinters of wood and a few teeth flew into the air as the ghoul's head rocked to the side, and dried skin the texture of parchment split to show the glistening muscle beneath.

The bridesmaid stumbled to the side, but then regained her feet, moving back towards Jimmy with grim determination. Jimmy eyed the dead man in the tuxedo, seeing he had a good thirty seconds before that ghoul would reach him, so he swung the branch over his head and brought it down like he was chopping wood.

The branch tip was solid and it was more than a match for the brittle skull of the bridesmaid. Like a grape being stepped on, the head caved in, brains squirting out like the insides of a squished tomato.

The dead woman, now truly dead forever, swayed on her feet and dropped to the gravel, gray and brown brain matter spilling onto the road to glisten in the sun like fresh dew.

Jimmy had been so preoccupied with the bridesmaid he'd forgotten about the tuxedo ghoul, the groom sliding up to his side before he realized the dead man was there. The sound of gravel crunching under shoes came to Jimmy's ears and he spun around, his eyes wide, when he realized his cockiness might just get him killed.

He tried to bring up the branch, but the ghoul swatted it out of his hand in one swipe, the other hand reaching for Jimmy's throat.

With pale fingers squeezing his windpipe, he gargled a few syllables, but not loud enough to alert Cindy to his predicament.

The groom had been a large man in life and he was no different now. Though he had lost a few pounds thanks to decay, the emaciated zombie was still more than a match for Jimmy in a hand-to-hand fight.

The ghoul actually picked Jimmy up off the ground a quarter of an inch, his heels leaving the gravel, but the ghoul dropped him and sent him sprawling across the driveway as he gazed up at the dead face of the groom. He tried to crawl away, but his feet slid on the gravel like a cartoon mouse trying to escape a cat.

Jimmy's hand slid down his torso to grab his .38, knowing the time for stealth was over, when the ghoul pitched forward on top of him like a fallen tree, the enamel-covered teeth flaring wide to take a bite out of his neck.

Realizing his luck had finally run out, Jimmy closed his eyes and prepared himself for the pain to come.

# Chapter 10

Jimmy's eyelids were clamped shut as visions of his life, and how he had arrived to this situation with a dead groom on top of him ready to make him lunch, flashed before his eyes.

He thought of his parents, now dead, and of his friends, now all lost as well, and realized in his last seconds on Earth that the only family he had left was Henry and the others.

The odor of death suffused his sinuses, filling him with a sickness that made his stomach flip flop inside him. The growl of the groom as it leaned down to sink fetid teeth into him was so loud he at first didn't hear the gunshot crack across the area.

But he did feel the groom jerk on top of him and felt the wet splash of liquid on the gravel driveway.

Opening his eyes, he saw the groom had the top of its head missing, the scalp now spinning in the air to land in the dirt, looking like a dead rat. But the ghoul was still alive, so to speak, and though half its head was missing, it recovered from the force of the shot and leaned down to finish what it had begun.

Another shot cracked across the driveway and this time the ghoul's head snapped savagely to the side, the exit wound large enough to put a fist through.

Blood, teeth and bone flew outward in an expanding arc to ride the air in a wave of pink mist.

The groom began to spasm over Jimmy and from a distance it would have looked like the zombie was trying to dry hump him. Then the body went slack, and with a heave and a yell, Jimmy tossed the corpse to the side, rolling away as fast as he could manage.

Cindy was next to him in seconds and she leaned down to check him for bite marks.

"I'm, okay, I'm okay," he gasped as he wiped blood and bits of brain off his face. "The bastard didn't bite me."

"Oh, God, Jimmy, I saw it happening but I couldn't get off a shot in time," Cindy breathed as she leaned down and hugged him like a mother to a lost child now found.

"Uhm, you're crushing me," he said to her as she realized she was squeezing too hard and she backed off a little.

"Sorry, but it was just..." a few tears appeared at the corners of her eyes. "I thought I was gonna lose you."

"Hey, this is Jimmy Cooper you're talkin' to, babe. I'm indestructible," he joked but inside he was filled with trepidation. He knew how close he had come to buying the farm and now that it was over, he felt the adrenalin rush seeping from his system, leaving him drained and exhausted.

Footsteps sounded behind him and he turned around, expecting to see the dead groom again, as if the corpse had defied the logic of the new world and was once again on the attack, but all he saw was Henry moving towards him, and behind him, Mary, Sue and Jack waited at the door. Mary's .38 swayed back and forth as the woman studied the area for signs of danger.

"You okay?" Henry asked when he was a few feet away. His Glock was still in his hand, the barrel smoking slightly like an extinguished candle.

"Yeah, thanks to you. It was you, right?" Jimmy asked.

"Yeah, it was. You got lucky, pal. I took a risk shooting from that far away, but I figured the odds were with me, and you. Guess I was right.

"Shit, yeah, you were right." He climbed to his feet with Cindy's help and Jimmy held out his hand to Henry, his face serious.

"Thanks, old man, thanks a lot."

Henry nodded, shaking the proffered hand.

"Just glad my shots were true, now come on, if you're done playing with deaders out here, we've got some stuff to discuss. Jack told me a few things you're gonna wanna hear."

Jimmy nodded, and with a glance to Cindy, the woman wrapping her arm around him protectively, they moved back to the gas station and the rest of the group.

"You all right?" Mary called from the doorway, stepping out a few feet so Jimmy could enter.

"Yeah, Mar', I'll be fine, thanks for asking," Jimmy told her as he prepared to step inside. But before he did, Jack blocked his way, arms crossed over his chest as he gazed up at Jimmy.

"That was pretty stupid, gettin' caught out there like that. I've gotta ask again. Just how the hell have you managed to stay alive this long?"

Jimmy's face grew hard as he looked down on what was basically a smaller version of himself, though he would never admit that to anyone.

"Shut up, Jack, if I want your opinion, I'll slap it out of you," Jimmy snapped and pushed past the kid.

"Pussy," Jack mumbled under his breath, but then cried out when Henry slapped the back of his head with the palm of his hand, causing the boy's head to snap forward. "Oww, quit it, you old bastard, what was that for?"

"For being a wiseass, son, now cut the shit and get inside, we've got a lot more to talk about before we head out and whether I like it or not, you're the key to the entire plan."

Jack rubbed the back of his head, but he smiled as he looked up to Henry.

"So you need me now, huh? I'm valuable."

"Yes, son, you're valuable, now shut up and get over there before I bend you over my knee and tan your ass."

Jack made a raspberry in defiance, but he did as he was told, stepping back into the building, while Sue moved next to Henry, a smile creasing her lips.

"You have a real gift with children, Henry, has anyone ever told you that?"

"It's all in how you talk to 'em, Sue, gotta be firm. Like teaching a dog new tricks."

"Uh-huh," she said. "Well, just be careful, honey, dog's bite back when they're pushed too hard."

She nodded away from him to join the others and Henry watched her go, then with a shrug, he followed.

They had plans to make and once those plans were finished, they had a mission to undertake.

And if all went well, when the mission was done, they would have enough ammunition to last them for a while and they would wipe the earth clean of this one camp of cannies. And in the new world of lawlessness and savagery, sometimes that little bit of justice was all he could ask for.

*   *   *

A little more than five miles away from the gas station, one of more than a dozen ghouls looked up from trudging along, its head moving back and forth as it searched for the origination of the gunshot rolling across the landscape.

At first it couldn't pinpoint the sound and would have eventually gone back to shambling through the thicket, its dead brain not knowing what to do if prey wasn't in sight,

But then another gunshot rolled through the trees and the zombie turned, pinpointing the exact direction it came from.

With one leaded foot after the other, the ghoul began plodding forward, its dull mind now having a destination.

Others nearby also heard the gunshot, and soon there were more than a score, which would double in size as the mob moved through the woods, gathering others with them like a parade.

They were more than five miles away, but that was all right.

They never tired and so were patient, and with each foot placed in front of the other, the undead crowd moved towards the gas station.

# Chapter 11

The sun was high in the sky as the group of five set off from the gas station, leaving Raven and Sue behind to wait for them.

As Sue wasn't a fighter, and didn't have the stomach for killing, it made sense for her to remain behind, and Raven was asked to stay to watch over her. Though the girl didn't want to at first, wanting to join in on the action, eventually she relented.

So they got as much information from Jack as the boy knew and decided to set off after midday, wanting to be at the cannie's camp before nightfall so they could recce the place and be ready once darkness had finally fallen.

The plan was simple.

Get in, kill all the cannies, and then take as much ammo as they could carry.

"You're sure about this place, right, Jack?" Jimmy asked as they trudged along the lonely highway in single file. The plan was to get as close as they could and then leave the highway and go overland, thus coming at the warehouse from behind and avoiding any guards that might be posted.

"I told you everything I know, shit, it's not like I was sightseeing when I was there. They were trying to eat me for Christ's sake!" Jack replied, his face turning bright red.

"Okay, calm down, son," Henry said to him. "Jimmy just wants to make sure we know everything we can."

Henry glanced to Mary and saw the concerned look on her face and he moved closer to her, slowing down until she was next to him.

"You look like you have something you want to say," he told her.

She shrugged. "Not really something I can put my finger on, that's all Henry, but it's..." she trailed off.

"Yeah, go on," he prodded her. Cindy and Jimmy were walking together, chatting about something that had Cindy giggling and slapping Jimmy playfully on the arm. Knowing Jimmy, it was probably something sexual again.

Come to think of it, it was *always* something sexual with Jimmy, Henry thought. If the man wasn't' horny then he was hungry.

"It's just, this is the first time we're going after real people, you know, living like us. I mean, it's one thing whenever we're in a situation where if we don't shoot first we're dead, but this." She glanced to Henry so their eyes met so she could make sure he heard her. "This time we're going on what is basically an assassination of an entire camp of people."

Henry sighed wearily. Mary was their unspoken conscience, and that same conscience had gotten the group into hot water in the past. But that same sense of morals had also kept the companions from becoming nothing but bloodthirsty mercenaries. Though Henry had a strong moral code, in the deadlands that code could become twisted and bent. In a world where your next meal was unknown, sometimes hard choices needed to be made and the consequences ignored.

He reached out and grabbed her arm, stopping her as the others continued on.

"Mary, how can you even say that? Especially after what happened to you in Kentucky. For Christ's sake, we almost didn't get to you in time." He shook his head, not letting her talk. "No, now it's my turn. They're cannibals, Mary, no-good, filthy cannibals. They're worse than the damn deaders. At least the deaders don't know what they're doing, they're acting on pure instinct, but those cannies, hell, Mar', they chose this. They're killing people and eating them. They deserve the hell we're gonna bring down on them. Tell you the truth, I just wish we could kill them more than once."

"Hey, you guys comin' or what?" Jimmy called from up ahead.

"Yeah, we're comin', hold your horses," Henry replied as he began walking away from her.

Mary watched him go, and then with a sigh she followed. With Henry bringing up what had happened in Kentucky she found she now had images in her head. She remembered being strapped down to a hospital bed while a married couple had been flayed alive; their insides taken out like the cannie had been carving a turkey. She remembered the stale scent of sweat and grime when one of the cannies had tried to rape her, and only when she had sunk her teeth into his neck, killing him, did she manage to escape. But then the leader, Sterling, had stopped her by knocking her out, and if Henry, Cindy and Jimmy hadn't arrived when they did, she would have probably ended up as supper for the cannies.

Still, to actually be going in search of murder was against everything she had been taught by her parents and the code she lived by, but then again she remembered the fear in her gut as she lay helpless, waiting to be slaughtered like a pig.

Though she didn't fully agree with Henry's decision, she still saw the merit in his actions and she wouldn't wish what had happened to her on anyone else. So, deciding if by taking out the cannie camp she would save one person from going through what she did, she realized it would be worth it.

And to hell with her conscience.

*    *    *

The five people slowed when they were a quarter mile away from the warehouse housing the cannie tribe.

Jack was in front, and he had a handful of rocks he was tossing at a ghoul lining the road. It couldn't get over the fence because the guardrail prevented it and it hadn't figured out how to navigate over the rusting metal barrier.

One rock after another bounced off its head and torso, leaving dents and pockmarks where rotted skin was exposed.

Off to their left and right the mountains loomed high, the peaks tipped with a dusting of snow. The sun was just beginning its descent, and in another few hours it would be dark, but they were right on schedule.

On the journey to where they were now, they had come across a few roamers along the way; zombies that had taken to migrating away from larger cities and towns in search of food.

Not wanting to shoot them for the same reasons he had at the gas station, Henry and the others dealt with the ghouls in hand-to-hand combat, though the outcome was never a concern. The ghouls were only a threat when they had numbers, but seven living humans against three or four zombies was a sure thing.

Each time they came upon the roamers they were taken down quick and fast with rifle butts, feet, and stones lining the road. Behind the companions was a trail of bodies, though no one would know that but the group who made it.

Another rock bounced off the head of the ghoul, the head snapping back an inch before righting itself.

"Damn it, the fucker won't go down!" Jack spit as he threw another rock only to miss.

"Jack, watch your mouth, son," Henry snapped as he moved up next to him. He studied the ghoul while Jack continued tossing rocks at it, seeing this one had been female, the tattered dress and pony tail making it obvious of the gender. But other than that, there was no real way to discern what the ghoul had looked like when it had been alive and breathing. The face was a mess of rotting flesh and maggots, flies buzzing around the head like it was a fresh turd left in the park by a large dog. The breasts were gone, having dissolved more than a year ago, and the clothing was so filthy the color was unknown.

Jimmy slowed when he was even with Henry and gestured with his chin at the ghoul.

"Want me to take care of it?"

Henry shook his head. "Nah, I'll get this one, you guys keep going." He turned to look down at Jack. "We're close right?"

Jack nodded yes.

"Good, then we need to get off the main road in case they have any kind of patrols out."

"They don't have nothin' like that," Jack replied.

"Don't care, son, when you get careless, you get dead." He pointed to the opening in the aspens on his left that would cut across a large field interlaced with trees. Past the field it became a dense forest, massive trees that had stood for fifty to a hundred years covering the landscape.

"You guys go that way and I'll catch up in a minute," Henry told them.

"You sure?" Cindy asked, showing Henry the butt of her M-16. It was covered with bloodstains and bits of gore despite the fact she had been wiping it clean on the clothing of the ghouls she'd taken down. "I can use this."

"I just said I got this one, now go, and watch yourselves. Stay sharp, there could be anything in the woods with us that's not an actual animal."

They knew what he meant, and with a wave, they headed off. The ghoul tried to follow them but Henry called out, waving to the zombie.

"Over here, honey, forget about them." He held out an arm, showing the ghoul his bare skin. "Wouldn't you like a piece of this?"

The ghoul's black tongue slid out of her mouth like she was licking her lips and she tried to climb over the guardrail again.

Henry waited for the others to disappear down a slight incline and then he moved towards the dead woman. At first he was just planning on taking her out with his panga, but as he moved to within a foot of the zombie, he felt a rage grow inside him.

This rage had always been there. It had been there when he had killed his wife, Emily, after she had turned into a zombie, it had been there when Gwen had been tossed off the roof of the shopping mall, and it had been there when Mary had been taken by the cannies and brought back to the abandoned hospital.

But through all these times he had kept a level head, knowing to lose control could get him killed.

But now, as he stood all alone on a lonely highway, just him and one of the undead, the same undead who had ruined his life and taken everything he'd ever loved away from him, he felt that pent up rage exploding outward, and he did something he'd never truly done since the world collapsed.

He let it all out in one massive, cathartic explosion of anger and frustration.

Reaching out so fast the ghoul never had a chance to try and bite him, he grabbed it by the shoulder blades and yanked it over the guardrail, slamming it to the pavement.

The ghoul was light, the body tissue having wasted away, and Henry punched the face as hard as he could.

He felt the jaw dislocate and teeth flew from the decayed mouth to roll across the asphalt like dice. Then he punched the other side, using his other hand.

He was so lost in anger he totally forgot he had the panga and Glock at his disposal.

The ghoul flailed at him, teeth, what was left of them, trying to snap at him, but he twisted his arms so his wrists were free of being attacked. Then he punched again and again until his knuckles were sore and the face was nothing but a bleeding mass of ichor and pus.

After more than a dozen blows he slowed, breathing heavily from the exertion as he gazed down at the destroyed face that had once been a human being before turning into one of the living dead.

The ghoul was still alive though, the crushed face irrelevant as long as the brain was intact. Now blind, the ghoul reached out to grab his arms and he let it, holding them in place as the ghoul tried to pull its head up.

After more than a minute of this bizarre tug of war, Henry spread his arms wide and threw off the arms.

Standing up, he stared down at everything that was wrong with the world today and realized, now that his anger had been spent, how foolish he'd been.

To blame this one single zombie for everything that had happened to him was foolish and reckless. The ghoul rolled to its side, trying to stand, as if it was still going to try and reach him.

His breathing slowed and he wiped his brow. As he looked up and down the quiet highway, he decided whatever he'd needed to set loose was now free of him.

A dead weight he had been carrying around for almost two years was now gone, and though he still had what felt like the weight of the world on his shoulders, as in being responsible for five, no wait, now six, others, he still felt immensely better.

Glancing over the guardrail in the direction the others had been walking, he realized he better finish this and get after them.

So with a swift kick to the head, he knocked the ghoul back to the pavement, and then raised his left boot high and brought it down like he was stomping a paper cup.

The head caved in under the sole of the heavy boot, brains squishing out of the skull like tapioca from a squashed pudding cup. He twisted his foot back and forth, and when he was through, he turned and walked away, hopping the guardrail and jogging after the others.

As for the ghoul, the body twitched a few times and then remained still. No sooner did the last nerve ending die, then three crows dropped out of the sky and began feeding on the splattered brains like seagulls at the beach.

And with the exception of their annoyed squawks at one another as they fought for the choicest tidbits, the lonely stretch of road became silent once more.

# Chapter 12

"So there it is," Jack said as he gestured to the warehouse at the bottom of the hill the companions were presently occupying.

All around them were thick trees and scrub brush, perfect camouflage for the recce they were now doing.

"That's the main doors they always use," Jack was telling Henry and the others. "Around back is where the loading dock is. They don't use it too much because they don't have any cars or trucks. I did hear an engine once and smelled exhaust fumes, but from where I was I couldn't see it."

"Uh-huh, and how many do you think are in there?" Henry asked as he studied the warehouse.

From the ground up it was a red brick building for the first twelve feet, the rest was covered in gray siding. It looked like a thousand other warehouses across the United States, nothing to separate this one from any other.

With the one exception that people were being slaughtered inside this one, that is.

"Not really sure," Jack answered. "At least twenty or so. Shit, Henry, it's not like I was counting at the time, I was too busy thinking about getting cut up for dinner."

"Don't sweat it, kid, we'll figure it out," Jimmy said with confidence.

Jack spun on him so he was glaring at Jimmy, his index finger stabbing at Jimmy accusingly.

"I'm not a kid, don't call me that," Jack spit.

Jimmy said nothing, but he did grin widely while he was thinking up the proper reply. When he opened his mouth, Cindy jabbed him in the ribs with her elbow.

"Owww," he said as he bent over slightly. "What the hell was that for?"

"It was to stop you from starting trouble," Cindy told him. "Now shush so I can listen to Jack."

Jimmy made a face and Jack beamed widely, glad he'd won this round with Jimmy.

"All right, you two, quit it," Henry snapped as he gazed out across the warehouse.

Then he saw a man walking with a dog, a guard dog by the looks of it. It was hard to tell from where they were, but he was pretty sure it was a Doberman. Even from the distance he was at, Henry could see the dog was all skin and bones; the taut muscle underneath easily visible through the light fur and flesh. But the animal's teeth looked as strong as ever. If Henry guessed correctly, the cannies probably fed the animal little so the dog stayed mean. That way, if it detected an intruder, the dog would tear into the intruder with no regard for its own welfare, its stomach ruling its thoughts.

"They got a watchdog, Jack. You didn't say anything about dogs," Henry said as he turned to glare at Jack.

The boy shrugged like it was no big deal.

"They didn't when I was here, I swear, they must have added it after I escaped. Maybe that's why."

Henry rubbed his chin, feeling the scruff there. There had been no time for niceties like shaving and his three day beard was already filling in. It was slightly ashen, as was his hair. His once brown hair had received a generous dose of white over the past two years, which added to his older look. Though he was a few years under fifty, he looked like he was past the big five-o. Jimmy had taken to teasing him constantly which was why he affectionately called him *old man*. Mary told him to ignore Jimmy's jibes, telling him he looked distinguished.

"If they have one dog then there's probably more," Jimmy mused.

"So what do you think, Henry?" Mary asked while she studied the layout below. She was still having second thoughts about what they were doing, but she knew if they were all going to make it out alive she needed to focus on the job at hand.

"I think we'll wait for it to get dark and then we'll go in," Henry told her.

"Sounds good," Jimmy said. "Hey, you notice there aren't any deaders down there? What gives? There should be a few anyway, shouldn't there?"

Henry looked to Jack to see if the boy had an answer for this.

"Don't look at me, I don't know everything," Jack said.

"Yeah, and don't you forget it," Jimmy quipped, but then quickly raised his hands up in a placating gesture when Cindy gave him an annoyed look. "Sorry," he mumbled.

Henry moved away from the crest of the hill to walk a few feet to the closet tree where he had set his backpack.

"Okay, people, listen up. One of us is on watch at all times till it gets dark and we move out. I want one of us walking the perimeter and keeping an eye on the warehouse. The rest can relax and rest up for what's coming. Any questions?"

No one had any, knowing what would happen next.

This was the most difficult part of any mission they undertook. The part where they had to wait until the right time to move arrived.

"Who's on watch first?" Jimmy asked.

"I'll do it," Mary said. "I'm too wound up to try and relax, anyway."

"Can I come, too?" Jack asked her.

"Sure, Jack, I don't see why not. I could use the company."

"Good deal," Jimmy said to Mary. "Let me know when you want a break."

"Okay," Mary said and moved off to check the area, Jack following behind her like a love sick puppy dog. No one had noticed yet, but he had been developing a little crush on Mary.

"Hey, Henry," Jimmy said as he turned to ask the older man a question, but when he did, he saw Henry sitting on his butt with his back pressed against a tree, his eyes closed and his mouth slightly open. After a second a soft snore escaped his lips.

"Christ, he's asleep already? How the hell does he do that?" Jimmy asked as he turned away to talk to Cindy.

No one had an answer for that one, but it was how it had always been. Henry could sleep anywhere, especially when he was tired.

So with Henry snoring softly, secure in knowing his friends had his back, Mary walked the perimeter with Jack, while Jimmy and Cindy chatted about life and love and waited for the time to attack.

*   *   *

Three hours later, the sun long gone, the half moon now watching over the dead world, the four companions moved down the hillside towards the warehouse.

Jack was still on the ridge, though he wasn't happy about it.

As Henry moved through the long grass and weeds, he thought back to only five minutes ago.

"But I want to come, too," Jack had said with anger in his voice plus a touch of whining.

"No, Jack, you're too young. We don't know what we're gonna find down there and I don't need to worry about you, too. You stay here and wait for us. If something happens to all of us then you get back to Sue and Raven. Here me?"

The boy had frowned deeply, reminding Henry a little more of Jimmy, but eventually he gave in.

"Fine," he said brusquely.

"Christ, Henry, why don't we just get day care for the brat," Jimmy had said as he began moving down the hill.

"Cut it out, Jimmy, without Jack we never would've known about the ammo or where the cannies were holing up. Give the kid some credit."

"He's just jealous, that's all," Mary had said with a grin. "He thinks Jack's gonna take his place with us."

"Shut up, Mary, I am not jealous," Jimmy snapped at her like they were siblings. And though they weren't related that's how they always acted. There had been a time, back when they had first known each other two years ago when Jimmy had thought he might have been with her, but later that hope had dissolved into something more. A family connection born out of survival and battle.

She was the sister he had never had and he loved her. But at the same time he could hate her too, like now.

"Both of you, knock it off," Henry hissed as he moved around a sunken hole left by some burrowing creature. The ground was treacherous and it wouldn't take much to turn a foot.

Cindy said nothing, always enjoying when Jimmy and Mary went at it. Without her soaps from the TV, they were the next best thing.

Five minutes after leaving Jack behind, the group slowed at the bottom of the hill. There were a few trees cut back and a large asphalt parking lot. A few rusted-out vehicles, mostly trucks, and one school bus, sat rotting into scrap, but they had been placed there long before the world fell into despair.

Henry pointed to the right for Cindy and Jimmy, then he and Mary took the left, the plan already worked out before they descended the hill. Mary and he would go in the front while Cindy and Jimmy would take the back exit. Both parties going in with guns blazing to catch the cannies by surprise.

Their wrist watches were synchronized for six minutes, none wanting to risk running out of time before the others were ready.

And it was good they had planned this in advance as no sooner did Cindy and Jimmy move to the side of the building then a cannie was spotted. The man wore a ragged black leather jacket, and if it wasn't for the small, bright-red tip of the cigarette in his mouth, Jimmy and Cindy would have missed him.

But the man had been lazy; not realizing smoking on watch could get him killed.

He was about to learn a valuable lesson.

As Jimmy and Cindy crouched behind a couple of rusted out oil drums, both watched the sentry. The man was mumbling a song to himself as he stood across the lot. He would constantly reach down and scratch his groin and Jimmy had a feeling if the guy went to a doctor, he would be told he had crabs or worse.

Cannies weren't the best on personal hygiene, he knew from experience.

"What are we gonna do?" Cindy whispered. "The second we try and reach him and he sees us, all he has to do is yell for help," she finished, her brow creasing in thought.

Jimmy nodded, agreeing with her, trying to think how they could get the cannie to come to them.

Then his eyes went wide and he grinned.

"Wait, I got it," he said as he reached a hand into a pocket. When he withdrew it, he had a battered and worn one hundred dollar bill.

"What the hell are you gonna do with that? Bribe him?" Cindy gasped, not understanding what Jimmy could possible be doing with a worthless bill.

"Just watch," he said with a sly grin.

There was a slight breeze blowing across the lot and Jimmy dropped the hundred near the barrel and then tapped the barrel slightly. Ducking behind it, he waited patiently for what he hoped would happen. The sentry heard the tapping and turned suddenly, his eyes wide, his cigarette glowing in the shadows.

Moving closer, he held a long six foot spear with a barbed tip. If he jabbed that into flesh and then yanked it free, the jagged tear would be impossible to staunch, and that was why he had made it like this.

The sentry slowly walked towards the barrels, but his guard was barely up. Small animals and birds were a constant annoyance and he figured this was more than likely the same thing. When he was only a few feet from the barrel though, the breeze blew the hundred a foot and the sentry's eyes spotted the movement.

When he leaned down to see what it was, his eyes lit up at the sight of the wrinkled bill.

Though the money was meaningless in the present world, avarice, greed and old habits refused to die and the cannie couldn't help himself. Reaching down, bending at the knees, he reached over to pick up the hundred, greed dancing in his eyes.

But when he was down to half his height, his hand now touching the bill, he stopped suddenly and glanced up just as the butt of Jimmy's .38 came down hard on the back of his neck, sending him into oblivion. The body folded like the legs of a rickety card table and he slumped to the ground, a soft wheeze escaping his lips.

Cindy came out from hiding and she nodded at Jimmy's clever ruse.

"Not bad, babe, I never would have thought that would work."

Jimmy shrugged. "Worth a try I figured." He glanced down at the cannie. "So what do we do with him?"

Cindy's face grew hard and the warrior she had become bled through her usually calm exterior.

"That's easy, Jimmy. We do what we came here for," she said and leaned down, pulled her hunting knife, and slit the cannie's throat from ear to ear.

Blood shot from the severed jugular and Cindy stepped away, not wanting to get the viscous fluid on her. The scarlet fountain shot three, four feet into the air but quickly died down like a spent water hose.

"Man, girl, remind me not to get you mad," Jimmy breathed as he stared at the twitching sentry. The man's eyes were open now and he was gazing up at the half moon. But Jimmy was pretty sure he was seeing something neither him or Cindy wanted to see for a very long time.

She didn't reply, but moved off further down the side of the warehouse. Jimmy stared at the dead guard for another second and then turned and followed, jogging a few feet until he was with her again.

On their right there were windows ten feet off the ground. The windows were leaded glass with wire mesh in them for security. They were also tinted white to keep out the sun and help keep the building cool in the summer.

Some of the windows were cracked, the glass missing in places, and from out of these holes the raucous laughter of a few men and women could be heard.

Cindy glanced to Jimmy. "Sounds like at least fifteen to twenty people in there. What do you think?"

Jimmy cocked an ear, listening to the multiple voices.

"Yeah, somthin' like that." He moved forward, taking the lead again. "Come on, we only have a minute or so left," he said as he checked his wristwatch.

Cindy nodded and the two shadowy forms moved on, blending into the gloom as they slid along the building.


Henry and Mary watched Cindy and Jimmy disappear around the side of the warehouse and then they moved towards the main doors.

The sentry with the guard dog had gone to the opposite side that Cindy and Jimmy had taken and Henry had been confident he and Mary could make it to the doors before he returned, but as he found out to his misfortune, he was wrong.

Just as Mary and Henry were halfway across the open area leading to the doors, Mary in the lead, the sentry rounded the corner of the warehouse. At first he didn't see Henry and Mary, the gloom of the night casting shadows everywhere, but then he turned to his left and spotted Mary standing stock still, looking like a deer caught in a truck's headlights.

The guard hadn't seen Henry yet, as he was off to the side, the shadows more complete where he was, and for one precious moment Henry didn't know what to do while his mind tried to figure out how he could stop the sentry from sounding the alarm.

It was Mary who was the one to save the day, so to speak.

Evidently the guard didn't consider Mary, a woman, as a threat and he didn't raise the alarm. Before he could ask her who she was and what she was doing here, Mary lifted up her shirt and bra, flashing the man her breasts.

The guard's eyes popped out of his head at the sight before him. Mary was in perfect shape, her abdomen tight, her breasts firm and creamy white. Both nipples were at attention, the chill in the air arousing them immediately.

The instant Mary raised her shirt, her back to Henry; he realized what she was doing and went into action. Dashing along the building, staying wreathed in shadows, he charged up to the guard and the dog before the sentry knew he was there.

As he ran, he pulled his Glock free of its holster with his right hand and drew his panga with his left. The guard stared at Mary with greedy eyes while she wiggled her hips, and then he caught movement and heard the slap of boots on stone. He turned away from Mary's breasts to see Henry coming at him, weapons aimed at both him and the dog.

In the same motion, Henry raised the panga and brought it down on the top of the dog's neck, severing the leash and spine in one fluid motion, while at the same time he shoved the barrel of the Glock into the sentry's gut to muffle the shots as a quick double tap of the trigger sent two rounds of death into the man's body.

The bullets tore upwards into the cannie's heart and lungs, one exiting out his left shoulder blade. The guard jerked like a puppet as the bullets shredded his insides and then dropped to the ground, spitting blood as he died.

He was dead before he hit the ground.

Spinning on his heels, Henry raised the blade to fend off the dog, but he saw his first strike had been true. The dog's head was hanging by thin threads of gristle and flesh, and as Henry watched, it toppled over to the side, its four legs finally giving out. Blood spread across the asphalt, looking black in the moonlight.

Mary had reached him and he turned to her while she was lowering her shirt.

"Now that wasn't what I would have thought to do," he said with a grin.

"Hell, Henry, I don't think it would have had the desired effect if you did it," she chuckled. She glanced down to the dog. "Poor thing, it was only doing what it was told to do."

"Shit, Mary, that poor thing would have ripped your throat out if given half the chance."

"Still," she replied.

Henry glanced at his watch to see valuable minutes had passed.

"Come on, we need to get into position, Jimmy and Cindy should be ready soon." He looked her in the eyes, his own hard and cold. "You ready for this? No mercy. If it moves, it dies, simple as that."

"I'm fine, Henry."

"You sure?"

Her features became annoyed as she gritted her teeth. "I said I'm fine, now come on, you just said we don't have any time." She moved off to the doors and Henry quickly leaned down, wiped his blade clean on the dog's short fur, and then followed her, making sure to avoid the growing pool of blood spreading out from both corpses.

Things were about to get real serious real fast and he wanted to make damn sure Mary's head was still in the game.

# Chapter 13

Jimmy and Cindy rounded the end of the warehouse with Jimmy in the lead. As he turned the corner, he walked straight into another cannie who had come outside to take a leak.

Before either man realized what was happening, they were on the ground, fists and legs entangled with one another. Jimmy's .38 was knocked from his hand to slide on the asphalt, just enough to be out of reach.

Jimmy ended up on the bottom, and as he looked up at the half moon behind the snarling visage, he realized he just might not make it to see the morning.

The reason for this was the teeth snapping at anything they could find, whether that was his ear, nose or neck. The cannie's teeth had the typical filed points and the breath of the man was as foul as it could get.

Jimmy's stomach rolled inside him and he saw images of road kill in his mind as the fetid breath flooded over his face.

Teeth clamped on empty air and the two foes battled, rolling across the ground.

Above them, Cindy remained silent; knowing to call out to Jimmy would only get them discovered. She moved closer, her M-16 raised like a club, the butt ready to come down on the back of the cannie's head.

But as the butt was coming down, the cannie's head was shifted slightly when Jimmy tried to push him off. With the head now a few inches to the right, the butt of the rifle missed the back of the cannie's head, only grazing an ear, and then continued down to crack Jimmy on the chin.

"Oww, what the fuck!" Jimmy hissed, stars filling his eyes from the impact.

"Oh, shit, baby, I'm sorry," Cindy whispered as she tried to line up another blow.

"You're sorry? Just don't do it again," he snapped back as he struggled with the man growling on top of him.

Jimmy managed to get a fist out to the side and he brought it back in, punching the man's solar plexus with all he had. He was greeted by a grunt of pain, but the cannie still tried to bite his face off.

Meanwhile, Cindy was dancing over them both, this time wanting to make sure she could club the cannie good, but when she realized it wasn't going to happen, she ran around so she had their butts to her and she pulled back her left leg and kicked out like she was going for a field goal.

The tip of her boot connected with the cannie's genitals and she felt something pulp. The cannie opened his mouth to scream but Jimmy managed to press his jacket sleeve over the man's mouth, stifling the howl of agony. Even in the gloom of the night, Jimmy could see the icy pain in the cannie's eyes and though this was an enemy, as another man with balls between his legs he felt just a little sympathy for him.

But not enough to want to spare his life.

With the cannie distracted, he reached down and pulled his Bowie knife from the sheath at his back and jammed it up and under the man's ribcage. The cannie's back arched an inch from the insertion of the blade, but then he settled back down as the blade pierced his heart by no more than an inch. A half inch of blood red steel jutted out the man's back, the knife impaling him through the chest.

Jimmy could feel the warm wetness trickling out of the wound and down his hand, but he ignored it.

Then Cindy slammed the butt of the M-16 onto the back of the cannies skull, cracking the base of the head with the blow and causing the man's head to snap foreword, the guy's forehead hitting Jimmy on the nose.

"What the fuck? He's already dead, for Christ's sake," he hissed and then pushed the corpse off him and extracted his legs.

"Well, how the hell was I supposed to know that," Cindy snapped back, her voice low.

Jimmy waved it of. "Forget it, all right? Just forget it, it's over, no thanks to you," he jibed, not able to resist. His nose hurt and his jaw was throbbing and he was pretty sure she had done more damage to him than the cannie.

"I said I'm sorry. What more do you want?"

"Nothing, babe, nothing. Come on, let's go, that cost us time," he said as he picked up his .38 and moved to the door the cannie had just exited.

With a frown on her face, she followed.

No more than a minute had passed since the silent brawl began and she knew they were still on time.

*     *     *

Henry was standing at the door leading into the warehouse with his eyes on his wristwatch. Mary was beside him, peering into the darkness of the lot to make sure there were no more surprises while her .38 moved slowly back and forth like a radar dish searching for a target.

Henry's lips moved slowly as he silently counted down the seconds until it was time to go in.

"Three, two, one..." he said, and with Mary nodding she was ready, he threw open the door and entered the warehouse, his Glock leading the way.

The instant Henry stepped inside the large space the odor of cooking meat flooded his sinuses.

To his left was a pile of clothing boxes, and other odds and ends looted and salvaged from nearby homes. To his right was a small area with furniture spread out. Couches of different colors and makes, mismatched chairs, and a large throw rug adorned the middle, like a living room made by someone who was colorblind.

There were about twenty people gathered in this area and a small propane fueled gas grill was in the center of them. The smoke drifted up to the high ceiling where it found an outlet through small skylights which were propped open.

Meat was sizzling on the metal grates, the fat steaming in the flames, but from where Henry stood he couldn't tell what kind it was.

Knowing the people he was dealing with, he didn't think he wanted to know.

At first, no one noticed Henry and Mary enter the warehouse.

The only illumination was a few kerosene lamps and candles, which were spaced around the main area. The doorway was wreathed in subtle shadows, but then a cannie appeared from around the clothing boxes and his eyes went wide when he spotted Henry and Mary.

This man was also armed with a gun.

Though Henry only had time for a glimpse of the weapon, he saw what looked to be a Winchester double-pump shotgun. But the stock had been removed and the barrel sawed off to make the shotgun a room sweeper.

"Hey, who the fuck are you guys?" The man growled in a gravely voice from too much smoking.

Henry didn't reply, knowing if the man realized he and Mary were foes, their chances of surviving the barrage of death from the small cannon the man held was nil.

So he swung the Glock up and double tapped the trigger, sending two 9mm rounds into the man's body. The first bullet smacked into the meaty part of his upper right arm, the nerve and muscle damage now preventing the man from squeezing the trigger to the shotgun. But it was the second round that sealed the deal and sent the cannie on the last train west.

The round slammed into his chest, flinging him backward against the boxes of clothing. The bullet struck his heart and the pump was shredded to chewed-up muscle in an instant. The cannie's mouth was open, as if he wanted to ask Henry another question, but the lines between brain and his body were already shutting down and nothing came out but a bloody froth of bile and drool.

With spastic movements, the cannie fell onto the boxes, blood splashing across the cardboard to stain it crimson and then he slumped forward like a broken doll. The limp body slid to the ground, leaving a trail of scarlet behind it, the Winchester clattering to the floor a foot from the fresh corpse.

One down, twenty to go, Henry thought quickly as he spun around to face the other cannies.

At first none of the people near the couches moved, that fraction of a second seeming to last forever, but then like a bell had been rung, they all went into action, reaching down for whatever weapons they kept near them, realizing they had intruders inside the building.

His finger still on the trigger, Henry aimed at the first cannie and shot him in the face, the bullet pulping an eye as it continued into the brain.

Mary joined the fight as well. No sooner had the first gunshot been fired, then Mary darted to the side to get behind a pile of old wooden crates and began firing indiscriminately at the scrambling cannies.

A small caliber round ricocheted off the edge of the crate she was behind and small splinters of wood peppered her face. She ducked back instinctively and then reappeared a foot lower, causing the shooter to have to readjust his aim.

Mary didn't give him the chance, but fired a shot into his abdomen which had the man bending over and screaming in agony.

After that it was chaos as the cannies dashed every which way as they tried to reach Mary and Henry.

Henry had to lunge to the left as bullets missed him by inches and he rolled to the cement floor and came up with his arm extended, firing three more shots into the closest bodies. One of his next shots went wide and hit the propane tank attached to the barbeque grill. The faded-white tank erupted into a blazing fireball that reached out and consumed more than half the cannie's numbers in an instant. Filthy clothing caught fire and hair became charred while eyes were melted from sockets and skin bubbled on bones.

The added smell of charred human flesh joined the original aroma of cooking meat and Henry realized the scent was one and the same.

A screaming woman ran at him, her body now blazing in yellows and oranges as the flames consumed her, cooking her from the outside in. But her face was relatively clear of fire, and though she was breathing in the smoke of her own burning body, her pointed teeth flashed in the glow as she charged at Henry, a long spear held in her melting hands.

Henry fired twice at her, striking her in the chest, but the woman felt none of it. The pain from the flames consuming her was so intense she never felt the impacts, like she was so high on crack her arm could be chopped off and it would barely make her blink.

The woman came at Henry like a living funeral pyre, screaming in rage, and he dodged to the right as the spear tried to take out his left eye.

Rolling to the floor, he came up again, ready to fire, but before he could, another round struck the woman in the back of her head, the skull exploding, cooking brains and blood sizzling on her glowing torso.

The body toppled over, the skin now black and charred, the red of muscle peeking through where the skin had been cracked and shifted from her exertions.

Henry glanced up to see Mary looking at him. She had shot the woman and saved his life. She flashed him a grin and then turned back to the other cannies, all who were now rolling around on the floor, bright red and orange flames licking at their bodies like living beasts.

Getting to his feet, Henry moved closer, and when he heard more gunshots sounding from across the warehouse, he looked up to see Cindy and Jimmy moving through the darkness of the building from the opposite end.

They were firing into whatever shapes they could find and slowly making their way to the burning couches. A shape appeared in Henry's peripheral vision and he spun to his left to see a small child, no more than twelve, charging towards him. Henry hesitated for a second, his moral code preventing him from shooting the little girl and it was only as the child grew closer, opening her mouth wide that Henry saw the pointed teeth and the evil gleam in her eyes.

In a flash he wondered why he had never considered this situation. Of course the cannies would have children. Though they consumed human meat, they were still human beings themselves. Of course they would love, laugh and have sex, as well as want to have children or protect the ones they already had.

The girl held a long hunting knife, and with a snarl of animal ferocity, she came at him like a wild beast.

Perhaps if the little girl's teeth had been normal, Henry might have done things differently, but the filed teeth said volumes to him that the girl never could. She was already one of them, and even if he spared her life, she would only continue doing what she had been taught over the past year or more.

And he didn't have the time or the resources to try and deprogram her.

It wasn't his fault; it was the goddamn world's fault.

Just before the girl reached him, he shot her in the chest, the bullet punching her backwards to sprawl across the floor. She twitched a few times and then remained still, a small pool of blood spreading out from her prone body.

Henry didn't watch her go down. Knowing he needed to look everywhere at once, he spun around, searching for another target.

But there were none. Off in front of him, near the flickering fires of burning corpses, Cindy and Jimmy were finishing up the last of the cannies. Mary came out and also moved forward, shooting any body still twitching, doing it for two reasons. Not to take chances and to put the poor bastards out of their misery.

Rolling black smoke hovered near the ceiling, most of it slowly finding its way out of the building the same way the grille smoke had.

The only illumination was from the burning bodies, the candles and kerosene lamps all knocked over and extinguished with the exception of the one shattered lamp which had caught fire, the oil now burning in a spreading pool resembling molten metal in the flickering shadows.

"Everyone all right?" Henry asked as he stepped closer, his Glock sweeping the way for danger. He caught movement to his right and he spun, shooting three rounds into the darkness. He was rewarded with a grunt of pain and another body tumbled out of the shadows to sprawl on the concrete floor. There was a seven inch knife in the cannie's hand which was why the man had waited in silence, hoping for his chance to attack.

"Stay sharp, everyone, there could be more hiding anywhere," Henry said as he turned back to the others.

"No shit, we found a bunch when we entered through the back. And there's something back there you might want to see, too," Jimmy said as he stared at the bodies of blackened corpses. The odor of cooking flesh was one that got into the back of your throat and clung there for days on end, and just knowing he was breathing in the remains of people, even though it was just ash, made him want to gag.

"Okay, let's make sure this is it and then we'll check it out," Henry told Jimmy as he moved around the perimeter of the burning couches. Mary was a few feet away and he moved over to her, his eyes constantly scanning the surrounding darkness.

"You okay?"

She nodded. "Yeah, I'll live." She had a small cut on her left cheek where a stray splinter had nicked her. Henry reached out and touched it, his finger coming back with a small droplet of blood on it.

"You're bleeding," he said softly.

She waved it away, wiping her cheek with her hand. "I said I'm fine, Henry, it's just a scratch, leave it alone." Her tone was cold.

He nodded, knowing that tone well. She may have done what was needed of her tonight, but was still bothered by it. He didn't say anything, however. That was what made her Mary and he loved her for it. Even in a world with death, despair, and darkness, Mary was a white light of hope that things could get better in time.

"How's it look on your end, Jimmy?" Henry asked.

"Looks good. We took seven out in a small room in the back and two outside before getting in here. That's got to be all of 'em."

"Yeah," Henry replied. "I was thinking the same thing. Okay, spread out and make sure. Once we're done, we'll have a look at what you found and then see about getting the ammo Jack said should be here," Henry said to Jimmy as he slapped in a new clip.

Jimmy and Cindy moved off to the north side and Henry and Mary did the same to the south; moving in pairs to watch each others backs.

It looked like they had gambled and won. The surprise attack had worked and though the cannies had more firearms than Henry had expected, they were still woefully under armed and unskilled compared to the companions and it looked like they were home free.

With the dying flames of the cooking cannies still casting the warehouse in a dim gloom, the four companions moved out to finish the job.

# Chapter 14

"You ready?" Jimmy asked Cindy as the two stood by a small door leading to a room at the back of the warehouse.

Across the large building, Mary and Henry were doing the same, searching all rooms for possible hiding cannies.

"Go for it," she said flatly, her jaw set tight, her M-16 held at the ready. She knew she had a quarter of a clip if she was lucky and had set the weapon to single shot to conserve ammo. She could only hope the battle was finally finished.

Jimmy pushed open the door and crouched low, his .38 aimed into the darkness. He figured by ducking down anyone with a gun would have shot over his head, but whatever he expected inside the room, it wasn't what greeted him.

Two sets of glowing eyes seemed to flicker three feet off the floor and it was only when he heard the low, muffled growls, though muffled, that he realized there were guard dogs in the room.

He caught a glimpse of hackles raised, jowls curled back to reveal sharp, yellow teeth, and just before he could shoot, the dogs rushed him, and in the dull gloom teeth and slavering mouths charged for his face.

Jimmy yelped in surprise and fear as he raised his arm in front of him for protection. The first dog sunk teeth into the heavy material of his jacket sleeve and bowled him over, the other dog right behind its brother.

But Cindy was ready, too, and she shot the second dog as it was in mid-leap. A horribly human scream left its mouth as it was punched to the side to fall to the floor outside the room in a tangle of pedaling limbs. But the animal wasn't dead and it tried to right itself, so Cindy sent another round into its head.

The small skull shattered; brains and blood splattering the wall behind it as the animal fell heavily to the floor, dead for good.

Meanwhile, Jimmy was in a battle for his life.

The dog sank its teeth into his arm, and only the thick material of his jacket saved him from torn flesh and severed muscles. Still, the tips of the teeth were penetrating and he grimaced in pain as he tried to fend off the vicious animal.

As he rolled on the floor, the dog snarling over him, he managed to bring his .38 up and under the dog's abdomen. The muzzle was now pressed tightly against the animal's fur, and when Jimmy squeezed the trigger the first time, there was only a muffled pop, the flesh and fur a natural silencer. With the dog growling in his ears, he never heard the first shot, so he squeezed the trigger three more times, wanting to make sure the gun was actually firing,

On top of him, the dog jerked with each shot like it was being yanked up an inch or so, then it would drop back down.

A few seconds after that final shot, the dog's aggression seemed to subside and Jimmy realized the pressure on his arm had lessened. With a groan, he pushed the dead animal off him and then used the barrel of his gun to pry the teeth from his arm.

"You okay?" Cindy asked as she moved over to him. She had been about to try and crack the dog attacking Jimmy on the head with the stock of her rifle but then she had heard the muffled shots and had paused. She didn't want a repeat of what happened with the cannie guard.

"Yeah, I'll live," he gasped as he rolled to his side and spit onto the floor. His arm was throbbing, but when he flexed his fingers and made a fist he found he could do it without much pain. He'd gotten off lucky, he knew. If he'd been wearing only a shirt, things may have gone very differently.

"What the fuck? More damn dogs," Jimmy breathed as he came to a sitting position. He stared at the two corpses and shook his head. In the gloom, he could see the dogs had scars on their necks where their vocal cords were. Someone had made sure to keep these dogs silent. That was why there had been no barking, only guttural noises.

"You guys okay!" Henry's voice drifted across the warehouse, echoing off the walls.

"Yes, Henry!" Cindy called back. "We found some more dogs, they're dead now!"

"Okay, stay sharp, we don't know what else is in here. Find any ammo yet?"

"Not yet," Jimmy called out as he stood up, swaying a little. "But we still got more doors to check!"

"Okay, watch your asses," Henry said and then he went silent, him and Mary continuing their search.

"I was worried there for a minute, lover, thought you were a goner," Cindy told Jimmy as she kissed him on the cheek.

"Hey, no mere dog can take down the great Jimmy Cooper; you should know that, babe."

She grinned, glad to see Jimmy was already making jokes. But she also knew it was his way of deflecting attention when he was hurting or in emotional distress. She glanced down to the two dead animals, the blood flowing in a semicircle from the carcasses, and shook her head.

"Wonder why they didn't just eat these guys if they needed food?"

Jimmy shrugged. "Cant eat 'em, if you need 'em as watchdogs, Cindy. They're either food or workers, right?"

"Yeah," she replied, "good point."

"Come on; let's check the rest of these rooms. I've had enough of this shit. The sooner we're done the sooner we can get out of here."

She answered him by kissing him on the cheek again, then she lowered her rifle and the two moved off to the next door, this time prepared for anything, not just human attackers.

\*   \*   \*

"Go 'head, open it," Henry hissed as Mary reached out and turned the doorknob on the faded wooden door. They both moved to the sides to hide behind the doorframe.

The door's hinges squeaked, sounding louder than they should have in the relative silence of the warehouse. The only other sounds was the crackling of the remaining fires still trying to survive, the couches and chairs now just smoldering lumps of ash. The bodies of the dead cannies were now nothing but twisted, blackened corpses, most curled up in the fetal position from the agony of being burned alive.

If Henry felt any sympathy for the dead cannibals he showed none.

From the other end of the building, Henry could hear Jimmy and Cindy still checking rooms. From the sound of it, there being no gunshots, they hadn't come across anymore trouble since being attacked by the dogs.

That was good.

Hopefully this last room would be empty as well and they could move on. But the ammunition hadn't been found yet and that was a cause for concern. While it was good the companions had cleaned out this nest of vipers, without ammunition to replenish their depleted stores they were in for a world of trouble. Only their firearms and their wits had kept them alive for as long as they had managed and with only their blades and fortitude the end result would still be the same.

They would die.

In the new world, a gun was more valuable than gold, sometimes more valuable than food. There was no way to avoid it. The undead were everywhere and they were relentless.

The door swung inward and stopped when it hit the wall. When no gunshots sounded and no voices screamed murder from inside the dark room, Henry tossed a burning torch made from a shirt taken from the boxes of clothing and a loose pipe found on the floor.

The torch landed in a spray of sparks and rolled a foot before stopping at the foot of a metal desk. Henry looked to Mary who only shrugged. Her shrug said volumes of what she was thinking

"Think it's safe?" Henry asked.

"Only one way to find out," she replied with a grin.

"Yeah, I know," he said and then without waiting for her reply, he dropped to the floor and rolled into the room, coming up in a half crouch, the Glock looking for a target.

The room used to be an office, Henry realized as his eyes tried to see everything at once. There was a cork board on the far wall behind a desk and what looked like work orders, still pinned with tacks across its facade. A few of the papers moved fitfully in the gentle breeze stirred by opening the door.

There was a couch to his right, the blanket and pillow showing it had recently been occupied, but so far there was no sign of the occupant.

To his left were what appeared to be metal cages. Five of them, one on top of the other, the fifth one propped on top so they looked like a pyramid. They were large, similar to the ones found at dog kennels. These would have housed large dogs such as German Shepherds and Dobermans. For a second Henry wondered if there were any dogs in here and the muzzle of his Glock flicked from left to right as he waited for a snarl and glowing eyes to appear from the shadowy corners of the room.

But nothing appeared and he relaxed slightly.

"Is it okay?" Mary whispered from the door.

"Yeah, looks like it," Henry said as he stood up.

That was when he realized there was a small form curled up in one of the bottom cages.

Behind him, Mary turned at the sound of something, cocking her head to the side in curiosity. She couldn't be sure, but it sounded like a voice. She could hear Jimmy and Cindy talking at the other end of the building, so she knew it couldn't be them, so without telling Henry, she turned and began moving towards the origination of the voice.

Henry never knew she had left and he began moving towards the cages, his guard up once again. When he reached the cage and knelt down next to it so he could investigate the shadowy form, another shadow crossed over him from behind.

Assuming it was Mary, he casually glanced over his shoulder to tell her what he'd found when he found himself staring up at the dirty face of a cannie, the eyes wide with hate and the yellow and pointed teeth flashing in the fading glare of the torch.

His battle hardened instincts going into high-gear, Henry tried to spin around and bring up the Glock, but when his arm was halfway there, a club flew out of the darkness to crack across his wrist. White stars flashed across his vision and the Glock dropped from numb fingers to clatter on the floor.

Before he could do anything but cry out in pain, the club was arcing back to strike him in the head. He managed to dodge to the side and the club only glanced off his shoulder, still causing him to grit his teeth in pain.

Rolling across the floor, his back struck the desk and he looked up to see the cannie lunging for him, the club already coming down to crack his head open. At the last instant, Henry kicked out his right boot, knocking the left leg out from under the cannie and the blow was deflected. Instead of landing on top of Henry's skull, the club struck the desktop, leaving a large dent in the metal.

Still on the defensive, Henry rolled away again just as another blow came down, missing him by an inch, the club rebounding off the cement floor.

The cannie grunted from the club's impact, feeling the vibration up his arm and into his pointed teeth.

Henry continued rolling across the room, looking like a kid playing a game of rolling down a hill, but this time he managed to come to his feet.

"Okay, you bastard, let's see what you got when I'm standing," Henry hissed.

The cannie said nothing, only growled like an animal and charged him. Henry waited for the last second and then side-stepped the charge, his fist coming down to crack the back of the cannie's neck. The man dropped to the floor and Henry danced away into the far corner, finally getting a chance to breath.

The cannie was big however and he rolled to the side and was on his feet before Henry had considered trying to keep him down for good.

"I'll crack your head open and suck out your brains," the cannie snarled as he licked cracked lips.

The dying light of the torch bathed the room in darkness and Henry turned slightly to the side so the cannie couldn't see his hand as it crept down to his panga.

With a throaty roar, the cannie charged, the club coming up for an overhand chop that Henry couldn't possibly escape now that he was boxed into a corner.

But whatever the cannie expected Henry to do, he didn't.

Before the club could come down, Henry drew the panga and stepped forward, throwing the man's aim off.

The panga slid into the cannie's stomach, all sixteen inches forced in by the taut muscles of Henry's arm and the cannie was stopped cold. He stood still, the club over his head while his mouth opened and closed like a fish, a thin red line of blood seeping out of the corner. Then the club slid from his fingers that didn't want to hold it anymore. On the way to the floor, the club struck the back of the cannie's head, causing yet more damage.

The two men were face to face, Henry's mouth curved into an evil grin. He didn't ask for this, but by God he would fucking finish it. Bringing up his other arm, Henry grabbed the hilt of the panga with both hands and pulled up at a sharp angle.

Entrails spilled out of the opening wound to splash onto the floor beneath the two men's feet. When Henry had reached as far as the blade could go, he bent it and then sliced to the side, severing the cannie's heart in twain and ending his life.

Pulling the panga free, the cannie stood on legs that were already growing soft. He stared with incredulous eyes that couldn't possibly conceive how his own organs were now on the floor in front of him. Then the light went out of his eyes and he pitched face first to the floor, hitting so hard he seemed to bounce an inch.

The odor of bile and death filled the room, then another aroma added to the rest.

The cannie had shit and pissed himself upon dying, his bowels and bladder releasing its contents.

Breathing heavily, Henry crossed the floor for his Glock and picked it up, feeling better with the weapon in his hand. He looked up when a shadow crossed the doorframe, and with his adrenalin still pumping, he raised the Glock and was about to squeeze the trigger, expecting yet more attackers, when Mary raised her hands in defense.

"Whoa, wait, it's me!"

He held off, releasing the trigger. Only a quarter ounce more pressure on the trigger would have sent a round straight into Mary's chest.

"Where the hell did you go?" He snapped, angry at her for almost getting him killed. "You were supposed to be at the door watching my back!"

She was about to snap back at him for talking to her like that when she saw the sprawled body of the dead cannie and was able to put two and two together.

"Oh my God, are you hurt? Are you okay? I'm so sorry, Henry. I thought we were all right here and I heard a voice."

"So you decided to go for a walk and check it out for yourself? Christ, Mary, that's a good way to get killed. It sure as hell almost got me killed!"

Her face went ashen and she felt terrible, Henry could see this in her eyes.

"I don't know what to tell you. I'm really sorry," she said ruefully.

With a heavy sigh Henry bent over, wiped his panga clean on the back of the cannie's shirt, and stood up.

"Forget it, it's over. Talking about it won't help. Just don't do anything like that again, all right? We're a team for a reason."

"Okay I got it." Then her face changed slightly and she smiled. "But I did find something you're gonna want to see."

"Fine, but first there's something in here you need to see, then we need to check in with Jimmy and Cindy."

"Okay, what you got?"

Henry picked up the waning torch and shoved it against the bars of the cage with the dark form inside. The torch banished the darkness and illuminated the inside of the cage and Mary gasped at what she saw.

"Oh my God," she said as she moved closer.

"Yeah, that's what I thought," Henry said. "Come on, let's get this cage open and then go see Jimmy and Cindy. They're gonna wanna see this, too."

# Chapter 15

"Okay, this is the last door," Jimmy said to Cindy, "go 'head and open it."

She nodded and turned the knob, then pushed the door open.

Jimmy was to the side, and after waiting a second or two to make sure no shots or attackers were coming at him, he poked his head around the doorframe to see nothing but darkness.

"Shit, didn't these people ever hear of using candles?" Jimmy groaned while glancing to Cindy.

"Don't look at me," she replied.

After waiting long enough to believe the room was empty, he stepped inside it. It was cooler in here, similar to outside, and he detected the odor of oil and grease.

"We need some more light in here," Jimmy said. "I can't see shit."

"Okay, give me a second, I'll be right back," she replied and darted away from him. He could hear her footsteps as she padded away.

He waited for what seemed like forever, but in fact was only a few minutes. Finally his impatience got the better of him and he decided to just go inside and check it out.

There was a faint glow seeping through the doorway from the fires at the opposite end of the warehouse, and as he stepped inside, he found he could see a little.

He waited for another minute while his eyes adjusted to the darkness and then he realized he could see vague shapes. There was a big one about ten yards in front of him, but that was all he could make out.

Moving to the right, he began skirting the outside of the room. He was fast realizing this wasn't a room at all, but another part of the warehouse that had been sectioned off from the main building. He kicked something metallic and it skittered along the floor. Moving the three feet until he felt the object again with the tip of his work boot, he picked it up and held it close to his face. From what he could see and feel, he realized it was an adjustable wrench. That made sense given the aroma of oil and grease.

He may have been wrong, but he was fairly certain he was in a part of the warehouse the cannies had made into a garage.

Footsteps sounded from behind and he turned to see Cindy with a burning torch similar to the one Henry had used. As she entered the large room, the darkness receded and he saw the workbench, tires and the large, brown UPS truck sitting in the middle of the one massive bay.

"Looks like we found the garage," he said to her as she moved next to him.

"Yeah, sure does," she replied as she walked in a circle. Then she noticed another door on the far side of the bay, just at the periphery of the flickering torch.

"We got another door over here," she said.

"Great, that's great, Cindy, you know how much I love opening these doors to see what's on the other side that wants to try and eat, shoot or kill me."

She chuckled at his remarks.

"Oh, be serious, we need to make sure this place is empty. If even one cannie gets away they'll just start all over again."

"Yeah, yeah, I know the drill," he replied. He began walking to the door. "Come on. Let's get this over with."

She nodded, the torch hissing as the material burned. She had rolled the material in kerosene oil from an oil lamp, the flames now burning brightly.

Jimmy reached door and he placed his ear to the wood. At first he heard nothing, but then he could have sworn he heard shuffling.

"Shit, I think it's more dogs,"

"Okay, well then this time let's get 'em before they get us," she replied. "Here, hold this."

She handed him the torch, raised her M-16, and shot five rounds through the wooden door at about knee height. The wood splintered and holes appeared as the bullets punctured the door. She paused, then raised the muzzle and fired three more shots higher, in case it was cannies hiding inside. Unfortunately then the rifle cycled dry.

"Damn it, that's it, I'm out," she said, lowering the M-16 and taking the torch back.

"It's okay, babe, that should do it. This is the last damn door, thankfully. Whatever's in there is dead now, that's for sure. Good thinking, babe, we should have done that before and saved us a lot of grief."

She grinned from his praise, like a proud child receiving a compliment from a teacher or parent.

"Okay, then," Jimmy said. "Open the door and I'll be ready just in case," he said to her as he raised his .38.

"Gotcha," she said and moved to the door. This door had a simple slide lock on it and she had to unlock it first, then she reached down to the knob. Jimmy placed the torch on the ground by his feet and then glanced at her one last time, nodding he was ready. The light flickered, now mixed with shadows, but it was still more than ample to see by.

With a curt nod of her own, she opened the door wide and Jimmy's mouth dropped when four people charged out of the room, their hands raised to grab him.

He fired the .38 at the first body and then swung the muzzle around to take out the next, but he already knew there were too many to stop. As they rushed forward, he just couldn't understand how they survived the bullets Cindy had sent through the door?

*     *     *

Henry and Mary were halfway through the warehouse on their way back to Jimmy and Cindy when they heard the first gunshot.

"That's Jimmy's .38," Henry said as he carried the frail form in his arms.

"Go, Henry, I got this covered," Mary said while reaching out with her hands to take the blanket covered form in his arms. Henry shoved the form at her and then took off, not waiting to see if she was prepared to take the full weight of their burden. She staggered for a bit and went to one knee, the weight too much for her to carry alone. She decided she would just stay where she was and wait for the others to return.

The warehouse was almost totally in darkness now, all the flames from the fires exhausted, but there was still some moonlight filtering in through a few of the windows lining the building.

In the middle of the empty structure, with the smell of cordite and charred human flesh hanging in the air, Mary raised her .38 while watching the surrounding shadows.

As she slowly rocked the silent form in her arms, she wondered if she was doing it to console her charge or herself.

*     *     *

Jimmy stared at the shadow-enshrouded faces as they came for him, not understanding why the two bullets he'd just fired hadn't taken down his attackers, when the first figure in line moved close enough to the torch for Jimmy to get a better look at its visage.

*It's a deader, goddammit*, Jimmy thought as he began to back-pedal away from grasping hands. And if the rotting face didn't give it away then the second figure in line would have.

This ghoul had once been a woman, but her left arm was snapped in half like it was folded, and the jagged ends of both radius and ulna bones were sticking out through the mottled gray flesh.

Realizing he was dealing with the undead and that was why Cindy's bullets had done nothing, he readjusted his aim for the faces.

He fired again, and this time the bullet struck the temple, a small hole appearing there, while the back of the ghoul's head exploded outward like an explosive charge had been placed inside and then ignited. The ghoul dropped to the floor, its brains leaking out like spilt jell-o.

Jimmy was still backpedaling and his shoulders came up against the wall, just to the left of the door he'd entered. He had miscalculated and now was trapped. Swallowing the knot of fear in his throat, he took aim at the next ghoul, the one with the snapped arm, and shot the dead woman square in the right eye.

The eye popped like a fried egg as the round punctured it, following through to take out the left side of her head in a brilliant spray of black ichor and brain matter. The ghoul next to her was baptized in gore, but it barely noticed.

Jimmy's back was against the wall and he swung the gun around to try and take out one of the last two, but he knew he was going to be too late when the one to his right suddenly pitched forward.

Cindy was behind it, the stock of her rifle having caved in the back of the ghoul's skull like it was made of cardboard. But there was still one more and Jimmy raised the .38 to take it down. Only when he squeezed the trigger, he was rewarded with a dry click.

*Oh, shit*, he thought, *I'm out of fucking ammo!*

He raised his hands, knowing to go hand to hand with a zombie was never healthy, when another gunshot cracked across the room. The ghoul's head snapped to the side and the left ear was blown clean off its head, the brains following right after it.

The ghoul toppled over like a drunk with liver failure and Jimmy turned to see Henry standing at the doorway, his broad shoulders outlined by the dying torch.

"You guys all right?" Henry asked as he strolled into the room, his eyes searching for more targets.

"Good timing, old man," Jimmy breathed as he lowered his empty gun.

"Happy to help. Any more left?"

"No, Henry," Cindy told him as she moved forward to check on Jimmy. "That was it. They were locked in that room over there."

Henry moved to the room, Glock up, but when he peered inside all he could see was a few empty boxes and puddle of slime on the floor. The redolence of decay and death was unbearable and he closed the door, cutting off the worst of it.

Moving back to the ghouls, he kicked one until it rolled over.

Picking up the dying torch, he moved it across the bodies, studying them.

"Here, Jimmy, have a look at this," he said as he waved the torch over the corpse's mouths. Using the muzzle of the Glock, he pulled back the lower lip of the dead man. The hot metal sizzled slightly on dead flesh, but Henry ignored it.

"Holy shit, what the hell?" Jimmy gasped.

Cindy move closer and peered over the men's shoulders.

"They got sharpened teeth, why's that?" Cindy asked.

Henry stood up, a few bits of burning torch dropping onto the bodies to smolder.

"They were cannies, too. They must've been bit and when they turned they were kept here."

"Why would they do that? Shit, Henry," Jimmy said, "even cannies know not to mess around with deaders."

Henry shrugged. "Maybe these people were relatives? Maybe they were just good friends? Who knows, hell, maybe they were gonna eat them if things got real bad."

Cindy pulled a face at the thought of it.

"Oh, gross, that's so sick, please, don't even joke about something like that," she said as she turned away. She looked around and realized Mary wasn't with them. Her face took on a worried look as she turned to Henry.

"Hey, Henry, where's Mary?"

"She's fine, Cindy, she's out in the warehouse waiting for us." He gestured to the UPS truck. "Does that thing work?"

"Don't know, we haven't had time to check," Jimmy said.

"Well, we can check later. For now, let's go get Mary. And then you said you wanted to show me something?" Henry said to Jimmy.

"Huh? Oh, shit, yeah, I did, didn't I. Okay, let's go, it's this way anyway."

Henry nodded, and with one last look at the four dead ghouls, the three of them headed out of the room.

At the last second, Jimmy fell back so he was last in line, and with one last look at the bodies, he closed the door leading to the garage.


Mary was right where Henry had left her and he spotted the relief on her face when she saw the others behind him.

"Thank God, I heard gunshots and was beginning to get worried," Mary said.

"No big deal, Mary. A few deaders were in a closet. Jimmy and Cindy got 'em and I finished off the last one," Henry told her.

Jimmy smirked slightly, the smile not reaching his eyes.

"Yeah, no big deal," Jimmy said, but inside he was still remembering the feeling of dread at being cornered.

He was really beginning to hate this place and wanted to get the hell out of here pronto. That was when Cindy saw there was someone with Mary; hiding behind her body like Mary was a human shield.

"Who's that?" Cindy inquired, moving closer.

"We found her in a cage. If I'm right, she was probably gonna be lunch one of these days," Henry said as he gazed down at the frightened woman. She was filthy with grime and feces from being inside the cage, but even in this state he could see she was a pretty woman. Her hair was covered in dirt, but it looked blonde or dirty blonde and her features were sharp and attractive with a slim nose and a high brow.

Her dark green eyes peered out of her face like two tiny marbles and she was shaking like a leaf in a storm.

Henry took a step forward and she moved closer to Mary.

"It's okay, honey, he's a friend, they all are," Mary said softly.

"Shit, Henry, she looks broken," Jimmy said, referring to her mental state. "So what, we gonna take her in, too? We already got the brat and now this? Christ, why don't we just settle down and start our own fucking town."

Henry spun on Jimmy, his eyes hard and angry.

"So, what, Jimmy, we're supposed to just leave here to die! Well, I won't do that! And as long as I'm leader of this group we'll do what I goddamn want! Is that okay with you?"

Jimmy gulped, not used to seeing Henry like this. He could barely remember how many times Henry had ever yelled at him, and never with this kind of anger.

"Yeah, Henry, fine, you want to take her, we'll take her. It's just we got enough to worry about without all these refugees."

"I'll worry about the refugees, you worry about your own ass, all right?"

Jimmy looked downtrodden. It was like his father was chastising him. Henry's demeanor was enough to make him back down as he respected the older man so much. Unless Henry was going to do something that would literally get him killed, Jimmy had already vowed to follow him anywhere.

"Yeah, old man, it's cool, sorry I said anything."

Henry's visage was still hard, but when he saw Jimmy's attrition, his face softened and his eyes relaxed a little.

He reached out and Jimmy flinched, but when Jimmy realized Henry was just placing a comforting hand on his shoulder, he relaxed.

"It's okay, Jimmy, sorry I blew up. This shit must be getting to me is all. Look, why don't we let the girls stay here and help her get cleaned up and grab her some new clothes at least," he pointed to the filthy woman. "And you can show me what you found earlier."

"Yeah, okay," Jimmy said, glad whatever had just happened seemed to be over."

As the two men began to walk away, Mary called out.

"Oh, Henry, don't forget I found something you're gonna want to see, too."

"In a minute, Mary, let me see what Cindy and Jimmy found first." He walked deeper into the darkness. "And, guys," he said to Mary and Cindy, "watch yourselves, I think we got 'em all, but don't take any chances."

"We'll be fine, Henry, you watch yourself, too," Cindy said.

He waved and moved off, Jimmy a few feet ahead of him.

Cindy looked down at Mary and the filthy woman and she pointed to Mary's .38.

"Hope you got bullets for that, 'cause I'm out," she said holding up her M-16.

She nodded. "Yeah, I got a full load in the cylinder and two dozen more in my pockets."

"But how?" Cindy asked, not understanding where the ammo was from, but Mary stopped her with an upraised hand.

"Just wait for the boys to get back and I'll show you all at the same time."

Cindy nodded, and with Mary helping the trembling woman up, they moved to the edge of the warehouse to find someplace to rest and then find some water and clothing for their new friend to get cleaned up.

Then they could relax and wait while the men went exploring, like they were two kids left alone in a museum after closing.

# Chapter 16

With Jimmy holding another torch, Henry entered the room first; the muzzle of his Glock facing forward like it was a sensitive snout that could sniff out the whereabouts of any prey in the area.

As Jimmy and Cindy had already been through this part of the warehouse, it was empty, but he wasn't taking any chances. Upon entering this section of the building, Henry immediately knew what the cannies had been using it for.

It was the kitchen.

Henry saw two things at the same time, the first being the bullet riddled corpse of the dead cannie lying face down in the middle of the room. The other was the large, wooden table that dominated the middle of the room.

On this table were the remnants of a male, human body, the severed head lying to the side as if it was nothing more than the discarded fat from a pricey tenderloin. The mouth of the head was agape, the tongue slightly protruding, and the eyes were wide with what Henry must have assumed was the horror of the man's impending death. There was a jagged nub of spinal column jutting from the severed neck.

Dark blood was covering the table and it dripped to the edge where it trickled to the cement floor, slowly spreading out to follow the slant of the concrete.

The chest of the torso had been sliced down the middle, like it had been in an autopsy, and the ribcage had been cracked to expose the tender organs within. A gaping opening greeted Henry's inspection and he turned away disgusted.

But there was nowhere he could look without seeing something distasteful in this chamber of horrors. On the floor, off to the side, were large plastic buckets filled with the severed arms and legs of other poor souls. To the right of the table, lining the wall was another, shorter table. On this table were the smaller limbs and hands of what had no doubt been children. The bodies had been sliced and diced, the pieces of flesh made into bites sized portions like they were going to be used for stew.

And if he wasn't sure at this assumption, the large steel pot still simmering to the side over a small gas stove proved his point. Next to that was a large bowl of boiling oil, and human fingers floated in it, overcooking like well done French fries.

Moving to the stew pot, he reached for a ladle and stirred the brown, lumpy liquid. He saw wild onions and potatoes, which was normal, but then a severed hand floated to the surface, a silver ring still on one of the fingers.

Evidently the cook was lazy, he thought.

But there was still more.

Large glass bowls were filled with human livers; the livers chopped up into bite sized pieces and then mixed with onions and peppers. Next to those were more large bowls, piled high with intensities, like it was nothing more than link sausages waiting to be boiled. Human hearts sat in a large metal wash bin with vinegar, waiting to be pickled. To the left was an old meat grinder, a human arm in the top, the bone peeking out like the remnants of a turkey leg, and a large pile of what resembled ground hamburger below the spout.

The scene was so unbelievable, Henry had to pause for a moment to gather his thoughts.

Glancing down at the dead cannie, he spit on him, wishing the man was still alive so he could kill him again.

"So this is what you wanted to show me?" Henry asked Jimmy, the young man standing behind him, waving the torch around so Henry could see.

"Yeah, un-fucking-believable, huh? I mean, look at this shit, these fuckers actually ate other people."

"And you doubted they did? Especially after what happened at the shopping mall and Barry and then at the hospital?"

"Yeah, well, uhm, what I meant to say is..." Jimmy stammered not knowing how to reply.

"Just forget it, Jimmy, it doesn't matter. Come on, let's go see the girls and finish up."

"Okay," Jimmy said and followed Henry out of the chamber of horrors. As they exited the kitchen Jimmy moved up so he was walking next to Henry.

"Hey, Henry," Jimmy said.

"Yeah?"

"Back there in the kitchen, all that shit by the grinder. Once it was ground up it did look like regular meat. What do ya think it tastes like? Chicken or beef?"

"I don't know, Jimmy, and I don't want to know, now quit talking nonsense and shine that torch in front of us so I can see where the hell I'm going," he snapped.

Jimmy nodded, and with the torch leading the way, the two men headed back to find the girls.

*    *    *

A few minutes later, the companions were gathered near the middle of the warehouse, the smoking corpses of the cannies still the focal point of the area. By now all the fires were about out and only a few sputtering flames still tried valiantly to remain lit. Soon, they too, would be extinguished, plunging the warehouse into total darkness with the exception of a few feeble rays of moonlight that seeped through the tinted windows.

Next to them, standing quietly on wobbly, weak legs, was the woman Henry had found in the cage. Jimmy and Henry were quickly filled in about the woman, her name, and how she had ended up in a cage in a cannie camp by Mary and Cindy.

Her name was Carol and she had been a wife and mother in a nearby town and had woken one night to see two cannies glaring down at her with knives in their hands. The cannies had scaled the wall of the town and her home had been near the perimeter and so had been one of the first to be invaded. She had found out later three other homes had been targeted that night and for a few weeks her and her family weren't alone in the cages.

Her entire family had been taken to the kitchens more than a week ago and she was the last to still be alive. Knowing her only son and husband had been cooked and eaten filled her with grief and she had already admitted more than once she wished she was dead and would have tried to kill herself in the cage if she'd had a weapon so she could join her family in Heaven.

But though filled with sadness, she had greedily taken the power bar Mary had given her from one of her pockets. After she had eaten, her dull eyes had taken on a brighter hue, the nutrients helping to vitalize her. Mary and Cindy both hoped once the woman was away from this terrible place and back in the sun, she may decide to live, if only to keep the memories of her family alive.

As everyone gathered themselves, Mary moved up to Henry, a sparkle in her eye.

"So, Henry, are you ready to see what I found?"

Gesturing with his right hand, his Glock back in its holster now that he was sure they were alone, he said. "Lead on, Mary, I'm right behind you."

She smiled widely, turned, and moved deeper into the shadows. Henry glanced to Jimmy and asked him if he wanted to come too, and after checking with Cindy to see if it was okay, he followed, Cindy remaining behind to watch over Carol.

The three crossed the warehouse floor and slowed when they reached yet another doorway. The door was open on this room and inside one small candle burned.

Mary was the first inside, and when she was to the right of the doorway, she held out her hands and said, "Ta daaa, look what I found!"

Jimmy blinked in surprise and moved to one of the boxes lining the side of the room.

"Holy shit, will you look at all this stuff?" He was digging in the top box and his hand came out holding bullets. Dozens and dozens of them.

In the flickering candlelight, he was able to make out the labels on the sides of the boxes.

"Shit, guys, this is the mother load. Will you look at all this ammo!"

"Calm down, Jimmy," Henry told him. "None of it matters if the caliber won't fit our weapons.

"Oh, but there is, Henry," Mary said as she walked over to a box on the end and picked up a small, five inch box of 9mm shells. She tossed the box to him and he caught it deftly. "There's boxes of this and it's all ours."

Henry said nothing, but instead quickly popped out his spent clip and began filling it with bullets from the open box. It took him a full minute, but when he was done he slapped the full, 17 round clip back into the gun. The familiar weight of the loaded gun felt good in his hand, and after checking to make sure it was cocked and ready, he slid the gun back into its holster. The safety stayed off and would remain that way until he knew he and the others were entirely out of danger.

"Oh, shit, rounds for my gun!" Jimmy called out as he reached into another box and picked up a box of .38 caliber rounds. His eyes noticed the next box and he barked out loud again. "And these'll fit Cindy's rifle!"

Henry was walking around the room, seeing what else there was to find.

"Great job, Mary, I just wished you'd said something sooner," Henry told her.

"When? Since I found it there's been no time," she replied.

He nodded. "Yeah, that's true, huh, well it looks like we got time now, so, hey, what's this?" He crossed the room to the opposite end of where the boxes of ammunition were stacked. There was a long table that went the width of the room, it was made of plywood and was strewn with gun parts of all shapes and sizes. Henry picked up a few pieces, but saw they were in poor condition. Now that he was closer, even in the gloom of the candlelight he could see there were more crates with gun parts under the table.

"Looks like they were trying to build some guns here. Glad they didn't figure it out yet or we would have been in for a world of hurt," Henry stated.

"Yeah, no shit in that one," Jimmy said as he slid rounds into his .38 and shoved handfuls into his pockets so he jiggled as he walked. Later, he would transfer them to his backpack, but he felt good knowing he was loaded with enough ammunition to take down a small army. Moving to another box, he reached down and picked up a vest. The letters SWAT were stenciled on the back and front breast.

"Hey, Henry, what are these for?"

Henry glanced over. "Looks like those might be bulletproof vests," he said. "Probably made of Kevlar, stop a standard round from a foot away."

Jimmy made a face and a raspberry noise. "Vests are for pussies," he sneered as he dropped it back into the box. Then he made sure to grab a few clips for Cindy's M-16, shoving them into the waistband of his pants and wincing when the cold metal touched his skin.

"Hey, Henry," Jimmy called. "I'm gonna go give a few clips to Cindy so she's got bullets, I'll be right back," Jimmy said, and with out waiting for a reply he was off.

Henry didn't hear him, as he was still studying the gun parts, wondering if there was anything worth salvaging, when his eye spotted an old, WW2 two-way radio in the corner of the table, where the two walls met. Mary saw that he had noticed the radio and she slid up next to him.

"That's why I left you before, Henry. I thought I heard a voice but it was this radio. But when I got here the voice stopped and I don't know how to use this thing."

Henry grunted slightly, his attention on the radio. His father had been a ham radio hobbyist and he had a little knowledge on how to use one. Stepping up to it, he reached out and checked the power cord, seeing it ran down to a car battery, an adapter in between to change the current. Someone had jury-rigged it and it looked like a decent job.

Satisfied he had power; he sat down on the old, worn chair and began playing with the row of buttons and switches until he was rewarded with a loud, high-pitched howling. He played with it some more and the howling stopped to be replaced by crackling static. Leaning in closer, he could have sworn he heard words amongst the static, but it might have been his imagination.

Twisting the dial, he kept at it while Mary looked on, biting her lower lip in expectation. There was really no reason to be excited even if they heard a voice on the other end of the radio, but it was just that simple things like cell phones and the internet, items that had been taken for granted only two years ago were now nothing more than lost relics from another time.

"There, Henry, go back, right there, you had it!" Mary exclaimed as she leaned over his shoulder, her hair falling over her face.

Henry heard it too and did as she asked.

"...message....help...willing to follow...west...42...repeat..."

"Hold on, almost got it," he said while he twisted the dial some more. He heard rustling behind him and he glanced over his shoulder to see, Jimmy, Cindy and Carol all at the door. His free hand had gone down to his Glock and he now removed it, focusing on the radio.

Cindy made sure Carol was all right and she and Jimmy moved next to Henry, wanting to hear the message trying to fight its way to clarity.

"...anyone hearing this message who is in need of help and is willing to follow the west bound road into the mountains by Highway 42 to Crescent Falls will be aided. Stay tuned to this frequency for further updates when available. I repeat, if anyone hearing this message..."

Then the message faded to be lost by a dull crackle and the lights on the panel began to dim.

"Damn, the battery's dying," Henry said as he slapped the side of the radio, as if that would make it work again.

"Wouldn't matter anyway, Henry, that was a looped tape. It was starting again before you lost it," Mary said.

"Still, it would have been nice to hear the entire message from beginning to end, he replied as he pushed away from the table. As he did, he was able to see the maps lying on the table. He hadn't noticed them at first, but now that he studied them, he saw there were circles where the possibility of towns could be hidden within the mountains.

"Looks like the cannies were planning on paying those people a visit," he said as he picked up the map so he could see it better in the candlelight. See, this one is circled and it's off of Highway 42. I'd bet my Glock this is the place." He pointed to the words next to the circled area. **Tomorrow** was written out in black marker.

"Looks like these bastards were gonna pay this place a visit tomorrow."

Cindy moved closer to see the map. "Looks like we just saved that town a world of grief, huh," she said.

"Yeah, shame they'll never know it," Jimmy said. "We might have gotten a free ride out of it."

Footsteps sounded from behind everyone, coming from the main floor of the warehouse and they were heading directly for the companions location.

"Cindy, get Carol out of the doorway," Henry hissed. Cindy moved to Carol and pulled the woman away. Carol was still weak and went where she was told, barely putting up a fight. Then everyone waited, weapons drawn and aimed at the doorway. The instant the owner of the footsteps appeared, they would be sent to Hell on a boatload of hot lead.

The footsteps grew louder and then seemed to hesitate, as if the owner realized something was wrong. Where there had been voices it was now silent. But then the footsteps continued and a shadow appeared near the doorway. Henry raised his Glock, his finger depressing the trigger. A quarter ounce of pressure was all that would be needed to send the figure on the last train west.

And then Jack entered the room, his eyes going as wide as dinner plates when he saw the barrel of four guns aimed at his head and torso.

"Whoa, guys, don't shoot, it's me!" He screamed raising his hands in front of his face as if that could shield him from a barrage of lead.

Henry paused at the last instant and released the trigger, the Glock dropping immediately. The others did the same, though Jimmy seemed to hesitate for a moment longer, as if he was considering shooting anyway and claiming it was an accident. Cindy saw this and she elbowed him in the ribs. He smiled bashfully, but lowered his .38.

"Jack, you almost got yourself shot. What the hell are you doing in here? You were supposed to wait on the hill."

"Yeah, and I did for like, forever. I got tired of waiting, all right? I heard all the shooting and then everything went quite. I wanted to see if you might need my help."

Jimmy made a disgusted noise. "Oh, yeah? And what were you gonna do? Yell at them?"

"Screw you, Jimmy, I could have done something. If you'd given me a gun then I could have used that," Jack snapped in reply.

"No, Jack," Henry said, getting into what would be a fresh argument between Jack and Jimmy. "I already told you, no guns, at least not until I think I can trust you with one. That's gonna take time."

Jack crossed his arms over his chest and pulled a face, but he knew not to talk back to Henry.

Mary crossed the room and rubbed Jack's back in consolation while he pouted at Henry.

"Actually," Henry continued. "Though I told you to stay on the hill and you didn't listen, it still might be a good thing. Did you bring our backpacks?"

Jack's face lit up a little. "Sure did, they're right outside, I had a feeling you'd make me go get them so I dragged them down with me."

"Well, you were right, son, I would have." Henry turned to Jimmy who still wore a face of annoyance. "Hey, Jimmy, I think it's time we check out that UPS truck in the garage. If that sucker works we won't have to walk back to Sue and Raven."

Jimmy grinned. "Was already thinkin' that, old man, but figured the ammo was more important. Want to go check it out now?"

"Yeah, but let's all go together. If it runs, I want to gather as much stuff as we can fit inside it. We can use most of it for trade if for nothing else. Might even get us into that town where they would have considered turning us away otherwise."

"So let's go," Mary said, eager to leave this place of death and horror.

Everyone grabbed more ammunition, as much as could be carried comfortably. If the UPS truck worked, they would come back for more, but they knew the value of traveling light. If you carried too much you would only end up tiring yourself out and would probably die before you ever got the chance to use it all. Plus, the more you carried the slower you became and more than once a split second was the razor line between living or dying.

After gathering more ammo, Cindy now ecstatic about having more clips for her rifle, the group of six moved out, crossing the warehouse on their way back to the garage. Barely a glance was given to the immolated corpses. The cannies had lived evil lives and had died evil deaths; no tears would be shed over those deaths.

In a few minutes they were all gathered inside the garage, the zombies still spread out on the floor where they had fallen. The air was ripe with death and noses were covered by hands. Flies had appeared to begin feeding and maggots had crawled away from the corpses to see if there was better feeding elsewhere.

Jimmy had a new torch in his hands, allowing them to see better than with a simple candle.

Henry moved to the UPS truck, casually walking like there was no trouble, and as he opened the sliding door and prepared to step up into the driver's seat, a guttural growl sounded from inside the rear of the truck. Before he could stop him, a man charged out of the darkness to attack him, pointed teeth flaring in the shadows. The cannie wrapped his arms around Henry, preventing the warrior from drawing either his gun or panga, and both tumbled off the truck to fall to the oil-covered cement floor.

As the two men fell to the hard floor, the back of Henry's head struck the concrete, rattling his brain and filling his vision with pinpricks of light. He felt himself sliding into unconsciousness, but before he went, he caught the glint of a sharpened blade reflecting the light from Jimmy's torch as the cannie raised the weapon in preparation of plunging it deep into his chest.

# Chapter 17

Though darkness was forcing itself on his waning consciousness, Henry fought it off, knowing if he dropped away to oblivion, he would never wake up.

With every ounce of will he could muster, he kept himself from fainting, though his head screamed at him from the trauma suffered after striking the oil-covered floor.

In the distance, he could hear Jimmy and the others yelling as they moved forward to try and help him. But he knew if he didn't stop the cannie from plunging the long, filthy dagger into his chest himself, then it was going to happen whether he liked it or not.

So with a growl of his own to stave off unconsciousness, he slid his left arm free of the cannie's body and reached up with that hand, stopping the cannie's descending arm a fraction of an inch before the dagger managed to touch his shirt. The tip hovered directly over his heart, the arm straining to plunge it into his chest, only Henry's arm halting it.

But the cannie was on top of him and he had the advantage, so he used it, forcing his weight onto Henry's arm, the blade slowly moving downward.

Henry felt the tip of the dagger kiss his flesh, the tip poking through his shirt. A small bead of blood began to form around the tip to spread out and stain his shirt a bright red.

The cannie was laughing while he tried to kill Henry, and though fighting for his life, Henry saw the man was wearing faded gray coveralls, the top part covered in oil and grease. Even while he battled, his mind pieced together what must have happened. The man must have been the mechanic for the cannies, and when all hell had broken loose he'd hid inside the UPS truck, waiting for a chance to escape.

Why he hadn't taken off when the companions had left the garage was anybody's guess, but the man had been there as Henry had opened the truck unawares.

So now, because of a lack in judgment, Henry was staring at his executioner.

The tip of the blade moved another half centimeter and Henry cried out, time seeming to stand still, but unbeknownst to him no more than ten seconds had passed since the cannie lunged out of the back of the truck.

The cannie groaned with effort and Henry could see the man was about to push again, and this time Henry had no doubt the blade would sink deep into his chest, slicing past his ribcage to puncture his sternum, his beating heart waiting within. He imagined the piercing pain as the dagger slid into his left ventricle, the gasp of shock when his heart stopped beating and he expelled his last breath.

And as his left arm shook with the strain of holding the man above him, his muscles taut like cordwood, he knew he was fighting a battle he couldn't win.

The darkness was rushing over him again and his fight with unconsciousness was once again overwhelming him, but just as he felt the cannie shift his weight to force the blade home, a gunshot cracked across the garage and the cannie was blown away from Henry.

A thin splatter, like mist, rained down over Henry's face and he had a quick glimpse in the flickering shadows of Jimmy, his .38 still leveled where the cannie's left ear had been.

Then Henry lost his battle and fell into the dark night, wondering if he would ever wake up again.

\*    \*    \*

Henry came to thanks to the sound of a rumbling motor, the vibration going right through his back and into his teeth.

Opening his eyes, he realized he was inside the UPS truck, the ceiling lost in the gloom above him. He could hear voices all around him, Jimmy's the predominant one of course, and the others as well. It sounded like Jack and Jimmy were arguing about something.

Sitting up, he touched his chest to feel a small bandage over the wound. When he rubbed it gently, it didn't hurt too much and he realized he had dodged death for another day.

As he sat up, his vision blurred for a moment, but then he realized it wasn't his vision, but the darkness inside the truck. So with a groan he stood up, wavering slightly for a moment before feeling he was up to the task of walking.

Turning to the rear of the truck, he saw the doors were half open. All around him were boxes with the caliber of ammunition labeled on the side. A few boxes had clothing in them and he saw his and the rest of the group's backpacks stuffed behind the driver's seat. Reaching down his body, he felt relieved to feel his Glock and panga safely on his person, and after taking a few deep breathes to clear his head, he opened the rear doors the rest of the way and stepped down to the garage, the cooler air hitting him and helping to clear the cobwebs.

There was still the stink of death in the air, and now the dead cannie mechanic added to that aroma, but someone had taken a moment to cover the corpses with an old tarp.

Mary looked up from carrying a box when she saw Henry climb out of the truck.

"Hey, there, I was starting to get worried," she said.

"How long was I out?" Henry asked, his voice sounding throaty like he was a chain-smoker.

"About two hours. I was worried you had a concussion. You know what they say about sleeping with one, right?"

He nodded.

"Yeah, well we tried to wake you up, but it wasn't happening. Finally we had to just pray you'd wake up on your own. So Cindy and me dressed your chest wound and put you in the truck so you'd be safe."

He nodded "Where's Jimmy? I just heard him," Henry said.

"You're welcome," she said, slightly annoyed at him.

"Huh? Oh, sorry, Mary, of course I'm grateful, thanks. I'm still a little groggy." He looked around at the boxes lined up near the rear bumper of the truck. "You guys have been busy, I see," he said, admiring the stockpile of supplies. "So where's Jimmy?"

Mary still held her box so she used her chin to point out the doorway that led to the interior of the warehouse.

"He's in there somewhere. Just yell out, he'll hear you or you'll hear him; the echo is awful around here," she said.

Henry turned and pointed to the UPS truck, seeing the smoke bellowing out of the exhaust.

"Someone shut that off before we all get killed by carbon monoxide," he said as he moved to the doorway.

Cindy heard him and stopped what she was doing.

"I got it," she told him. She climbed up into the driver's seat and turned off the motor. "Jimmy said we should let it idle for a few minutes, we're almost ready to go," Cindy called as she hopped back to the floor.

Henry paused at the doorway. "It sounded fine, Cindy, and you should never take what Jimmy says at face value, right?"

She grinned. "Yeah, that's true, I guess."

"Damn straight, okay, I'll be right back."

The women waved and Henry strolled into the main part of the warehouse, feeling better with each passing second.

When he was in the middle of the warehouse, he cocked his head when he heard voices, arguing of course, and he turned and followed the sounds until he reached the kitchen again, the charnel house smell preceding the room before he entered it.

As he entered, the voices of Jimmy and Jack came to him and it seemed they were arguing yet again.

"And I say some of this stuff is okay to eat," Jimmy was saying.

"That's bullshit, Jimmy and you know it. All of this stuff is contaminated. Fuck, I'm a kid and I know that."

"Yeah, you're a kid who doesn't know how to keep his goddamn mouth shut."

"Oh, yeah? And whose gonna make me keep it shut?"

"I will if you don't shut the fuck up!" Jimmy snapped in reply.

"Hey, hey, you two, knock it off!" Henry yelled, silencing both young men. He immediately got a headache from yelling, but he ignored it, not wanting either of them to see him show weakness.

"What the hell are you two arguing about now?"

They both began talking at once, each trying to override the other and Henry raised his hand again, then brought it down in a chopping motion.

"Enough! Christ, you two are worse than brothers. Why can't you get along?"

That only started them talking again, each trying to be the one who got Henry's attention.

Henry was seriously considering taking his Glock out and firing a shot into the ceiling when Jack picked up a hunk of meat. It looked like pork for all purposes.

"This is why, Henry! Jimmy wants to take some of this meat with us!"

"No I didn't, you little brat, I said we should bring any vegetables we can find."

"Bullshit, you said meat, too!" Jack yelled back.

"Enough! Christ, shut the hell up, both of you!" He turned to Jimmy. "You, did you really say that?"

Jimmy was about to talk when Jack opened his mouth. Henry spun on him and jabbed a finger at him accusingly. "Uh-huh, you'll get your turn, now be quiet."

Jack looked like he was going to talk anyway, but Henry jabbed the finger again and raised his eyebrows in a *just test me* look that he remembered fondly from his own father.

Silently Jack relented.

Jimmy, now getting the chance to speak, filled Henry in on his idea. When he was finished, Henry shook his head.

"I see where you're going with this, Jimmy. Sorry, but I don't want to eat anything that came from this kitchen and I'm pretty sure the girls don't want to either."

"Ha, told you, asshole," Jack spit in victory.

"I said to stop it, Jack," Henry said. "Jimmy makes sense, though, we need to find food where we can get it and later if we end up on the road with nothing to eat even I'll be regretting if we leave this stuff behind. But I'll take my chances and I think the others will agree with me, too."

"Fine, Henry, whatever," Jimmy said and turned to leave. "I'm going back to help the girls. We're just about done. The truck's got a quarter of a tank so at least we got fuel."

"Good, okay, we'll be right behind you," Henry said as he watched Jimmy leave. When Jimmy was gone, the light from his torch vanished with him, bathing the kitchen in dull shadows, the body parts now looking even more sinister.

Jack crossed his arms over his chest and looked at Henry with a smug look.

"That guy is an idiot," he stated blandly

"No, he's not, Jack, and you better remember who's who around here." He stepped closer to Jack so all he had to do is whisper. "If you two can't get along then one of you has to go. And guess who that's gonna be?"

"Him?" Jack said sarcastically.

"No, Jack, you, so I suggest you stop it or else. Now go back to the truck and help the others."

Jack looked like he was going to say something but something inside him realized there was a time to concede and this was it. So with a heavy sigh, he scooted around Henry and trudged out of the kitchen, leaving Henry alone with his thoughts.

Henry leaned against the table, the severed corpse moving slightly like it wanted to get up and leave, not at all pleased with being sliced and diced for supper, and he raised his hand to his temple.

Closing his eyes, he could feel the headache pounding behind his eyeballs, a steady staccato like a drum solo. He knew either Mary or Cindy had aspirin in their packs, salvaged from somewhere on their previous travels, so with one last look at the chamber of horrors, he turned to leave.

It was as when was passing the gas stove that he slowed for a moment, his eyes studying the contraption of valves and hoses attached to the gas canisters. The oil wasn't boiling and the stew was getting cold, evidently Jimmy or one of the others had turned off the gas.

Nodding to himself, he got a spark of an idea, but there would be time for it later. For now, he left the kitchen, leaving the body parts and organs alone once more to rot in the darkness.

# Chapter 18

The UPS truck was filled with as much stuff as the companions could fit in the racks lining the insides. There were thousands of rounds of ammunition for their weapons as well as for others. When they reached the next town, they would live like kings, the bullets worth far more than money or gold ever had been in the old world.

There were boxes of clothing, ammunition, bullet proof vests, and other items in one corner, piled so high they looked like they would topple over the instant Jimmy stepped on the gas pedal. A few old and stretched-out bungee cords were wrapped around the cardboard containers and then attached to hooks on the walls, the best they could do to secure them from falling.

Everyone was ready to leave this place of death.

Carol was sitting on a box in the back of the truck, her head held low, along with Sue and Raven. Jimmy and Jack were in the front seats, arguing as always, and Henry, Mary and Cindy were standing in the garage looking up at Jimmy in the driver's seat.

"Okay, so give us five minutes and then start the engine, when we come back there's not gonna be anytime for screwing around. You got me?" Henry asked.

"Yeah, old man, I got it. Jesus, lighten' up a little," Jimmy remarked casually.

Henry's brow furrowed in annoyance.

"I'm not messing around here, Jimmy, when we get back it's go time."

Jack leaned over Jimmy's lap with a mischievous grin.

"Don't worry, Henry, I'll make sure this idiot does what you tell him," Jack said with a sly glance to Jimmy, like the man wasn't listening.

"Screw you, Jack, we should leave your ass here and be done with you," Jimmy snapped back.

"Maybe we should leave you here instead!" Jack yelled back.

Henry let out a weary sigh and turned away from the two squabbling young men.

What he had told Jack earlier wasn't true of course, he would never tell the boy to leave, his conscience wouldn't allow it, but there had to be something he could do to make them get along.

Hopefully in time, Jimmy and Jack would learn to at least tolerate one another, but for now every second the two were together was nothing but difficult. He turned to Mary and Cindy who had agreed to help him with his idea when he'd left the kitchen.

"You girls ready?"

"Sure, let's go," Mary said. "The sooner we get it done, the sooner we can leave this horrible place."

"Ditto for me," Cindy agreed.

Henry grunted an agreement of his own and they left the garage, heading back to the kitchen. As they entered the main warehouse the remnants of cooking meat still hung in the air. The smoking corpses were where they had dropped, the fires all but out. A few salvaged candles were lit here and there so the darkness wasn't complete. Henry picked up a doused torch, lit it, and the three of them moved through the shadows until they reached the scattered boxes of clothing. Each of them picked up a box and then walked to the kitchen for the last time.

Mary pulled a face when she saw the horror show of the kitchen, but she remained silent. Cindy had seen it all before and was stoic.

"Okay, let's get to work," Henry said and began taking out sheets, clothing, and towels from inside the box he'd carried into the kitchen while the girls did the same with their boxes.

In minutes the clothing was scattered across the kitchen, the sheets draped over the human meat like white shrouds. Henry made a loose rope and carried it out to the warehouse, dropping it to the floor just outside the kitchen doorway. After this, while the women waited, he went and grabbed two kerosene lamps he'd found earlier. Though they had been knocked to the floor in the battle, they had managed to remain intact. Quickly, he doused the clothing scattered about and then the rope of pants, sheets, and shirts that led out of the doorway.

"Okay, we're almost finished here. You girls can head back to Jimmy and tell him to start the engine. When I get back we'll be leaving hastily to put it mildly."

"Okay, you be careful," Mary told him, and with Cindy waving, the two left, going back to the truck.

Henry finished soaking the clothing and then moved to the gas valves and hoses. Pulling his panga, he cut the hoses, the hiss of gas immediately shooting from the openings. Holding his breath, he bent the hoses away from his face and left the kitchen, taking a last glance at the mutilated bodies spread about, knowing one night when he couldn't sleep the images he now had locked in his mind would come back to haunt him, especially the images of the children's body parts.

Pulling his lighter, he lit the end of what was nothing more than a large wick, and as he backed away, the kerosene soaked wick began to burn, the flame rolling across the rope to enter the kitchen.

Henry didn't see this though. When he knew the clothing was burning well, he was already dashing across the warehouse floor, the adrenaline in his system driving him forward like he was powered by jet fuel.

He was moving so fast he bounced off the doorframe to the garage, taking a second to close the door, then he was charging to the UPS truck, waving his hands for Jimmy to get ready.

"Go, Jimmy, go, don't wait for me to get in! Go!" Henry yelled as he ran around to the back and jumped in through the rear doors. Mary was waiting and she slammed them shut behind him, one of the doors almost crushing his left boot between the jamb.

Jimmy floored the gas pedal and the truck surged to life, the front bumper heading straight towards the bay door.

Henry was lying on the floor of the truck and was about to say something when the front grille crashed into the bay door, the sound of rending metal and a jarring force sending him sliding across the floor to be buried under a box of clothing.

The UPS truck was more than a match for the thin metal door and a second later the cold night air was surrounding the truck as Jimmy spun the wheel and headed for the only exit to the lot.

Behind him, in his mirror, he saw the ruined bay door flapping back and forth like a torn poster hanging on a wall by a lone piece of tape.

And then what Henry planned for happened.

There was a horrendous thunderclap and a section of the warehouse exploded, windows and bits of concrete flying into the air to rain down like deadly hail.

Jimmy slowed the truck and Cindy opened the rear doors so they could all get a good view of the destruction of the warehouse.

"Holy, shit, Henry, what the hell did you do?" Jimmy asked as he stared at the rising fireball.

"I rigged the kitchen to blow up. There was a bunch of propane tanks in there, but I never had any idea that was going to happen," he said as he gazed at the growing conflagration.

"Maybe there was something else in there you didn't see," Cindy suggested. "Maybe there was natural gas trapped in the lines of the gas pipes and you ended up setting that off, too."

"Yeah, maybe," Henry said.

"Whoa, that was fucking awesome," Jack gasped as he watched the flames rise higher. Most of the warehouse windows had shattered, the white tinted glass now spread across the ground like crystal snow. Jack's eyes reflected the fire and it seemed to give him the look of a sprite or small demon. His smile was wide and he was relishing the flames like a firebug.

"So, Henry, what was the point of doing that exactly?" Mary asked.

Jimmy had put the transmission in drive, and as Henry closed the doors, they headed off down the long driveway that would lead them to the main road.

"I wanted to make sure if there are any cannies still around these parts that there's no way they can set up shop here again," he said as he moved to find a place to sit. His elbow hurt from when he jumped inside the truck and he rubbed it like a five-year-old with a boo-boo.

"Makes sense, but you do know that though we took out this camp there's plenty more of them elsewhere," Mary told him.

"Yeah, Mary, I know, but at least this is one place that'll be clean for a while."

She nodded, getting what he meant perfectly. Though they never planned it, it always seemed wherever the companions would end up and whatever they got themselves into, they seemed to leave the place just a little better than how they found it.

Henry moved to Jimmy and leaned over the driver's seat.

"So, Jimmy, what's the deal with crashing through the garage door? This isn't a movie, ya know. We might not have made it. Why the hell didn't you unlock it and roll it up."

Jimmy grinned that smartass grin he was known for. "Where's the fun in that, Henry? I checked the door and I knew it was thin. There was never a chance we weren't gonna get through it, trust me."

"I told him not to, Henry," Jack said "I said it was a bad idea."

"Shut up, brat, no you didn't," Jimmy snapped back.

Henry lifted his hands into the air in a *why me, God,* gesture, then moved back to the girls. Carol was still sitting silently. She wore a denim jacket found in one of the boxes over her shoulders and Henry wondered if the woman would ever snap out of the trauma she had been through. But the woman had witnessed her family killed and eaten in that order. How the hell does a person overcome something like that?

That made him think of his own wife and what he had done to her, killing her with his own hands when she had turned into a ghoul. It had taken him a long time to come to grips with what had happened to her and only recently was he finally able to let her go.

And then he'd found Gwen only to have her ripped from him before their relationship could even begin.

But here it was, two years later and he was moving on. Now he had Sue, Mary, Jimmy and the others who were the family he'd never had in the old world.

In many ways he was better off now than ever before, though it was hard to look at it that way on a day to day basis.

"Oh, shit, will you look at that?" Jack gasped from the passenger seat.

The motor changed pitch and Henry looked to the back of Jimmy's head.

"What's wrong? Why are you slowing down?"

"Uh, Henry, I think you might want to come up here and see this. It looks like we got ourselves another problem," Jimmy said.

With yet another weary sigh, wondering if this night would ever end, Henry stood up to see what was so interesting in front of the truck. Upon reaching Jimmy, he glanced forward, the headlight beams cutting through the night like razors, forcing the shadows away like a squad of policemen to an unruly mob.

"Oh, you've got to be kidding me," Henry breathed while staring through the windshield at the unbelievable scene before him.

"Yup, told ya," Jimmy said.

Henry didn't reply, but just gazed out the windshield like it was his own death peering back at him.

While the UPS truck's engine ticked softly, and the exhaust rumbled, a few crickets added to the cacophony of noise, and the surrounding tree branches seemed to wrap the brown-painted vehicle in their gentle embrace.

Or perhaps they were merely preparing to squeeze the life out of it.

# Chapter 19

"Well that explains why we haven't seen any deaders around here," Henry said softly while he stared out the front windshield of the UPS truck.

About fifty feet in front of the vehicle was a large, metal chain-link security fence. On either side of the gate, the fence moved off until it was lost amongst the trees.

But the fence and gate wasn't what was concerning Henry and the others at the moment.

It was the two hundred plus ghouls gathered at the gate, all pushing and shaking it like a mob of teenagers trying to get into a sold-out rock concert.

Even in the headlights glare Henry could see a massive black cloud of flies hovering over the heads of the zombies. The putrid, rotting animated corpses rattled the fence seeking to gain entry, but there was a large chain running through the gate's main posts where they met in the middle, and though the ghoul's determination was commendable, raw and rotting flesh was no match for hardened steel.

On the ground at the ghoul's feet, many bodies were laid out, most flattened to resemble road kill. It was obvious what had happened as Henry stared at the shifting mass of undead humanity. Some of the ghouls had lost their footing and had then been knocked to the road, only to be trampled by their brethren like empty cans of soda.

"Jimmy, kill the engine," Henry said, and when Jimmy did so the moaning of the dead came to his ears through the windows of the truck.

Their wailing was pitiful in nature, like a morose mother crying out for a dying child, but despite this, Henry knew they were in a hell of a situation.

Sure, they could drive the truck back to the warehouse, abandon it, take what they could carry and then walk back up the incline. From there they could travel over land, by the same way they had first reached the warehouse, to return to Sue and Raven at the gas station. But even Henry was tempted by greed in a situation such as this. What they had in the UPS truck was a find of a lifetime and he'd be damned if he was going to throw it all away because of a crowd of roamers.

"I say we just drive through 'em," Jimmy said as he leaned on the steering wheel.

"Yeah, you would," Jack said. "Idiot."

Jimmy spun on Jack. "What the hell does that mean? All we have to do is drive through 'em and keep on going, piece of cake."

Jack made a raspberry and shook his head like Jimmy was the child in their conversation. Henry leaned forward and touched Jimmy's shoulder, silencing him.

"No, Jimmy, Jack makes a good point," Henry said. "Look at how thick they are out there. I don't think the truck could make it through them all before getting bogged down. And if there's a chance that could happen I don't want to do it."

"So, what? We're just gonna leave all this shit behind? That sucks, man. What we found is the haul of a lifetime."

Henry couldn't argue with him, having thought the same thing only moments ago.

Mary and Cindy moved up behind Henry to see what was going on.

"Oh my God, will you look at all of them?" Mary gasped as she stared out the windshield.

"Tell me about it," Jimmy said. He turned off the headlights, wanting to save the battery, but kept the parking lights on. The glare of the lights disappeared to be replaced by a dull yellow glow from the parking lights, the ghoul's visages taking on an even thicker pallor than before. It was as if every ghoul had a bad case of jaundice.

Jimmy shifted sideways in the driver's seat as he looked Henry square in the face.

"Well, old man, this is the time you're supposed to come up with a plan to get us through there in one piece."

"Uh-huh, and maybe if you'd shut up for a second I might be able to think of one," Henry snapped back, though his voice lacked venom.

With a huff of annoyance, Jimmy crossed his arms over his chest and Jack let out a short bark of laughter. Jimmy glared at the boy but stayed quiet. Henry peered out the window at the shifting bodies, but nothing came to mind.

And as he watched the gate, he realized it wouldn't be long before it finally collapsed under the onslaught of bodies. And now that they were there the ghouls were even more worked up, pushing and forcing themselves against the chain-link like animals.

After more than five minutes had passed and Henry had nothing, he finally gave in.

"I'm sorry, guys, I got nothin'," he said sadly.

"Getting' senile in your old age, huh, Henry?" Jimmy cracked.

Henry slapped him on the back of the head, but it wasn't hard, just a reminder not to be a wiseass.

Cindy moved up a little closer to Henry, Mary moving to the side so Cindy could see. The blonde haired woman stared out at the sea of rotting corpses and then to the rear of the truck at all the cardboard boxes. Then she smiled as she winked at Henry.

"I got an idea," Cindy said triumphantly.

"That's my girl," Jimmy said. "So what is it?"

She turned and pointed over her shoulder.

"Okay, we have more ammo than we know what to do with, right?"

"Yeah, go on," Henry said intrigued. If she was thinking of shooting them, she was nuts, there were far too may to take out with bullets. Though there were at least two hundred in front of the gate on the road, there were even more lining the fence on both sides, their shadowy forms disappearing where the light couldn't penetrate. The entire complex must be surrounded and only the incline where the companions had reached the warehouse was safe, no doubt because of the hill keeping the warehouse hidden from the ghouls. He had no doubt they arrived from time to time, but the cannies would have been able to easily dispatch them.

"Well, what's in bullets?" Cindy asked.

"Gunpowder, why?" Henry replied.

"Right, gunpowder. So all we have to do is crack open a bunch, find something the size of a pipe and we can make pipe bombs."

"Pipe bombs?" Jimmy asked. "I don't know, Cindy, that sounds awfully familiar to me. Didn't we use them before, like a year ago in Chicago?"

"So what if we did," she snapped. "If it works then who cares?"

"She's right, Jimmy. Goddamn it, Cindy, that's a great idea," Henry said as he reached out and kissed her happily on the forehead.

She grinned like a little girl praised by her proud parent, and then took a step back to get started.

"Okay, Jack, you stay up here and keep an eye on that gate," Henry said. "If it moves more than a few inches let me know, those posts on the sides are looking weaker by the minute."

"Okay, got it," Jack said.

"The rest of you, come on, we've got work to do," Henry clapped as they all moved into the rear of the truck. There were small overhead lights running down the center of the ceiling and they were perfect to work by.

Knives were pulled from sheaths to use as a way to pry the bullets open and in no time they were getting to work.

The next problem would be where to find something to use as pipes for the housing of the gunpowder. But one thing at a time, Henry thought.

So with the undead wailing for their blood outside the walls of the truck, the companions got to work, and when they were done the ghouls were in for a treat.

*    *    *

One hour later they were almost finished. The UPS truck had been backed up as far away from the gate without losing sight of it as Henry could get it. Just in case the fence gave out he wanted as much warning as possible, but he knew to drive too far would be a mistake as well. Now that they were invested in getting through that gate, they needed to monitor the situation until the end.

Jimmy was hovering over Cindy as she used a pair of pliers to crimp the end of the exhaust pipe protruding from the muffler, but she wasn't strong enough and Jimmy had to do it for her. Even he had trouble, but the same reason that had allowed him to take off a large portion of the exhaust was why he was able to squeeze the end shut, he just had a little more upper body strength than here.

The exhaust was old, rusty and in desperate need of changing. The thin metal was easy to mold and Jimmy had all but torn it off the undercarriage, bits of rust raining down on him. The hard part had been disengaging the hangers, the rubber outlasting the metal attached to it. But he had persevered and had accomplished his task in due time.

Jimmy's face was covered in dirt, grease, and rust. He became this way thanks to being on his back underneath the truck.

When they had decided the pipe bombs would work, they then had to figure out what to use as casings and it had been Jack who came up with an idea.

"How 'bout the muffler and the rest of the exhaust?" Jack had suggested, interrupting the others while they talked about what to use. Before his suggestion nothing had come to mind.

"Sure, brat, why not? But how are we gonna get it off?" Jimmy had asked.

Jack reached down behind the driver's seat and picked up a small bag, similar to a gym bag. It was only a foot long, but inside were a few tools and other odds and ends. Pliers, a small hammer, two different screwdrivers, Phillips and flathead, a voltage tester and some black electrical tape.

Tossing the bag at Jimmy's feet, he grinned. "Use these, Einstein."

Henry reached down and picked it up instead, and after investigating the contents, had nodded in approval.

"It might work at that, Jack," Henry said. There was a tire iron on the floor as well and Henry picked it up, handing it to Jimmy.

"Here, use this too, Jimmy. All you have to do is pry the exhaust off. We're not being picky here. And get going, there's only so long before that gate gives out." He flashed a look through the front windshield to the zombies up the road, but things were still the same.

"Man, why do I always get the grunt work?" Jimmy moaned as he took the tire iron from Henry.

"'Cause you're young and fit, that's why, now quit whining and get moving. While you're doing that the rest of us will get started on the bullets."

So Jimmy had exited the truck, grumbling about how unfair life was and the others had begun to separate the gunpowder from the bullets. Carol had been useless and Henry had let her sit quietly. The woman was almost comatose and he hoped she would snap out of it soon.

In this new world weakness wasn't tolerated and was usually a death sentence.

"There, is it done?" Jimmy asked Cindy as he finished crimping the rusty metal.

"Yeah, now be careful," she said as she picked up the muffler. It was heavy now, a giant bomb waiting to detonate. There was a thin piece of string coming off the top, the added hole thanks to Cindy and the Phillips screwdriver.

Inside the muffler was more than half the gunpowder they had collected from the bullets, as well as the empty shells themselves, and another two boxes of sealed bullets for good measure. The spent shells and new bullets would act like shrapnel when the bomb exploded and hopefully would do some major damage to the undead crowd.

Besides the muffler bomb, there were two smaller ones no more than a foot or so in length. These had been broken off from the exhaust pipe Jimmy had torn free. The tire iron had worked well as a hammer to flatten one side and then the other had been flattened just enough to allow them to pour the gunpowder inside. When they were through, Henry had squeezed the end some more, sweating as he did it, praying the pliers didn't create a spark and blow them all to Hell in a hundred bloody pieces.

"Okay, I'm done," Henry said as he wiped the perspiration from his brow. Was it him or was it getting warm inside the truck? He stood up, cradling the two, one foot bombs in his arms while Jimmy carried the muffler with Cindy right behind him.

"Mary, you stay here and wait for us with Jack and Carol," Henry told her. "Get in the driver's seat, and just before we toss these over the fence you start the engine. After the bombs go off you drive up, we'll get in and off we go."

"Okay, you guys be careful," she said to all of them.

Jimmy flashed her a wide grin. "Aww, Mary, that's so sweet, I didn't know you cared."

She frowned, "I don't, now shut up and go," she snapped, though there was just a hint of a grin there to belay her words.

The rear doors opened and the cool air swept into the interior, washing away the stink of sweat and gunpowder. It was almost totally dark, only the parking lights chasing back the night.

As they climbed out, Henry paused by the driver's door.

"Hey, put on the headlights, will ya? I want to see what we're doing," Henry asked Mary as they all moved away, Jimmy gabbing like a school girl about what was going to happen next. He loved explosions and he loved blowing up zombies with a vengeance, no matter how big or small the number.

As they moved up the road, the stench of decay and purification grew worse and the buzzing of thousands of flies filled the area. The headlights snapped on, casting long shadows in front of the companions and Henry wished he had his hands free so he could draw his Glock. Just having the weapon in his hand would make him feel better, even if it was imagined hope.

They moved to within a few feet of the fence, and in the glow of the headlamps they stared at the faces of the dead. Some were so decayed their faces were sloppy messes of flesh and gore, maggots and roaches crawling about as they fed on the rotten flesh. Rats scurried about between the feet of the ghouls, feeding like kings as they gorged themselves on the sagging meat.

A few were more adventurous, and they crawled up pants legs, digging into the torsos to eat the insides of the bodies. The ghouls barely noticed they now had houseguests as they struggled to push the gate in.

Cindy flicked a lighter and she waved Henry over to her.

"Okay, Henry, let's use the small one first to see how well it works," she said.

Henry nodded and walked over to her, setting one pipe bomb down and holding out the other so she could light it.

The wick had the subtle scent of gasoline on it and that was for the simple reason Henry had the idea to take a little from the fuel tank so the wick would burn without question. He wasn't about to toss the bomb over the fence only to have it fizzle and die.

"Oh, man, this is gonna be good," Jimmy said. He turned to the crowd of undead faces. "Get ready for a surprise, you dead fucks!"

The wick was lit and Cindy gestured for Henry to toss it, though he needed no encouragement. Turning, he ran another three feet and tossed the bomb like it was a heavy stick.

The pipe sailed over the gate and the heads of the zombies, then bounced off the head of a female ghoul, leaving a dent on her scalp. But no sooner did the pipe rebound off the head then the wick reached the end and the night was filled with an explosion with the strength of about two hand grenades. The female ghoul's scalp wound didn't matter anymore because the ghoul was now nothing but vapor, as she had been at the epicenter. More than a dozen ghouls took the blast full on, another half dozen peppered by shrapnel. If there had been a large hole made in the crowd, Henry and the others couldn't see it from where they were standing on ground level.

"Shit, Henry, that did nothing," Jimmy said. "Here, Cindy, give the next one to me," he said as he set the muffler bomb down. With a shrug, Henry handed Jimmy the second pipe bomb. He didn't care who threw it, as long as it happened.

Cindy lit it and Jimmy tossed it high and up. The wick sputtered in the dark as it arced over the heads to fall back to the earth. Just before it would have dropped into the crowd, the bomb exploded, severing heads from shoulders and taking limbs off like giant razor blades.

At the front of the line, the ghouls swayed from the blast and Henry saw a slight recession against the gate.

"Good job, Jimmy, that one must have made a dent in the ones closest to the gate."

"And you doubted me, old man?" Jimmy asked with a grin.

Henry ignored him, his eyes only on the target. He could hear the UPS truck and he saw Mary was moving closer, but she was taking her time. He nodded; all was going as planned.

"Okay, last one. This is for all the marbles," Henry said as he picked up the muffler."

"You want me to throw it?" Jimmy asked.

Henry shook his head. "Nah, I got this one, there's still some energy in these old bones," he joked. Cindy looked into his eyes and Henry nodded. "Do it, honey."

She lit the wick and Henry turned, ran like he was a football quarterback, the muffler over his shoulder, and let it fly, the weight of the bomb causing him to yell as he threw it into the air.

It was like chucking lead, but he was up to the task, and the bomb went up and over the fence to begin its descent only five feet from the gate.

The companions stood silently, waiting for what they thought would be an explosion like the others, but what they didn't take into account was all the gunpowder Cindy had packed into the muffler.

When the bomb ignited, the night went white and a massive shockwave rolled across the road, blowing zombies, the gate, and the three companions around like dry leaves in a storm. Henry was struck in the head by first an arm, then a head, and then the legless corpse of a ghoul, the torso knocking him over as he rolled on the ground like he had been dropped into the middle of a hurricane.

Cindy and Jimmy reached out for one another and they became entangled in each others arms as they rolled to the side of the road.

Henry felt a wash of heat flow over him and he was glad the torso was protecting him from the worst of it, and though it seemed to last forever, in truth it was only seconds.

He lay on the asphalt, staring up at the night sky and he realized he couldn't hear a thing. There was only a dull ringing in his ears.

As he looked up at the sky, dazed, he saw lots of little objects floating in the air, and he wondered if he was seeing stars plummeting to earth.

But then one of those objects grew larger as it fell back to the ground and Henry realized it was a severed head. As the head came at him, he could see the white eyes blinking and the teeth gnashing and he rolled to the side, the head spattering on the road like a rotten peach. Then he realized it was raining, but not with raindrops.

It was raining body parts, and with thickening thuds, the rotting meat struck the road and surrounding area.

Pushing the torso away from him, he felt something land on his head. Reaching up, he pulled off a bloody ear, a stud still in the earlobe, and tossed it away with disgust.

Then more pieces of meat were falling around him and he realized the bomb had sent the destroyed zombies into the air, and what went up would eventually come down.

Looking around the road, he saw Cindy and Jimmy lying on the shoulder and while arms, legs and hands fell all around him, he dashed to his friends, helping them up as it rained human beings.

"Come on, we need to get back to the truck!" Henry screamed over the sound of body parts slapping the road.

"Huh, what?" Jimmy said, still dazed by the explosion. There was blood on the side of his head and Henry didn't think it was from being struck by a flying body part. He must have whacked his head on something as he rolled, probably the road itself.

A high moan pierced the air over the sound of falling organs and he saw more than fifty ghouls moving towards them, climbing over their decimated brethren.

Where the gate had once stood there was nothing but two bent and warped metal posts. The bomb had been strong enough to blow the gate clear of its hinges and more than a hundred bodies into bloody pieces.

The companions had their opening, but only if they took the chance now.

From behind him, Henry heard the sound of a car horn through his frazzled ears and he saw Mary in the driver's seat. She was flashing the headlights trying to get his attention while she leaned on the horn,

Henry lost his train of thought, still dazed himself, and knew he was supposed to do something as he helped Jimmy up. Then he snapped back to himself, realizing he'd drifted off for a second.

"Come on, let's go, help me with Cindy," Henry barked.

Jimmy was dazed, but at the sound of his woman's name he nodded. The two men picked up the dazed woman and together they half-carried, half-dragged, her to the UPS truck while two score ghouls came for them.

"Get ready!" Henry yelled as he ran around to the back of the truck. Jack was waiting and he helped Cindy into the interior,

Henry climbing up and slamming the doors as Jimmy fell inside next to him.

"Go, Mary, go!" Henry yelled as he dropped to the floor, exhausted. There was nothing he could do now but trust in Mary's driving skills to see them through the danger.

Mary slammed the transmission into drive and with a surge of power the vehicle jumped forward just as the first zombies reached the front bumper.

They were struck head on, their spinning bodies flying off to land in bloody heaps on the side of the road, and Mary powered through the crowd. Only now the mob was spread out thanks to the bomb and she had traction to accelerate each time she struck a ghoul.

There was a constant thumping, like thunder, each time a head connected with the front bumper and the tire wells ran thick with blood and gore, red and yellow pus dripping off the edges like slush. The tires ran over bodies, the insides of the ghouls squirting out like pie filling to spread across the road.

Mary swerved around the worst knots of bodies, her higher elevation in the driver's seat allowing her an excellent vantage point.

She came to a spot where there was no way to avoid the massive crowd so she floored the gas pedal and yelled out. "Brace yourselves, this is gonna get rough!"

Then the UPS truck was plowing into the thickest part of the mob, bodies falling like wheat to a scythe as the vehicle drove over them. The vehicle began to rock as if it was going over a dozen speed bumps and Mary fought to right it, not wanting it to tip over. And as she drove over a carpet of human bodies, that soon became a definite possibility.

But as soon as it began, it was over and the front tires dropped down to the road and then the back followed suit.

The bouncing ended and Henry turned on his side to gaze up at the back of Mary's head; her long hair moving back and forth like it was a living creature.

"Well?" Henry asked as he felt the vehicle level out.

"That's it, Henry, we made it, the road ahead is clear!" Mary called out, the others clapping and congratulating each other.

Carol was the only subdued one in their party. She merely stared at the floor with her jacket draped over her shoulders, her blonde hair covering her face, hiding her features.

Jimmy rolled over to check on Cindy and was relieved to see she was fine, her eyes were clear and she wore a big smile from ear to ear.

"Christ, babe," Jimmy said to her. "What the hell did you put in that muffler?"

She chuckled and dropped back to the floor, her head lolling from side to side with the movement of the vehicle.

"A little too much gunpowder I guess. Wow, I didn't think the blast would be that big."

"Oh, really, well, next time how 'bout making sure."

"Jimmy, it's not like I build pipe bombs on the side for a hobby, you know. I never made one before. How the hell was I supposed to know?" She said with a chuckle. She was high on the explosion, the blast still fresh in her mind. It had been more powerful than she could have ever imagined.

"It was your idea. Maybe it's just me, but I just assumed you knew what you were doing when you suggested it," Jimmy snapped back, sitting up. His head was still bleeding, but it was just a small scalp wound. No big deal. Just one more to add to the list, he thought.

"Well, I know about them, you know, what I read and stuff when I was in Pittsfield. My uncle had all kinds of survivalist books. I didn't think it looked too hard, is all."

"You didn't... you didn't think..." Jimmy gasped as he stared at the woman he loved in shock.

"Jimmy, give it a rest, she did good," Henry said as he sat up and slowly climbed to his feet, which wasn't easy thanks to the shifting floor. It was like being in a boat in choppy water.

"Yeah, Jimmy, leave the woman alone, she knew more than you did," Jack quipped, taking his shots at Jimmy when he could. Which wasn't hard.

"Shut up, brat, no one asked for your opinion," Jimmy spit back in anger.

"I don't need your permission to talk, so go screw yourself!" Jack yelled back and then the two were going at it like brothers trapped in the same bedroom for a week with only one television.

Henry was too tired to stop them and he moved to the front of the truck, dropping down into the passenger seat Jack had vacated. His head was throbbing like a drum, but his hearing was better, though with Jimmy and Jack bickering in the back he wished for the droning again.

"You know which way to go?" Henry asked as he peered out the front windshield. The glass and hood was a mess of gore and Mary had the wipers on to try and wash the worst of it off so she could see where she was going.

"Yeah, think so," she said. "There was a road sign a little bit back and I think it'll take us to the gas station in about an hour or so."

"That's good," he replied. "We've been gone for a while and I want to get back to Sue and Raven."

She flashed him a knowing smile. "I'm sure they're fine, Henry. After all, the gas station is in the middle of nowhere. What could possibly happen in only a few hours?"

"Yeah, you're probably right. After all, we're in the middle of the mountains. If we can't catch a break here then where can we?"

"That's the spirit, Henry. Think positive thoughts," she said, and with the high beams on, the truck drove deeper into the night, blasting the darkness away.

# Chapter 20

Mary slowed the UPS truck on the road leading to the gas station, preparing to finish the last leg of the return trip back to Sue and Raven. When she decreased speed, the roaring exhaust quieted down to a dull roar.

With no muffler and half the exhaust missing, the vehicle sounded like a locomotive, but it couldn't be helped, so they covered their ears with their hands and dealt with it as best they could.

For now, it was still a lot better than walking and carrying the supplies on their backs. But once they made it to the next town, they would have to either fix it or ditch it, the noise a beacon to every raider, cannie and ghoul in a five mile radius.

It was when she crested an incline, and was about to drive downward to the gas station, that she slammed her foot on the brake pedal, jarring everyone in the rear.

"Oh, wow," Jack said from the passenger seat, his eyes facing forward.

"Mary, what the hell?" Jimmy called out when he was knocked from his perch on a box of ammo. Luckily, Cindy had reached out and saved him from a bad fall to the metal floor.

Mary ignored him and turned to Henry, a solemn look on her face.

"Henry, get up here, there's something happening at the gas station."

"Oh, for the love of..." Henry sighed as he stood up and crossed the few feet separating him from the back of Mary's seat. But when he reached her and gazed out into the darkness beyond, his jaw dropped and he gasped in surprise.

"How the hell did that happen?" He whispered to no one in particular.

"Don't know," Mary said, "but we need to decide what to do and fast, 'cause if they're still alive in that building they won't be for much longer."

Henry wasn't listening to her, his mind racing with the terrible possibilities that struck him like lightning. To have finally found Sue after almost two years alone to lose her again so suddenly.

It wasn't right, hell, it wasn't fair. No man deserved so much loss in one lifetime. No man deserved to keep loving and losing like he seemed to be doing on a regular basis.

"Holy shit, there's got to be a hundred out there. No, wait, a thousand!" Jack said aloud as he leaned forward to stare out the windshield.

That had Cindy looking up and Jimmy stood and moved next to Henry, wanting to know what was going on.

"Hey, what's the deal, why aren't we..." his question went un-asked when he stared out the window with the others.

Down the road, at the bottom of the incline, was the gas station. And, yes, it was still standing, but where there was once a quiet, dilapidated building, the half-moon now shed its feeble light on eighty-two ghouls, all clamoring to fight their way into the gas station. Henry's heart sank in his chest when he watched the shifting crowd change position so a ghoul could exit through the front door of the gas station.

Then another exited and three more went in, the screen door flopping on broken hinges thanks to the zombies battering it repeatedly.

The inside of the gas station was overrun with the undead.

He imagined Raven and Sue hearing the first thump of dead hands on the door. Raven would have investigated and easily dispatched the ghoul, then would have returned to be with Sue again. But then another would arrive, and then another after that until there was far too many for any one person to stop, whether they were armed or not.

And sooner or later, in the hours he had been gone; the zombies had battered in the door and entered the building. It was possible Sue and Raven were still hiding in there somewhere, but as he watched the ghouls moving around the entire building, he knew it was highly unlikely. He had been inside that gas station and knew there was nowhere truly safe from that many attackers, living or dead.

His legs felt weak and he reached out for the back of Mary's chair to stabilize himself. While he was lost in thoughts of doom, the others were all chatting excitedly, Cindy and Mary, as well as Jimmy, all worried about Sue and Raven.

Jack even had a concerned look on his face. Though he hadn't known Sue or Raven for too long, he'd taken to them and would miss them both if they were dead.

That was when Henry looked up and out the windshield again, his eyes playing over the massive crowd of walking dead.

At first he didn't notice movement on the roof, but as he creased his eyes and strained, he saw the distinct form of a human being waving its arms back and forth to get the occupants of the UPS truck's attention.

It was Sue, it had to be. He wouldn't even consider the possibility it wasn't.

"Mary, let me drive, now, please," Henry said and almost pulled her out of the chair as she tried to get up.

"Okay, Henry, but, whoa, what's the hurry?" She asked, not understanding why he wanted to drive. Each of them had silently agreed it was highly unlikely Sue or Raven were still in the gas station. Either they ran away or had become trapped and were now dead. But not Henry, he still had hope they were still alive.

Henry ignored Mary's protests and jumped into the driver's seat. Before anyone could brace themselves, Henry stomped on the gas pedal, the truck surging forward with a throaty roar from the severed exhaust.

Boxes tumbled and toppled as everyone yelped in surprise. Henry paid them no mind, but flew down the hill, the front bumper heading directly for a large knot of ghouls.

A few zombies had turned away from the main mass of bodies when they heard the loud exhaust system. They began walking up the road, arms outstretched as they moved like automatons without a master.

Henry never slowed his speed, but began plowing into body after body like they were nothing more than bowling pins as he forced his way to the gas station walls, sounding the horn like a warning cry.

By the time he was only a few feet away from the main doors, more than a dozen prone and mutilated bodies lay in the road behind the truck. One ghoul had its head severed from its neck, only a few bits of gristle keeping the head attached at all. A thick, viscous fluid seeped from the jagged neck wound to bubble on the asphalt, the darkness only making the murky fluid resemble ink.

Henry slammed the transmission into park, the truck already shaking as countless hands battered its metal sides. A headlight was knocked out by a foot and the light coming off the front of the grille was cut in half.

Henry was already on his feet, sliding open the driver's side window and shooting at the closest ghouls near him. He wanted to clear a path for the next part of his plan.

He began climbing outside the window.

Jimmy's eyes went wide as he dashed over to Henry, who was already halfway out the window.

"What the fuck are you doing? Get back in here!"

"Can't, Jimmy, there's someone on that roof. It's got to be Sue or Raven. I'm gonna go get 'em."

"What? That's crazy! You'll die out there!"

"Then so be it, I'll die!" He snapped back and then he was outside, his feet now on the sill of the window.

The vehicle was rocking back and forth on its shocks like a boat in choppy weather as the ghouls turned their attention to it. They could see Henry on the side of the truck and they wanted him badly. With one hand holding the strut to the side mirror, Henry shot a few ghouls below him who were trying to grab him, then he began climbing up the side like a chimp in the zoo. He managed a few footholds but then lost his footing, the metal slick against the soles of his boots, and he dropped two feet, his left hand preventing him from falling. Rotting hands reached for his swinging legs and he kicked out with his right one, cracking a ghoul in the nose and crushing cartilage into pulp. With his Glock still firmly grasped in his right hand, he shot two more ghouls in the face, then regained his footing and began climbing once again.

By this time the others inside the truck had joined in to help him. Whether Jimmy agreed or not, his friend's life was now hanging by a thread and he would do everything in his power to see him through it in one piece.

Cindy and Mary were also firing from the opposite window. The sliding door was locked and the small window was cracked as each forced the muzzle of their weapons through. Cindy's M-16 chattered on full auto, shredding faces and heads like confetti, blood and bone spraying other ghouls like shrapnel from a grenade. Spent shell casings rained down by her feet to roll about the floor, causing them to watch where they stepped.

Mary took her time, wanting each shot to count. Though they had plenty of ammunition, it still took time to reload and that fatal second she stopped might be Henry's last.

Henry had made it to the roof of the truck and as he slid to the opposite side, he lost his balance, falling hard, his right knee cracking hard enough to make him wince. Gritting his teeth in pain, he shook his head to clear it and tried again, having to fight the rolling roof like it was a bucking bronco.

Timing it right, he jumped the five foot gap between the truck and the roof of the gas station. Though looking flat when he'd approached it, there was a slight incline to help keep snow off it, and he landed badly, shingles sliding and falling away from under his scrambling boots and hands.

He dropped to his knees, reaching out with his free hand, the other still grasping his Glock, and yelped in pain when his bruised knee told him that wasn't such a good idea.

He felt himself sliding backwards, and as he swung his head around, he realized this time he wasn't going to be able to stop himself from falling off the roof to tumble into the dead arms of the waiting ghouls below.

All he could do was pray it would be quick.

*  *  *

The noise was unbelievable, Jimmy thought, as he shot a ghoul in the face and then shifted his arm, firing so fast the bullet almost missed its mark. But that wasn't really a problem at the moment. There were so many zombies packed so close together that as long as he aimed into the crowd, his bullets found a home.

The inside of the truck was like being inside a massive drum with a hundred fists banging on it at the same time.

Talking to one another was impossibility and eye and hand signals were how they communicated, the dim interior light on the ceiling of the truck the only illumination.

But he knew his shots needed to be head shots or it would be a wasted bullet.

Jimmy had never given the actual zombie apocalypse much thought.

He had always been the kind of person to take things in stride. Whether that was working as a janitor at Pineridge Laboratories, or running around what was left of America hunting and killing zombies, to him it was all in a days pay, so to speak.

He could hear Henry's boots stomping on the roof overhead and then they were gone. Jimmy assumed his friend had jumped to the gas station's roof, because if he had fallen off the truck, there wouldn't be enough of him left to bury in a sandwich baggie.

His .38 clicked dry and he yanked it back inside the window. Opening the cylinder, he shook out the spent brass and quickly began sliding in new rounds. Next to him on the passenger seat, Mary and Cindy fired indiscriminately into the crowd of undead faces, the rounds destroying visages and pulping features to mush.

Jack stood in the rear with Carol, his eyes wide with fright. Though a tough kid, even he couldn't help but be intimidated by the situation. They were surrounded on all sides and as he looked every which way at once, he jumped each time a pale fist slapped the sheet metal walls of the truck.

Jack didn't want to think what would happen to him if they didn't get out of here soon, but he was a kid, and despite wanting to grow up overnight, even he knew there were some things he couldn't do.

Jimmy slapped the cylinder closed, cocked the weapon, and shoved it back out the window. A ghoul had its face near the opening and the muzzle was forced into its gaping maw. It bit down hard on the barrel, breaking teeth like they were made of ice. Then Jimmy squeezed the trigger and the back of the ghoul's head disappeared in a tuft of red mist and bone fragments, splattering the faces behind it.

The mouth slid from the barrel and Jimmy ignored the blood on the metal, firing again and again. He couldn't help but wonder how the hell they kept getting into these situations. Where most people were running away from the undead, it seemed time and time again, he and the others were charging into the thick of it, guns blazing like an old television western.

He glanced up to the roof one last time; hoping Henry was doing all right so they could get the hell out of here before it became too late to even try.

*   *   *

Just as Henry felt his boots leaving the roof, a shadow appeared in front of him, the moonlight at such an angle he couldn't see who it was, and reached out for his flailing hand.

Like a drowning man reaching for the last life preserver, he stretched his arm towards his only chance for survival.

His wrist wrapped around warm flesh and he was halted from his downward descent. Then he was being pulled away from the edge and back to the roof. He dropped to the shingles, breathing heavily and quickly slid his Glock back into its holster so he could have two hands to keep himself upright.

Behind him, in the night, gunshots could be heard interlaced with the moans and pounding of the undead on the UPS truck.

His head was down as he sucked in great gasps of oxygen and when he looked up, he saw Sue's smiling face gazing down on him. His heart filled with hope as he looked into her eyes. Swallowing the knot in his throat, he tried to talk, but his mouth was too dry. Wetting his mouth, he tried again and this time the words came.

"Sue, thank God you're all right. I'm here to save you," he said in a hoarse whisper. "We all are."

"Oh, really, a second ago it looked like I was saving you," she said as she shifted position on the roof.

"Whatever, it doesn't matter now," he said, slightly embarrassed. "The fact is, I'm here to get you off the roof and back with us." He looked past her into the night. "Where's Raven. Is she..."

"No, Henry, she's fine. She's on the other side of the roof. There's a dumpster there, that's how we got up here, but the roamers are trying to use it, too. She's been there for hours, Henry, and every time one climbs up and gets close, she kicks it away. She's like a machine. I asked her to let me help and she said she was fine. That girl is inexhaustible."

Henry sat up, nodding. "Good, I'm glad she's okay. When I saw all the roamers around the gas station, I just assumed..." his voice cracked a little and he stopped talking. She leaned down close to him and kissed his lips, the kiss lingering for a moment.

"I'm fine, Henry. I told you I wouldn't leave you like your wife and Gwen and I meant it." The left side of her mouth curved into a smile. "You're stuck with me for quite a while."

"That's the way I want it," he said and stood up, swaying a little, but soon getting his balance back.

"Hey, Henry! Now or never!" Jimmy's voice called out between gunshots.

That got Henry moving. He knew they were on borrowed time and he needed to get Sue and Raven back to the truck, and they needed to leave, fast!

Another shadow appeared from the opposite side of the roof and a second later Henry saw it was Raven. She looked tired. Her ebony hair was a tangled mess and her razor-sharp nails were bloody from the damage she had inflicted on the ghouls, but her face was full of determination.

"'Bout time you got here," she said as she moved over to him.

"Sorry, honey, we got stuck in traffic," he replied, then reached out and squeezed her shoulder with affection.

She smiled then, a thin one, but a smile nonetheless. She may have been a quiet girl, but every now and then her hard facade would crack, such as now.

"Come on, we need to go. We've gotta jump back to the truck," Henry said.

"And what do we do then? How'd you get on the roof of the truck in the first place?" Sue asked.

"I climbed out the driver's window, up the side, and then onto the roof; and here I am."

"And you want me to do that, too? With all of them around here trying to get at me?" Sue gasped.

Henry sighed, his adrenalin pumping at maximum. He wanted to move and this standing around chatting was driving him crazy.

Cindy's M-16 chattered on full auto, the bursts shredding bodies by the dozens.

"Look, Sue, one thing at a time, all right? For now, let's get off this roof and get to the truck."

As he finished his words, more shadows appeared behind Sue and it took him a moment to realize there were roamers on the roof with them. With Raven abandoning her post to leave, the ghouls had begun climbing up the dumpster and onto the roof.

"Shit, deaders!" He snapped and drew his Glock like a whip, snapping off shots and dropping the first two bodies. But there were many more behind and it was fast becoming obvious the roof was now a no go. He turned to Raven with a look of anger and she shrugged.

"What? I thought we were leaving," she said, defending herself.

"Yeah, you're right, we are, come on, you go first," he told her and then double-tapped the trigger twice more, the four rounds penetrating skulls and torsos. One ghoul was hit in the chest and though the bullet wouldn't kill it, the force of the round knocked it off balance. With flailing arms it rolled off the roof to fall onto its brethren.

Raven didn't need to be told twice. She gauged the distance, moved to the edge, and backed up a few feet. Then she took three steps and lunged over the gap. She landed like cat, slid a foot on the smooth metal and spun around, waiting for Henry and Sue.

"Okay, I'll go next," Henry told Sue. "And then I'll be there to catch you. All right?"

She nodded, the look of trepidation apparent on her face.

They walked to the edge of the roof and Henry kissed her quickly for luck, then he backed up and jumped back to the truck. He landed hard again, whacking his knee, and he muttered a few choice imprecations, but he shook off the pain of his now throbbing knee and turned to Sue. The entire time gunshots were sounding and the roof was rocking like a tugboat caught in a tsunami.

"Come on, honey, I got you," he said, reaching out a hand to her.

She squeezed her hands into fists so hard that her nails pinched her palms, but she knew there was no choice. Since the world had collapsed, she'd done things she never would have thought herself capable of and now was no different.

Henry saw her hesitation and he called to her, pointing to his eyes.

"Sue, just look at me, nothing else, just back up a little, run, and jump, but don't look down. Nothing matters but me!" He had to yell, the gunshots and moaning so loud. He could hear Jimmy yelling below him now, followed by Mary's muffled comeback. The smell of cordite filled the air, mixing with the stench of death and decay.

"Come on, Sue, just go for it," he coaxed, his face impassive, though inside he was worried she couldn't do it.

Then she nodded, set her jaw tight and did what he told her. She backed up and began running for the edge, but she was moving too fast in her panic. As she jumped over the gap, Henry already knew she was going to land too close to the edge of the truck's roof and spill over the side.

He lunged for her, catching her in mid-air, both of them now falling to the side to land so hard on the roof they dented it.

Henry was only worrying about her, not willing to lose her, and as he pulled her back on, he found himself slipping off the rear of the truck, right over the back doors.

Sue was able to catch herself thanks to Henry and she was sprawled at an odd angle, but Henry found himself rolling off the edge. He flailed out and his hands managed to catch the lip, and he found himself hanging down, his feet a few inches above the first ghoul's grasping hands. They reached up and rotting fingers caressed his boots and he couldn't repress the shiver that ran up his back like ice.

There were small windows on the rear doors and he looked into the one he was facing to see Jack's startled face glaring back at him.

"Jack! Jack! Wake up, son, tell Jimmy to go! You hear me! Tell Jimmy to drive the goddamn truck. Now!" His fingers were hurting and he wondered how much longer he could hold on.

Jack's face disappeared, and a second later the truck's exhaust roared louder, drowning out the moans of the dead. As Henry hung there, trying to lift his legs up and out of the ghouls' reach, he felt the truck lurch forward.

His body was thrown outward and then it swung back again, an *oomph* leaving his lips.

"Henry? Henry, are you okay?" Sue's voice called down from above.

"Yeah, I'm fine; just hold on, the truck's moving. Get down flat and stay that way!" He called up to her.

The truck lurched forward again as Jimmy tried to push his way through the undead crowd. Henry felt like a sack of potatoes hanging from the back of a pickup truck. Every time Jimmy moved the truck, Henry's body would swing back and forth and his fingers threatened to let go.

Below him, the faces of the dead were moving by him, and as he glanced down to the ground, he could see a red mush of crushed and bloated bodies each time Jimmy ran over the corpses and flattened them into something resembling tomato paste.

He couldn't hear a thing, the exhaust so loud, and he looked into the rear door window to see Jack's worried face again.

"He's going!" Jack called.

Henry wanted to reply, but he didn't have the energy. His feet were flying everywhere as Jimmy fought the wheel, the thumps of bodies vibrating through the frame and into his fingers.

It seemed to go on forever, and he was lost in his own world of pain and battering flesh. He gritted his teeth as his fingers grew white hot, then slowly became numb. His eyes were closed and his body swung back and forth like a pendulum, but he knew to let go was certain death.

But eventually his fingers could hold him no longer and he let out a cry of frustration as his digits slipped from the edge.

He felt himself falling for a mere second and then he was on the ground, his legs curling up under him as he rolled to the side on instinct. He expected to feel a hundred grasping hands on his body as they began ripping him to shreds, his limbs torn from him like he was a roasted chicken tossed in front of starving men, but nothing happened.

Slowly, he opened his eyes to see the thin, half-moon gazing down on him. Footsteps could be heard and he turned his head in time to see Jimmy rounding the truck, his .38 in his hand. That was when Henry turned his head to the other side and saw they were nowhere near the gas station.

The road was quiet, the aspens lining the shoulder resembling silent guardians of the forest, the small guardrail lost in the gloom. A few crickets began sounding, their symphony silenced at the arrival of the throaty exhaust, but now that it was off, they resumed once again.

"Hey, old man, you still in one piece?" Jimmy asked as he reached out a hand to help Henry up. Numb fingers tried to grasp Jimmy and the younger man had to use two hands, holding Henry by the wrist.

Standing on wobbly legs, Henry looked around and then up. Sue's face was lost in shadows, but it was her. Then Raven appeared, and with the agility of youth, she climbed off the truck, landing gracefully in the dust on the shoulder of the road where Jimmy had parked.

Mary, Cindy and Jack exited the truck, Jack opening the rear doors.

As the doors opened, spent shell casings poured out of the interior to trickle onto the ground like water. The companions had used more ammo than they could count fending off the ghouls while Henry saved Sue and Raven, but luckily for once they didn't have to keep count.

Carol stayed inside, still in her own world of misery.

With the rear doors open, Sue was able to climb down, Jack helping her.

When her feet touched the ground, Henry stopped talking to Jimmy and moved to Sue, scooping her up in his arms and hugging her tightly.

She returned it, hugging him tightly, the two standing silently in the night while the others talked amongst themselves. Raven was sharing what had happened and how the dead had slowly come out of the woods as if they had known they were there.

When Raven had realized it was too late to run, she had taken Sue out the back and they had climbed onto the roof, then waited for the rest of the companions to return.

Henry and Sue joined the others and Henry punched Jimmy in the shoulder playfully.

"Nice driving, there, sport, you almost got me killed."

"Me? You were the one that told Jack to get going, *right god-damn now*, if my memory's correct," Jimmy snapped back, though his tone was also playful.

"Yeah, guess you're right at that. Well still, that was too close for my tastes," Henry said.

"Amen to that, Henry," Sue said as she slid closer to him, Henry wrapping an arm around her. He tried not to think how close he'd come to losing her only moments ago.

Jack was chucking rocks, already bored with the adult's conversation and Jimmy interrupted Henry and Sue while they talked.

"So, what's next? We got a shitload of ammo and not a lot of gas left."

Cindy spoke up. "Why don't we try for that town we heard about on the radio?"

"Hey," Mary said. "That's a good idea. Besides, where else are we gonna go?"

Henry looked at each of their faces and then to Sue's.

"What do you think?" He asked her.

Sue shrugged. "I'll go wherever you guys want to go, you know that."

Henry rubbed his chin. He'd been thinking the same thing. If the radio message was true, then they might be going to the only place in America that hadn't been touched by the plague or whatever the hell had caused the dead to rise years ago. At first it had been the rain, a deadly bacterium in it, but soon the clouds had burned off the infection and were now safe again. But like many viruses, the strain had mutated and now to be bit by a ghoul would cause the victim to die and become one. Suddenly those old Italian horror movies weren't so silly.

Henry clapped his hands together and immediately regretted it as they still hurt. There were thin cuts on the inside of his finger joints where they'd been wrapped around the lip of the truck as he'd hung on for dear life.

Sue noticed this and took his hands into hers.

"That looks bad, Henry, let's get those cleaned and dressed. An infection is the last thing you need right now," she said like a mother to her child.

Henry reached up and touched his chest where the dagger had pricked him hours ago, and realized he was a walking factory of cuts and bruises.

But that was okay. As long as he had wounds and bruises they meant he had more trophies in the race of life versus death. So far he was winning and he would cheat like hell to keep it that way.

"Okay, gang, if we're going then let's go. If we're in luck maybe we can find this place by morning."

"The maps inside," Cindy said.

"That's good, hopefully that's all we'll need," Henry told her.

Jimmy turned to look at Henry with a quizzical look.

"You mean you want to drive at night? We don't usually do that."

Henry nodded. "No, Jimmy, you're right, but if you hadn't noticed already there's nothing out here with the exception of those roamers and they're behind us now. With the headlights on we should be fine."

"One headlight you mean," Mary said as she inspected the front of the vehicle. "Looks like one got broken."

"That's fine, Mary, one's enough to get us there," Henry said.

"You hope," Jimmy added.

"Yeah, maybe," Henry said and then turned to Jack. "Jack, we're leaving!" He called to the boy who spun around, tossed one more rock at the tree he was using for target practice, and dashed back to the rear of the truck.

The others joined in and soon all were inside, doors slamming and the throaty howl of the exhaust filling the road once again.

The bloody, gore-covered, dented truck with the missing exhaust headed off into the darkness, leaving the dusty shoulder of the deserted two lane road behind.

Three minutes after the last bellow of exhaust was lost and faded, the crickets started up again, their night symphony the only sound to pierce the air once more.

# Chapter 21

A little more than three hours later the UPS truck was still winding its way down the empty road. There had been no road signs for more than an hour and Henry had thought this was a little suspicious. If it had been daylight, he may have been able to check for posts that had once held signs, but with the darkness heavy and only one headlight, such things were impossible. The map found in the cannie warehouse was spread out on the dashboard. For what it was worth, they were fairly confident they were going the right way, but with each passing minute Cindy was beginning to grow concerned they had taken a wrong turn somewhere in their back trail. The horizon, or what she could see of it through the hanging branches, was just beginning to lighten, signifying the coming dawn.

It couldn't be soon enough for her.

Cindy was driving at the moment, having spelled Henry more than an hour ago, and Mary was next to her in the passenger seat.

They had planned on each of them driving for an hour or so, and by switching up no one would grow tired and miss something important or be caught unawares.

The tree branches overlapped the road like massive arms trying to block out what ambient moonlight there was, and inside the truck the mood was slowly growing worse as the gas gauge on the dashboard continued to slowly drop to empty.

They all knew when they finally ran out of gas they would be in for yet more walking. And with them seeming to be in the middle of nowhere, none of them were looking forward to it.

In the back of the truck, the others tried to grab some shut eye, knowing the next day would be hard. Not that it would be anything special, mind you; everyday was hard and all the companions played the cards they'd been dealt.

"Hey, Henry, I'm, starving, what've we got left to eat?" Jimmy asked from the darkness. The throaty roar of the exhaust was like a motorboat, the vibrations through the undercarriage somewhat soothing.

Henry shifted position on the box he was on and began rummaging through a backpack. A few seconds later he tossed something to Jimmy.

"Heads up," Henry said while tossing the object.

Jimmy caught the object easily and groaned loudly when he realized what it was.

"Oh, man, a power bar? I am so sick of these damn things."

"Fine, then give it to me," Jack said from the shadows and swooped in and snatched it from Jimmy's hand, like a deeper shadow amongst the others.

"Hey, you little brat, that was mine, give it back!" Jimmy snapped.

"Tough shit, Jimmy. You said you didn't want it," Jack replied as he ripped the wrapper open and began munching happily.

"No, I didn't. I said I'm sick of 'em, that didn't mean I wasn't gonna eat it. So help me, if you don't give that back to me now," Jimmy threatened.

"Blah, blah, blah," Jack needled back.

Cindy called back from the front seat. "If you kids don't behave I'm gonna turn this truck around, so help me," she joked, causing Mary to chuckle.

"Tell me about it," Mary said. "Jimmy acts like he's ten when he argues with Jack, doesn't he?"

Cindy nodded. "Not that much of a stretch for him really, Mar'," Cindy joked. The road was so dark only the single headlight showed her the way. She was only going thirty, not wanting to outrun the single headlight in unknown territory. As she studied the road ahead, she felt herself urging the sun up, knowing it would rise when it was good and ready.

Henry sat up and slapped the side of the truck, though with the growling muffler it was barely heard.

"Will you two cut the shit? Christ, this is getting old, already."

"But, Henry," Jimmy protested like a child.

"But nothing," Henry snapped back. "I told you two you need to get along, we can't have you both bickering like brothers all the time, it puts the rest of us at risk." Even in the darkness, both

Jimmy and Jack knew how Henry looked. His jaw would be taut, his eyes creased in anger. His tone told them all they needed to know, even without visual aides.

Cindy was still chuckling up front when she spotted something flashing in the middle of the road. The vehicle was now moving down an incline and her speed had jumped to almost forty, her foot barely on the gas pedal as she let gravity do her work for her.

At first she thought the glitter might have been some broken glass, as only a few pieces here and there seemed to sparkle, and it was hard to see on the left of the road thanks to the missing headlight. If she had been more cautious, she would have slowed down, but way up here in the mountains, even though she was wont to admit it, she had let her guard partially down. It wasn't hard to do when no signs of civilization had been seen for hours.

So the truck continued on, with Cindy casually asking Mary if she had spotted the glitter.

"Hey, Mary, do you see that sparkle in the road?" That was all she got out because the instant the front two tires rolled over the glitter, there was a loud popping, the sound overriding the noisy exhaust. Both front tires deflated and Cindy began to swerve to the right, but no sooner did the front two tires go, then the back two tires struck whatever was on the road. The tires punctured and went to the metal rims in a flash, the grinding and scraping of metal on asphalt filling the inside of the truck, which was soon followed by screams and shouts of surprise.

"What the hell!" Henry called out, but Cindy was too occupied to reply. The steering wheel was fighting her and she was doing everything she could not to crash into the guardrail on either side. There was no way of knowing how deep the ravines went either. It could be ten feet or a hundred, all she knew it was likely they could all die if she left the road. But the truck wasn't cooperating and with all four tires blown, Cindy fought a losing battle.

"Oh my God, we're gonna roll!" Cindy screamed when she felt the vehicle sliding to the left.

No one replied, all too busy holding on for dear life. The truck hit a bad dip in the road and the left side jumped into the air, the right side now becoming the bottom. The truck had been moving at good clip thanks to the hill and it began to slide across the road, spark shooting up to light the fading night.

Inside the truck, boxes went flying and Henry found himself upside down, then he felt something smothering him and he pushed it away, realizing it was Jimmy's butt.

The noise was deafening, scraping metal, exhaust opened wide, and shouts and screams as everyone tried to hold on to whatever they could find. Eventually the truck stopped and other than the exhaust sputtering, the night grew silent.

Then the engine died and it seemed like a void of silence descended, though that was the farthest thing from the truth.

Henry was lying on his side and he was able to look out the back window. As he stared out at the night, he saw a flare shooting into the already lightening sky.

Immediately his mind went into action.

The truck somehow crashing and then a flare set off in the middle of nowhere? He knew it could only mean one thing.

They had driven right into an ambush.

Rolling onto his side, he scanned the truck's interior.

"Everyone all right?" Henry called as he sat up, his hands instinctively reaching down for his Glock and panga. Both were where they should be and he breathed a quick sigh of relief.

"Yeah, I'm fine," Jimmy called. "What the hell happened?"

"An ambush, that's what, I saw a flare shoot up, that means we set off a trap. We're gonna have company any moment so lick your wounds and let's go before they get here," he snapped. "Sue, where are you?"

"I'm here, Henry, I'm fine," Sue said as she pushed a box off herself.

Henry nodded to himself, thankful she had been unharmed, and was up now and moving to the front of the truck, which was an ordeal in itself.

"Raven you here?"

"I'm okay," Raven said from under a pile of boxes, her voice slightly muffled.

All the boxes of bullets and supplies taken from the cannie warehouse were now torn open and scatted everywhere. And worse, when he reached Mary, he saw she was unconscious, or so he prayed.

There was a small amount of blood seeping from her scalp just over her forehead, but it wasn't bleeding too badly.

Reaching down and touching her neck, he let out a gasp of relief when he felt her pulse strong and steady. Cindy was just recovering and she turned to see if she could help. While Cindy pulled Mary to a sitting position, she shook her head in anger.

"Shit, Henry, I never saw what hit us, I can't believe I was so stupid. Right before we flipped I thought I saw something gleaming in the road but then it was too late. I could have killed us all," she chastised herself.

"Doesn't matter, Cindy, what's done is done," Henry told her. "Right now we need to deal with the present. Come on, get your stuff, we need to move fast." He turned to the rear of the truck. "Jack!"

"Yeah?" Jack called out.

"Henry pointed to the bullets on the floor. "See what you can get together; use whatever you can find as a container. We're gonna need some of these bullets in a few minutes if my guess is right," he told the boy who went into action.

"How are we gonna get out of here?" Cindy asked as she cradled Mary's unconscious body.

Henry looked to the front and rear and decided there was no time for games. Pulling his Glock, he shot the front windshield three times, the loud retort sounding like a cannon had gone off. With the windshield already spider-webbed from the crash, the bullets were enough to weaken it so that Henry could kick it out of its bent frame. The glass fell to the road with a shattering of a thousand crystals and in seconds Cindy and Henry were carrying Mary out onto the road. When he set her down, Henry pointed to the truck.

"Leave her for a second, Cindy, we need you inside to grab as much gear as we can get."

She nodded, her blonde curls falling over her face and then ran back into the truck, Henry behind her. He glanced over his shoulder once to see Mary lying prone on the road and it sent a shiver down his spine as he watched her. She truly looked dead as she lay still on the black asphalt.

Then he was at the truck and the hustle and bustle inside took his attention.

Jack had managed to fill a few boxes and Henry directed him to drag them out of the open windshield. Jimmy had managed to gather their packs but one, the stray lost in the debris and there was no time to look.

"Good, Jimmy, get Carol and go outside with Mary, we'll be right behind you," Henry told him. Carol had been unhurt in the crash and she was now led like an automaton by Jimmy.

Jimmy, not going to waste using her, draped a backpack over her shoulder. The woman acted as if it wasn't there.

They climbed out of the truck with glass crunching under their feet and Henry looked out the now horizontal rear doors to see a set of headlights approaching from the top of the incline, the tight beam of the headlights cutting through the trees.

His best guess was they had less than three minutes before whoever had set the trap was upon them.

Henry's mind raced and as he watched the headlights grow closer, he knew the companions were never going to be able to get away in time, especially not with one of their number wounded.

So they would need some sort of distraction. Something to keep the approaching force occupied while they tried to escape, or if not escape, perhaps they could take out the driver of that vehicle and take it for themselves.

Henry's eyes darted back and forth inside the truck and out the back window, and as he did this an idea began to formulate in the front of his mind.

But he would need help.

"Jack, Raven, I think I have an idea that will keep our new friends busy while we try to escape, but I need your help," Henry told the boy and girl.

"Sure, Henry, just tell me what to do," Jack replied, his teeth flaring in the shadows, Raven only nodding slightly as she fixed herself after climbing free of the tumbled boxes.

Nodding, Henry began pointing to this and that, Jack and Raven doing what they were told without argument. Jimmy appeared at the front of the truck, and he reached in and grabbed Cindy's M-16 where it had fallen in the crash.

"You guys okay?" Jimmy asked. Then he looked through the truck and saw the headlights. "Oh, shit, we got company coming," he finished.

"Yeah, I saw them too," Henry replied. "You know what? Seems you're here, come in here and help us."

Jimmy slung the M-16 over his shoulder and climbed back inside.

"What's up?"

"A welcome gift for our friends, that's what. I want to thank them for wrecking our transportation," Henry said, his teeth gleaming in the shadows. "This wasn't an accident, the chances they're friendly is slim to none, you agree?"

"Yeah, agreed, what's the plan?"

Henry began filling Jimmy in as Jack and Raven worked fast, now working together with Jimmy. For once the two younger men weren't arguing, knowing both their lives, and the rest of the companion's, were now on the line.

And with the ocher-colored sun now beginning to kiss the horizon of the Colorado Mountains, the headlights to the approaching vehicle moved closer, the unknown force barreling down on the trapped companions.

# Chapter 22

The beat up, red Ford pickup approached the rolled over UPS truck, the driver slowing the vehicle to a heavy stop when he was no more than two car lengths away.

From off the back of the pickup, five out of the seven armed coldhearts who had been riding in the rear bed hopped down and began to investigate the crashed UPS truck, while the driver remained behind the wheel.

The remaining two men stayed on the truck, their higher elevation perfect for picking off any prey they might spot.

While the men moved across the pavement, the passenger side door opened and another man stepped out.

His face was narrow, with a hawk-like nose, and a large scar, which was white against his tan face. The scar adorned his right cheek, from eye socket to the top of his lip. It had been given to him by a woman who hadn't taken too kindly to being raped by him.

Of course, no one else knew this.

The whore was long dead and he made sure to tell anyone who didn't already know about it that he caught the scar in a bar brawl with a man twice his size.

"Spread out and check the area. Whoever was in this wreck's got to be around here somewhere," he called out as he hefted his pump-action shotgun to a better position. Glancing up at the lightening sky, he knew the prey couldn't have gone far thanks to the amount of time it had taken for him and his men to reach the crash site.

One of the men in his camp had come up with the idea to lay spikes across the road, camouflage them with dirt, and then attach a flare to a zip line. That way if someone came down the road, not only would they crash with all their tires blown, but his men would get the heads up they had a target out on the road.

It had been luck that he and his men had been awake when the flare had touched the sky. They had just finished beating the shit out of a man and women they had found a day ago and were about to begin having some fun with what was left of the woman when the flare had changed their plans drastically.

It had taken them less than a minute to load onto the old pickup and head down the road. Their camp was less than two miles from where the spikes had been set; deep in the mountains, and it had taken them mere minutes to arrive.

This section of road had been picked for the simple reason there was nowhere to go if someone lived through the crash. On either side of the guardrails were steep embankments, which were too steep to climb down, unless one wanted to risk breaking their neck.

So if the prey wasn't in the immediate area, they must have gone down the road on foot, and it would be a simple task to catch up to them with the pickup truck.

They had done so in the past, and recalling the screams of the running prey when they were mowed down still kept him warm at night.

Oh, yes, the man with the scar liked the way the world was now. Up here in the mountains, where the zombies pretty much didn't come, he was a law unto himself. No one fucked with him and his men and that was the way he liked it. He took what he wanted, screwed what he wanted, and killed who he wanted, and pretty much just did whatever the hell he desired and there was nothing and no one who could stop him.

Well, there were some people, but they stayed out of his business and he left them alone, at least for now. Part of the reason was he didn't have enough men to take on the security force of the only village within walking distance. But soon he would have enough men and then he would rain death down on the small village, taking what he wanted and leaving the rest to rot in the sun.

"Well, what's up, where are they?" Scarface yelled as he stopped walking about ten feet from the overturned UPS truck. In the gloom of the coming morning, he could smell gasoline and see small rocks spread around the crushed vehicle, especially by the undercarriage, littering the road like spare change.

He gave it no further thought.

"They're not here," one of the men said, a fat specimen of a man with sagging jowls and greasy hair. The man hadn't bathed in more than a month and was proud of it. He didn't mind that he was always told to ride in the rear bed, that he would never, ever get to ride inside the vehicle.

Scarface turned to two of his men. "You and you, get inside that wrecked truck and see what's in there, and watch it."

Maybe there were bodies in the wreck, he thought. It had happened before. Sucks not to have anyone to play with, but there was always the supplies they would find.

Both men nodded and did as ordered.

Scarface was the leader and both men knew not to disobey unless they wanted a knife in the gut.

The two men moved to the rear doors slowly, just in case someone was waiting with a leveled blaster. It had happened before. Survivors of a wreck, too hurt to run, would wait until one of the hunters would arrive and then shoot them before they knew what hit 'em. Scarface had lost three men over a two month period before he got his people to wise up.

The two men took it slow, and after making sure the interior of the truck was empty, one man went inside, then waved the other one to follow.

Scarface waited for more than five seconds, and was about to call out to them when one of the men stepped out, a smile on his cracked lips.

"Holy shit, boss, we hit the fuckin' jackpot. This thing is full of ammo!"

"What are you talkin' about?" Scarface snapped.

"Ammo, Boss, boxes of it. The shit's everywhere!"

Scarface's grizzled face split into a wide grin while the other men began to whoop it up. Sure there were no survivors, whoever had been inside the truck had taken off, but they could be run down later. In the meantime, it looked like they'd scored the find of a lifetime.

Scarface took a few more steps closer to the truck, and when he did, he glanced down at what he thought were rocks and pebbles, figuring they'd been torn up out of the road when the truck had flipped. But as he moved closer and the sun continued to rise, chasing the darkness away, he began to see how the rocks seemed to reflect the light, like little mirrors. Moving closer, he kicked one with his foot, and as the rocks rolled across the road he heard the distinct sound of metal. His eyes followed the bits of metal to the undercarriage and he realized there was a massive pile of these items poured against the rear tires, right where the gas tank was. Now that he was closer, the distinct odor of gasoline tickled his nose, stronger than before, and when he looked down he realized the gas wasn't just seeping out of the tank in a small trickle, but was coming out like the tank had been punctured with something sharp. The fuel then wound its way around the vehicle and off into the forest, right up to the guardrail, like a long, fluid snake.

But then he also realized the gas was trickling uphill. That didn't make sense at all and he was about to yell out, to tell his men there was something off about this particular crash when he looked up to see a man with wide shoulders, and a grim countenance on his face near the guardrail. The man stepped out of the forest right where the gas trail stopped.

Scarface and the man made eye contact and held it for less than three seconds, but in that time, Scarface saw the man in front of him was no simple trader who'd been caught off guard on a lonely road in the middle of nowhere.

The man's once brown hair, though now peppered with white, was cut short and the eyes that peered back at him were hard. They were the eyes of a killer. Of a man who would show no mercy when none was warranted. His upper torso was nothing but muscle under his torn shirt and his tanned arms were corded like taut, steel cables.

The man was armed too. A Glock 9mm was in a holster on his right hip and a massive knife, at least sixteen inches long, adorned his left hip.

All this Scarface took in at a glance.

It was as he was opening his mouth to order his men to shoot the bastard who had the balls to step out into the open like it was *he* who was the hunted, when the man with the ash gray hair lit a small cigarette lighter in his hand, the tiny ball of light flickering in the morning gloom.

With an evil grin, the man dropped the lighter to the gas trail at his feet, and before Scarface could do more than gape in shock, the gas trail erupted, and in less than five seconds traveled across the road to the rear of the overturned UPS truck.

And then there was nothing but noise and light as Scarface was blown off his feet and the world exploded into chaos.

No sooner did the UPS truck explode, the entire vehicle jumping into the air three feet to fall back down like a flaming meteor, then the bullets around the truck and undercarriage began to cook off, rounds shooting off in all directions.

On the road, Scarface was rolling around, the side of his body on fire, but no sooner did he go down then one of his men was near him, slapping the flames out and helping him up.

But if the leader of the coldhearts thought that was the worst thing that was going to happen to him today, he was sorely mistaken.

Only seconds after the initial blast of the truck, with the shockwave still reverberating across the road, the companions stepped out of the forest on either side of the road where they had been hiding, clinging to the top of the ravine by the guardrail like wayward children as they waited for the right time to strike.

Surprise, Henry knew, was the companion's only chance. They had to take down as many of these coldhearts before the men realized what was happening.

Henry and Jimmy split to the left while Cindy, her M-16 spitting death, took the right, wanting to split up so as to avoid giving any shooters too simple a target.

At this close range, almost every shot Henry took found its mark, the rounds finding the soft flesh from less than twenty feet away.

Spilled guts sprinkled the ground with red, and twitching bodies quickly found the road as he emptied his clip in seconds, popped out the spent mag and slapped another fresh one all without missing a shot.

To his left, Jimmy was moving across the road, firing at the two men on the back of the pickup, knowing both of them had good vantage points to return fire. Jimmy's first shot took the man on the left high on his temple, the .38 slug taking off half his head. The second man ducked down, but not before taking a round to the shoulder. As he fell away, Cindy picked up the slack and riddled the man with lead.

Through his peripheral vision, Henry saw Cindy gun down two more of the coldhearts, the front of their bodies turning bright red as the rounds tore them apart. Cindy climbed her shots up the second man's torso, until finally ending by shooting the man in the head four times. The head exploded, skull fragments and brain matter flying off in all directions. The headless body swayed back and forth where it stood, not aware it was missing a head, and then it toppled backward, the hands still twitching in death spasms.

As Henry stepped onto the road, a man enveloped in flames holding a large knife came at him. How the man could even see was amazing. All his hair was burned off and his face and arms were one massive, red welt, the flesh cracked and charred from being caught in the explosion of the UPS truck. The smell of burnt hair and meat filled the air.

Henry spotted the knife coming at him and he twisted around, smashing the butt of his gun down on the murderous hand, then he raised the muzzle and shot the man in the chest. The body attached to the hand flew backwards in a spray of blood, knocking down another attacker as he came at Henry with murder in his eyes. Henry glanced down at the gun in the man's hand and realized he wasn't going to be able to take him out in time, when a multitude of bullets caught in the explosion cooked off and one struck the attacker in the chest, just to the left of his heart.

Henry stared at the man as he took a step back, then saw the red spot appear on his chest. The man looked down and then back up, his eyes meeting Henry's with a curiosity, as if he didn't understand what had happened to him.

After all, Henry hadn't fired a shot at him.

Then the man toppled to the road and bled out.

Knowing someone or something was on his side just now, Henry spun around and continued the fight, but as he did he saw the battle was over. Jimmy and Cindy were standing in the middle of the road, their weapons moving in fast arcs as they waited for another target to appear, but all the men were down.

It was while Henry was moving towards them he saw a man with a large scar, half his body burnt to a crisp, step out from behind the pickup truck, his shotgun already leveling out to shoot Cindy in the back.

"Cindy, behind you!" Henry yelled out, but it was painfully obvious he was going to be too late as he brought up his Glock to stop the coldheart from shooting her.

Jimmy heard Henry's shout and spun on his heels, seeing the man about to fire. Knowing his woman was in danger, he acted fast, not thinking of his own life, but only for the woman he loved.

With his .38 coming up and firing twice, Jimmy was lunging for Cindy, his body now between him and the coldheart leader.

Scarface managed to fire one shot before he was hit twice in the chest, his heart and lungs exploding out his back in red tendrils as the .38 slugs ripped his insides apart. But with his last living action on Earth, Scarface kept his aim true, and though Jimmy pushed Cindy to the road, sending her sprawling forward, more than half the shotgun blast caught him in the chest, knocking him to the pavement in a heap of arms and legs.

"Jimmy! Oh, Christ, no!" Henry yelled as he darted across the road, his heart beating a staccato in his chest as he went to help his fallen friend.

But he'd witnessed his friend take a shotgun blast straight to the chest and there could be only one result.

That his friend was dead.

As he reached Jimmy's face-down body, he was already gearing himself for the bitter truth, though he hated it just the same.

# Chapter 23

Cindy was rolling onto her side as she turned back to Jimmy, seeing him spread across the pavement like a slain deer.

"Oh, God, no! Jimmy, he can't be..." Cindy gasped as she began crawling to his still body.

From out of their hiding place in the woods, Sue and Jack also came running, but Raven stayed behind to be with the still unconscious Mary and quiet Carol who was agitated from the sounds of battle.

Henry reached Jimmy and he knelt down by his side, his eyes already beginning to tear up at the sight that was about to greet him as he began to roll Jimmy onto his back.

He knew the young man's chest would be a mass of red and torn flesh, blood coating him from neck to waist. He wondered if Jimmy's eyes would be open, the now lifeless orbs staring out into the infinite void between life and death.

Henry hoped not. That might be too much for him to bear.

"I'm so sorry, buddy, it's not fair," Henry whispered as he turned over the body.

So it came as a shock when he rolled Jimmy over, expecting to see blood and a dead face, that this wasn't the case.

Instead, Jimmy's eyes were wide open, filled with life, and his mouth was curved up into a wide grin, that wiseass grin that his friends knew so well and yet hated at the same time.

"It's nice to know you care so much about me, Henry. You're not gonna give me a kiss now are ya?" Jimmy cracked as he stared up into Henry's shocked face.

"What the...? But how? I saw you take a blast to the chest," Henry stammered as he helped Jimmy to sit up.

Groaning as he did so, Jimmy nodded to Henry, then smiled as Cindy reached him, the woman hugging him hard in relief.

"Yeah, you did." He slapped his chest where there were multiple holes in his shirt from where the pellets had penetrated the material, wincing when he did it. "But I'm wearing a vest, one of the ones we took from the cannies."

"You're wearing a..." Henry let the words hang in the air for a second. "Wait a second. I thought you said bulletproof vests are for pussies?"

Jimmy nodded as Cindy helped him to stand. "I did, but what's wrong with being a live pussy? Better than being a dead hero any day," he joked as he winced in pain. Though the vest had stopped the blast, it was possible he had a few cracked ribs, most definitely bruising.

"Well, I'm just glad you're still alive," Cindy said as Susan and Jack came up to join them. "I'm not finished with you yet," she finished as she kissed him again." Then she leaned in close. "Thanks for saving me, baby, the first chance we get I'm gonna rock your world," she whispered seductively.

Jimmy's eyes went wide now that he had something to look forward to. Jack took a look at Jimmy and saw the holes in his shirt and nodded curtly.

"Hey," Jack said. "You okay?"

Jimmy nodded. "Yeah, brat, you not gettin' rid of me that easy. It takes a lot more than a shot to the chest to take out the great Jimmy Cooper."

"Amen, buddy, amen," Henry said as he slapped Jimmy lightly on the shoulder. "Look, if you're really okay then I could use your help makin' sure we're good here. Then we can see if we can use that pickup truck over there."

Though he winced slightly, Jimmy nodded. "Yeah, Henry, I'm fine. Just got the wind knocked out of me, that's all. I'll be better in a bit."

"Good," Henry said. He turned to Susan. "Raven with Mary? How's she doing?"

Susan shrugged. "She's okay. She's still out of it, but her pulse is steadier. But if she doesn't wake up soon I think we should begin to get worried."

"Okay, sure, but let's deal with one thing at a time," Henry said. "Go get her and Carol, will you, please? Bring them out here with us. I want to be out of here in five minutes. There's no telling who heard all that shooting and the explosion. I don't want to be around here if anyone else turns up to investigate."

"Got it," Susan said, moving away to Mary, Carol and Raven. They were about six feet down the slope past the guardrail, as that was as far as they could go safely.

Henry turned and walked to the battered pickup, Jimmy and Cindy beside him. All had weapons ready, but were fairly confident the battle was over. Behind them and to the side, the UPS truck still crackled with the heat of the original explosion. Bullets still exploded inside the truck, but the ammunition that had been poured against the undercarriage was all cooked off by now. It sounded like there were fireworks going off, and one stray round shooting in the wrong direction could still kill. The warped and burnt sheet metal looked like Swiss cheese after the cooked rounds that had shot their way out and into the open air. Henry had taken a chance in what he'd chosen as a distraction, but the alternative was worse, and he'd taken the chance knowing full well what he was doing. Luckily, all the companions had come out unscathed, though Jimmy had been close to not walking away in one piece.

As they approached the pickup, Henry saw the driver slumped over the steering wheel. There was a bullet hole about head height in the center of the windshield. When he got to the driver's door and opened it, the odor of feces and urine washed over him.

Reaching inside, he grabbed the dead driver by his shirt and yanked the man out of the cab. The body tumbled unceremoniously onto the road, the odor following him.

"Looks like he caught one in the brain pan," Jimmy said. "I wonder which one of us shot him?" He mused as he stepped over the body and peered inside the vehicle. The rear glass of the cab was covered in brain matter and the seat was slick with urine and moisture from what had soaked through the dead driver's pants after he'd shit himself.

"Damn, it stinks in here," Jimmy said.

Henry moved closer. "Don't care about the smell, Jimmy. Just as long as it works." He reached around the steering column and turned the key, grinning when the engine sputtered to life. "Outstanding, looks like we got wheels again."

He turned to see where Jack was. "Hey, Jack, how 'bout grab-bing the boxes of ammo we hid and get them loaded into the back over here," Henry told the boy as he pointed to the rear bed.

Jack waved and ran across the road. Just over the guardrail were a dozen boxes of ammunition and other miscellaneous items salvaged at the last minute before they'd prepared the UPS truck to explode. It had broken Henry's heart to see all those rounds of ammunition destroyed, but he needed a plan fast and there was no time to unload it all. After all, there was always more ammunition in the world, but there was only one each of the companions.

In the end, he was happy with the trade he'd made. Though the ammo was gone, they were all alive and well, though Mary had been knocked around a bit, and they now had another vehicle, preferably one with a working exhaust where anyone in the area wouldn't hear them coming from miles away.

Henry cut off a few shirts that weren't so bloody from some of the corpses of the coldhearts and used them to try and wipe the inside seat of the pickup as clean as he could. When finished, he went to see if he could help anyone load up the supplies.

He spotted Jimmy leaning down over the dead body of the man who had almost killed him. He was rifling through the corpse's pockets. A second later, Jimmy stood up with what he had been searching for. Shells for the new shotgun taken from the dead man.

"Ha, I got me a shotgun again, and shells, too," Jimmy said in victory.

Henry nodded. So be it. The raider was dead and Jimmy was alive, whatever the man owned now went to Jimmy if he wanted it. It was the way of the world, simple as that.

Mary was walking with Sue and Carol, and when Henry moved over to her, Mary lifted her eyes and glanced up at him. He leaned down next to her and wiped a few brown strands of hair off her sweaty brow.

"Hey, there, Mar', nice to see you awake. How you doin'?"

She moved her head back and forth slowly, but that was all she could manage. Her head wound had stopped bleeding and Sue was making sure it stayed clean.

"I'm okay, Henry, just a little dizzy. Sue filled me in on what happened. You got them all? We're safe?"

"For now, yeah, we're as good as we can be, I suppose. At least we got wheels and there's almost half a tank of gas. Should get us to that town, that is if we can find it."

Sue looked up then from her ministrations to Mary. "Why, you think we won't be able to find it?"

"Well, yeah, maybe, there's a lot of land out here and if there was a town nearby don't you think those raiders would've been there? If they're attacking whatever might come down this road then I highly doubt they have. There's a lot easier picking from a town then what might turn up on this stretch of empty road."

Sue didn't reply, not having that much experience with raiders and the like. She had been a normal woman before the dead began to walk and she hadn't changed much since. She had been captured by cannibals along with Raven, and if it hadn't been for Henry and the others, both of them would be long dead by now. Henry told her she needed to get hard if she was going to survive in this new world, but to be cruel and kill went against her nature. Henry told her he would watch over her, but still, at times she wished she could do her part more.

"Hey, Henry, we're done!" Jimmy called out from the pickup.

Henry glanced to Jimmy, saw everyone was waiting on him, Sue and Mary, and he leaned down to help Mary up, practically carrying her. Sue helped Carol up, the small woman saying nothing as Sue led her into the rear bed of the pickup. Henry watched them and wondered what they were going to do with the quiet woman. They couldn't keep her as she was a definite liability.

"I got it, I can walk," Mary said as she pushed him away, but he wouldn't let her.

"Nah-ah, nothin; doin'. You took quite a hit on the head, Mary. You'll let me help until I say you're okay. And you ride inside with me, too. The smell's not the best, but we can leave the windows open," Henry told her as he helped her across the road to the passenger side of the pickup. Raven was there and helped Mary as well, Jimmy watching from a few feet away.

"Hey, Mar', good to see you back in the land of the living," Jimmy said with a grin.

"Thanks, Jimmy, good to be back," Mary replied as she was helped inside the cab.

Jimmy turned to Henry when he moved beside him. "So, who's gonna drive?"

Henry pointed to himself. "I got it, Jimmy, you were just shot, remember? At the moment I'll fly this bird." He glanced to Raven and Jack who were talking together, both with angry faces.

"What's up with you two?" Henry inquired.

Jack said something to Raven and she nodded, then Jack turned to Henry.

"We're both still pissed because you wouldn't let us fight, too. Especially her, she can kick ass like the best of 'em," Jack said, sticking up for Raven.

Henry nodded. "Sure she can, but those killer nails of hers can't stop a bullet and she doesn't want to carry a gun." He looked to Raven. "Am I right?"

She shrugged, her black hair flowing over her shoulders. "Don't need one, got these," she said, flashing her razor-sharp nails in the air.

"Exactly, and you're amazing with them. But we just had a gun-fight, and you don't bring knives or similar items to a gun fight, you bring guns, got me?" He was looking at Jack as he asked his question.

Jack frowned, but didn't reply.

"I said, got me, son?" This time Henry added a touch of cold-ness to his voice that Jack picked up on.

"Yeah, Henry I got it."

He nodded. "Good, then if this discussion is over the both of you hop in the back, we're leaving." Henry turned and moved around the front bumper and slid behind the steering wheel. Next to him was Mary and Sue, Mary in the middle.

"You guys ready?"

"Sure, Henry, all set," Sue replied.

Henry leaned out his window, the fresh air better than inside the aroma filled cab.

"Jimmy, you guys ready to go?"

Jimmy slapped the top of the cab. "We're ready, old man, let's get the hell out of here," he said as he turned to make eye contact with the others in back with him, and the boxes salvaged from the

UPS truck. Raven, Jack and Cindy all looked back at him, but Carol merely stared at the metal floor of the bed, taciturn as ever.

Putting the transmission in drive, Henry stepped on the gas, the truck jerking forward for a second as he got used to the feel of it. As he drove away, he veered around a few of the corpses in the road, then he had no choice but to drive over a body that was directly in his path.

The sounds of brittle bones cracking filled the air as the tires rolled over the corpse, leaving a larger indentation on the chest where the tires had crushed the rib cage.

Then he was around the UPS truck, still smoldering, while flames were still licking out the sides and windows. A bullet cooking off from time to time, though the worst was over, and in seconds the wreck was behind them, the pickup moving down the road. Though the companions were a little lighter for supplies, they were still alive and in good shape. There had been other past situations where they had come out a lot worse than this one, so with a smile on his face, Henry drove onward, the road open to what he and his friends may find.

\*    \*    \*

No sooner did the pickup round the bend in the incline of the road and disappear from sight, then a murder of crows appeared from the nearby trees. The ebony birds had watched from afar, scenting the aroma of spilled blood, and with the departure of the pickup, they dove in, quickly digging into the bodies of the raiders. The eyes were first, the soft morsels a delicacy amongst the birds, followed by the tongues, which were pried out of closed mouths like they were digging in the dirt for worms. Eyelids were next, pulled like they were made of rubber as the beaks pecked and severed skin from muscle.

Soon, insects appeared. Ants, flies and roaches, all crawling from the sides of the road, seeking the spilt blood and gore.

A coyote arrived, picking a corpse near the guardrail, its sharp teeth ripping into the soft belly of the dead raider as it feasted on the still warm innards.

Whether zombie, animal, or insect, man was always food for something, and thus is how it would always be.

# Chapter 24

The next hour and change went by slowly, the battered pickup truck winding its way deeper into the mountains as the road twisted and turned like a snake. Conversation was light, each of the companions lost in private thoughts, and like usual it was Jimmy who broke the silence, slapping the roof of the pickup so Henry would pull over.

Steering to the side of the road, Henry found a clearing. The guardrail had dropped away more than thirty minutes ago and there were almost no signs of man with the exception of a stray, empty and crushed soda can and a newspaper blowing about on the edges of the road.

Even here, in the most personal part of Mother Nature, man had to leave his mark. When the vehicle pulled to a stop, Jimmy hopped down, and with a grin, pointed to the woods as he hobbled on one leg.

Henry chuckled as he cast a glance to Sue. "I swear, that man's got a bladder the size of a walnut," he joked. He turned to Mary sitting next to him. "How you feeling, better?"

"Yeah, Henry, I'll be fine, just took a knock on the head." She touched the lump gingerly, wincing slightly. "It'll be okay in a day or so."

"You got lucky, Mary, you know that?" Sue stated as she shifted in her seat. "Henry, I want to get out and stretch my legs, is it okay?" She inquired.

He nodded, then decided he could use a stretch, too. "Sure, but be careful, we don't know this area, who knows what could be beyond those trees. Just stay in eye sight in case there's trouble."

She smiled, hearing it all before, and opened her door. Henry opened his as well and glanced back to Mary.

"How 'bout you? Wanna stretch?"

"No, Henry, I'm good, I'll just sit here and wait." Mary leaned back and closed her eyes, her chest rising and falling gently.

Henry closed his door and turned to see into the rear bed. Raven, Carol and Jack were still there and Jack nodded to Henry. He retuned the greeting and moved to the front of the pickup, wanting to inspect the truck now that he had a chance. It was beat up, but seemed in decent shape. The tires were worn, but still had some tread, and the paint, though chipped, was still serviceable.

That was when he noticed the light-green fluid dripping out from under the front bumper, and he frowned, going to one knee to inspect it.

Sure enough, the radiator was leaking. As he poked around some more he found a small hole in the bottom of the radiator, probably from a stray round. It looked like it had been leaking for a while, and because it hadn't touched anything hot on the undercarriage, no steam had issued from under the hood, yet.

Popping the hood, Henry waited until the radiator had relieved pressure and he took off the small red cap. Just as he expected, it was low.

"Damn it," he hissed.

Jimmy came up behind him, looking over his shoulder. "What's up, old man?"

"The damn radiator's leaking, that's what. How much water do we have left?"

Jimmy gave it some thought. "Not too much, especially if you want to put it in the radiator. Why, you gonna?"

"Don't see how we have a choice, do you? It's either that or use the water while we sweat it out as we walk when this thing craps out on us."

Jimmy considered that and nodded. "Yeah, good point. Okay, I'll get some." Then he was off to the rear of the truck. He asked Jack for help, and of course a second later they were arguing as Jack told Jimmy he could shove it and to do it himself.

While Henry dealt with the radiator, Sue walked around. She had begun strolling down the road, just enjoying being out where it seemed to be the old world, where the undead didn't seem to be, hadn't contaminated with their decay.

As she rounded a tight hairpin bend in the road about fifty feet from the pickup truck, she realized the landscape opened up before her. She was now able to see out across the mountains, and what she saw nestled in a small valley to her left, along with a small lake, caused her to gasp.

Immediately, she turned and ran back to Henry and the others, wanting to share the news of what she'd found.

*   *   *

"You think that's Crescent Falls?" Jimmy asked as he stared intently into the valley below.

The others were all standing together, with the exception of Carol who was still in the truck. The frail woman was falling deeper into herself and Sue was worried about her. Henry told her there's only so much they could do for the woman. She would have to get hard to survive or she wouldn't, it was as simple as that.

The companions gazed out across the wide-open landscape, the smaller mountains surrounding the small village on all three sides, and the last side, the one facing the companions, seemed to go all the way down to the edge of a small lake. There was a large collection of buildings scattered around a central road, with a few branching off to the sides, and one road disappeared around the edge of a bluff, which was protruding on their right. A few of the buildings had smoke coming from their chimneys, and from where the companions stood, they could see there was electrical power. There was one intersection in the middle of town, and even from high on the ridge, they could see the red stop light blinking on and off.

It was a picture perfect image, suitable for framing on a postcard. As the companions stared at the majestic town, it was easy to believe there had never been an outbreak of the walking dead, no rains of death falling from the sky, and the world was the same as it always was.

"Hey, Henry, you hear me? You think that's the town from the map?" Jimmy asked again.

Henry shrugged, pulled from his reverie. "Could be, it's not like there's a lot of villages out here in the middle of the mountains." He pointed north. "The Rockies are that way and they're a bitch to get through. Looks like we found it," he turned to Sue, "Great job, honey."

She grinned. "Well, thanks, but it was there, all I did was look out and see it," she said with a wave.

"So, what's the plan?" Mary asked as she admired the beautiful vista. The fresh air was doing wonders for her. Her head was clear and didn't throb as much as before. At this rate she'd be up to her old self in another hour or so. Luckily, she had some aspirin in her backpack, wanting to save them when she really needed them. Henry had taken a few the day before and now she figured it was her turn. Henry rubbed his jaw, his chin rough with stubble. He had been on the go for what seemed like days and there hadn't been time to shave. He preferred to keep his face clean, not wanting to fall into a rut. When he shaved, it reminded him of how things were, plus Sue didn't like his beard, telling him it scratched her when they made love, and he wanted to please her.

"Okay, listen up," Henry called out. "The pickup's got a busted radiator, but it'll still drive. But figuring as we don't know what's in that town, I don't want to lose our only mode of transport, so here's what we'll do." He began filling them in as the others nodded and asked questions.

And with an azure sky painting the awesome picture of Nature's beauty, they planned for their next move before heading into the small village.

*   *   *

"I hope this idea of yours works, Henry," Jimmy remarked as they all walked down the middle of the mountain road. If Henry was correct, the small village was no more than three miles away, give or take. Behind them, hidden in a recess off the road was the worn pickup truck. It was now hidden under cut branches and dried leaves. Now, if they ran into trouble in the small village and had to leave in a hurry, at least they knew they had wheels waiting for them.

Henry had a good reason to be concerned. More than once they had walked into a town and found it hostile. This way they had an ace up their sleeve if needed. Though their backpacks were full to the brim with ammunition and remaining food supplies, the rest was hidden in the rear bed of the battered truck. They had already lost more than ninety percent of what was taken from the cannie warehouse and none of them wanted to lose the rest.

"Yeah, Jimmy, me too," Henry replied as he placed one foot in front of the other.

"You have any idea on what we might find when we get there?" Cindy asked as she walked askance of Jimmy. The two were holding hands, like two young lovers out for a stroll. Jack had made a remark a few minutes ago about them, but Jimmy had actually shrugged it off. Cindy had kissed him for that and Jack had made a disgusted noise. Henry and Sue had laughed at that.

In the rear of the group was Raven and Carol. The ebony haired girl was looking after the withdrawn survivor and had told Sue she didn't like watching her. But Sue had known Raven the longest and the two had a good relationship, similar to a mother to a daughter, so Raven had agreed to watch the silent woman...for now.

Henry shrugged slightly at Cindy's question. "Half hour or so if I had to take a guess but don't quote me on it," he said.

"Did you see how clean and neat everything looked?" Mary said. "There weren't any fences to keep out the dead, either? Did any of you guys see any?"

No one said they did.

"Yeah, no shit," Jimmy said. "It's like the deaders never got this far. Hey, Henry, you think that's possible?"

"Anything's possible, Jimmy, but listen up everyone, when we get there we don't do anything to call attention to ourselves. We step light and try and find out who's in charge, make sure we get a warm welcome."

With nods of agreement they continued down the road, the sun slowly rising in the crystal blue sky.

\* \* \*

A black as night crow sat on the edge of the lilting sign, like a sentry guarding its charge, its wings fluttering as it struggled to keep its balance.

They all stared at the faded sign like it was a relic of the past.

**Crescent Falls, Alt. 4, 398.**
**Population, 2,038.**

And printed neatly below that in dark red paint were the words: ***Walk the Yellow Line and You'll Be Fine***.

"Well, that certainly gives us an idea what we might expect," Jimmy said as he crossed his arms over his chest.

Henry nodded, his jaw taut. "It's good advice, too. We follow their rules and we should be fine. Let's go, we're wasting daylight."

Everyone shuffled along, Mary giving the sign one last look as, she too, moved out. The crow cawed at the group as they passed it by, as if giving a warning not to go that way.

It was when they were about a half mile from what Henry thought would be the edge of the village that they saw signs of life.

"Check it out, the road's clean," Jimmy said as he walked on point.

The others followed where he was pointing and sure enough, they now noticed the weeds and leaves that had been in the pavement behind them was now gone.

"Someone's cleaned the road of debris," Henry said as he reached down for his Glock. "Maybe that's good, they take some pride where they live."

"Hey, Henry," Cindy said. "I hear something coming, a car or truck maybe," she said while gesturing down the road with the muzzle of her M-16.

"Wait a second, yes, I hear it, too," Mary said. "What do we do?"

It was a good question. Where they were standing in the road, there was nowhere to run or hide. Both sides of the road were mountainous and even if they tried to run they wouldn't get more than sixty feet before the vehicle arrived. Whether on purpose or by accident, the companions had walked into a very bad situation.

"Okay, no one panic, for all we know they're friends. Let's go on that assumption until told otherwise," he said as he looked at each of their faces.

It was good advice. In the deadlands, you usually had to work on the assumption that every stranger you met was your enemy and should be killed before they could do the same to you. But the other side of the coin was that most people living in the remnants of America were reasonable, good people, honest and hard working, and didn't have blood in their eyes or murder on their minds the instant they met you.

The wind was blowing toward the village, making it hard to hear anything coming from that direction, but within another moment they all heard the powerful revving of an engine.

Each of them saw the vehicle as it breasted a rise in the road about three hundreds yards away. It was a small, open jeep, but this one was a dark black with roll bars that looked reinforced with extra metal and welds.

Five men were seated in it, all holding wicked looking blasters.

"Just stand easy, people," Henry said as the jeep pulled up and stopped in a squeal of brakes about forty yards away. "We don't want to bring the entire village down on us."

As Henry waited for what would happen next, he studied the firearms the men carried. Though not a complete expert with all weapons now in use in the deadlands, he did recognize the ones the security force carried.

"Winchester carbines. Selective fire, M-2 models, twenty caliber, if I'm right," Henry said, remembering the description from the magazine he'd read a month back.

"Nah, Henry, those puppies are thirty caliber," Jimmy said as he moved up next to him.

Henry took another look and realized Jimmy was right.

"Yeah, sorry, thirty. It's good to know the size of the bullet when it rips into you," he muttered.

Four of the men jumped out of the jeep and formed a skirmishing line across the road while the driver climbed into the back and pulled off a black tarp, exposing a gleaming, mounted machine gun. Henry recognized it immediately. The 7.62 model. That weapon would make Swiss cheese of him and his group in seconds.

Things just went from friendly to unfriendly in the blink of an eye.

As Henry stared at the security force in front of him, he wondered if he shouldn't have sent the newcomers to buy the farm as soon as the jeep pulled up.

If he had, they wouldn't be in the standoff position they now found themselves in.

As he stared at the men with their weapons now pointed at his people, he got a good look at their outfits. They wore black jump-suits with shoulder and knee pads. Knee-high leather boots and black caps with shiny tops, as well as dark sunglasses that hid their eyes, giving them the look that one man was the same as the others.

"Goddammit, Henry, these guys are some kind of security force," Jimmy hissed as he reached over his back for his new pump-action shotgun taken from the scarfaced man as spoils of war.

"Take it slow, Jimmy, we're already in a bad spot, let's not make it worse," Henry told him out of the side of his mouth. His hand was on the grip of his Glock, but he didn't want to pull the handgun, not until he was sure he'd needed it.

There was still a chance the security force's motions were all for show.

The center man of the quartet called out to them, the tone of his voice neither harsh nor friendly. "You people strangers to these parts?"

Henry didn't answer right away, giving the question some thought. It wasn't that it was such a hard question, of course, but from previous experience it was the sort of query that had a lot more behind it than the one simple question. It was the sort of question where the wrong answer could end up bringing down a hail of lead that would sweep the companions off the road in bloody chunks.

"What do you mean by strangers?" Henry finally said, his eyes on the hands of the security force. If he saw one finger twitch near a trigger, he knew all talk was off and it was time for people to die.

The security guard who had asked the question shifted his feet. "If you have to ask me then that means you are," he said bluntly. "Where're you folks from?"

"Different places," Henry said, treading lightly.

The security man gestured with the muzzle of his carbine. "You look well armed. You mercies, raiders, maybe?"

"Neither, we're just friends passing through the mountains."

"Passing, huh? Where to exactly?"

"Where ever we want to go," Henry said, clearly becoming angry with the questions.

"Uh-huh. Way I see it, you were heading to my little village, is that it? You want to come and visit us in Crescent falls? That the idea?"

"Maybe, how's that sit with you?" Henry asked, his eyes staring at the man whose own eyes were hidden behind dark sunglasses.

"Well, you're here now so you might as well come along. Why don't you walk ahead of us and we'll talk on the way."

"We got a choice if we don't want to?" Jimmy asked.

"Sure you do," the man said, this time grinning. "You can walk ahead or we can cut you down right here and leave your bodies for the buzzards." To illustrate his point, the man behind the machine gun flicked off the safety, the click loud on the empty road.

Jimmy scowled deeply, but he began walking, and so too, did the others.

"Huh," Jimmy said, "some fucking choice."

# Chapter 25

The jeep growled behind the eight travelers as they made their way down the road and finally to the beginnings of the village. One of the guards kept watch over them the entire time behind the machine gun, the muzzle never wavering far from their backs.

It was an unpleasant feeling, but there wasn't much any of them could do about it at the moment.

The leader of the patrol called out to the companions when they reached a barrier across the road, consisting of a single red and white striped pole which was connected to a small stone and wooden hut.

As Henry waited with the others, once again he was able to see how neat and clean everything was. There was no trash on the road and even the cracks had been repaired, using a sticky black tar.

Two more visored guards stepped out of the shack, both holding shiny polished carbines that gleamed in the sunlight. Both Henry and Jimmy saw how the men's heads turned right to the women in the group of travelers, as if they had never seen the female form. Henry was about to ask them what the hell was their problem when the leader of the security patrol barked at them, telling them to snap out of it and get to opening the barrier.

Mary, Cindy, Jimmy and Henry all shared a close look, but no one spoke, not wanting the guards to know they had noticed the furtive glances from the men.

The pole was lifted and the security leader ordered Henry and the group to get moving. Once again they began walking, winding their way through the village. The homes were mostly one-story, a few with two, but they seemed to be mostly commercial property.

While they walked, people out on the streets stopped to stare at them.

The words strangers and women were heard by Henry and Jimmy and they both looked to one another. What was odd was there were no young or middle-aged women on the street, only men of all ages and very aged women, all with bent backs and wrinkled visages. A few of the older women stopped and made the sign of the cross while shaking their heads in what appeared to be sadness when the companions passed by them.

Mary saw this and made a note to mention it to the others to see if they had noticed the same thing.

Fifteen minutes later and they slowed in front of a two-story brick building with flower pots on the window frames and a wreath made of wheat and barley on the main door, a large, four foot wooden job that looked like it could fit a wagon easily with room to spare on the sides.

"This here is the boarding house," the patrol leader said. "You people go right inside and Lucy will fix you up with a place to sleep tonight. Tomorrow you're gonna need to meet the Doc."

"A doctor? What kind is he? Medical, physicist?" Mary asked.

The security guard grinned again, which was hard to tell if it was truly a real grin as his eyes were still hidden behind the dark glasses.

"A little of both I guess, miss, but you can ask *her* tomorrow. For now, just go on inside and get some rest."

"And that's it, just like that we can go in and relax," Henry said. He had been waiting for the guards to make them relinquish their weapons, but so far no one had asked them too.

"That's right, just go on in. We'll have some food sent over in a bit."

With nothing else to say, Henry turned to the others and motioned them inside the building. Jimmy opened the door and it swung inward on greased hinges, then Cindy and Mary stepped inside, followed by the rest. Carol was second to last which left Henry staring at the guard.

"Go on, get inside, later we'll send someone by to get your names and where you're from. Just give the info to Lucy. She's got the book you'll all need to sign in. We like to keep track of all visitors who come here. As you can imagine, we don't get much."

Henry looked at the man, trying to peer past the dark shades.

"You do know what's happened out past the mountains, right?"

The man nodded. "You mean the biters? Sure we do, we're not idiots here. But you don't have to worry about them around here. See all the mountains around the village?"

Henry nodded.

"Well, those mountains protected us from the rains. Somethin' to do with high pressure systems or some such shit. All I know is the clouds couldn't get to us and we stayed safe."

"No kidding," Henry said.

"Yeah, no kidding," the man replied, annoyed. "Look, pal, you're the leader of your little group, right?"

"Yeah, I guess I am," Henry answered.

"Yeah, that's what I figured. So listen up. Keep your people in line and follow the rules and you'll be fine around here, got it? Walk the yellow line and you'll be fine, that's our motto and it's worked well so far."

Henry nodded. "You won't get any trouble from us. We just want to rest up for a while and then we'll leave. We can pay for what we use, too."

The guard grinned again, his teeth flashing in the sun. "That's good, got to pay your own way round here. And I already know I won't have any trouble with you or your people."

Henry wasn't sure if the man's statement was ominous or genuine so for the time being he ignored it.

Then the guard gestured with the muzzle of his carbine to the door of the building. "Now get inside. I'm not gonna ask again nicely."

As there wasn't anything else to say, Henry nodded and stepped inside. When he did, three guards left the jeep and took up a perimeter around the building. As the door closed, Henry caught a glimpse of the guards getting orders and heard the patrol leader instructing them not to let Henry or the others out of the building. Then the door clicked shut and that was it.

Turning around, Henry saw the rest of his group standing in a large foyer. There was a big desk at the opposite end and a middle-aged woman was waving to them.

Now that Henry was with them, the companions crossed the floor to the woman.

"Hi, there, I'm Lucy, welcome to Crescent Falls," she said cheerfully.

"Well, hello yourself," Mary said. "It's nice to see another female face under sixty. We didn't see any on our way over here. Where are all the young women?"

Lucy's smile faltered, but only for a second, then she pushed a journal in front of Mary, obviously changing the subject.

"Would you please sign in? It's for the town records," she said.

"My friend asked you a question," Cindy said. "Any reason why you don't want to answer it?"

Lucy smiled, but it was a half-smile.

"No, of course not. Uhm, most of the younger women are working in the fields, and the rest are with their children. It was just dumb luck you didn't see anyone under sixty on your way here, that's all."

Mary glanced at Cindy, and then Sue, who only shrugged.

"Makes sense, doesn't it?" Sue added.

Mary stepped aside and let Cindy sign the journal, then the rest did the same.

"I want to go next," Jack said, shoving Jimmy aside.

"Fine, brat, go, I don't care," Jimmy snapped back, annoyed.

"Boys, cut it out," Henry threatened as he looked about the room.

It was sparse, with only one window near the front and a plush rug around the desk. It took Henry a second to realize that when he glanced up at the ceiling, there were fluorescent lights on, which made him remember the blinking traffic light in the middle of the village.

"Hey, wait a minute, you people have electricity?" Henry gasped as he stared at the flickering tubes like they were the most amazing thing he had ever seen.

Lucy shrugged. "Sure, why wouldn't we?"

Mary leaned against the desk so she could see Lucy's face better. "I guess you haven't been out of these mountains in a while, huh?"

"No, not since things began to happen. Heck, none of us have, well, that is except the security patrols. They go into the city every month or so to get biters for the doctor and his staff."

"Biters?" Cindy asked. "Oh, you mean deaders?"

Lucy looked perplexed as she rolled the word over in her mouth, then she nodded, figuring what Cindy meant.

"If you mean the dead people, then yes, deaders, neat name."

"Why do the patrols go and get them?" Mary asked, curious.

Lucy opened her mouth to reply, but then footsteps sounded from behind her and a man stepped out of a small doorway. He was in his late sixties or early seventies. He had a large nose with a black wart on the tip and his forehead and pitted cheeks were cratered like the moon. Despite this, he had a grandfatherly quality to his appearance.

"Now, now, Lucy, don't bore or new guests with the private business of our benefactor," he said as he stepped out and placed a hand on her shoulder. Henry noticed when the old man's hand touched Lucy's shoulder he squeezed it, the muscles in his arm going taut, Lucy wincing slightly. It wasn't hard to see he was silencing her.

The old man looked to Henry and the others, a twinkle in his eyes. "Welcome, friends, welcome, it's so nice to have guests again, it's been a while. I'm Theo, this is my place."

"Why's that? Don't you get a lot of guests here?" Jack asked curiously.

"Jack, hush," Henry hissed, but the old man waved a hand to stop Henry.

"No, leave the boy be, it's a fair question," Theo said, turning to look Jack square in the face. "Up here in the mountains we don't get a lot of visitors, but from time to time people find their way here," he told Jack and the others.

"So, how come you have power? Is it a generator or what?" Jimmy asked, following Henry's initial question to Lucy.

Theo nodded. "No, son, no generator. We're fortunate enough to have a nuclear plant near the village. It's not really for us of course, but we get the power nonetheless."

"Nuclear, huh?" Henry said. "Now why the hell would a small place like this need a nuclear reactor?"

Theo moved around the desk and patted Henry like he was his father. "Now, now, there's plenty of time for all your questions to be answered, but not from me. Come, come, I'll take you to where you can sleep. We do things simple here. We don't have separate rooms, but one large one with bunk beds. Is that acceptable, sir?" He was looking at Henry as he asked this, assuming he was the leader of the companions.

"That'll be fine, Theo, thanks, we're not shy. And call me Henry, please."

"Of course, Henry, nice to meet you, all of you," Theo said as he led them away from the desk and down a small hallway.

Mary glanced over her shoulder while they were led away and she saw Lucy wasn't as cheerful now that she thought no one was watching her. Her brow was creased with concern and her eyes looked troubled.

"Hey, Mary, you comin'?" Jimmy asked.

"Yes, Jimmy, I'm coming," she said as she turned and followed the others.

Lucy watched the new people leave the room and shook her head sadly.

She knew what was in store for them, and though she wished she could have said something, she knew all that would have happened was she would end up getting herself killed with them.

No, there was nothing she could do for the new visitors to Crescent Falls.

It was a shame really, they seemed nice, especially the one called Mary.

Picking up the journal, she hugged it to herself like it was a small child needing protection.

Oh, well, she would just have to deal with her guilt, after all, she had gotten over it eventually when other strangers had come to the village to then be taken by the doctor and his malevolent staff.

As she walked away from the desk, she glanced one last time to the empty hallway the companions had used to exit the room.

At least she could pray they wouldn't suffer too much, there was that at least.

# Chapter 26

At the end of the long hallway, Theo stopped everyone and opened a door on right hand side.

"Go right in folks and I'll have some food sent to you in a bit," he said with a pleasant smile creasing his wrinkled visage.

"Thanks, thanks a lot," Henry said, stepping through the doorway, followed by the others. It was a large, windowless room, roughly the size of a standard two-car garage. There were twenty bunk beds lined up in two rows, as well as another door at the far end. All the beds were made up with gray blankets and white sheets. The floor and walls were a dull white, but clean.

Henry had the feeling he had stepped into a large hospital room.

When everyone was inside, Theo stopped at the doorway, his eyes taking in each of them.

"There's a bathroom at the other end, that door there will get you there. There's a full shower and sink. If you want to get cleaned up there are shampoos as well as fresh towels, too."

"Oh, sweet, I would kill for a shower," Jimmy said as he moved around the room.

"Yes, well, luckily you don't have to," Theo said with a wry grin. "Okay, so if you folks are all set I'll leave you to yourselves?"

"Yes, Theo, thanks, we're good for now," Henry said.

Theo nodded, and with a brief wave closed the door, a soft click issuing from the lock. Henry, Jimmy and Mary all turned to look at one another as they each had heard the click, and it was Mary who walked to the door and tried to open it.

"What the...it's locked," she said as she turned the knob with no results. Now that she was at the actual door and touching it, she realized it wasn't painted wood, but was made of a heavy metal. Tapping it, the door sounded solid.

"Relax, Mary," Henry told her. "I'm sure it's nothing. They probably don't want us wandering around the place unescorted. After all, we are strangers here. They just want to keep tabs on us."

Mary frowned while she turned around to lean her back against the door, her arms crossed in front of her. "I hope you're right, Henry. We've been locked up before and I don't like it one bit."

Jimmy nodded. "I'm with her, locked up is locked up, Henry; and what's with this room? There's no damn windows. That's a little odd, don't you think?"

Henry nodded. "Sure, but they let us keep our weapons, right? Listen, Jimmy, relax. If they wanted us dead, I think they would have tried something out on the road. They had the firepower. No, whatever's going on I doubt it's as evil as you think." He patted his Glock. 'Sides, they try something and they know we can defend ourselves."

Cindy was at the bathroom door and she opened it, whistling at what she found. Though sparse, there was a pile of white fluffy towels and a porcelain toilet. An actual working toilet. She hadn't seen one in quite a while. It takes crapping in the woods time after time to appreciate the small things civilization brings.

Crossing the tile floor she reached out and turned on the faucet. Immediately a sharp spray of water shot out, splashing onto the shower stall floor. She had turned it to hot and within seconds there was a pall of steam hanging in the air.

Her skin pricked as she imagined herself under the spray.

Reaching out, she turned it off and went back to the others who were talking amongst themselves.

"Still, Henry," Mary was saying, "we should have seen at least one younger woman when we were brought here. There were none. I don't care what Lucy said, something isn't right around here."

"Oh, please, Mary," Jimmy told her. "You just don't want to admit we found something good here. We got a nice place to sleep, our weapons are still with us, and running water and electricity. And soon we're gonna eat. To me this is pretty damn good, hell, maybe this is the place we've been looking for all these years."

"I hate to say it," Jack added, "but I'm with Jimmy, this place is cool."

Jimmy flashed Jack an annoyed face. "Shut up, brat, you don't get a vote."

Jack flipped him off, but Henry moved between them, not wanting to let them have at it.

"Stop it, you two. Look, maybe you're right, Jimmy, but we just got here so I wouldn't go making any plans to settle down just yet. For now, why don't we just get cleaned up and maybe grab some shuteye."

"Can I go first in the shower?" Cindy asked.

No one objected, and with a wide smile on her lips, Cindy ran into the bathroom and closed the door. While she undressed, she noticed small holes near the top of the ceiling, but she didn't give them much attention.

Then she was under the warm, soothing spray and loving every second of it.

Outside in the main room, the others unpacked their supplies and did a quick inventory while Sue went to Carol. The woman was sitting on the lower bunk of a bunk bed, staring at the floor. Jack approached too and he leaned down to look into Carol's face, mainly her eyes.

"I don't know, Sue, she looks pretty fried," he said softy.

Sue nodded, placing a hand on Carol's shoulder. "You might be right, Jack. She's been through a lot. Some people need time, but others just can't deal with it."

"So what happens if she doesn't snap out of it?"

Sue sighed heavily. "I guess that'll be up to Henry." She stood up and rubbed the boy's greasy hair. "You're gonna get a nice hot shower, young man."

"Aww, do I have to? I'm fine."

Sue wrinkled her nose. "No, dear, you're not, come on, as soon as Cindy is finished you're next."

"Aww man, this sucks, I take back what I said about this place."

Sue chuckled and pushed Jack over to the others.

Henry was going through what they had for ammunition. He had a dozen clips now for his Glock as well as extra ammo for Mary's and Jimmy's .38s. The others had about the same with Jimmy carrying a handful of clips for Cindy's M-16. All in all they weren't doing that badly.

If push came to shove, they had the ammunition to defend themselves as long as they had a good place to hole up.

The bathroom door opened and Cindy stepped out with a bil-
lowing abundance of steam. She was wrapped in a towel as well as
one wrapped around her head.

"Oh my God, that feels good," she gasped. "I didn't want to get
out, but I know you guys want to get in there, too."

Sue nodded, then pushed Jack in front of her. "He's next, he
needs it the worst," she said. Jack mumbled but he did as she was
told. Sue then turned and pointed to Raven. "You're next dear, we
both know those dark locks could use a good washing."

"Okay, fine with me," Raven said. She was sitting up on a bed
with her back against the wall, her legs crossed at the ankles, her
arms behind her head. Wherever she was, she took it in stride; it
was her nature.

For the next hour, each of the companions washed and relaxed.
Even Carol, with Sue's help, went into the bathroom and took a
shower.

It was almost two hours later, all of the group now resting on
the beds, when Jimmy brought up the subject of food, wondering
where it was.

"It'll be here," Henry told him as he looked up from cleaning his
Glock. "Let's just give it a little longer. Tell you what, if no one
comes in the next hour we'll make some noise, all right?"

"Fine," Jimmy said as he reached for a power bar from his
backpack. He only had a few more left and then it was back to
whatever they could find on the road.

For the next ten minutes they all talked about this and that and
then Mary stopped talking in mid-sentence, her head moving back
and forth like she was trying to hear something faint.

"What's wrong?" Cindy asked.

"Don't you guys hear that? It's like hissing, but softer," Mary
said.

Henry sat up in the bed he was on, while he slapped in the clip
for his Glock, checking the slide to make sure it was working
properly. Then he stood up.

"Hey, wait a second, yeah, I hear it, too," Henry said while looking around the room.

Then Jimmy scrunched up his nose when he got a whiff of
something foul. "Hey, what the hell is that smell?"

Then Jack jumped off his bed. "Hey, under the bed, look, there's gas coming out of holes in the wall!"

All the companions moved to the middle of the room while Henry and Jimmy went to one of the beds and shoved it away from the wall. The bunk bed's legs screeched on the tile, leaving deep grooves.

"What the hell?" Jimmy snapped when he saw the gas. It was slightly opaque, but only just, and he covered his nose with his sleeve, feeling lightheaded now that he was inhaling it more.

"Goddammit, they're gassing us!" Henry yelled as he turned to look at the others. Everyone, get some sheets and try to stop up the holes; hurry, dammit!"

They got moving, ripping sheets from the beds, pillows and blankets flying everywhere as they tried to plug up the holes, but it was Sue who pointed up near the ceiling.

"Henry, up there, in the corners, there's more holes!"

Henry followed her finger, and sure enough, there were small, one inch holes lining the ceiling, just at the edges. Even if they managed to plug all the holes near the floor they couldn't get to the ones near the ceiling in time.

"Dammit, what the hell are they playing at?" Henry yelled, coughing as the gas filled his lungs. "We're friendly?" He turned around, now wondering if there was a hidden camera somewhere watching them. "You hear me? We're friendly; you don't have to do this!"

If someone heard him, no one answered.

Cindy dashed for the bathroom, hoping the small room might be safe, but as she pushed open the door, she saw the same gas hissing out of the small holes she had seen earlier before taking a shower. She was going to spin around and leave the room, but she became lightheaded, and before she could stop herself, she dropped to the floor in the wet shower stall, unconscious.

Out in the main room, Henry and Jimmy were still trying to stop the gas.

"Cover your mouths with rags, maybe it'll help," Henry ordered them, but though they tried to cut sheets into manageable rags, their actions were already slowing as the gas took effect.

One at a time, each of them dropped where they were. Sue fell onto a bed face first, Raven following soon after. Carol had never left her bed and she simply closed her eyes and drifted off into oblivion.

Jack was younger and tried to fight the effects, but even he couldn't stop the gas and he dropped to the floor, his left arm hanging out like he was stretching, his legs crossed at the ankles. A small amount of drool slid out of the corner of his half-open mouth.

Mary was next, and as she felt dizziness fill her mind, she slumped to the floor, her head landing on a stray pillow, saving her yet another bump on the head.

Henry and Jimmy, coughing and wheezing, fought to stay awake, but as Jimmy opened his mouth to say something to Henry, he pitched forward onto a bed, his head hitting the metal of the top bunk. As he fell to the bed, a small trickle of blood now seeped from his tiny scalp wound over his forehead. Henry was last to succumb to the gas and he covered his mouth with a sheet and tried to stay awake.

He moved to the farthest part of the room and hunkered down, hoping the gas had the same consistency as smoke and the air near the floor might be clearer.

Then the door to the room opened and six men wearing gas masks, black boots, and the uniforms of the guards, dark glasses and all, stomped inside.

Seeing them, Henry reached down and raised his Glock from a hand that didn't want to work. He managed to actually aim the Glock at the first man and he got off a shot, but then his arm dropped to the floor and the gun slid away.

As for the guard he had aimed at, the round found its target. When the man entered the room, the 9mm slug caught him in the throat, ripping out his larynx and shredding his jugular. The man gasped for air as blood geysered out and across the room, staining the pristine white walls scarlet.

The man dropped to the floor as his life's blood seeped out and was dead before his body had settled.

A man in black knelt down beside the downed guard, checking for a pulse, but shook his head. He glanced over to Henry, and with a snarl stood up, drawing his carbine and aiming it at Henry's glazed eyes. Henry stared down the barrel of the muzzle but he was too drugged to do anything but breathe.

"You fuck, you killed Andy," he hissed as he prepared to blow Henry's head off.

Another guard stepped up and knocked the carbine to the side just as the guard squeezed the trigger. A loud report filled the room and the wall exploded to the left of Henry's head. A few bits of plaster nicked his face, causing small scratches to seep red, but Henry could do nothing. Then, though his will was great, he closed his eyes and his head slumped forward.

"No, you idiot, the Doc wants them alive, all of them," the leader of the security men snapped. "It's Andy's fault for just charging in, the Doc said to wait until the gas took full effect."

The guard shook his head, whatever emotions were on his face hidden under the gas mask. He stood up, but pointed down at the unconscious Henry. He kicked him in the side and said, "You and me, buddy, I'll get my payback." Then he moved out of the way.

The leader of the security team nodded. It was good enough for him, and besides, he'd liked Andy, too, even if the man was an idiot.

"Okay, men, let's get started. The gas is only good for about two hours. The Doc wants them in the complex and ready to go before they wake up."

The men began gathering the companions' weapons and packs, tossing them onto a small cart one of the men rolled in. Then as the guard called for more help, wheelchairs were brought in.

While the eight companions lay helpless and unconscious, the security team got to work transferring the unconscious group to the chairs so they could be transported.

The leader of the team grinned under his mask.

These people were in for a world of hurt, and as always, he was just glad he wasn't one of them.

# Chapter 27

Dreams of the past filled Henry Watson's mind.

But though he'd lived through thousands of experiences before the dead began to walk, for some reason his mind only focused on the past two years, as if his life before the world crumbled was irrelevant and wasn't worth the neurons to process those memories.

Past enemies flooded past his mind's eye, gibbering countenances that laughed and screamed at him.

He saw Sam from Pittsfield, the tall dark man who had began as an enemy, but had ended as an ally.

Barry, the evil boss of the shopping mall flashed into his head, and how the man had killed Gwen, a woman he'd only begun to care about. The Groton Naval base, where Mary and Cindy had been captured by the sadistic crime boss, Raddack, and had come very close to being killed; and then there was the Reverend Carlson, a mad reverend who tried to use the undead to wipe out a rival town. But Henry had served him up to God on a platter and the man was burning in Hell even now.

All these images flashed through his mind as he struggled to pull himself from his drug induced sleep. Slowly, he came to, and when his eyes finally opened, he immediately had to close them, the bright, white light piercing into his brain like a laser.

Giving it a second, he then tried again, only this time he took it slowly, cracking his eyelids and then opening them a fraction at a time.

Spots danced in his vision, but eventually they cleared and he saw he was in a room, stark white with nothing but a bed bolted to the wall and a hole in the floor for his waste. Glancing down, he saw he was wearing nothing but a pair of white boxer shorts.

Sitting up, he stared at the bland room, for the moment still too groggy to wonder where he was. Glancing down to his chest, he saw his side had received medical care. Touching the wound gingerly, he saw what appeared to be surgical glue on it. His small cut on his hand was also cleaned and dressed. As he bent over and forward, his side ached, as if he'd been kicked by a mule. Figuring it must have happened when he'd passed out, he ignored it.

Looking to the front of the room, he saw it was wide open, no bars, or doors, so he stood up, waited a second for his equilibrium to align, and he crossed the room.

And promptly walked into a glass wall.

"What the hell?" He mumbled to himself as he reached out to touch the glass. There was now a smudge where his nose had bounced off the large pane, otherwise it was crystal clear.

Tapping the glass, it sounded thick and he wondered if it was bullet proof or just heavy like the safety glass used on shopping mall doors. As his eyes scanned the outer hallway, he saw he was in what could only be called a cage, futuristic though it was.

Across the hallway was another cage and when he put his face to the glass and looked both ways, he saw there were what appeared to be at least a dozen cages.

Then he caught movement to his left, in the cage there, and a second later he was able to see Jimmy, also clad only in a pair of white boxers. Jimmy looked like he'd just woken from an all night bender and he scratched his hair while looking around in curiosity.

"Jimmy, hey, Jimmy, over here!" Henry called out.

Jimmy didn't look at first, but when Henry yelled louder, Jimmy turned and saw him.

"Henry?" Jimmy said, but though Henry saw his mouth moving, he couldn't hear the younger man.

"I can't hear you through the glass, you have to speak up!" Henry yelled.

Jimmy touched the glass and tapped it, then slapped it hard. Henry heard the dull vibration, but the glass stayed intact.

"Can you hear me now?" Jimmy called. It was muffled but intelligible.

"Yeah, just barely. You okay?"

Jimmy nodded. "Yeah, you see the girls? Or Jack?"

Henry shook his head. "No, I just came to, but I don't see them, unless they're in one of the other cages. Can you see into some of the other ones from where you are?"

Jimmy twisted and turned his head from side to side so he could see into a few more cages, his face pressed hard to the glass.

"I see someone's feet. I think it's Jack. If it's him, he's in the cage across from me, but it looks like he's still out it. No sign of the girls, though." His face crossed with concern. "You think they're all right?"

Henry shrugged. "We'll just have to hope so."

Jimmy looked down at himself and then Henry. "Hey, what's with the underwear? Where the hell are our clothes?"

"That's a good question, hopefully we'll get to find out," Henry said as he leaned his head against the glass. Inside, he was fuming with anger. They had been captured and imprisoned for some reason, and worst of all, they'd been separated.

"Hey, I think Jack's waking up," Jimmy said as he watched the boy stir on his bed. Henry waited, while Jimmy, being closest to the boy, filled him on what they knew so far. Jack went through the typical questions and in a few minutes was up to speed.

Well, as up to speed as the rest of them.

They yelled through the glass to each other for the next half hour until finally Henry had enough. There wasn't really much else to talk about so he told Jack and Jimmy to just relax and save their energy and be alert for a possible chance to escape.

Two hours later a door at the end of the hallway opened and five security guards stomped in. All wore dark sunglasses, caps, and their ebony uniforms were a stark contrast to the whiteness of the hallway and cages.

Four of the guards took up position outside Jimmy and Jack's cage and the leader of the team stopped in front of Henry's. All were armed with carbines.

Even with the dark glasses and cap, Henry recognized the man as the first security guard he'd met on the road into the village; the one who had told him to watch himself.

"You three are to come with me, the Doctor wants to meet you," the man said.

"What if we don't want to come with you?" Henry asked, crossing his arms over his chest. It was tough being defiant when he wore nothing but underwear, but his powerful frame helped.

"I have orders to bring you with me. If you don't comply, my orders are to shoot you dead and dispose of the bodies. Your choice."

Henry stared at the dark sunglasses, wishing he could see the man's eyes, at least try and gauge how much he said was true. But as he stared at the set jaw and stiff posture, he decided it wasn't worth the risk that the man was bluffing.

With a wide smile, Henry nodded agreeably.

"So, what are we waiting for?" Henry asked. "And by the way, can I get some clothes for me and my friends? It's freezing in here."

"We'll get you something to wear on the way, now step back from the barrier." He pointed a finger at Henry threateningly. "And one wrong move by you or your friends and you're dead, you understand me?"

Henry smiled from ear to ear, his teeth flashing in the fluorescent lights. "Crystal."

The guard pressed a button on the wall and the glass door slid up into the ceiling. Henry watched it go up, fascinated. There was a thin slit where the glass was now recessed.

The man gestured the muzzle of his carbine for Henry to exit the cell, then Jimmy and Jack were released.

"Move out, and remember, no funny stuff," the guard warned.

"Wouldn't think of it," Henry replied as he began walking with Jimmy and Jack.

At the end of the hallway, a door slid up, reminding Jimmy of *Star Trek*. He commented to Henry on it who only shrugged. Jimmy would have said more, but he received a nudge in his back with the muzzle of a carbine so he decided his commentary could wait

Though they were in their underwear, the air was relatively comfortable and the reason was the twelve inch vents set near the ceiling and floor. As they passed by them, warm air blasted out, filling the area with heat.

Studying the vents, Henry wondered if they could be used to escape in. He had done the same thing back at Pineridge Labs, all the companions hiding in the ceiling while the place had been ransacked. But as he studied the size of the gratings, he didn't think it was a possibility here, they were all too big to fit.

Then an idea fluttered into his head. Maybe one of them *could* fit.

They were escorted down a hallway, and then another seven minutes were spent traversing winding corridors, all painted a stark white. It was like a maze, filled with twists and turns.

It was as they were passing by yet another doorway, that it opened and Henry got a glimpse over the exiting man's shoulder. He saw a few things at a glance, the first being the man exiting the room wore a lab coat and an ID badge of a lab technician or doctor. His small wire-rimmed glasses were sliding off his nose and he looked startled when he looked up to see three males in underwear and a compliment of guards.

But what was most interesting to Henry was what he could see over the technician's shoulder.

He saw a large room filled with lab equipment and in the center he counted five glass cages on the left side of the room. These cages were occupied, but what Henry saw made him blink in disbelief. What he saw in those cages was unimaginable and he found it hard to believe what he was witnessing with his own eyes.

The door closed and the lab tech scurried away, while Henry got a poke in the back for his trouble.

"Nothing to see here, keep moving," one of the guards said.

While they walked, Jimmy leaned closer to Henry and whispered. "I saw you looking into that room, anything interesting in there?"

Henry nodded, his jaw set tight as he processed what he'd just seen. "You could say that, Jimmy. I don't know what the hell is going on around here, but these people are into some sick shit."

For talking, he received yet another poke in the ribs, this one causing him to grunt. Stopping, he turned slowly and glared at the guard who had struck him.

"You do that one more time, pal, and I'm gonna shove that gun up your ass, you hear me?" Though in his underwear, his tone was menacing and the guard actually paused for a second, unsure of what to do. He wasn't used to being threatened by the prisoners. Normally they just cowered and begged not to be hurt.

The security leader moved between Henry and the guard. "That's enough of that, Watson, don't try my patience," he said, his tone clear. "Now keep walking."

Henry stared at the dark glasses of both men for another three seconds, then he turned around and began moving again. He could be wrong, but he was pretty sure he got his point across. He had a feeling the guard would give an extra moment of thought before poking him again unless he really had to.

"That was cool," Jack said as he followed next to Jimmy. Henry reached out and rubbed the boy's hair.

"Thanks, Jack, just stay sharp. And if you see a chance to escape, take it, okay?" He whispered the last part out of the side of his mouth, only Jack hearing and then just barely. Jack actually blinked, wondering if he'd heard Henry correctly.

Henry looked down on the boy and nodded, wanting him to be ready if the chance came.

They walked another five minutes and were told to stop in front of yet another door.

"Go inside and get dressed, and hurry up," the guard said. "There's only one way in or out so don't try anything funny."

Henry grinned as wide as he could, as if the guard was an old friend he hadn't seen in years. "Wouldn't think of it," he said as the door opened and they entered, Jimmy waving with his fingers like he was saying *toodle loo*.

The door closed behind Jimmy and he turned to see Henry and Jack already getting dressed. The room was sparse as all the rooms seemed to be with only a shelf in a corner with white jumpsuits on them, all folded like someone from the Gap had dropped by. On the floor, lined up neatly, were different size canvas sneakers, all white, of course

Henry waved Jimmy over while he shrugged into his jumpsuit, wincing slightly as he stretched the wound on his ribs.

"Listen up, you two; I can't believe they've actually left us alone for a few seconds. Now we can talk."

Jack was slipping into his jumpsuit, which was a little too big on him. Evidently the people of this place didn't get a lot of child visitors.

"Maybe they're watching us with a hidden camera or some-thing," Jimmy suggested while he got dressed.

"Maybe, but I doubt it," Henry said while putting on a pair of sneakers. Then, after tying the laces, his eyes scanned the room. There were two vents in this room, one near the ceiling and one near the floor.

"Hey, Jack, come here," Henry said as went to the vent near the floor.

"Yeah?"

"Could you fit in there?"

Jack kneeled down and looked inside the vent. His hair was ruffled when the warm air shot out.

"Sure, I could fit in there, might be a little tight, though."

"Good, then do it. I said you needed to escape when the chance came and this is probably the best shot. See what damage you can do to this place."

Henry leaned down and kicked the vent as hard as he could, the racket filling the room. Immediately, the door leading out to the hallway opened and the guards charged in.

"Hey, get away from there!" The first man yelled.

"Go, Jack, go!" Henry yelled as Jack dropped to his knees and scuttled into the vent like a rat.

Carbines were leveled at Henry and Jimmy who raised their hands in surrender, but as a guard ran forward to stop Jack, Henry casually kicked his right foot out and caught the man in the side of the leg, knocking him off balance. The guard toppled head first and his forehead whacked the wall, Henry and Jimmy wincing slightly.

"Oooh, that's gotta hurt," Jimmy said as he raised his hands higher, not wanting to get shot.

Jack was gone, his knees striking the metal ductwork echoing as he disappeared around a bend.

The lead guard, cursing a blue streak, shot into the hole, Henry and Jimmy looking at one another, hoping Jack had managed to get away. The lead guard leaned down and peered into the vent, seeing nothing but a few stray bits of dust disturbed from Jack's passing.

With a snarl on his face, the man whirled and shoved the muz-zle of the carbine under Henry's chin. After being fired, the muzzle was hot and Henry kept his face clear, not wanting to give the man the satisfaction of seeing him in pain.

"Get him back here now, or so help me..."

"So help you what?" Henry asked like he was chatting with a friend. "He's gone, face it, you fucked up."

The man's finger hovered on the trigger and Henry's eyes glanced down to see the trigger finger twitching.

"Think before you do what I think you're gonna do, pal. I have a feeling whoever wants us here wouldn't be too happy with you for shooting my head off."

"He's got a point there, Stark. The Doc wouldn't be too happy if you killed this guy."

Ah, so Henry finally had a name for the leader of the security team.

"Yeah, Stark, think about it long and hard," Henry smiled. But his heart was beating fast and he was wondering if he was going to be boarding the last train to Hell in a second.

Stark groaned with anger, but he took the carbine away from Henry's chin. Henry let out a soft sigh of relief, but before it fully left his mouth, the butt of the carbine was coming at his chin. There was a loud *crack* and Henry was thrown backwards to hit the floor hard. Jimmy was about to jump at the guards, wanting to help Henry, but four carbines were leveled at him with their safety's off, the men ready to blow him away.

Stark grinned slightly, but his eyes remained cold.

"I wouldn't if I were you," Stark snarled. "The Doc doesn't want Watson killed, but I don't have the same orders for you or the kid."

Jimmy stopped his aggression, then turned to Henry who was on the floor, his right hand rubbing his chin.

"Can I see to him?" Jimmy asked politely, knowing Stark held all the cards.

"Yeah, go 'head," Stark said. Then he turned and faced his men, singling one out.

"Get a few more guys and find that kid, now," he ordered, the guard nodding and leaving the room.

By now Henry was sitting up, rubbing his chin. There was a large bruise there and his teeth felt like someone had been banging on them with a hammer, but he knew he had gotten off lucky.

Stark had pulled his blow at the last second or Henry would be spitting teeth right now instead of just a cut lower gum.

"Come on, get the fuck up. You still have an appointment to keep."

Henry spit a wad of blood and phlegm onto the floor, the scarlet froth bright against the white tiles, then he wiped his mouth with his sleeve, leaving a long streak of red, as he was helped up by Jimmy.

Henry glared at Stark, but did nothing, the guard leader staring Henry down. Henry had already made up his mind that when he had a chance to escape, he would make sure this man was taken down on his way out if he had the opportunity. Henry and Jimmy were led out of the room with a wave of carbines.

As they left, Jimmy leaned forward. "You think Jack's okay?'

"All we can do is hope," Henry replied.

Then he shut up, not wanting to get another poke in the ribs. His ribs already felt like someone had been playing the drums on them and he knew when to quit.

With Jimmy and Henry in the lead, the guards behind with carbines leveled at their backs, they moved deeper into the complex.

# Chapter 28

Mary came to first.

With blurry eyes she realized she was strapped to a hospital bed. Memories of what had happened to her when she had been captured by cannibals in Kentucky flooded into her mind and she resolved she would die before she let some bastard try what had happened to her before.

Looking around herself, she spotted Cindy and Raven on other side of her with Sue across the room. They were unconscious at the moment, but Cindy showed signs of stirring.

Then she looked past her strapped feet to see Carol also strapped down across the room to the right, but where Mary and the others were in beds, with sheets and pillows, Carol was on a steel table, her feet in stirrups like she was at the gynecologist.

She wore a white hospital gown and her eyes were wide with fear as she gazed around the room like a frightened child. When she saw Mary was awake, her eyes locked with hers.

"Help me, please," Carol whispered.

Pulling on her bonds, Mary knew she was as helpless as the woman and she frowned, shaking her head.

"I'd love to, Carol, but as you can see I'm in the same spot you are. Just hang in there." She turned to Cindy and called out. "Cindy! Hey, Cindy, wake up, we got a serious problem here!" Cindy stirred a little more so Mary sucked in a deep breath and yelled. "Hey, Cindy, wake up!"

A low groan issued from Cindy's lips, and her eyelids did flutter slightly. It took another three minutes, but eventually Cindy was finally awake, her eyes darting in her head like a deer caught in a semi's headlamps on the highway.

"What the hell?" She said as she strained to free her arms. "Where are we? Last thing I remember..."

"Yeah, I know, we got gassed," Mary said.

Cindy saw Raven on the opposite side of Mary and she asked about her.

"She's out like we were, let her sleep, its not like there's anything she can do right now," Mary said.

"Where the hell are we?" Cindy asked.

Mary shook her head, her brown hair falling over her shoulders. "Don't know, but it can't be good if the guys aren't around and were trussed up like pigs for the slaughter."

Cindy made a face. "Thanks for the optimism, Mar'."

"It is what it is," Mary replied and shifted her head to get more comfortable.

Then both women turned at the sound of a door opening at the far end. Like a whisper it slid into the ceiling and a man in a white lab coat entered. As Mary watched him, she saw a heavy-set man with thinning hair and black eyes that were dead, devoid of emotion.

"Ah, it looks like out guests are awake," he said. He carried a clip board and wore an ID badge on his lab coat. As he got closer to the women, Mary was able to read the badge.

"Dr. Martin Stanley," she said out loud. "Doctor of what?"

"Oh, many things, my dear. I never wanted to get stuck in one field so I hold many doctorates, none of which you need to know about at the present time." He turned away from her then and walked to Carol who was crying.

"Oh, no, sweetheart, there's no need to cry. I promise you that all your pain will be gone in a few short minutes."

Carol whimpered some more and both Cindy and Mary struggled to get free.

"What are doing to us, you bastard, let us go!" Cindy yelled, her blonde hair falling across her face.

Dr. Stanley turned and smiled at her while wagging his index finger as if he was speaking to a petulant. "All in good time, my dear, now why don't you be quiet or I'll have to scdate you, hmmm?"

Cindy growled in her throat, but she held her tongue. She had been in similar spots with the companions and she knew when was a good time to speak and when to be silent. At the moment, this Dr. Stanley held all the cards, antagonizing him wouldn't get her anything. Plus, if she was sedated she wouldn't be in true form if there was a chance to escape. So better to bite her tongue for now.

Glancing to her side, she saw that Mary appeared to be thinking the same thing, her eyes creased in anger. Looking past the brown tresses of Mary, she saw Raven was awake. The teenager was quiet as usual, not saying anything, only listening while she took in what was happening around her.

Cindy nodded as Raven glanced at her. The young girl was tough and she would also be looking for an opportunity to escape if one presented itself. Sue was still out of it but her chest rose and fell slowly, telling her the woman was alive and well. Perhaps she had inhaled a higher dose of the gas?

Another man entered the room with a hiss of door hydraulics and from his garb it was clear he was some sort of lab attendant or helper. He glanced at Mary and Cindy, but then went to the doctor, who began giving instructions. The attendant began moving about the room setting things up.

Meanwhile, Dr. Stanley was moving about the room, getting a table with surgical supplies ready. Then he went to the far corner of the room and began wheeling over what looked a lot like a salon hairdryer, though this one was connected to a small computer terminal with wires draped across the floor.

The helmet itself was covered with wires and meters, and in the center, on the inside, exactly where the head would be when the helmet was lowered, were two six-inch long syringe-like prongs with wicked points that glistened in the white fluorescent lights of the room. The machine was wheeled up to Carol until it was hovering over her head and then he began lowering it, his smile never faltering.

The helmet was attached to a stainless steel arm and it was hinged so that when the helmet was lowered, it was able to bend. By doing this he was able to adjust the height of the helmet with ease, and after raising Carol's head an inch off the table, he was able to slide the helmet over her head, the top just touching her forehead, and now half her face was hidden from view. The twin steel surgical probes hovered a bare inch over her skull and the entire monstrosity resembled a diving helmet. The doctor pressed a button on the computer terminal and two foam pads, connected to the inside of the helmet, began to ease out until they were pressed against Carol's temples. She struggled in her fear, but her head was now completely immobilized.

Both Cindy and Mary stared in horror and curiosity while Carol was placed in the helmet. Despite themselves, they couldn't help but wonder what was going to happen next. Those hypodermic needles, what were they for?

The attendant moved to the computer terminal, and began turning dials and flicking switches. A second later there was a low hum filling the room. After a minute the attendant turned to Dr. Stanley.

"It's ready when you are, sir."

"Good, excellent," he said more to himself than to the attendant. He set down the clipboard he had been scribbling on and looked down at the bare spot of scalp on Carol's head. Mumbling to himself, he lowered the prongs until they were touching the smooth flesh at the very top of her skull.

"Perfect," he said like a mad scientist, his eyes now filled with an electricity that wasn't there when he first entered the room. He crossed the room and stopped at a large control panel on the wall. Turning on the monitors, the screens flickered to life. Readouts scrolled across the screens and a computer-drawn CATSCAN of Carol's brain appeared. It was being taken by a small camera hidden in the top of the helmet every five seconds.

Reaching across the panel, he flicked a button labeled **LASER** and immediately a row of red and yellow crystal diodes flicked on along a shiny metal cabinet situated behind Carol's head.

Dr. Stanley nodded to himself. "Good, good, everything is working properly," he mumbled, not even aware he was speaking.

He crossed the room until he was hovering over Carol's supine body. He touched her arm almost sympathetically and said: "Now my dear, this is going to hurt a lot, but when it's all over I promise you, you won't feel pain ever again. I suggest you just try to relax and don't fight the procedure, it will only make it more painful."

"You bastard, let her go, so help me when I get free I'll kill you!" Mary screamed, losing her temper. Some may have called Mary's compassion for others a flaw, but she considered it one of her greatest strengths, despite the fact it had gotten her and the companions in trouble more than once.

Dr. Stanley spun on the balls of his feet, his face twisted into a snarl. "I warned your friend, dear lady, and now I'm warning you. Shut up or I will have you sedated, though I would prefer not to. It sometimes interferes with the procedure."

Mary stared into those dead eyes and knew the doctor was telling the truth. Gritting her teeth in frustration, she remained silent. Cindy said a few words of encouragement, but Mary barely heard them.

While the doctor warned Mary to be silent, Raven was busy worrying at her left hand strap, the one hidden from view by the way her bed was positioned. Her razor-sharp nails were slowly working at the strap around her wrist, though the angle was bad. Still, she continued, trying to part one single strand of fiber at a time.

Dr. Stanley turned back to Carol, reached out with his right hand, and threw a switch on the top of the helmet. Immediately, two brilliant colored lights shot out of the tips of the prongs. They were a deep yellow, like a burning sun, and incandescent as they flickered in the air as they crossed the small distance to Carol's head.

The doctor slowly began to turn a lever that began lowering the prongs closer to Carol's skull. The heat of the fine, thin laser beams immediately cut through flesh and bone at the top of Carol's scalp.

Carol began screaming then, a high pitched shrieking that filled Mary, Cindy and Raven to their very souls with dread. The laser beams continued downward at a slow, eight millimeters per second. The thousands of degrees, yellow beam of the laser burned and sizzled Carol's brain tissue as it sliced deep into her grey matter.

Bits of her brain began to bubble inside her head and the smoke of said destruction seeped out of the hole, smelling putrid and rotten.

Dr Stanley turned to the attendant who was monitoring the screens and he frowned deeply, waving the smoke away from his nose.

"That seems to be the only problem; unfortunately, the brain smells quite horrible when it burns."

"Yes, sir," the attendant said. He knew the doctor wasn't really talking to him, only airing his words out loud. He had worked with Dr. Stanley in the past and knew not to speak unless asked an exact question.

"Perhaps we can get a small ventilation fan connected overhead to suck out the smoke and odor. Yes, that would work quite well if we can't correct the problem," Dr. Stanley said absent-mindedly.

The doctor glanced over at the monitor showing Carol's CATSCAN. Every layer of her brain was now displayed as the laser beam cut deeper into the central tissue of her mind.

"We're about to reach the cerebral section, sir," the attendant said as he adjusted the monitors.

"Ah, excellent," Dr. Stanley said as he turned to Mary and Cindy who were watching with mouths agape. He was proud of his invention and was glad to have an audience for a change. "Now is when it gets really interesting. You see, I'm going to burn away her memories and put her into an entirely different consciousness. When I'm through, she will do whatever I tell her. Similar to hypnosis but far, far better. When I'm finished, this woman will be a blank slate, only following orders blindly."

"But why? Why the hell are you doing this to her?" Mary asked.

"Because we need breeders, my dear, and we can't have breeders with a mind of their own. Get's too messy. When I'm done here this woman will be an automaton made for only one reason, to have babies."

"But that's insane, why would you do that?" Cindy gasped.

"Because the world is dead, dear lady, and its up to us, perhaps the last research center still functioning in America, to make sure we repopulate the country. To do that we need babies, lots of them. Only then, when they are old enough to fight, can we ever have a chance to take this country back from the dead creatures that now walk the land. As you may know, they outnumber us a thousand to one, perhaps a million to one. No, dear, we need numbers and fast."

The doctor had to speak up, having to talk over Carol's screaming. The woman's hands were squeezing and releasing while her back arced, her legs spasming like she was an epileptic suffering the worst seizure of her life.

Because she was strapped to the table there was nowhere to go and she nearly cracked her bones inside her muscle and flesh, her limbs twisting in utter agony. Razor sharp teeth of pain dug deep into her brain, wiping out her personality and tearing the memories of her family, her husband, her children away like they were ghosts. In many ways this was a blessing, the woman not wanting to think about how she had witnessed her family killed and eaten by the cannies, but there were good memories, too. The ones she held on to, the birthdays and anniversaries, or playing in the park, all this was wiped away like a scrubbed hard drive.

Carol was still screaming, but now she didn't even realize she was, her body eventually crashing as she fell into a state of unconsciousness.

"Very good," Dr. Stanley muttered to himself as he reached up and turned the lever and pressed the **OFF** button to the laser, the beam flicking off and the prongs withdrawing.

Smelling salt was waved under Carol's nose and she came to, blinking as the helmet was withdrawn from her head. There were now two charcoal circles on her skull from where the laser had seared into her brain. Carol opened her eyes and stared about the room blankly.

"There, now, my dear, that wasn't so bad, was it?"

Carol only blinked back, now with a mind like a baby's.

The attendant powered down the machine and turned off the monitors, then walked over to Dr. Stanley.

"Take her to recovery and as soon as she's ready I want to harvest her eggs," the doctor ordered the man.

"Yes, sir," the attendant said. He lifted the brakes on the steel gurney's wheels and began pushing Carol to the door.

Mary, Cindy and Raven all stared at Carol as she was wheeled past. They saw the woman's eyes, and though before they were haunted with the loss of her family, now there was nothing there. Her eyes were as dead as the walking corpses wandering the deadlands

The door slid up and then she was gone.

Dr. Stanley was finishing up with the laser machine, making sure it was in perfect working order. While he worked, he mumbled to himself. "Such a good machine, yes you are, so good," he said as he wheeled the helmet back against the wall, practically stroking it lovingly.

When he was satisfied it was safe, he turned and strode to the foot of Mary's bed, looking into the eyes of each of the three women.

"I have to examine the data to see if I need to recalibrate. Until then you three may relax and wait for your turn. Don't worry, it's really not as bad as it looks, in fact, think of it this way. Once you have been indoctrinated, all your worries and concerns will simply fade away. And it's not like you're sacrificing yourself in vain. What you will be doing will save this country in the years to come."

"Fuck you, asshole," Cindy said, Mary nodding in agreement.

"Tsk, tsk, such foul language from such a beautiful woman, well, no matter, that too will be wiped clean." He turned and walked away, as if the three prisoners were nothing to worry about. "Someone will be in to check your vitals shortly to get you ready. Wouldn't want you to have a heart attack on my table, now that would be a shame," he chuckled.

The door lifted and he exited, the door swishing closed once again.

Mary and Cindy exchanged glances, then both looked to Raven.

The ebony haired girl shook her head. "We're fucked," she said blandly.

"Raven," Mary said as she pulled on her bonds to no effect, "you took the words right out of my mouth."

# Chapter 29

"Hold up here," Stark said coarsely, Henry and Jimmy doing as they were told.

They had walked for another six minutes what to Henry seemed like a maze that went around in circles. There were even a few times when he had the strange idea he had been in the same corridor twice.

But it was hard to tell as the corridors were all bright white with no identifying features. He had to wonder how the hell the guards found their way around at all.

Yet another door stood in front of them. Stark moved to the front of the line, glared at Henry and Jimmy, and then pressed a small recessed button to the right of the doorframe. Henry realized he wouldn't have known the button was there if he hadn't seen the man press it with his own eyes, it was that well hidden.

"Yes?" A stale voice from a hidden speaker said somewhere near the door.

"I have the male prisoners here, Doc," Stark said, his voice sounding slightly uncomfortable. It wasn't hard for Henry to see whoever he was talking to obviously held some sort of authority over him.

"Send them in," the voice replied, cold and stony.

The door hissed up and Stark gestured for Jimmy and Henry to get moving again.

Jimmy grinned at Stark with a wide, friendly smile, but Stark wasn't amused.

Both warriors were ushered inside, and with Stark and only two other guards with them, the door swung closed with a soft hiss of hidden hydraulics while the other guards remained in the corridor.

Henry looked to Stark and the other two guards and wondered if it was worth trying to take them out. Two to one odds could have been worse, but then he realized even if he and Jimmy succeeded, they still had to get out of the room, the other guards now taking up positions in the hallway.

Jimmy looked to Henry, waiting for a signal, but Henry shook his head no. It wasn't the right time.

Henry studied the room and saw it was mostly the same as the other rooms he'd seen. White with no pictures or windows. But there were two subtle differences in this one. One was there was a white curtain hanging on the far wall and there was a larger circular-sized table, made of wood, but bleached bone white, in the center of the room.

Henry and Jimmy waited for what, they didn't know, and then, a minute or so later, they heard the clip, clip of clogs or hard soled shoes. But this wasn't a steady gait, it was a hop, slap, that continued in a steady rhythm.

Both warriors looked up to see a woman entering from a side door, her limp more pronounced now that she was in sight. Henry saw her left leg was nothing but a withered limb, thin as her arm, and the clop, slap was her walking.

The woman herself was an odd assortment of looks, the personality of this woman obviously in odds with herself.

For starters, she was barely five feet tall, with skin that was so pale it was a wonder if she had ever seen daylight. Her hair was done up in a messy bun, the gray and brown mousy locks slipping out of the pins holding it, and there were at least three pens and pencils in the bun, sticking out at odd angles.

It lent her an air of forgetfulness, as if she kept putting her writing utensils in her hair and would forget where they were; only to do it again five minutes later with another one.

She wore a lab coat, white, but it was buttoned all the way up to the collar, looking like it would pinch off her airway if she moved her neck too fast. She had an enormous bosom, which was vastly out of proportion to the rest of her small frame, and her eyes were surrounded by large, coke bottle glasses which made her tiny orbs seem like insignificant specs of blue and white.

And to add to this incredibly weird picture, she wore the brightest, darkest red lipstick any woman could ever find, along with thick pancake makeup that still didn't hide her pallid complexion.

"Welcome to Project Delta. Please sit down, gentlemen," she said as she dropped down gracelessly in the chair at what had to be considered the head of the table. Though she had the look of a woman in her fifties, her voice had the soft lisp of a woman twice her age.

Jimmy glanced to Henry and he nodded, the two of them grabbing chairs at the table. Henry leaned forward in his chair, staring at this small woman. Still, if she was the leader of this place then her appearance had to be deceptive.

"My name is Doctor Bernida Tandy and I am the leader of this complex. You are our first visitors in quite a while, how did you manage to find us? Why did you come to us, journeywise?"

"We picked up a radio transmission saying to come here, that it might be safe from the deaders here in Crescent Falls. We're friends; we don't want to hurt you. I'd like to know where the rest of my group is, the women we were traveling with. Are they okay?" Henry said this all politely, but inside he wanted to stand up, slam his fist on the table and demand to be told where Mary and the others were. But he knew that would get him nothing, so he held his tongue and played the diplomat...for now.

"Ah, yes, we monitor all communications around this complex and the village. We found the person who sent that transmission and they have been dealt with harshly."

Jimmy glanced at Henry his eyes saying what *harshly* really meant.

"Your women are fine. They have been examined and have now been conscripted into the greater works we are doing here. With them and others like them, we will build a new generation of Americans that will be strong enough to take back the country from the undead creatures that now walk the earth."

Jimmy raised his hand like he was in grade school.

"Yes, you wish to ask a question?" Dr. Tandy said.

"Yeah, I do, what's up with this place. Are you military or what? In case you didn't know it, there's no more military, it's all gone, lady."

Dr. Tandy frowned, but it looked more like she was pursing her lips for a kiss.

"I know that, we all do here, but that still doesn't mean we have to stop what we were put here to do."

"And that is?" Henry asked. God he wanted to jump over the table, take Stark out and then shoot anyone who got in his way, but still he held his ground, knowing he and Jimmy were at a disadvantage. Looking at Jimmy's body language, he could see the young man felt the same way.

"Research and development, but that has changed drastically since the dead began to walk. You see, the mountains on all sides of us protect us from the storm fronts. The cumulous clouds filled with whatever made people become the walking dead never reached us and we have relatively been immune from the ravaged lands around us. Tucked up here in the mountains, we have also been safe from the hordes of living dead. They do manage to come here of course, but it is nothing to destroy them.

"And where is this exactly?" Henry asked. "Are we still in Crescent Falls?"

Dr. Tandy shook her head, resembling a bobble head. "Yes and no, Mr. Watson." She glanced to Stark and waved for him to go over to the curtain. "Open it, please."

Stark did as he was told, pressing a button to the side of the curtain. A small motor began to whirl and the curtain parted, exposing a large window.

"Oh, shit, you've got to be kidding me," Jimmy gasped as he stared out the window. "This has got be some kink of a joke."

"No joke, Mr. Cooper, I assure you. What you see is reality," she said. "Let me fill you in a little more about who we are and what we are doing here. Only then will you understand how important our work is and how, you too, can be a part of it."

Henry pulled his gaze from the window, still shocked at what he was seeing, and he nodded to Dr. Tandy.

"All right, we're listening," Henry told her, his eyes constantly flashing back to the window. It was unbelievable, like he was living in a sci-fi movie. Well, instead of the everyday horror that he and every other human being left alive on the planet had to deal with.

For the next hour, Dr. Tandy, in her silly little voice that was forty years off-sounding, squeaked her way through a detailed account of the complex she controlled and the people who worked under her and how they came to be.

Though hard to deny, the tale of Project Delta was still hard to accept. It was the kind of story that would have made a conspiracy nut drool, one of underground redoubts and military secret installations.

Afterward, when he'd heard the entire tale, he tried to keep it all straight in his head, but could only remember the bare essentials of the story.

During the middle of the 1990's, multiple secret projects were set up across the United States. Though there were protests from activists high in the political food chain, in the end it was useless and secret military bases were built deep underground, and in the case of Project Delta, deep under the lake of the village of Crescent Falls near its center. Here, a huge and intricate complex was established and staffed with top scientists and security to watch over them and do the dirty work. At the time the village of Crescent Falls never knew what was going on; as they were told the construction had to do with a fault line in the lake that needed to be corrected.

According to Dr. Tandy, by the year 2000, only scientists involved with the military were receiving any funding to fuel their research.

Bigger and better weapons of mass destruction were usually the agenda of the day.

Then two years ago, the dead began to walk and the country was thrown into chaos. Civilization was destroyed and the military became scattered as each branch fought to consolidate their power and survive the coming apocalypse.

With a massive storage room stacked to the rafters with food, a water purifying system, plus a small nuclear reactor which used the lake water as coolant, the scientists were soon left alone to their own devices when all contact with the outside world disappeared. Of course, there were expeditions into Denver to see how bad it truly was. The first expedition never returned, assumed lost, and the second did return but with casualties. That was when the scientists got their first hand look at the living dead when the hosts died and then returned to a state of *unlife* after being exposed to the deadly rain. By the end of the first year the bacteria began to mutate within the ghouls and what was once a nontransferable virus was now a contagion that could be transferred from host to victim.

Left to their own designs, it was soon apparent there were much more important things to worry about than building better weapons. As the first year came to an end, it was realized how truly terrible the zombie invasion was, so the complex began to alter its program schedule, realizing they were now the country's only hope to ever return it to what it once was.

And to do that they would need people. So they changed their mandate and began working on ways to breed the female of the human species as fast as was allowed without killing the subject. Of course, to put a thinking woman through the process of birth again and again for as long as they lived was inhumane, so they came up with Dr. Stanley's laser probe. The probe was originally going to be used for interrogation. As the laser ate away at the prisoner's brainstem, eradicating the mind piece by piece, so the answers needed could be taken at will. But the laser proved equally useful as a mind wipe, washing the slate of the female's mind clean so they were in essence brain dead, but with the basic motor functions still running on automatic. Thus a perfect breeder, who felt no pain or discomfort.

"And when there was no one else, we went into the village and harvested all the available women, the only ones not taken were the ones who are incapable of breeding from age or disease."

Henry nodded. "There was a woman at the boardinghouse, Lucy, I think her name was."

"Yes, Mr. Watson. She was afflicted with ovarian cancer five years ago and is incapable of child birth, so she was excluded from the project. So, too, are the very old and extremely young." She leaned back in her chair. "Of course, the young will come of age soon enough," she tried to smile, but it looked horrible on her painted face.

"But, lady," Jimmy said. "This is nuts. The people who gave you your orders, the ones who put you down here, they're probably all dead. There's no one left."

"Of course we know that, Mr. Cooper, we're not fools, but someone has to do something, don't you think? Are we supposed to just let those dead creatures take over the planet while we run and hide like scared children?" Her voice went up an octave, and Henry could see she did believe what she was saying, though insane as it was.

"And what about the women in my group, what about them? Are they going to be part of your project?" Henry asked.

Dr. Tandy nodded. "Of course, in fact the process has already begun with one of your group and soon the others will be wiped so they can join her and the others in the breeding facility in the west wing of the complex."

"What the fuck? You're not gonna do that to my Cindy, you crazy bitch!" Jimmy snarled while standing up, his chair flying out from behind him. Immediately all three guards leveled their carbines at him. If he made one inch of an advance towards Dr. Tandy, he was about to be shot full of holes.

"Easy, Jimmy," Henry said, reaching up and grabbing his friend's arm. Jimmy's muscles were taut, veins in his neck pulsing as anger filled him.

"The good doctor may have a point. At least she's trying to do something about the deader problem."

Jimmy turned and looked down at the still seated Henry.

"Are fucking crazy, old man? What the hell are you talking about?"

Henry glared at Jimmy, trying to will him to calm down. "I said there's nothing we can do about it so we might as well get with the program, that's what; now pick up your chair and sit back down, please." His tone was low but it pierced Jimmy's haze of anger. Though his face was red and he was breathing fast, he swallowed the knot of fury in his throat and picked up his chair, sitting back down. Slamming his hands on the table, Jimmy glared at Dr. Tandy, his eyes like small daggers of hate.

"Well said, Mr. Watson, well said. It's nice to see you are a reasonable man. That was one of the reasons I didn't have you shot when we captured you. You see, we need information about the outside world, and from what I hear, you and your counterparts have traveled far and wide. It would be a shame to wipe all that wonderful knowledge away."

Inside he was a ball of absolute rage. He had visions of reaching over the table and wrapping his hands around the frail neck of the woman, squeezing until her eyes popped out of their sockets like ping pong balls. But the three carbines aimed at his head stopped him cold.

"Just glad to be part of the team," he said happily, though his jaw was taut.

Thinking about what could be happening to Mary, Cindy, Raven and Sue was too much to bear and it took all of his will power to remain seated.

Then something came to him. The doctor had said nothing about the escape of Jack and he had a feeling the woman didn't know about it. Had Stark kept that tidbit of a screw-up to himself? Not wanting to let her know of his mistake? Henry wondered if the fact he knew this would help him, but in the end he didn't think so. He decided to remain silent on the subject. Only now, knowing they were underwater, what hope did Jack have of escaping?

Stark glared at Henry from across the room, as if daring him to say or do something that would give him an excuse to kill him. Henry wouldn't give the man that reason, at least not on purpose.

Dr. Tandy stood up, signifying the meeting was over. She glanced to Stark, waving him closer to her.

"Take these men back to their cells and later I want them interrogated," she ordered him. She turned to Henry and Jimmy one last time.

"You two can cooperate as you've said and tell us everything we want to know or we can make your lives very difficult." She began to walk away and then paused, turning back around. "That is, what will be left of it after the laser probe is through with you." Without waiting for a reply, she hobbled out of the room, the slap, clop echoing off the bare walls.

Stark pointed to the door for Henry and Jimmy to get going, and they complied, both soon moving down the hallway.

Another man in similar black garb came up to Stark and whispered into his ear, his voice low so Henry and Jimmy couldn't hear what was being said. When he was through, Stark nodded, said a few terse words, and sent the man off, this time with another guard.

"Hey, Stark," Henry called, "you find Jack yet?"

"No, Watson, not yet, but I'm not worried, after all, it's not like he can hold his breath long enough to reach the surface. We're pretty damn deep down here and you'd need a scuba tank to reach the surface before running out of air. No, Watson, we'll find the kid and when we do he'll pay for the grief he's putting me through. You all will."

Henry didn't reply; there was no reason to.

With a poke in the back, Henry began walking again, Jimmy by his side.

"What the hell was that for?" Jimmy asked. "We need to find the girls before God knows what's gonna happen to them."

"I know that, Jimmy, I really do, but we can't do a thing for them unless we figure out how the hell to get out of here once we find them. And every bit of info helps us do that."

"Quiet you two, you can be gagged you know," Stark snapped.

Henry turned and glared at the man but did as he was told. Nodding to Jimmy, the younger man returned it with one of his own. Though impatient to the last, he knew Henry was right. Even if they saved the girls, without an exit strategy they were still trapped in the underwater complex.

# Chapter 30

Another sneeze was coming to Jack and he forced it down, knowing the ductwork would echo the sound throughout the complex.

After sliding into the vent, he had paused near the corner, still able to see out to Henry's feet. Then he saw the guard's feet and there was an altercation. When the guard began shooting into the vent, Jack had jumped back, seeing the small round holes appear in the side of the metal five inches from where his head was. Then he'd turned and began moving off, not knowing where he was going, but wanting to keep on the move.

He crawled for ten minutes, pausing every now and then to peer through the gratings into the rooms below. He found it odd how he had entered the ductwork near the floor and through a gradual rise had ended up near the ceiling. The large metal ducts he was now in weren't empty either.

Besides being used for ventilation and heating, there were cables for power, communications, such as phones, and other items such as alarms and fiber optics, plus a dozen more he couldn't name.

The first room of interest to him was the cafeteria. As he peered through the metal slats, he saw men and women in white lab coats, as well as security guards, all eating and talking as they sat around large, circular tables. The aroma of the food made his stomach growl and he fought the urge to want to eat down. It was hard, but it wasn't the first time he had been hungry.

Moving on, he next came to what appeared to be living quarters. There was a bed and desk in each room along with a few personal items scattered on the walls and floor. One of the rooms had a couple having sex in it. The woman was on top of the man and she was riding him like he was a wild bull. Her breasts were full and her hips shapely and Jack found himself becoming aroused. He watched for another three minutes and then realized he needed to get moving, so with a sigh of regret, he left the couple to their sexual devices, the woman's moans of pleasure following him into the ductwork.

Fifteen minutes later brought him to yet another room of interest. Gazing down, he saw shelves and lockers full of all sorts of weapons and explosives--large blocks of what looked like clay for one-- and best of all, in the far corner of the room, were the companion's weapons. As he looked inside, he saw Henry's Glock and Jimmy's .38, as well as Cindy's M-16. And their clothes were there too, all neatly folded after looking like they had been laundered.

He pushed on the grating, wanting to see if he could get down into the room and see what he could take with him, but the grating was screwed to the wall on all sides with sheet metal screws. Sure, he might be able to kick it in, but then someone would know he was there and he knew his only advantage at the moment was stealth. So with another sigh of regret, he committed the armory's position to memory compared to where he thought he was and moved on.

The next room was the most amazing to his young eyes. It was a laboratory, filled with dozens of beakers and test tubes. But that wasn't what was so interesting.

It was the cages with glass walls and the occupants therein.

Swallowing a dusty knot in his throat, he stared at the creatures in the cages. One cage contained three zombies, but they weren't normal looking. Their legs had been chopped off just above the knees and then sewn up so that the ghouls resembled midgets. They waddled around on their nubs as they slapped the glass with rotting hands, leaving pus and ichor behind with each consecutive slap. The next cage had a zombie with no arms or legs. Nothing but a torso and a head, it rolled around the cage floor like an earthworm.

The next cage contained five ghouls with different appendages. One had legs where arms should be and vise versa. Like circus freaks the ghouls moved about the cage, bumping into one another as they moaned and wailed.

But it was the last cage that made Jack gasp in horror.

Inside the glass enclosure was a giant of a zombie with two heads and arms that were not the ones the ghoul had owned in life.

The second head was attached slightly to the side of the first and the stitches on the neck gave it the look of Frankenstein. The new arms on the ghoul had been taken from someone who had been a body builder in life, the muscles flexing and pulsing under the dead tissue. The ghoul's left head roared in rage, the other head wailing, while meaty fists slammed against the reinforced glass, shaking the room with each ferocious blow.

With his heart beating in his chest from fear of the abomination, Jack crawled deeper into the complex, still searching for some way to help Henry and the others.

Twenty minutes after leaving the lab of mutated zombies, he peered through another grating to what resembled a hospital. There were rows and rows of beds on both sides of the room, all filled with women who looked pregnant. But as he studied their faces, he saw nothing but blank stares that reminded him of the look zombies had. He watched a lab tech taking a woman's blood pressure and the woman never flinched, never moved. It was like she and the other women had been hypnotized or something.

Deciding he'd seen all that mattered here, he moved on yet again, and five minutes later came to a four way junction with a service ladder. Climbing downward, he came to another large junction and in this one were two things of interest. The first was what looked like a large transformer, like what was on telephone poles, and the other was a door leading out into the main complex.

An idea struck him as he stared at the transformer and he went to the door and opened it a crack. Peering out into the white corridor, he searched for what he hoped would be there.

Sure enough, on the far wall was a fire ax, hanging next to a bright-red fire extinguisher.

With his heart beating fast with adrenalin, he crossed his fingers and dashed into the hallway towards the axe.

Reaching it, he looked both ways and thanked God it was empty. But then he heard voices and footsteps and knew his luck had changed. Grabbing the axe from the wall, he charged back to the door, and just as he closed it with a soft click, two security guards came around the corner, their carbines held out in front of them.

As they passed by the door, one slowed for a moment, but then continued on, deciding he didn't feel like checking the small room.

Letting out the breath he'd been holding, Jack opened the door and peeked out one last time.

It was empty...for now.

Turning around after closing the door, he hefted the axe in his hands. The transformer stood in front of him, the power conduits spreading out of it and into the nearby ducts like the legs of a massive spider.

And as he raised the axe over his head, he grinned widely. Henry told him to see what damage he could cause, and if there was one thing in this world he liked to do, it was break stuff.

# Chapter 31

"How's it coming, Raven?" Mary asked from the bed askance of the young girl while Raven continued working at the strap with her nails.

"Almost there, few more minutes," the girl said tersely.

"Either that crazy doctor or his assistant should be here any minute," Cindy said.

"You're not helping," Raven said curtly.

She knew time was running out, but slicing her straps with nothing but her finger nails, sharp as they were, took time. She had been at it for more than an hour, ever since she came to, but it was slow going. She was just glad whoever had tied them to the beds had used material straps and not leather, or worse, handcuffs.

"I still can't believe what you said happened to Carol," Sue said from across the room. After finally waking up, and hearing what had happened to Carol from Mary and Cindy, she was heartbroken. Worse, she was terrified the same thing was going to happen to her.

"Well, believe it," Cindy told her. "'Cause we both saw it with our own eyes. The sick bastard burned out her brain and made her a vegetable. Now she's gonna be a breeder for these fuckers." She was so mad her face was bright red. All she wanted to do was get out of her bonds so she could kill some of these no good scientists.

"It was horrible. The smell was unbelievable," Mary said as she scrunched up her nose. There was still a slight aftertaste hanging in the air from Carol's burned brain and it made her stomach roll like she was seasick.

Sue glanced to Raven. "Please hurry up, you're our only hope," she pleaded.

"I know that, Sue," Raven said. "I'm trying, now leave me alone."

"Where do you think the guys are?" Cindy asked Mary. "Ya think they're safe?"

Mary shrugged. "Good question, but as they don't have wombs it's possible they're fine." She shook her head. "This crazy place, these people are out of their minds. We have to get out of here soon or it's vegetable city for all of us."

And then all eyes went to the door as it hissed up, the assistant for Dr. Stanley now entering. The man carried a clipboard and a few other items which he set on a nearby rolling metal table.

Then he picked up a syringe and went to a square wall cabinet which contained numerous small bottles. The man took one out, stuck the tip of the syringe into it, and sucked a few centimeters of fluid into the needle. After returning the bottle to the cabinet, he turned and smiled at the women, squeezing the syringe so a small amount of fluid was ejected.

"Wouldn't want any air bubbles, now do we," he grinned malevolently.

"What the fuck's in there?" Cindy asked, gesturing with her chin to the needle.

The assistant shrugged casually and crossed the room to Raven.

"Just a mild sedative so you don't fight us when we move you from the bed to the table so we can melt your brains," he said evilly.

"Bastard, you'll pay for this, I swear on my grave!" Mary said, her nostrils flaring in anger.

"Oooh, a fighter, I like 'em when they fight. Maybe after you're a veggie burger I'll pay you a visit in the breeder farm. After all, if you're already knocked up there's nothing I can do but have a little fun. 'Sides, it's not like you'll know any different."

"Fuck you, you prick!" Mary yelled back. She usually didn't curse, but this was drastic. This man was about to assist in cooking her brains in her head, then later raping her.

The assistant chuckled as he moved around the bed to Raven. As he did this he let his free hand trail up the teenager's leg. "Mmmm, I like 'em young," he said heavily.

Raven said nothing, her nails still sawing at the strap. She knew she was close, just a little more. The assistant was on the opposite side of strap she was working on and his eyes were focused entirely on her legs which were exposed after she'd kicked off the sheets.

He grinned even wider when he saw where her nightgown collected at the juncture of her thighs.

"Now, let's get you ready. You get to go next, sweetmeat," he said as he reached over to a small table next to the bed and grabbed some cotton and alcohol to clean her arm in preparation for the shot.

It was when he was looking away that Raven felt the strap part, the last of the threads finally giving way. There was a soft rip as Raven pulled her arm free, and the assistant turned, his mouth opening in surprise. But Raven didn't give him a chance to do anything but gape as she swung her free hand around and sliced at his throat. Though three of her nails had been dulled by sawing at the strap holding her, the other two were still razor sharp and they parted the flesh under his jaw like it was made of paper.

Blood shot out of his split throat to bathe Raven in hot plasma, but she ignored it. Reaching out with her free hand, she now grabbed the man by his shirt and pulled him closer to her. As he fell onto her lap, she leaned over and used her teeth, sinking them into the side of his neck, tearing out the thin layer of flesh protecting his carotid artery. More blood shot outward and into her mouth and she spit the foul tasting fluid out while the man twitched on top of her. He tried to get up, but she held him down, his head now between her legs. If his wish had been to visit that tempting spot, he'd gotten it, only it was the last wish he would ever get in this life.

While Raven held the man's head down, the body spasmed in its death throes, the blood seeping out across the bed in what seemed like gallons. Finally, the man's legs stopped kicking, and after another minute, Raven pushed the body off her to fall to the floor in a heap. Mary glanced over the side of the bed where the man was now prone and she nodded happily.

"Great job, Raven, he's dead all right. Now get free so you can do the same for us," she said quickly.

"Hmmph, you're welcome," Raven said, but she did reach over and begin undoing the other straps holding her to the bed. Once she was free, she climbed out of bed and moved to the others; quickly unfastening their straps while wiping her face and neck clean with a sheet.

"Are you hurt?" Sue asked, seeing all the blood covering the front of Raven's gown.

"No, fine, it's all his," she said curtly then moved to Cindy to free her.

In less than two minutes they were all free and rubbing their wrists from where their straps had bitten into their skin.

Mary ran to the door, but when she tried to get it open it wouldn't go up. There was a small button to the right, and though she pushed it repeatedly it wouldn't activate.

"Damn, we're locked in," she said as she turned around and crossed her arms over her chest.

"What?" Cindy asked. "Let me try, we saw Stanley and that guy going back and forth." She went to the door and pressed the button, but nothing happened.

"I just did that, what makes you think you doing it is gonna change anything?" Mary asked, annoyed.

Cindy turned, also dejected. "I don't know, I just thought…well, nothing I guess."

Raven was across the room where there was another small steel table on wheels. It was about a foot in diameter and on it were gleaming stainless steel scalpels and clamps, all the necessary tools to save a life or take one.

"Here, we can use these," Raven said while holding a few up in her hands.

"Good idea," Mary said. "Come on, everybody, take at least one, it's better than nothing."

When everyone was armed with a blade, they stood in the middle of the room, discussing their options.

"We'll just have to wait for Dr. Stanley or one of his helpers to come back," Mary said as she looked around the room.

"We can wait by the door, and when he walks in, ambush him," Cindy suggested, then shrugged. "It's not like we have a lot of options here."

Sue looked to Raven's bed, the first one by the door. "We should see about cleaning up all that blood or at least hiding it so when he comes in he doesn't see it all."

Mary nodded. "Yeah, good idea, Sue. If he comes in and sees all that he's gonna know something's wrong." She turned to Raven.

"Hey, Raven, grab some blankets from the other beds and toss them over the mess you made." She grinned as she told her this and Raven grinned back, getting the joke.

After grabbing two blankets she went to her bed and made it. Though some of the blood began to seep through almost immediately, it still looked better than before. The body of the assistant was hidden from view between two of the beds so it was fine, though Sue did grab a sheet and cover him up.

"Waste of time," Raven said.

"Maybe," Sue replied, "but he's dead and I want to show some respect, it doesn't cost a thing."

"Your time, not mine," Raven replied and moved off to another part of the room to inspect the laser probe.

Sue had frowned, not liking that she'd been questioned. "Yes, it is my time," she whispered.


The door hissed up fifteen minutes later and the women were waiting for whoever entered.

It was Dr. Stanley, carrying a clipboard and a cup of coffee.

Mary and Cindy were on both sides of the door, and Raven and Sue had returned to the beds so when someone entered they would see nothing amiss, at least for a few seconds. Raven had taken Mary's bed, not wanting to sit in the blood and no one had argued. By the time whoever came in figured out she was in the wrong bed, they would have taken him down...hopefully.

As Dr. Stanley walked in, his eyes immediately went to the empty bed Raven should have been in, and though he knew something was off, at first he didn't get concerned. He knew his assistant had come in earlier to get the next woman ready so perhaps he had moved them around for one reason or another.

The first insight he had that something was amiss was when he was struck from a blow from Cindy, the back of her elbow connecting with his nose. Sharp pain filled his head and he dropped his clipboard and coffee, one splashing on the floor, the other clattering away.

Before he could cry out, Cindy had grabbed him by his shirt and had yanked him out of the doorway. The door began to close, but

Mary was there and she rolled the small steel table under it, stopping it halfway. There was the whine of hydraulics as the door continued to try and close and then it stopped; a safety feature similar to an elevator door installed in the mechanism.

After jamming the door open, Mary joined Cindy in pummeling Dr. Stanley.

By the time they were finished, his face was a bloody ruin with two black eyes and a fractured nose. He tried to talk, but only managed to spit bloody teeth across the floor. A red drool slid out of the corner of his mouth as he rolled to his side and coughed up phlegm.

When the man was beaten to within an inch of his life, a gasping Mary and a heaving Cindy glanced up from him and looked into each other's eyes. Both had bloody knuckles from the beating they'd just handed out.

"What next?" Cindy asked, but then her eyes lit up. Crossing the room, she went to a small steel table near one of the beds and picked up a scalpel. Walking back, she leaned down over the weeping, bloody doctor and placed the blade to his throat, ready to draw it across his neck and kill him.

"You can't kill me," Dr. Stanley spit. "If you do, you'll never get out of this place alive."

"Screw you, asshole," Cindy snarled and flexed her arm to kill the man and be done with it."

"No, wait, maybe he's right, and I think I have a better idea," Mary said to Cindy, holding her arm before she could kill the doctor.

Dr. Stanley's vision was fuzzy, and though he tried to hear what Mary and Cindy were saying about him, he was in too much pain to focus. But he figured they must have come to their senses, realizing that to kill him would seal their fates.

Finally, he lost consciousness, sliding into the void between life and death while the two women continued to discuss his destiny, but now he knew he would live, the woman called Mary had believed his words.

Dr. Stanley came to six and a half minutes later, his entire body feeling like one massive bruise. His eyes were swollen and puffy from the beating he'd sustained, but he could still see through the slits. His world had become smaller, but he could see he was still in the laser probe room, but he was now across the room in the corner. As he looked over his supine body he saw the monitors for the CATSCAN and other screens were lit up. As he tried to move, he found his head was secured tightly, like it had been placed in a vise.

The women were still in the room, too, and they were talking, no wait, arguing about something.

Sue was in a heated discussion with Mary, while Raven watched the corridor. They all knew it was only minutes before someone arrived and found out what they were doing. Dr. Stanley knew he would also be saved as soon as a security patrol came by this area. Which should be anytime now.

"I don't like this, Mary, it's barbaric," Sue was saying to Mary as she pointed to the doctor who was now strapped to another metal table. "You can't do this to him."

"You know what, Sue? I don't give a damn what you think, all right? You weren't awake when we had to watch that bastard make Carol into a vegetable! You didn't hear her screams or smell her brains cooking in her head! Look, I get you don't accept this world we now live in, and most of the time it's rather endearing, but right now I really don't have the patience for it. So you need to shut up and let us do what we need to do!"

Sue took a step back, not used to the vehemence in Mary's voice. Cindy approached her from behind and placed a hand on Sue's shoulder.

"She's right, Sue, you didn't see what we saw. Tell you what, why don't you go wait by the door, we're about ready to leave anyway." Then she thought of something. "Actually, why don't you get the scalpels and anything else we might be able to use as a weapon when we leave here, okay?"

Sue looked at Cindy and then Mary who was red with anger. Finally she nodded. "Fine, I'll go get the supplies we might be able to use. But I still don't like this one bit."

"Fine, it's been dully noted," Mary said angrily.

Sue moved away and Cindy stepped closer to Mary.

"You know how she is, Mar', she means well," Cindy told her.

Mary didn't reply, instead she pointed to the monitors, switches and dials.

"Let's just get this done and get out of here. The boys must be wondering where we are," Mary said, her voice cold.

Cindy chuckled then, trying to lighten the mood a little. "Knowing them, they're probably in a sauna or something relaxing while we were here waiting to get our brains sucked out."

Mary gave Cindy a wan smile. "Yeah, no doubt."

Cindy followed Mary across the room and they began flicking dials and turning knobs, trying to remember what they'd seen Dr. Stanley do. Finally the diodes behind the helmet lit up and Cindy called out. "Hey, we got power here!"

Mary crossed the room and nodded. "Good, looks like we figured it out. She reached up and pressed the small buttons she thought the doctor had pressed with Carol, and after a few failures the needle probes finally extended. Then, without so much as a goodbye, she reached out and pressed the **ON** button for the laser.

The yellow beams shot out and began boring into the doctor's skull, the smell of cooking flesh filling the room immediately.

"Come on, let's get out of here," Mary said coldly as Dr. Stanley began screaming.

"I told you I'd kill you, you bastard," Mary said before she turned to leave the room. Dr. Stanley didn't hear her; he was too busy being lobotomized.

Cindy glanced at the man in the helmet as his legs and arms, though tied down, began to thrash and spasm. Pleased with his fate, she turned and walked away.

Raven was waiting at the door with Sue, and when Cindy and Mary ducked under it, Raven kicked the metal table out from under the door, the door now closing once again.

As the door slowly closed, the doctor's screams began to grow in pitch, but were soon muffled as the bottom of the door connected with the floor.

One at a time, Sue passed out the scalpels to each of them.

"Come on, let's go find the boys and get the hell out of here," Mary said, her eyes hard. Sue was staring at her accusingly, but Mary ignored her gaze.

The four women set off, Raven taking point as she checked the hall ahead to make sure it was clear.

Mary paused for a half-second and listened to the screams of the dying Dr. Stanley. With no one there to stop the laser, it wouldn't simply make the man a vegetable, but would instead bore completely through his brain and then into the metal table underneath his skull. She hoped it was painful, very painful, knowing as the man died his brain would be fried in his skull.

As she moved away, taking up last position, the shrieks and cries of Dr. Stanley filtered through the door, and Mary smiled, slightly, hoping the bastard suffered for a long time before his brains were finally burned out of his head.

She wasn't able to save Carol, and though she hadn't known the woman for very long, she knew what justice was. And whether what she did was justice or vengeance, in the new world she now existed in, sometimes they were both the same thing.

# Chapter 32

Henry and Jimmy were both sitting in their cells when the lights first began to flicker, and then went out all together. Immediately the large room was bathed in a red glow as emergency lights came on.

But the best thing to happen with the cessation of the lighting was the glass wall of their cells began to slide up. Henry stared at the glass as it rose into the ceiling, surprise clearly written on his face, when the lights came back on again.

No sooner did the power return then the glass began to descend once more.

Acting quickly, he jumped up and dashed through the opening, almost catching his foot on the bottom lip as the glass seated into the floor once again.

Rolling to his feet, Henry saw Jimmy also on the floor, having charged out of his cell when the glass had ascended.

"What the hell's going on?" Jimmy asked.

"Dunno, maybe Jack's gotten into something he shouldn't have," Henry said as he looked around the room. "But let's not look a gift horse in the mouth."

They were the only occupants locked up at the moment and there were no guards around. After all, why would they be needed to stay? Once Henry and Jimmy were in their cages they were trapped.

"Come on; let's see if we can find the girls. And pray we're not too late," he added.

Jimmy nodded, punching his fist into his other palm as the two ran for the door.

Pressing the button to the side of the frame, the door slid up easily.

"That's a lucky break," Henry said. "I figured it might be locked."

"Why?" Jimmy asked. "Once we're in the cells it's not like we can just walk out."

"Yeah, good point," Henry agreed.

With Henry in the lead, they stepped out into the hallway, but it was empty.

"So far so good," Henry said. "Come on, I think we want to go this way."

Jimmy nodded and they headed off. They made it to the second intersection before they heard the sound of footsteps approaching.

Henry pressed his back against the wall and raised his index finger to his lips. Then he raised his hand and held up two fingers for Jimmy.

Jimmy nodded, understanding. Henry then used hand signals to tell Jimmy to take the one on the left and he would attack the right one. They didn't know who was coming, whether it was guards or simple lab techs, but whoever they were; they were an obstacle to be removed.

Henry took one side and Jimmy the other so that whoever was coming would walk right past them before either man would strike.

The footsteps grew closer and Henry heard the voices of two men, both deep.

His heart began to beat faster as his adrenalin filled him with liquid strength, and he clenched his fists together while he waited for the two security guards to stroll right past them. Neither man was thinking they needed to be on guard as they walked down the corridor.

Obviously they weren't concerned about the power fluctuations.

When the guard closest to Henry walked past him, Henry swung a dreadful clubbing blow to the back of the man's neck, then followed with another punch to the small of the guard's back, just over his kidneys. The guard gave a cry of pain and shock as he stumbled forward. While this was happening, Jimmy charged in and punched his guard on the side of the face, rattling teeth and rocking the man's head like it was made of fragile glass. As the man reeled from the blow, Jimmy reached out and snatched the guard's carbine from limp fingers.

Henry was still dealing with his guard, and as the man crumpled to his knees in pain, paralyzed by the powerful double-punch to his body, Henry slapped the man's cap and glasses off his face.

Deep brown eyes looked up at him, tears forming at the edges of his sockets, as the man tried to say something, perhaps pleading for mercy.

Henry never hesitated, but instead chopped at the man's throat with the side of his hand, pulping the thyroid cartilage and crushing the laryngeal branch of the vital vagus nerve, sending the guard flailing to the floor as he gagged on blood.

The man was dying fast as his arms spasmed and his hands grasped empty air.

Jimmy had just finished dealing with his own guard. After rocking the man's head to the side, Jimmy jumped him, using the butt of the carbine to cave in the man's temple. The body dropped like a ton of bricks, a large crack now in his skull. Pink brains could now be seen as they tried to escape the bone prison of the guard's head.

Henry nodded in approval and then held his hand up for Jimmy to remain quiet. Listening intently, Henry waited to see if there were signs the killings had been heard by others, but there was no alarm.

Jimmy glanced up to a corner of the corridor where the wall met the ceiling and pointed with the muzzle of the carbine.

"Look, cameras."

"Damn, figured as much," Henry growled.

"You think anyone's watching?"

Henry shrugged. "Maybe, but I doubt it. If there was, I think we'd be hearing an alarm or something by now, don't you?"

"Yeah, I guess so."

"Either way, Jimmy, we've got to find the girls. Whether these people know we're free doesn't matter."

"That's a given, so let's get going, already."

"Fine, you lead the way," Henry said as he picked up the other guard's fallen carbine. He checked it quickly and was pleased with what he found. The weapon was in great condition and smelled of gun oil. Whatever these guards were, they respected their armaments.

The two men headed off and five minutes later came upon their next obstacle. There were three security guards standing in the corridor. Both Jimmy and Henry waited, hoping they would eventually disperse, but when almost ten minutes had passed and the three men still were talking, Henry grew impatient.

"This isn't working, we don't have time for this crap, we need to take 'em out before someone finds those guards we took down," Henry told Jimmy.

Jimmy grinned. "So let's go," he said as he hefted his carbine. Jimmy was never one for waiting when action could be used instead. His impetuousness had sometimes been a problem for the companions, but other times Jimmy's willingness to charge in shooting had saved the day. This was one of those times.

"Okay, you take the two on the right and I'll get the one on the left."

"Why do I have to take two guys? Why can't you take the two on the left?"

Gritting his teeth, Henry moved closer to Jimmy so they were nose to nose.

"Jimmy, now is not the time for your bullshit, all right? Think of the girls. Now take the two on the right and shut up."

"Fine, all right, I got the two," he said like a spoiled child.

Henry nodded and moved to the edge of the hallway. He looked to Jimmy, raised his hands in the air with three fingers and began rolling each finger closed until he was down to one.

When he lowered the last finger, he said the word, "Now," and both men jumped into the corridor and sprayed the guards with their carbines.

Only Henry's jammed after the first round and he only shot his target a glancing blow. Jimmy sprayed his two targets with lead slugs and they went down with bloody chests and angry back wounds. But Henry's man was a fighter, and as soon as he heard the shots, he spun, took the glancing blow from Henry's shot and raised his carbine to return fire.

With nothing else to do, Henry threw the jammed carbine as hard as he could at the guard's face. The muzzle struck the man below the right eye and clattered to the floor. The guard cried out in pain as his head was knocked back, and when he looked up, Henry was charging him like a linebacker.

Both men were about the same height, but Henry had about ten pounds on the guard. He sent the man crashing back against the far wall with a spine crushing impact. The guard's gun went flying from his hands as Henry wrapped his hands around his throat.

But the guard could fight and he brought up his arms between Henry's and forced Henry's hands off his throat. Acting fast, Henry jammed two of his fingers into the man's nostril's and yanked forward as hard as he could.

Tearing flesh filled the air as the man's nose was parted from his face. A bloody hole, now dripping blood and mucus, gaped as the man screamed in pain, but Henry barely gave him the chance. With amazing lightness on his feet, he pivoted sideways and used his forearm to strike the man across the front of his neck. Unable to breathe, the guard slumped to the floor, his face purpling as he waved his hands in the air for help.

Henry spun around the man, stepped up from behind and wrapped his hands around the guard's chin. Bracing himself like he was pulling a cork from a large bottle, and breathing in with the effort, he snapped the guard's neck like a dry tree branch.

Letting go, the body slumped to the now bloody floor and Henry went and picked up the dead guard's carbine, hoping this one was in better shape, despite the appearance of the last one.

"That's three more down and a hell of a lot more to go," he said as he sucked in a deep breath.

Jimmy nodded. "That was something else, Henry, way to think on your feet," he said as he kicked the dead guards to makes sure they were truly dead.

"Thanks, now come on. Let's get moving. We need to find a map or something of the layout of this place. "Otherwise we'll wander around here forever and sooner or later someone's gonna find these guys and us."

With a curt nod from Jimmy in agreement, they strode down the corridor, leaving the three dead guards to find out what lay beyond this fragile life.


As the two warriors moved through the complex, they stealthily avoided armed patrols now searching for them. It was slow going, as they wanted to check each room, hoping that would be the one the women were in.

Coming upon the next door, Henry pressed the button on the wall and the door slid up.

"You stay out here, I'll be right back," Henry told Jimmy. "But be ready to run or hide if a patrol comes by."

"Gotcha," Jimmy said with a grin, hefting the carbine.

Henry stepped inside the room and his eyes went wide when he saw the cells, then he scrunched up his nose at the odor of death which permeated the large room.

No sooner did he enter the room then the lights flickered and the door slammed shut. Turning, Henry pressed the button on the wall, but the door remained closed.

"Hey Jimmy. You okay!" Henry called through the door.

"Yeah, the lights just went out. How 'bout you?"

"I'm fine. But it looks like the door won't open. Try on your side," Henry told him.

Jimmy did and but the door stayed closed.

"Damn it," Henry said in frustration. "All right, listen up, seems I'm stuck in here I might as well check it out. If the power hasn't come back on by the time I'm through, we'll figure something out."

"Okay, if I'm not here I had to disappear for a while, but I'll come back when I can," Jimmy called through the door.

"Fine, just be careful," Henry said.

"Yeah, you, too," Jimmy replied as he leaned against the wall, his eyes peering into the dull gloom. Only the red backup lights near the ceiling illuminated anything and that wasn't much.

Henry stepped back from the door and had another look at the massive room. In the center were large lab tables with test tubes and vials. The red lights near the ceiling cast everything in a scarlet hue, giving him the creeps. Shadows were everywhere, filling the corners and crevices where a second ago there had been light.

Deciding he should get a move on, he stepped deeper into the room, searching for the women. For all he knew, they were in one of the cells near the opposite end. The only way he would know for sure is to check.

As he stepped lightly, he began to hear sounds, chewing noises to be more precise.

With the carbine leveled at chest height, he stepped around a large table overflowing with tubes and charts and found what was making the sounds he'd heard.

Zombies, four of them, all looking like midgets in the darkness.

At first the small deaders with half legs ignored him as they fed on a lab tech they had caught when their cells had opened, but one at a time they each turned to glare at Henry. Their faces and arms were covered in blood and gore and they hissed and moaned at the sight of him.

As one team, they turned and left the fallen lab tech as they began hobbling towards him.

"Now I've seen everything," Henry said as the dwarf ghouls came at him, rocking back and forth like they were drunk or off center.

With the carbine in hand, he lowered his aim and shot each midget-zombie in the chest, not wanting to take chances he might miss in the dark. Then he realigned his aim and shot each one in the head as they flailed about on the floor.

Shaking his head at the deformed ghouls, he waved the gun smoke out of the air and moved onward.

In the next cage he found the next creature. The torso zombie rolled about and almost tripped him when he reached its cage.

"What the hell?" He gasped as he watched the torso rolling about, barely able to discern what it was in the gloom and shadows. Teeth gnashed at his boots, trying to bite him and he jumped back.

Not wanting to have to worry about this ghoul later, he placed the muzzle of the carbine near its head and blasted the skull to bloody chunks. The torso rolled around like a landed fish, but soon it stopped, the blood and ichor seeping out of the severed head and gaping neck wound thanks to the power of the blast.

For the moment there was no danger so he examined a few charts on one of the tables, seeing if he could figure out what they had been doing here. Though not a scientist, Henry got the gist of some of the writings.

Obviously the researchers here were messing with the walking dead for one reason or another. To him it just seemed like they were playing with the dead, as if they could figure out what had happened and why they walked. Though how chopping off the arms and legs of a zombie would help them with their research was beyond him

Shaking his head yet again at the house of horrors, he turned and looked into the shadows for more monstrosities, praying the girls weren't inside this large room somewhere.

He began walking again, passing open cells on his right as the soles of his sneakers crunched on the shattered remains of test tubes. In the flickering shadows, he peered harder, hoping he might spot Mary's face or Cindy's smile, but no, it looked like all that was in this laboratory were the dead corpses of the ghouls he'd shot and slaughtered lab techs.

And then he did spot movement off in the corner of the lab, near a large file cabinet.

The metal cabinet was partially blocked from about the waist down thanks to another of the ponderous lab tables in the way. Here as before, test tubes and beakers were knocked askew or crushed. Bunsen burners were spread out and knocked over like a science high school class had ravaged through the place without a care.

And then he heard it as he moved closer to the shadow. The unmistakable sound of tearing meat.

"Hello? Mary, Sue, Cindy?" He whispered, praying beyond hope that it was one of them, though for his life he couldn't imagine why they would be making those foul noises.

His left sneaker kicked an intact test tube and it rattled across the floor, sounding like a church bell in the silence.

Suddenly, a shadow the size of a head, no wait, two heads, popped up behind the table and seemed to be looking at him. But Henry couldn't tell who was there thanks to the emergency lights pale illumination. And to top it off, this section of the room happened to be a section where the lights didn't overlap, so behind the table was even more darkness.

"Whoever's back there, come out with your hands up or I'll send you straight to Hell," Henry warned as he moved closer.

It had to be a couple of lab techs who had hid when the power had gone off and the cages had opened. Must be a glitch in the first case. Maybe when the power went out it had been tied into the fire suppression system, and as a contingency the cages opened so no one would be trapped inside while a raging blaze had been happening. It made sense; this place never should have been a place to hold prisoners in the first place.

There was a huffing sound like what a horse makes and Henry took three more steps, stopping a few feet from the table.

"I said come out with your hands up. Look, fellas, don't make me come and get you, you won't like it if I do," he warned again, the carbine swinging back and forth as he searched for more movement. But since the heads had appeared, they had then disappeared again, and the sounds of tearing and feeding returned.

Henry was beginning to realize it probably wasn't lab techs behind the desk.

"More damn deaders," he mumbled under his breath. And as he prepared to step around and blow the ghouls straight to Hell, the heavy lab table suddenly exploded upwards and out, spinning in the air like a child's toy.

Taken completely off guard by the projectile, Henry fired at the table, the rounds punching into the underside of it as the table flew at him with immense speed. Just before it would have hit him, probably taking his head off, he crouched low, the table spinning over his head like a massive boulder.

The crashing of the heavy table landing was awe inspiring. Everything on the other tables was knocked to the floor and the second table hit imploded, collapsing in on itself in a sea of crystal and wood shards, the debris flying through the air, seeking tender flesh.

Henry felt bits pelting his back and he rolled away, wishing he was wearing something heavier than a thin white jumpsuit, but he knew now was not the time for *could haves*. With the noise of the table hitting the floor still reverberating through his feet, Henry realized there was now another vibration, one moving towards him. Looking back from where the table had shot up, he saw a massive shape coming out of the shadows.

At first he blinked in surprise, not believing what he was seeing, but as the behemoth of walking death and rot stepped into the vicinity of one of the emergency lights, he blinked his stupor away and raised the carbine to fire.

Two shots at the heads went wide, the creature faster than Henry would have expected. The massive two-headed ghoul came for him, its large feet crushing anything that was unfortunate enough to fall under them. Henry rolled to the side, bringing the muzzle of the carbine up yet again. He fired twice more, only one of the rounds catching the side of the left head. The right eye was shattered and the distinct smell of burnt hair filled the chamber, but otherwise the giant ghoul continued forehead.

Shaking his head with utter disbelief, Henry rolled away, still trying to wrap his head around what was now chasing him.

Back in California, he'd been forced to fight a large zombie, more than six feet tall. The ghoul's arms had been huge and it had towered over him. He had been lucky then, having taken a grenade from a nearby soldier cheering on the fight, but this time there would be no grenade to save the day and his carbine felt woefully inadequate.

The zombie roared with both mouths and swung its massive arms towards him. Henry jumped out of the way, coming up in a crouch. He fired again at the heads, but the blast went through the middle of them, almost as if the heads had sensed the shot.

His jaw tight, Henry decided he would have to belay shooting the heads and take the easier targets of the massive torso.

Jumping onto a lab table and bending at the knees, he spun and fired twice into the zombie's chest. Rotten flesh exploded outward, but the ghoul shrugged off the impacts, the blows of the rounds barely fazing it. With a roar and ham-sized fists swinging, the ghoul charged Henry.

Firing again, Henry took off three of the ghoul's left fingers and then had to retreat yet again. His left sneaker came down on one of the dead lab techs and the squishing of entrails caused him to slip like he'd stepped on ice.

His feet went out from under him and he fell heavily to the floor, the vibration of heavy feet still growing closer. Rolling onto his side, he raised the carbine and shot the ghoul at point blank range. The blast went into the zombie's lower abdomen, blasting flesh and bone away, but when Henry went to fire again, the carbine clicked dry.

"You've got to be kidding me," Henry breathed as he looked down at the now impotent weapon.

He had fired his last shot, and now, with this massive ghoul coming for him, he had no weapon.

With nothing to use as an offensive weapon, he took to the defensive, and as the ghoul came at him, he crawled under another table, his palms crunching in the glass on the floor. He ignored the hundreds of slivers, knowing his time was short, and as he came out the other side, the ghoul turned and gazed down at him. Three eyes, all dead white seemed to bore into his skull, and the large mouth opened on the right face, a bone chilling wail issuing forth. Swallowing the knot in his throat, Henry crawled on hands and knees until he'd given himself some much needed distance. The ghoul, angry his prey was escaping, reached down and pushed the lab table to the side, the legs scraping across the floor.

Henry looked left and right, trying to find something he could use as a weapon, but once again he came up blank.

Then, in the shadows of the emergency lights, he saw the gaping chest cavity of the giant ghoul glistening red and brown. As the ghoul moved closer, Henry could see organs and a shattered ribcage within.

An idea came to him, though risky, but at the moment he was out of ideas. The power was still off and Jimmy couldn't help him. All he had was his own bare hands, and as the ghoul stomped closer, he prayed that would be all he needed.

Moving to the left, the ghoul charged and Henry tried to get out of the way, but he tripped over another corpse of a hapless lab tech. The zombie seemed to rage in victory, and before Henry realized it, he was being picked up by two hands that wrapped around his waist like he was a small child. He screamed in pain as he was lifted into the air. He was about a foot from the ghoul's two heads. The arms of the zombie were held outright and it was like Henry was a rag doll a small child was inspecting.

But his hands were free, and as the miasma of fetidness washed over him, Henry held his breath and used both hands to reach into the gaping chest cavity before him, tearing out whatever he could reach.

His hands wrapped around something that resembled a kidney, and upon pulling it out, he brought up the organ and jammed the foul meat into the left head's mouth. Teeth clamped down on the dripping organ, blood shooting out of the sides like a wet sponge as yellow teeth began to chew. Henry reached into the cavity for more, his arms up to the elbows in gore. This time he came out with what he thought was a liver and he turned his head and aimed for the right mouth, slamming the liver into the gnashing teeth and pulling his fingers back before he lost them.

Though he was dangling in the air, the two heads were placated for the moment, chewing on organs from its own body.

Henry reached in again, digging at the cavity like he was playing in the mud. Out came a pancreas, followed by a spleen, then he began tearing at the cracked ribcage. The heart came next, a massive organ thanks to the size of the owner, and he force fed it to the left head after it finished with its previous bloody morsel. By now the right head was looking for more to eat and its eyes were now looking straight at Henry.

Acting fast, he ripped out the half-eaten heart from the teeth of the left head and slammed them into the open mouth of the right. Then he got back to work, digging at the opened chest cavity like he was digging for gold.

He knew he had seconds before the two heads finished off their meal and decided to just eat him.

His hands and arms were a bloody mess of blood and pus, viscous fluids dripping down his elbows and splashing on his chest. The front of his jumpsuit was now stained red and black, but still he dug deep, pushing aside greasy gelatinous organs for what he knew was his only chance for salvation.

Then the two heads finished their appetizers and three eyes looked down at Henry, wanting him for the main course. With his teeth gritted and his face covered in gore, his two hands found what he was looking for inside the giant ghoul.

Wrapping his hands around the spinal column like it was a large tree root stuck in the ground, he yanked with all his might, screaming loudly with the effort.

There was a loud ripping sound and the spine of the ghoul tore free, looking like a red snake in Henry's hands. It seemed to flop around with nervous life and he held it away from him. The ghoul roared in what sure as hell seemed like pain, and then, as suddenly as the roar had begun, it stopped, the massive body toppling to the ground like a fallen oak.

Henry felt himself falling four feet to the floor and he curled up into a ball, hitting hard. The hands around him let go and he rolled to the side, glass and blood seeping into his jumpsuit.

He lay there, staring up at the ceiling when one of the zombie's meaty fists began to twitch, the fingers jerking like it had been pumped with electricity. Henry's eyes went wide and he began scrambling away, but as soon as it began, the fingers stopped moving.

Just some residual energy in the dying zombie's system.

Henry was now aware there was banging coming from somewhere. Looking around, he realized it was from across the room, where the door was.

Standing up, he swayed on his feet as he sucked deep lungfuls of air into his tortured lungs. His ribs ached from where the giant hands had held him, knowing they could have crushed him if the ghoul hadn't decided to play with its food for a while.

Reaching down, he found the empty carbine, and on weak legs, hobbled back to the door.

Just as he reached it the power snapped back on, the door sliding up and Jimmy charging in, his carbine pointing every which way.

"Jesus Christ, Henry, you okay? I heard the shots and what sounded like a fucking earthquake in here, but I couldn't get in." He then saw the state Henry was in. "Holy shit, are you hurt?"

Henry shook his head. "Nah, not really. Got a few cuts on my hands, but believe it or not I'm fine."

"What the hell happened in here?" Jimmy asked as he stared around the large laboratory. Now with the lights on, the carnage was easy to see. Bodies were everywhere, lab techs and ghouls alike. Jimmy spotted the massive feet of the giant ghoul and the two heads, but the rest was hidden behind an overturned table.

"What the hell is that?" Jimmy asked.

Henry glanced over his shoulder at the dead giant and he shrugged.

"That was something I never want to do again for the rest of my life. Come on, the girls aren't in here. Let's keep moving," he said as he began walking out of the lab.

As he stepped into the corridor, he saw the cooling bodies of three guards. Jimmy came up behind him, seeing Henry had spotted his handiwork.

"Yeah, uhm, had some company while you were in there. I hid to the side and got them all when they came around the corner. I'll tell ya, Henry; these guys aren't much for fighting, thank God." Henry said nothing, but instead moved to the closest guard's corpse. The man had been shot in the head, and though there was blood everywhere, his black jumpsuit was relatively clean. Henry leaned over and began stripping him of his clothing.

"Hey, old man, we don't have time for that," Jimmy said as the door to the lab slid closed behind him.

"I need his clothes, Jimmy, look at me," Henry said as he slid a limp arm out of the black sleeve.

"Fine, but I don't think you want the guy's pants," Jimmy said, pointing to the wet spot where the man had fouled himself when he'd died. The distinct aroma of urine and feces came to him.

"Yeah, good point, but the shirt will work just fine. Just keep watch."

Jimmy nodded, and while he moved about the hallway, Henry quickly shrugged out of his jumpsuit. The guard had a small knife and Henry quickly cut the top half of his jumpsuit off, then slid into the black shirt. It was an off contrast, but he felt a lot better. Using the inside and back of the old jumpsuit, he wiped his face as clean as he could get it, then dropped the bloody rag to the floor.

He was still pretty filthy, but it would do for now. At the moment there was more important things to worry about than being dirty.

The sound of running footsteps came from the opposite corridor and Henry knew they had seconds if that.

"Okay, let's move out, company's coming," he said as he stood up, now holding two of the dead guard's carbines. One he slung over his shoulder, the other he held in his hands.

Jimmy said nothing, hearing the thudding footsteps, and pointed to the hall they had been moving down before Henry had entered the lab.

Without a word, Henry nodded and the two men charged down the corridor, not wanting to engage more guards if they didn't have to.

The girls were somewhere in the complex and their time was running out.

# Chapter 33

"**D**amn, this place is huge," Jimmy said as they turned down another corridor.

"Yeah, I know, can you imagine what it must have cost to build this place?" Henry mused.

"No shit, and they did it all underwater in the middle of the mountains, messed up," Jimmy said while shaking his head.

Henry grinned. "Your tax dollars at work."

"Huh, not mine. Back at Pineridge was my first job; I just started paying taxes when the shit hit the fan."

"Yeah, well, I guess all that cash I put into social security is a wash now," Henry said. "Now enough talk, it's been quiet so far, but that's got to change sooner or later."

Jimmy nodded, knowing what Henry meant.

Since leaving the lab with the zombie freaks, they had come across ten guards or so. They only had to fight once, and they had taken the two men dressed in black out with their hands and the butts of their carbines. The other times they had managed to remain hidden. But they knew their time of being able to move about the complex unhindered was growing short. Any second now they knew one of the bodies they were leaving in their wake would be discovered and then all bets were off. While they remained hidden, they were able to study the guards' movements as they passed, and it was strange how they acted. They did seem to be searching for them, but then if they did, why wasn't an alarm sounding? It was then that he realized they still weren't searching for him and Jimmy, but were probably still on the hunt for Jack. That was good, it gave him an edge he knew he would need. The complex was vast and it seemed there weren't enough men to patrol the entire place, which would explain why no one had found the guards they had already taken down. But sooner or later that luck would change, it had to.

They had found a schematic on one of the walls, the paper map trapped behind plexiglass. After studying it for a few seconds,

Henry had a good idea where they were and where they needed to go.

As they passed yet another hallway, working their way to what they believed to be the breeding wing, Jimmy paused when he thought he heard a voice.

Henry stopped when he realized Jimmy wasn't with him and he turned.

"What's the matter?"

"Did you hear something?" Jimmy asked, cocking his head to the side.

Henry walked back to Jimmy and listened and then he heard it to. Someone was calling their names.

"Hey, guys, over here," the voice said.

Jimmy turned and walked a few feet and looked up at one of the metal gratings for the heat and air conditioning.

"Hey, Henry, I think someone's in here," Jimmy said while standing on his toes.

"Of course there's someone in here, you idiot," Jack said in a whisper. "What do you think I am, a talking rat?"

"Pretty damn close," Jimmy said with a grin.

"Help me out of here, I can't get the damn grating off," Jack said in a frustrated tone.

Henry moved next to Jimmy, and after a few seconds the two managed to pry the grating off. Henry had to use the muzzle of the carbine as a pry bar, but the strengthened steel was stronger than the thin grating.

Twenty seconds later, the grating was hanging from bent hinges and Jack was on the floor, wiping dirt and dust off his once white jumpsuit which was now a dull gray.

"Wow, thanks, I've been in there for like forever. I thought I was never gonna get out," he said and then sneezed.

"Bless you," Henry said.

"Thanks," Jack replied.

"Okay, so it's good to see you, Jack, but we need to move. There's guards everywhere and sooner or later there's gonna be..."

His words were cut off when an alarm began to sound, shrill like a klaxon.

*ATTENTION... ATTENTION... THE CAPTIVES HAVE ESCAPED, LETHAL FORCE IS AUTHORIZED. ATTENTION, ATTENTION, THE...* and the message continued to repeat itself.

"Dammit, our times up, boys, let's move," Henry yelled over the loud alarm and metallic voice.

Footsteps were coming down the hallway and Henry grabbed Jack by his dirty jumpsuit dragging him the other way. All three of them plastered themselves against the far wall, carbines up, and waited to see what would happen next.

The heavy stomping grew louder until six black-garbed security guards, complete with dark glasses, charged past where Henry and the others were hiding. Henry crossed his fingers the men would miss the grating which had been pushed back, but now didn't fit right, and he got his wish as the footsteps receded down the corridor and were soon lost thanks to the loud alarm.

"Good, we got lucky, but it's gonna run out sooner or later," he said. "Come on, let's go find the girls."

"I think I know where they might be," Jack said as he began to follow Henry and Jimmy.

Henry never slowed, barley listening, "Go on," he said almost absentmindedly, his ear cocked for the sounds of more guards.

Jack quickly filled him in on what he'd seen while crawling through the ducts, and finished by telling Henry about the armory and the supplies and shelves of ordinance stored inside, including the blocks that looked like Playdoh.

That got Henry's attention and he stopped so fast Jack ran into his back.

"Wait a second, so you know where the armory is?" Henry asked.

Jack grinned. "Yeah, well, uhm, pretty sure. I mean, I was in the walls and stuff, but I think I know where it is compared to where we are now."

Jimmy rolled his eyes. "Which is it, brat? Either you do or you don't."

"Shut up, Jimmy, I said I was in the ducts!" Jack yelled back over the alarms.

Henry gritted his teeth in anger at the two young men.

"Knock it of, both of you, there's no time for that shit now! We need to work together," he snapped.

"Sorry, Henry," Jimmy said ruefully.

"Yeah, me too," Jack added.

"I don't care about apologies, goddammit, we need to find the girls and get the hell out of here. Now, Jack, can you find that armory or not?"

Jack nodded, sure of himself. "Yeah, I can find it."

"Okay, then let's go. Which way, Jack?"

Jack looked at each of the hallways that would lead to different parts of the complex. Doing the math in his head, he then pointed to the right.

"That way."

"You're sure?"

"Yeah, well, pretty sure," he said.

"Forget it, it's good enough. 'Sides we gotta go somewhere," Henry said. "Okay, move out and stay sharp." As they began walking down the hallway, Henry handed Jack the extra carbine from off his shoulder.

Jack's eyes went wide. "No, shit, for me?"

"Yes, but only if it's life or death, you hear me? The safety is here, it's on now," Henry said while pointing.

"Cool," Jack gasped.

"Just point and shoot, but watch where you aim that thing, hear me?" Henry warned.

Jack barely did.

"I said, do you hear me?" Henry said, his tone hard.

"Yeah, yeah, I hear you," Jack replied, his chest now thrust out, feeling like one of the team.

For the next seven minutes the three of them worked their way through the complex, avoiding guards as they charged past like German stormtroopers from an old movie. Henry found it odd the way the men were acting. They weren't searching, just rushing around like mice in a cage. Not that he was complaining.

"Hey, Henry, what's the point of trying to find the armory?" Jimmy asked. I mean, we got guns, so let's find the girls and get the hell out of here."

"I hear you, Jimmy, but Jack said the armory had blocks of what he thought looked like Playdoh. You know what he really saw, right?"

"Shit, C-4?"

Henry nodded. "Has to be, and with that we can make sure to leave these bastards a little present before we leave."

Jimmy grinned widely, understanding what Henry meant.

"Damn that's sweet, okay, I'm with ya, let's do it."

"Fine, but remember, we need to find the girls first; we're not leaving without 'em. Either we all leave or none of us do, right?"

Jimmy nodded, his jaw tight and his features serious. "Damn straight, all or nothing."

"All or nothing," Jack repeated.

Then the alarm cut out and it became deathly silent.

"The alarm, it stopped," Jimmy said. "Is that good or bad?"

"Don't know, probably bad," Henry answered.

Suddenly there was the sound of more footsteps and clipped voices could be heard, all rapidly growing closer. Henry and Jimmy looked around, but there was nowhere to hide. They were in a long hallway with no doors or indents, just flat wall on both sides. They could try to turn and run back the way they'd come, but by the closeness of the footsteps he knew they would never make it in time.

"Shit, they got us cold," Henry spit. "Against the wall, now. As soon as the guards turn the corner, take 'em out. All we can do is hope we get them before they get us." He looked down to Jack. "Sorry, son, but it looks like you're gonna get to try that gun sooner than I would've liked."

Jack gazed back stoically. "I'm ready, Henry."

Henry smiled, proud of the boy.

Only seconds had passed since the first detection of the approaching footsteps, and as the three warriors raised the muzzles of their captured carbines towards the end of the hallway, they prepared to ambush the guards, and prayed it wouldn't end their own lives in the coming shootout.

# Chapter 34

Henry's knuckles were white as he squeezed the carbine, ready for the firefight to come. Next to him, Jimmy's jaw was firm, and Henry could see the determination in his eyes. Even Jack was prepared to die if it came to it. Though young and full of life, the boy's world was now one of death and decay, darkness seeming to be everywhere. But every once and a while a light would burst through the shadows.

"Wait for them to show themselves then let 'em have it," Henry said through tight lips.

Jimmy and Jack both nodded, and as the footsteps grew closer, Henry raised the carbine so he would be in perfect alignment with the chest of the first target.

So when the people who belonged to those footsteps appeared, his finger was hovering on the trigger, only a quarter ounce of pressure needed to let loose a barrage of death.

But at the last instant, he held his fire, seeing the unmistakable face of Mary, her long brown hair now tied back into a pony tail. And next to her were Cindy, Sue and Raven, the women unaware they were walking into a shooting match.

"Wait, hold, your fire, it's the girls," Henry said as he raised his carbine, his finger so close to squeezing the trigger and shooting Mary. Jimmy did the same but his eyes were only for Cindy.

But Jack was new to the whole guns and ammo thing and he was too filled with adrenalin to slow his trigger finger. Henry glanced down at the boy the instant he called out to hold fire and saw Jack going to shoot.

Using the muzzle of his carbine, Henry reached out and whacked the tip of Jack's gun, the muzzle now dropping to the floor. Jack still squeezed the trigger, but the shot went into the floor, leaving a long groove and scorch marks a foot long.

"Sorry," Jack said when he realized he had almost killed one of the women.

"No harm done, Jack, just listen better next time," Henry said, relieved he'd managed to stop Jack in time.

Across the hallway, Mary went into a crouch, as did Cindy, Raven and Sue. Mary had a carbine of her own and she prepared to fire at the source of the gunshot.

Henry stepped out and held his arms wide, so she could see who it was.

"Wait, Mary, don't shoot, it's us!" Henry called out as he looked down the muzzle of her blaster.

Mary's face was first filled with anger at everything she'd been through this day, but then her features softened and she lowered the carbine.

"Oh my God, Henry? Is it really you?"

"Who else would it be?" He said as he held out his hands to her.

She took off at a run, closing the distance in seconds. Henry was waiting for her and as the two met, he crushed her to his chest in a bear hug.

"Oh, Henry, we've been looking for you guys, but this place is a rat's maze," she said as she hugged him tightly. Behind Mary, Raven and Sue were jogging up, Cindy going to Jimmy and Sue moving up next to Henry. He held out his free arm, and Sue came into his embrace, while Raven and Jack said hello to each other.

"Tell me about it," Henry said. "I feel like the mouse searching for cheese in here. We've been looking for you, too, but as you said, this place is huge."

"So what now?" Cindy asked. Jimmy was grinning at the women's outfits. They were still in their hospital gowns, their bare behinds exposed for all to see. She saw Jimmy's lecherous smirk and she pointed a finger at him threateningly, warning him to be silent. He nodded he would, though his grin grew even wider.

"Simple, we blow this place to Hell and get out of here," Henry said as he stepped away from Mary. "Okay, listen up. We're in a bad situation right now, but we've been in worse, so stay sharp and follow my lead."

The women nodded, all knowing there wasn't time for more than one leader.

That was when Henry realized they were missing someone. "Hey, where's Carol?"

Mary shook her head sadly, and through gritted teeth, told Henry what happened in quick, short words, knowing there wasn't time to go into detail now.

Henry shook his head, the anger apparent. After what Mary had said it could have easily been one of them in the laser probe instead of Carol.

Jimmy was watching their backs, and as he waited for them to get going, he saw a security guard come walking around the bend. The guard didn't expect to see seven intruders standing out in the open, and why the guard was alone Jimmy never found out. The man's face lit up with surprise when he realized he'd found what he was searching for.

But Jimmy was ready the instant the man stepped into view, and as the guard lowered his carbine, Jimmy shot the man three times, the first round striking his groin, and then as Jimmy let the muzzle climb, the other two shots walked up his torso, until the third took out the man's neck in a spray of blood that painted the white wall scarlet.

Everyone turned at the gunshots, weapons coming up, but Henry told everyone to relax, seeing Jimmy had taken care of the problem.

"Nice shooting, Jimmy." He turned to Raven. "Raven, go get that guard's weapon, we'll need it," he ordered her as he turned to the other women.

"Okay, let's go, we'll fill you in on the rest of the plan while we're moving."

Raven returned and Cindy took the carbine, feeling better now that she was armed. Jack took point, leading the way and Jimmy and Cindy took up the rear in case anymore guards showed up.

One advantage the companions had was with the complex being so large, there were only so many men to search it.

Rounding a tight bend in the hall, Jimmy and Henry stopped short when five lab techs gaped at them with open mouths, their eyes flicking from the companion's faces to the carbines in their hands.

Henry's carbine was aimed at their chests, but when he saw they weren't armed, he held his fire.

"Wait, don't shoot, we're not armed," the first tech yelled. His blonde hair was cut short and there were pimples on his chin and forehead.

"Don't move, and keep your hands where I can see 'em, all of you," Henry ordered. The lab techs complied, some raising their arms so high in the air it was comical.

"Do you know where the armory is?" Henry asked. Behind him, the others waited, carbines leveled at the techs.

The blonde man seemed to be the spokesman for the lab group and he nodded.

"Go down this hallway, take a right, then go to the next junction, take a left and then another right at the second junction after that. The door will be on the right side."

Henry turned to Mary, Sue and Cindy. "You guys get all that that?"

Sue nodded as did Cindy. "Yup, right, left, and right, the door is on the right hand side," Sue repeated.

"What are we going to do with them?" Mary asked. We can't just kill them in cold blood."

Henry looked at her and nodded. "Yeah, I know, these guys might not be guilty of anything." He turned and looked at the blonde haired tech. "You, where's the nearest storeroom or stockroom, or a janitor's closet."

The lab tech pointed behind him, over the other lab tech's shoulders. "Back there, about twenty feet, there's a supply closet, why?"

Henry gestured for the group of lab techs to turn and get moving. "You'll find out, now move, to the supply closet."

With mumbles of protestation the lab techs moved out, Jimmy taking up the rear once again. Stomping footsteps could be heard coming from a short distance behind them, but they echoed in the hallway. For now they seemed to be alone.

In less than a minute the lab techs were standing in front of the supply closet.

"Okay, get inside, all of you," Henry told them.

One of the men next to the door opened it and they shuffled inside. The closet was small and the lab techs had to cram themselves inside. Henry thought they looked like a bunch of college kids trying to see how many people could fit into a phone booth. By the time the blonde haired man was inside, they were nut to butt and not too happy.

"You can't do this to us, there's no room in here," the man protested vehemently.

With a scowl Henry shoved the muzzle of the carbine under the man's chin. "Would you prefer I just kill you all and be done with it? I can't leave you to run around, you'll tell the guards where we are."

"No, we won't, I swear," the lab tech said, the others all agreeing they would never tell.

"Sure, and I'm Mary Poppins, now one last thing. How do we get out of here, where's the exit?"

The man clamped his lips tight and Henry pushed harder on the carbine, the tech's chin rising a few inches.

"There's an elevator on the north side of the complex, about ten minutes walk from here. He pointed to the hallway wall. See that thin black line near the ceiling?"

Henry and the others turned, and though they hadn't seen it before, they now saw there was a very thin black line that ran the length of the ceiling. It seemed to go on till the end of the hallway where it dog-eared to the right.

"Yeah, what about it?" Henry said.

"Well, that's how you find the elevator. They don't put it on the maps on the walls, same as the armory; for security reasons."

Jimmy nodded from where he stood watch. "That explains why we didn't see them on the maps, Henry."

"Yeah, it does." Henry grinned as he removed the carbine from the man's lower jaw, leaving the circular impression in his skin from the muzzle.

"Thanks, pal, you're all right, now you stay put in there and it'll all be over in a bit. 'Cause if you get out and I see any of you again I'm gonna blow your heads off; you get me?"

The tech nodded, as did the others.

He closed the door and used the butt of his carbine to smash the doorknob, trapping the men inside the closest. There were protests from inside, but what they didn't seem to realize is that they should have been glad to be alive.

"Okay, so we know where to go, let's move out. Cindy and Jimmy, you two stay in the rear and watch our backs. Mary, you're with me on point. Sue, Raven and Jack, in the middle," he instructed as they headed out, now with a true destination in mind, not just wandering and hoping they found the armory.

As they jogged down the corridor, Mary asked. "Hey, Henry, it's great we didn't kill those men back, there but won't they just die in the explosion we're gonna set?"

Henry shrugged as he jogged. "Maybe, maybe not. Look, Mary, we can't save the world. If they're innocent then I hope they survive, if they're not, then what happens, happens. Now forget them and focus on the hear and now, we're not free yet."

As if to prove his point, they rounded the first junction and came upon the backs of four security guards. The men were facing the wrong way and never realized they were in trouble until the first round struck the middle guard, blowing out the front of his shirt in a spray of blood and entrails. The other three men had begun turning, but it was too little too late. Mary fired high, used to killing ghouls, and her bullets struck the next guard in the neck, literally severing the head from the shoulders. The head flopped to the side, only a thin tendril of flesh preventing it from falling away from the torso. A brilliant spray of blood shot out of the stump to bathe the other guards in red. Shocked by the death and warm spray of one of their own, they were too shook up to return fire and Henry took out the other two with well placed shots.

As the bodies twitched on the floor, the companions reached them. "Get their guns," Henry told the others. "We'll need them."

The four carbines were gathered and the companions moved off, weaving their way through the corridors.

They came upon one more security patrol, but once again were faster on the draw. As they turned into the last junction, the bodies spasmed on the floor behind them, blood seeping out of jagged wounds as the corpses finally came to rest after falling in a tangle of arms and legs across the floor.

# Chapter 35

The door to the armory was sturdier than most of the other doors in the complex, but it yielded to a succession of powerful kicks from Henry's right foot. The door was a standard one with hinges, and with a squealing of weakening metal, the hinges finally split and the door burst open, revealing shelves and lockers full of munitions.

"Let's keep it moving, people," Henry said as he entered the room. Jimmy stayed in the corridor, keeping watch for security patrols while the others entered the room. Upon finding their laundered clothing, they tore off their jumpsuits and hospital gowns and quickly dressed.

Henry was elated to find his Glock and panga sitting on a shelf, looking the same as when they were taken from him. Jimmy's new pump-action shotgun was there, too, and so were Jimmy and Mary's .38's. Next to them sat Cindy's M-16, plus their hunting knives. Even their footwear was there and Henry couldn't imagine a better feeling then when he tore off the bloody sneakers and put on his worn work boots.

It took less than five minutes for everyone to get dressed, gather their weapons and belongings, and get ready to leave.

Jimmy traded places with Jack so he could get dressed in his original clothing, the starched odor of the shirt somewhat off putting. In the world of the walking dead, something like starched shirts just felt wrong.

"So what's next?" Cindy asked as she hefted her M-16. She preferred her own rifle over one of the carbines.

"Next is we take all the C-4 we can carry and find somewhere to plant the stuff to make sure this place goes sky high when it goes off," Henry said as he moved deeper into the armory. There were small munitions bags on a bottom shelf so he grabbed one and began shoving blocks of C-4 into them. "Mary, see if there are any timers, they've got to be here somewhere," he told her.

"Okay," she said and began searching lockers and shelves, Raven helping her.

"Found 'em," Mary said as she began pulling the timers out of a locker and shoving them into a bag.

"Good, take all you can, better to have more than not," Henry said. "Oh, and grab some of those flash bangs, too."

While Mary worked, she thought of something. "Hey, Henry, what happens if when we get to the elevator there's some kind of security code or something and we can't get it to work?"

Henry shook his head. "That's a good question, but for now let's deal with setting these charges. We'll deal with the elevator when the time comes."

"All right, but I don't want to be standing at the doors without a card or code when the bombs go off," she said.

"That makes two of us," he chuckled as he shoved the last of the C-4 bricks into a bag and prepared to leave. Sue, Cindy, and Raven were gathering extra ammunition, shoving them into gray satchels. Whatever happened next, at least they would be armed and ready.

Henry spotted a small .22 pistol on a shelf and he picked it up. Ammo was next to it and empty clips so with practiced ease, he filled the clip, then did two more.

"Hey, Sue, come here, will you please?"

She entered the armory, now dressed in her original clothes. "Yes?"

"Here, I want you to take this."

She frowned. "But, Henry, I told you before I don't like guns and I'm not good with them. I'd likely shoot one of you by accident then who I'm aiming for."

"Maybe, but it would still make me feel better if you had one. This is small, there's almost no kick. Here are the safety's," he pointed. "That's it, just point and shoot, piece of cake." He handed it to her. "Please, for me."

She looked into his eyes, the eyes of the man she now loved, and she melted,

"Fine," she said as she took it.

"Good, thanks, just put it in the small of your back or back pocket, that way your shirt will hide it."

She did as she was told and he sent her back into the hall.

There was another map of the complex on the wall of the armory and Henry pulled his panga, hitting the plexiglass with the hilt. The plastic shattered into big chunks and Henry used the tip of the blade to pry off the large shards that hadn't fallen so he could get at the map beneath. Mary was watching him and she had her head cocked to the side in curiosity.

"I'm tired of not knowing where we are. With this we can find what we need." He looked at it, studying it quickly. There was a red dot to signify where they were and he drew a line with his finger to where he thought would be a good place to set the charges.

"Okay, found a good place. We're done here, let's go," Henry said as he left the armory, the others right behind him.

Jimmy was on watch and nodded curtly, "So far it's been quiet," he said.

Henry shouldered the bag of C-4, and had the others do the same with theirs. They all needed their hands ready for when trouble found them. And it would, it was matter of *when*, not *if*.

"Okay, me and Mary are on point," Henry told them. "Jimmy and Cindy take the rear, the rest of you in the middle. From now on there's no stopping, whoever gets in our way, they're dead. If they aren't for us, they're against us, period. We've been lucky so far with the guards, but as we get closer to where we're going that's gonna change."

"Where are we going?" Cindy asked.

"The main control room," Henry said. "It's not far from here. We blow that and all the systems will crash, simple as that."

"So stop talking and let's get this show on the road," Jimmy said as he hefted his shotgun. The carbine was slung over his shoulder now. The shotgun was the perfect weapon in the close confines of the hallways. One shot to the floor in front of the targets and the pellets would ricochet in all directions, taking out everything in their path. It was called a room sweeper and it worked very well.

Suddenly, two sunglass-wearing guards stepped out from a side corridor only twenty paces from where Henry and the others stood. The problem was; they were all gathered close together, a perfect target for the two guards, there was no way the men could miss hitting one of companions.

The 9mm Glock was at Henry's side and already coming up the instant he spotted the two guards. With lightning speed, he took aim and fired, bracing himself even though the Glock didn't have much kick. He double-tapped the trigger, firing two rounds so close together they sounded like a single shot.

No sooner were the first two rounds out of the barrel then he shifted his aim slightly to the right and fired again, hitting the second guard. The two fresh corpses slid to the blood covered tiles of the hallway, their weapons clattering to the floor with them.

"Sweet," Jimmy said, admiring Henry's marksmanship.

The first guard had been hit in the center of his chest, both bullets no more than an inch apart. The force of the shots had lifted the man clean off his feet, throwing him backwards to bounce off the wall. The second two rounds had hit the other guard slightly higher, spinning his body as his sunglasses flew from his head, the glasses still sliding across the floor as the guard dropped to the floor, dead.

As the companions headed off, the hidden speakers in the wall began to hiss and crackle, then the distinct voice of Dr. Tandy filtered through. "*Report, section B, report, intruders have been spotted in section B, all patrols to section B, report. Terminate them all, repeat...*"

Somewhere in one of the hallways behind them a siren began to sound.

"Looks like the jig is up," Jimmy said as he looked around like a caged animal.

"Yeah, that's our cue to leave. Let's get moving," Henry said and they began walking down the hallway.

Though their position was known, it looked like all the guards must have been in other sections and were still making their way to the companion's location, because they moved through the corridors unhindered. They had almost made it to the nearest entrance to the control center, which was just around the next turn, when two attractive female researchers walked around the corner with a security guard behind them.

For a moment no one did anything, each staring at the other. Though Henry had just said anyone blocking them must die, he wasn't a cold blooded killer and for all he knew, the two women in front of him were innocent, merely victims in Dr Tandy's crazed ideas. But then, any thought of showing mercy vanished when the women on the right, with red hair, screamed at the guard.

"Kill them! They're the intruders!"

Mary was the first to react, and before the guard could get his carbine up, Mary shot the man in the forehead, blowing pulpy red and pink brain tissue mixed with bone fragments out the rear of his skull. In the hallway, the shot was deafening, and the two scientists were shocked into inactivity for a half-second.

Raven moved up to Henry. "They're mine," she said and attacked the two women, her hands a blur of action.

The red haired woman seemed to know how to fight and she jumped back when Raven came at her, arms windmilling as her razor-sharp nails blurred in front of the woman's face. The red head tried to fight back, but Raven was too fast, and after a swift kick to the chin, which rocked the red head's skull backwards, Raven slid in for the kill. She still had the scalpel taken from the lab and she used it now, slicing it horizontally across the woman's throat and sending a torrent of blood spewing from the severed artery. The scientist reached up with shaking hands to try and staunch the warm flow of plasma, but it was hopeless, and she was already falling to her knees in death. The second woman screamed with rage at the death of her partner and charged at Raven with vengeance in her eyes. From somewhere on her person she pulled a small knife and Raven prepared to meet her.

Suddenly, there was another gunshot and the attacking woman's open mouth received a .38 round which penetrated her skull and then rebounded and exited an inch above her left ear. The exploding round took off a large portion of her dirty blonde hair and the earring in her ear was blown clean off, along with the ear.

The force of the impact was so great that as the exit hole appeared in her head, it sucked out most of the woman's brain, the pinkish mass splattering to the floor like kidney pie.

Raven spun on Cindy with anger in her eyes.

"I had her, you didn't have to do that."

Henry spoke first. "I told her to, we don't have time for this shit, Raven. We need to keep moving, well done though."

Raven calmed her breathing and nodded, understanding immediately. This wasn't the time for fighting when a bullet would do the job. Both women scientists might have survived if they hadn't turned and attacked them.

"It's a good start, though," Mary said as they headed out. "If these two were like Dr. Stanley then they died too easy."

Henry nodded. He had no real idea what Mary and the other women had been through, so he wasn't going to judge. All he knew was the two scientists had saved him a dilemma and he wondered if his resolve would hold firm the next time they came upon noncombatants, though not wanting to believe it, it seemed everyone in this crazy place was their enemy.

Behind them the sirens began again, rising and falling in pitch. Henry was beginning to think he was asleep and this was all some kind of insane dream. They were moving through the empty hallways of a complex, which was deep underwater in a lake which was nestled in the beautiful mountains of Colorado. They were taking out security guards and scientists one after another, and yet despite this, there was no comeback, no armed massive assault from the facilities security personnel to kill them.

At least, not yet.

# Chapter 36

There was only one guard blocking the door to the control center when the companions came within view of it. The guard had his back to them, his carbine pointed to the floor.

His sunglass-covered eyes were watching something across the hall and Henry craned his head and saw it was a light, flashing on and off.

Next to the door was a sign that read. **Authorized Personnel Only, all others will be terminated without warrant or approval.**

"I got this one," Jack said excitedly at seeing such an easy target. Before anyone could stop him, he'd hefted his carbine and was charging into the hallway, wanting to take out the guard and pull his weight.

But this guard was slightly faster than his predecessors, and when he heard the sounds of Jack's sneakers slapping the floor, he spun, his carbine coming up as the man's finger squeezed the trigger.

One second Jack was smiling as he prepared to take out his first enemy, and the next he was flying backwards, his chest a mass of red as the blast from the carbine blew him off his feet.

"Nooo!" Henry yelled and raised his Glock, pumping three rounds into the guard's torso without stopping. The man bounced off the door to the control center and hit the floor hard, spitting blood and laying immobile.

With the guard down, everyone ran into the hallway and Jimmy stood watch while Sue and Henry kneeled over Jack's small form.

"Jack, Jack, can you hear me?" Henry pleaded as he tried to see if he could staunch the flow of blood seeping from the massive wound. But Jack's chest was hamburger, and there was no way.

Even if the boy had been in a hospital it was highly doubtful he could have been saved. He'd been shot dead center in the chest.

Spitting blood, Jack opened his eyes and looked up at Henry. His eyes were glazed and he smiled wanly, his lips coated red.

"Did I get him? Did I take the guy out?"

Henry's voice was tight in his throat as he nodded. "Sure did, son, you took him out good, he never saw what hit him. Thanks to you we're all set."

"See, told you I could do it," he said, his voice barely a whisper. He coughed, more blood coming from his mouth to drip onto the floor. His eyes lost focus for a second and then he was back. "Hey, Jimmy," Jack gasped. "I got him before you."

Though Jimmy had fought with Jack from day one, he liked the kid and now his voice was fraught with emotion.

"You sure did, brat, you got him before I had a chance to raise my shotgun. Great job."

Jimmy turned his head slightly to cover his grief and Henry looked back down at Jack, this small boy who had joined them a short time ago, a boy he'd said he would protect.

"So does that mean I can stay with you guys now? When you leave here, can I come, too?"

Henry's eyes were blurry and he wiped them clear with the back of his sleeve. "Sure you can, there was never any question of that."

Jack nodded, but his breathing was slowing. "That's great, Henry, that's real great. You know, I always wanted a real family, never really had one. I just wish..."

His head slumped to the side and Sue let out a soft screech as she turned away, crying. Cindy and Mary had tears in their eyes, and Raven, though stoic to the last, had to turn away, her eyes cloudy with loss.

Henry reached down and closed Jack's eyes with tears running freely down his cheeks now. He'd known it had been too good, their luck had finally changed.

Wiping his eyes again, Henry stood up and walked over to the prone guard. The man was still alive, the shots to his chest not fatal.

"You no good fucking bastard," Henry said through gritted teeth. "You just killed a boy, a fucking boy!" His tone went up in pitch until he was screaming.

The guard was awake and he stared up at Henry with fear in his eyes. He tried to back away, his head coming up and banging against the door to the control room.

"Henry, what are you gonna do?" Mary asked, tears filling her eyes as she hovered over Jack's still form.

"I'm gonna do what we should've done from the beginning. Killed them all and without hesitation. He reached down and picked up the fallen guard's carbine, unhooking the strap. Then he straddled the guard and wrapped the strap around the muscular neck, pulling it taut.

"You just killed a friend of mine, you bastard, a good kid who was under my protection," Henry growled. Spittle flew from his lips as his anger grew. As he pulled the strap tighter, it bit into the man's neck, cutting off his oxygen. The guard feebly raised his hands trying to fend Henry off, but he was too slow, the strap biting deeper and deeper into his throat. Henry jerked the strap hard, pulling the man forward, the man's body now so close he could smell the stink of him. The sunglasses fell from the man's face and were crushed by Henry's left boot as he prepared to pop the fucker's head clean off.

"*Die, you no good bastard!*" Henry screamed as he kneed the man in the groin, feeling the satisfying impact as he caught the guard's genitals between his knee and pelvic bone. The man slumped sideways but Henry still didn't let up, his arms tight, his muscles pronounced like steel cords as he squeezed tighter and tighter, the strap cutting so tight it could barely be seen in the folds of purpled flesh. The man's tongue began to swell, the hands fell limp to his sides, and his eyes burst from their sockets. A small rivulet of bright scarlet trickled out of the corner of his mouth and out his nose to splatter on the floor. As the body relaxed in death, Henry could smell the redolence of urine and feces as the man's bowels were voided.

Stepping back, Henry dragged the corpse away from the door, then waved the others on.

"Leave Jack there for now, we've got work to do," he said, his chest heaving with the exertion of killing the guard, but feeling slightly better.

There would be time to mourn Jack properly later, but for now they needed to finish the job, or Jack would have died in vain.

All it took was a piece of plastic explosive the size of a quarter, a ten second fuse, and a tiny copper detonator to blast their way inside what was essentially the brains of the complex. The small explosion made their ears rattle as the door was blown out of its frame to clatter on the floor.

With smoke still hanging in the air, Henry peered around the bent doorframe.

He was greeted by a handful of security guards who had been waiting patiently, all lined up to greet the invaders. They began shooting immediately, and Henry ducked back as bullets struck where his head had been a second ago.

There were six guards in total, and as soon as Henry stuck his head around the corner again to check, the guards began firing. Henry ducked back and looked to the others.

"We need to do this hard and quick. You guys with me?"

They all nodded.

"Okay, listen up, me and Jimmy will go in low, and then head right, Mary and Cindy, you go left. Raven and Sue, you stay out here till the coast is clear. Anyone comes down the hall, you get your butts inside with us, but make sure it's safe first."

"Okay, Henry, just be careful, we already lost Jack, God rest his soul, I don't want to lose one of you, too," Sue said softly.

He nodded. "Ditto for you, too." Then he turned to Mary. "Give me one of those flash bangs you got from the armory."

She handed him one. He held the small canister so the ring was on the top. That was all that was there in the armory, but it made sense. Grenades with shrapnel wouldn't be what you would want to use in an underwater complex, no, flash bangs were better. Lots of light and sound, but no explosion. Still, it would work well for him now.

He looked to Jimmy. "You ready?"

"Yeah, old man, let's go, you know how I hate all this sneaking around. Let's take the damn fight to them for once."

He grinned, knowing Jimmy's personality well, and after crouching low, he tossed the flash bang into the control room while bullets bounced off the wall and shot out of the doorway. After it went off, he dived through the doorway and rolled across the floor to come up in a shooter's stance, his carbine searching for a target. Jimmy rolled up next to him and Mary and Cindy did the same on the other side of the door.

The flash bang did its job well, immobilizing the guards with light and sound, and for a few precious moments they were blind and deaf.

As each of the companions rolled across the floor, the smoke hanging in the air helping hide them from view, they came up firing, their blasters firing on full auto when possible or in Jimmy's case as fast as he could pull the trigger.

Taken unawares by the flash bang, the security guards were each gunned down in a hail of lead, their bloody corpses jerking along the floor. Henry didn't slow down once the men were taken out. He jumped over their corpses, almost slipping on the spilled blood, and searched for more targets, knowing anyone else in the area would have suffered from the same effects of the flash bang.

Coming up behind him, Jimmy was looking back and forth, but there were no more targets.

"Where is everyone? That's it, just six guys?" Jimmy asked as he looked around. His shotgun was ready to go with a full load and he was eager to use the rest. The carbine slapped his shoulder and his .38 was back in its holster on his hip.

"Must be," Henry replied, Cindy and Mary walking up behind them.

"Think it's clear?" Jimmy asked.

"Looks to be, doesn't make sense though. Maybe with the alert, they're all out looking for us and only six were left behind to guard the control center. I mean, think about it, if you were trying to find us, would you think we'd come here?"

Jimmy nodded. "Yeah, good point, we'd have to be fucking crazy to do that," he replied sarcastically.

Henry turned to look at his friend, and when Jimmy didn't follow up, Henry looked away, studying the control room.

"I don't care why there's only six, it doesn't matter, now let's get to work," he said. "Sue, we need those bags!" Henry called out, and a second later Sue dragged the bags with the C-4 and timers into the room. She saw the dead bodies and made a disgusted face. Though she had traveled with the companions for months and was now considered one of them, she still had a hard time dealing with blood and bodies.

"Thanks," he said and unzipped them, taking out the bricks and timers. Sue looked around the control center, amazed at its vastness. Though all of them had an inkling to the size of the complex, the massive control room was truly amazing. Spidery scaffolding rose five stories high, interlocking with other frameworks of gray-painted metal. A nest of conduits, wires and pipes wound in and out of the darkness, seeming like they would go on forever.

As she stared at the scaffolding, she could see there were other doorways up there, which led to places she could only imagine. Realizing that the entire complex was man made and that man had built it under water, as well, she had to wonder how that same man could let the walking dead take over the world so easily.

"Sue, hand me one of those bricks, will you?" Henry said as he inspected a support beam. It was a foot thick and went high up into the shadows above. There were dozens of them scattered about the control room. Henry had a feeling if enough of them were taken out, the entire roof would collapse.

Pulled from her reverie, Sue did as she was asked, then walked over to Henry. "This place is amazing isn't it?"

Henry grunted a yes. "Maybe, but it's gonna be rubble in a bit, now go back to the door with Raven and keep an eye out. I can't believe we've been left alone for this long." He looked to Mary and Cindy. "You girls all right?"

"Yes, Henry, we're fine," Mary replied as she stuck a timer into a brick. "What do I set the timer for?"

"Thirty five minutes, that should give us five to finish up and then another half hour to get out of here," Henry told her. "And make sure to hide them, we don't want 'em found until it's too late, if at all."

"Gotcha," Mary said and headed off to begin setting bombs across the control center.

"Ditto for me," Cindy called from across the control room, hearing Henry's instructions. She had found a large bank of computers and was placing a brick behind them. No one would ever know it was back there until it was too late. After that one she went to the farthest point in the control room and placed a brick behind an electrical panel. Hundreds of two inch conduits led off it and went up into the darkness. Whatever it was, it sure looked important.

Taking another brick and timer, Henry crossed the room, wondering where to put the next one. There was a large switchboard, like a massive desk with gauges and lights flashing to his right. It reminded him of something out of a sci-fi movie or a console you would find at NASA. Moving up to it, he let his eyes play over the knobs and switches, finally stopping when one particular switch caught his eye.

**WINDOW**, was written in black marker over the switch. That had his curiosity peaked. Why would there be a switch for a window in an underground complex?

Deciding he had to see what it was, he reached out and pressed the button.

Immediately there was the whine of hydraulics and the sound of grinding came from in front of him, against the wall.

A massive steel panel was slowly rising, leaving behind a large glass window that looked to be three feet thick. The panel alone had to be a foot of solid steel.

As the metal panel rose, the glass began to reflect ambient light, filling the room with waves of what looked like shimmering, but was the water from outside diffusing the light.

"Will you look at that," Henry breathed as he gazed out into the underwater world of the lake.

The window was twenty feet by fifteen and there was now a panoramic view of the bottom of the lake. Plant life and fish could be seen and the entire picture looked like something from *20,000 Leagues Under The Sea*. Compared to the window Dr. Tandy had shown Henry and Jimmy, this one was huge, at least three times as large.

Jimmy, Mary, and Cindy all stopped what they were doing and walked up next to Henry.

"Wow, that is so awesome," Jimmy gasped as he stared out into the dark depths. There were spotlights on the wall of the complex, their beams pointing out into the water, otherwise it would have been nothing but blackness.

Henry gazed into the murky depths for another twenty seconds, then snapped himself out of it.

Remembering the C-4 in his hand, he had an idea. Climbing onto the console, he walked across it until he was standing in front of the window.

"What're you doing?" Mary asked.

"Making damn sure this place is destroyed," he said as he set the timer and pressed the molded brick into the left hand corner of the window, right where the glass went into the wall. "When this goes off, the entire lake is gonna come in here, so we need to pick up the pace."

"But, Henry," Sue said, "what about all the people inside this complex, like the women who are trapped here as prisoners."

Henry turned to her. "Mary said they're all vegetables now, so they're already dead, they just don't know it yet. As for the rest of 'em, they better learn how to swim or hold their breath under water, now get to work, we need to hurry."

Everyone got back to work, and four minutes and thirty seconds later they were ready to leave, the C-4 now hidden in nooks and crannies across the control room. The timers were set, and with time now ticking away, Henry rushed Jimmy, Cindy and Mary out of the control room and into the hallway, where Sue and Raven were waiting anxiously.

His eyes went to Jack's still body a few feet away and he felt his chest go tight with loss, but then he pushed it down. Jack was gone and they were still alive, that was what mattered now. When the complex went up, Jack would have a billion dollar coffin to rest in forever.

After consulting the map he'd taken from the armory, he knew where they had to go next. The elevator was about a fifteen minute walk to the south wing, yet more hallways and corridors between them, as they weaved their way through the maze of a complex.

There were three bricks left behind that hadn't been hidden, so he'd set the timers and left them on the floor, near where the six security men had been gunned down. Hopefully, if the scientists came inside to see what had happened, they would assume the three bricks of C-4 were all there was, and after defusing them, would stop searching for more.

He also left any searchers who were careless a few presents. He managed to rig a few clever boobies on shelves and in a couple of lockers, all of them now ready to be triggered if a security guard or scientist wasn't attentive. All the flash bangs had been used for the traps but one which he'd saved, but it was worth it.

Either way, the subterranean complex should go up in about twenty-six minutes. When the bombs detonated, the entire underwater structure should flood. And when the chain reaction of bombs continued, half the complex would go with it, the explosion so deep in the bottom of the lake that the force wouldn't have anywhere to go but down, thus protecting the village of Crescent Falls from damage.

There wasn't much time in the schedule for delays and Henry knew they were cutting it close. Now all they had to do was reach the elevator to the surface and escape while battling their way through the security patrols they were sure to encounter along the way.

With faces set in concern and determination, the six weary survivors began running through the hallways to freedom.

# Chapter 37

"Twenty minutes to go," Jimmy said as the group dashed down a side hallway, one that looked like all the others. But the thin black line near the ceiling was there, like a trail of breadcrumbs for the companions to follow.

Just after leaving the control room, they came upon their first encounter with a patrol. Four men dressed in the black garb yelled out and raised carbines to shoot Henry and the others.

It would have gone very wrong; the patrol keeping the companions pinned down and on the defense as the clock continued ticking, trapping them in the complex when the bombs detonated, if not for Mary producing the last flash bang from a munitions bag.

Henry had grinned widely when he saw the small canister and he'd taken a second to kiss her on the forehead proudly. Then he'd pulled the ring, waited a heartbeat so there would be no chance the guards could kick the canister out of the way, and tossed it around the corner.

There was a rattle when the can landed on the floor amidst the men and then a chorus of yells as one of them tried to get rid of it. One man managed to pick it up, but no sooner did he wrap his hands around it then it went off, directly in his face. Though relatively harmless, the flash bang only used to immobilize a target, it was still deadly when it went off two inches from a living face.

As the canister erupted, the guard's eyes caught the brunt of it and they were blown into his head from the force of the exploding canister. As white light and loud noise filled the corridor, the guard now screaming with his empty eye sockets dripping blood, Henry and the others charged into the smoke, firing their weapons repeatedly.

The guards were gunned down like carrion, and a second later the companions were stepping over the spasming corpses, careful not to splash in the spilt blood.

"Almost there," Henry said excitedly as he turned into one of the last hallways leading to the elevator, when Dr. Tandy appeared out of a side door armed with a wicked looking assault rifle, polished a deep black with a one inch muzzle and wide barrel. There was a telescopic sight on the end and a place to clip on an added grenade launcher. The long magazine jutting out the bottom was twice as big as a standard M-16 clip and the see-thru case showed steel-tipped hollow points that would shred the companion's bodies to hamburger in seconds.

Behind the frail looking doctor, was Stark, along with three of his best men, all wearing the standard dark sunglasses Henry had come to hate.

Though the powerful looking assault rifle looked comical in the small woman's hands, there was no doubt in the close confines of the corridor it would be lethal.

If the companions so much as raised a weapon, they would be dead before they hit the ground.

The small woman smiled at them, her red lips twisting to the side and her eyes distorted by her large glasses. When she spoke, her lilting voice showed no sign of anger.

"Drop your weapons, please, everyone, slowly, it would be a shame to get yet more blood on the walls for the cleaning crews to have to deal with."

Slowly as instructed, Henry and the others set their weapons down, carbines, M-16 and .38's, all laid neatly on the floor. Henry still had his Glock in his holster on his hip, and if the security guards or Dr. Tandy noticed, they said nothing, so he decided not to volunteer the handgun. Maybe that could be his ace in the hole. He also didn't see Jimmy's .38, only the carbine and pump action shotgun the younger man had been carrying, now on the floor.

"Excellent, now take a step back, please, all of you."

They did as they were told, moving back two feet from their weapons. Henry glanced at Jimmy and the younger man mouthed the words, "Tick tock."

Henry nodded subtly in reply, painfully aware their time was running out.

"My, my, Mr. Watson, you and your merry troop have been very busy today, haven't you. Even with our security cameras it has been quite a challenge keeping track of you. Manpower, you see. I've lost count as to how many of my people you've killed this day. You may have caused some small problem for Project Delta, but I assure you it is nothing we can't overcome." She glanced over Henry's shoulder to Mary and Cindy. "And you young ladies did a very bad thing. We found Dr. Stanley. Most unpleasant. He will be missed." She shook her head sadly.

"I don't give a shit what you think, lady," Henry said. He hesitated about trying to shoot the small woman and then the guards with his Glock, the short hairs standing up on the back of his neck as he stared at the wicked looking blaster she held and the guard's carbines.

"Bitch," Cindy muttered under her breath, but it was too soft for the diminutive scientist to hear.

Dr. Tandy noticed Henry's eyes on the automatic in her hands and she smiled slightly more.

"This is a modified Heckler and Koch G-12 caseless 50-shot automatic. The barrel had been changed out for a longer bore and the magazine has been doubled in size. The night scope has been enhanced to use even in the smallest amount of light and the frame is so light a child could hold it easily." She nodded to Henry. "You see, Mr. Watson, we do so much more here than just breeding, we have an entire weapons lab where we are creating better weapons to destroy the undead menace. Bombs, nerve gas and explosives, all ready once our army has been created." She could have been lecturing to a class of students at Harvard, her tone was so calm and controlled.

Henry gritted his teeth, still wondering if he should just go for it and pull his Glock, firing as many rounds as he could before the guards and Dr. Tandy could return fire, but he saw her finger was hovering over the trigger and he knew it would be a death sentence for them all.

"You're mad," Mary said as she stared at the small woman framed by the four security guards.

"On the contrary, my dear, my sanity is very much intact. I'm just doing what needs to be done to save this country. We are its saviors."

"Bullshit," Henry spit, "you're nothing but another crazed bitch with delusions of grandeur. We've come across your kind before."

"You are so very wrong, Mr. Watson. We are the last hope for a dying world. We are the ones who will bring light to the darkness, food to the hungry, we will be the ones to wipe the dead from the world and bring back the living to their former glory."

She was beginning to sound like a prophet quoting from the Book of Revelation, about how the world must be cleansed before it could be reborn. She went on for another two minutes until Jimmy slid up behind Henry, his .38 in his hand. Unlike Henry, he decided they were out of options and it was time to do something other than talk.

"Move your hand another inch and you will be so much dead meat, Mr. Cooper," the small woman said, the muzzle of the evil looking blaster now aimed directly at his chest. "Drop the weapon, now!"

With a sly grin, Jimmy dropped the gun, letting his boot catch it so it wouldn't be damaged. It was still at his feet though and Dr. Tandy didn't seem to mind.

"Hey, can't blame a guy for trying," Jimmy smirked.

"Indeed," Dr. Tandy replied. "Good, now the only reason you are all still breathing is because I need to know what you've been up to. We know you raided the armory and took all the plastic explosive, and timers. We already found the explosives you set in the control room, plus the traps you left behind. Three more of my men are in the infirmary thanks to you. But there were many other blocks of C-4 in that armory and I need to know what you did with them. What are you thinking? Don't you understand the good we are doing here?"

Henry took a step forward.

"Easy, Watson," Stark said, his carbine pivoting to aim directly at Henry's chest. Henry ignored him.

"Look lady, me and my friends travel around what's left of this country and there's been times we've had to do some killing. We've found that sometimes there's people that need it. I like to figure the world is just a little bit better after we move on, leaving whatever evil son-of-a-bitch is trying to take his piece of what's not his in the first place in the dirt. Nowadays there's no justice, only vengeance, but I say the two can be one in the same, and though we might not make that much of a difference, at least we're trying, we're not giving up out there without a fight. That's not what you're doing down here, what you're doing here is wrong."

"On the contrary, Mr. Watson," Dr. Tandy replied, "what we're doing down here is..."

There was a sudden gunshot in the hallway, and a neat hole appeared in Dr. Tandy's right eye, shattering the large lens over her eye as the bullet entered her head and the small caliber round bounced off the inside of her skull, mashing her brains to pulp in less than three seconds.

"That's for Carol, you sick bitch," Sue said from the side, where no one had noticed her draw the small .22 pistol Henry had given her earlier.

As the frail scientist slumped to the floor, her automatic rifle slipping from limp fingers, all hell broke loose in the tight confines of the corridor.

# Chapter 38

As Dr. Tandy slumped to the floor, Stark and his three men stood transfixed for a heartbeat, shocked to see their leader pitching forward with a hole in her head. Stark was the first to react, and with a throaty yell he aimed his carbine towards the companions.

But Henry was faster, and though Stark came close to shooting into the group, Henry's lightning fast draw saw his Glock out and his finger already double-tapping the trigger. He'd begun squeezing the trigger before the gun had barely cleared its holster. The first round ricocheted off the floor, but the second one found its target and Stark was slammed back as a 9mm slug found his heart.

Raven went into action just as fast. She still had the scalpel taken from the laser probe room and she flicked it underhanded, the stainless steel blade soaring across the space in an instance, the tip embedding itself in the left guard's throat.

Cindy was next, and with her hunting knife already in her hand, she tossed it at the right hand guard, the tip finding his shoulder, throwing off the man's aim. The carbine fired, but the bullet went into the ceiling, and by then Henry had shifted position and fired twice into the man's chest, pulping his heart and exploding his ribcage in a spray of blood and bone.

Jimmy had his Bowie knife palmed in his right hand, frustrated he'd been caught with his .38, and he threw the blade across the hall, the tip finding the throat of the next man, severing his carotid and killing him in seconds.

As the four guards slumped to the floor, joining their dead leader, Henry turned to the others, pointing the way to the elevator.

"Come on, there's no time to waste," he snapped as they grabbed their weapons and packs and took off at a ground eating pace. But as they moved out, Mary paused and ran back to the corpse of Dr. Tandy. Henry slowed and turned to see what was taking her so long. He saw the ID badge Mary had taken from the doctor's lab coat and he looked at her with a quizzical expression.

"What was that for?"

"A hunch," Mary said.

Then there was no more time for talk as the two chased after the others.

They almost made it to the elevator this time, but once more they encountered more security guards. The men dressed in black blocked their way, and after a vicious and brief firefight that ate up almost ten minutes, Henry's group managed to take them down, luckily not sustaining serious casualties on their end, though Cindy suffered a flesh wound to her left arm from a stray bullet.

As they jumped over the bodies, Cindy's sleeve was stained red, but she ignored the wound. She would live, and they needed to keep moving.

Upon reaching the elevator, Mary produced the ID badge, and sure enough, there was a card reader to the right of the elevator. After wiping blood from the back of the card, Mary swiped it through, all eyes staring at the two red and green lights.

After a second and nothing happened, Henry punched the closed elevator doors.

"Shit, this can't be happening!" He screamed.

"Wait a sec', Henry, let me try again," Mary said.

She rubbed the card against her shirt one more time to clean it and then slid it through the reader. Everyone was breathless while they waited for the light to flash and tell them if they would live or die.

But the green light flashed and the elevator door opened with a soft *ding, ding*.

"Get inside, now, there's no time to lose!" Henry yelled as he pushed Jimmy inside and pulled Sue with him.

The group of six piled into the elevator and Henry slapped the close button, the doors closing painfully slow.

Jimmy checked his watch. "It's gonna be close," he said nervously as the elevator began to rise. They could feel the slight sensation, but otherwise it was like they weren't moving. There were no numbers to say how long it would be to reach the surface, they just had to cross their fingers and pray.

The box of steel seemed to rise with agonizing slowness, but finally there was another *ding* and the doors opened. As the doors parted, the sound of a muffled explosion came to their ears and the elevator shook slightly.

Like they were escaping a burning room, the companions charged out of the elevator, just as the lights in the car blinked out. The door slammed closed and they heard the distinct sound of the elevator car falling back into the depths from which they had escaped.

Jimmy checked his watch one last time and frowned. "Damn timers were faulty. They went off a few minutes early."

"Can't trust anything these days," Henry grinned as they found themselves in a small building with no windows and a concrete floor. Under their feet, the floor began to shake, like seismic vibrations from an earthquake.

"Come on," Henry said. "Let's get out of here, who knows what's gonna happen when that place implodes or explodes or whatever the hell happens to a place that big that's underwater to boot."

Stepping out the single door of the small building, they found themselves on an island in the middle of the lake. Off in the distance, they could see the village of Crescent Falls. Overhead, the sky was a clear, unsullied azure and a bright sun sent rays to warm their faces. A hawk floated majestically between the closest mountains and a light dusting of snow could be seen topping the farthest peaks.

It was a beautiful day to be alive.

The entrance to the building wasn't guarded and there were half a dozen motor boats of different makes and sizes moored to a small dock.

"Look at the water," Cindy said. "It seems like its moving."

All eyes went to the smooth surface of the lake to see the once still surface now rippling with agitation. Tiny waves were rising and breaking against the docks, making sucking sounds as they retreated.

"Hey, wait a second, I can feel it now," Mary said as she cocked her head to the side.

"Must be the C-4, it's done its job then," Henry said.

Now that he was aware of it, he could feel a vibration through the souls of his boots. The complex was buried so deep in the lake there was no sound of its destruction, only an ominous vibration.

"We better get moving," Henry told them as they all headed for one of the boats. "Who's driving?"

"I will," Jimmy said as they all climbed inside, tossing their packs onto the bottom of the boat.

There were no keys for the boats as none were needed, just a button to push to start the motor. In less than half a minute the boat was moving away from the dock as the surface of the lake grew more unsteady with each passing second.

Henry spotted a steep goat trail on the land that was away and to the side of the village and he directed Jimmy to aim for it. By using the trail, it looked like they could bypass the village completely and then pick up the road they had used when first meeting the security patrol.

Upon hitting the shore, everyone climbed out just as a massive rumble shook the land.

"Holy shit, will you look at that," Jimmy gasped as the others watched with him.

The lake was beginning to bubble and seethe, almost like a giant pot of boiling water. On the island, smoke began to pour out of the open door of the small building, escaping the underground complex via the elevator shaft. Even from where they stood on land, it was possible to hear the distant explosions as the complex was ripped apart by both the bombs and the pressure of the water. It sounded like distant thunder, cracking on the horizon, and steam began to appear on the surface of the lake.

"Think that's it?" Mary asked.

"Has to be," Henry replied as the lake rolled and jumped like a living beast.

As they turned and began walking up the goat path, behind them there was a massive geyser of water shooting a hundred feet into the air, then it rained back down and the lake began to settle. All around the water's shore, animals ran from the disturbance, not understanding why their world was in turmoil, and birds fluttered from the trees, but in time all would become calm once more.

\*    \*    \*

It was near dusk when the companions reached the road that would bring them back to the hidden pickup truck taken from the raiders from what seemed like a month ago, but was in fact only a day. They walked in silence for a while, Jimmy and Cindy holding hands, while Sue walked so close to Henry she kept bumping into him. He didn't mind one bit.

"Hey, what was that with the gun? Thought you didn't want to use one," Henry said with a grin. "Glad you did though, you might have saved all of our asses back there."

Sue shrugged. "Like you said to me one time, Henry, adapt or die, I chose the former."

"Amen, honey, amen." He leaned to the side and kissed her on the cheek. "There's more of that later when we find a safe place to make camp."

She smiled. "Looking forward to it."

Jimmy let go of Cindy's hand and fell back to talk with Henry for a bit.

Raven and Cindy now began chatting, Cindy doing most of the talking. The road was quiet, only a flock of birds in the nearby trees flapping their wings at the disturbance of the passing group to break the silence. The rumbles of the destroyed complex had stopped hours ago and the world was back to what it had been, the animals coming out of hiding once more.

"I'm gonna miss the brat," Jimmy said to Henry. "He was a pain in the ass, but I liked him."

"Yeah, I know what you mean," Henry replied. "Still, he got a hell of a funeral pyre. Couldn't ask for a better memorial. Carol too."

"But he was so young," Sue said askance of Henry.

"Yeah, but when it's your time, and all that, Sue, we can't change fate," Henry told her sadly.

"Still, he was just a boy," Sue whispered.

"Yeah, I know," Henry replied softly.

They walked for another hour and finally came upon the hidden truck. Under branches and shrubs, it had gone undisturbed, and the companions loaded up into it, Jimmy taking the driving duties once more.

Cindy, now with a fresh bandage on her arm, sat next to Jimmy, her head on his shoulder. Raven sat next to her, the three filling the cab nicely.

Henry slapped the roof of the cab so Jimmy would get going, as he, Mary and Sue took up residence in the rear bed.

With a slight honk of the worn-out horn to say he was moving, Jimmy pulled onto the road and turned the pickup around to steer them back the way they'd come, the ties crunching on the stray gravel. Eventually, they passed the burned out wreck of the UPS truck and picked apart corpses of the raiders. By now all the soft tissue was gone from the remains and bones could be seen protruding from torn clothing as scavengers fed on the bloated bodies.

Sue was morose as she thought of Jack, and as the wind blew through their hair, refreshing after being trapped indoors, the sun slowly began its descent over the land.

Henry turned and wrapped his arms around her, consoling her.

"Look, Sue," he said. "We lost Jack and that sucks. More than I can tell you, but the rest of us are alive and that's what matters. If you hadn't noticed, the specter of death is always at our backs, just waiting for one of us to make a mistake. The trick is to outsmart the bastard and beat him at his own game."

"Is that what we did today, Henry? We outsmarted death?" Sue asked.

"Yup, damn straight. We won today, though we took a loss, but we still won. And we will next time, too."

Sue wiped a tear from her eye as she looked into Henry's piercing gaze. "But how do you know that for sure?"

"I don't, but I have faith. Faith in myself and faith in my friends. You, Jimmy and the others." He glanced at Mary who was now looking back at him, wanting to hear the conversation. "And Mary, too, of course, and sometimes that might not seem like enough, but if it's all we got then that's okay with me. We're a family, Sue, and families stick together."

"That's sweet, Henry, you old softy," Mary quipped, a wide smile creasing her lips.

"Hey, I'm a sweet guy, always have been."

Sue turned and squeezed his cheek like a grandmother to her grandson. "Yes, you are."

They drove on into the night and made camp when it was too dark to see where they were going. With each of them taking turns on watch through the night, it passed uneventfully, and with the sun touching the horizon, they headed out once more.

Soon they were near the town and the warehouse that the cannies had been in.

That was when Jimmy spotted his first zombie.

It was a decrepit piece of rot. Half its face was gone, only one eye still peering out of the mass of torn skin and blackened gristle. Maggots were squirming in the putrid flesh and its stomach was so bloated it looked like a simple pin would have it exploding like a large bubble. There was a massive hole in its chest, one you could look through, and field mice and cockroaches fed on the fetid meat of the wound, a buffet of immense proportions to their small bodies.

Jimmy swerved the pickup so he was aiming for the ghoul, and the front bumper struck the walking corpse head on, snapping its spine and then rolling over it, the tires snapping bones and crushing its pelvic bone.

"Ah, it's good to be back in the real world again," Jimmy yelled out the window so Henry could hear him. "Where the deaders only have one head and there's no hidden underwater complexes with crazy scientists in it. Just give me good old fashioned deaders and roamers and I'll be happy."

Laughing, Henry called back, "I'll see what I can do to grant you your wish." It was a beautiful morning; the blue sky filled with a warm sun that blazed the way to their next destination.

Henry didn't know where that would be or what they would find, but he had to hope it was better than where they'd been.

He knew there had to be someplace out there in the deadlands where the walking dead hadn't sullied, a place where the world was like it was before and he and his friends could live happily ever after.

All they had to do was find it.

## DEAD RECKONING: DAWNING OF THE DEAD
By Anthony Giangregorio
## THE DEAD HAVE RISEN!

In the dead city of Pittsburgh, two small enclaves struggle to survive, eking out an existence of hand to mouth.

But instead of working together, both groups battle for the last remaining fuel and supplies of a city filled with the living dead.

Six months after the initial outbreak, a lone helicopter arrives bearing two more survivors and a newborn baby. One enclave welcomes them, while the other schemes to steal their helicopter and escape the decaying city.

With no police, fire, or social services existing, the two will battle for dominance in the steel city of the walking dead. But when the dust settles, the question is: will the remaining humans be the winners, or the losers?

When the dead walk, the line between Heaven and Hell is so twisted and bent there is no line at all.

## RISE OF THE DEAD
by Anthony Giangregorio
## DEATH IS ONLY THE BEGINNING!

In less than forty-eight hours, more than half the globe was infected.

In another forty-eight, the rest would be enveloped.

The reason?

A science experiment gone horribly wrong which enabled the dead to walk, their flesh rotting on their bones even as they seek human prey.

Jeremy was an ordinary nineteen year old slacker. He partied too much and had done poorly in high school. After a night of drinking and drugs, he awoke to find the world a very different place from the one he'd left the night before.

The dead were walking and feeding on the living, and as Jeremy stepped out into a world gone mad, the dead spotting him alone and unarmed in the middle of the street, he had to wonder if he would live long enough to see his twentieth birthday.


# THE DARK
By Anthony Giangregorio


### DARKNESS FALLS

The darkness came without warning.

First New York, then the rest of United States, and then the world became enveloped in a perpetual night without end.

With no sunlight, eventually the planet will wither and die, bringing on a new Ice Age. But that isn't problem for the human race, for humanity will be dead long before that happens.

There is something in the dark, creatures only seen in nightmares, and they are on the prowl.

Evolution has changed and man is no longer the dominant species.

When we are children, we are told not to fear the dark, that what we believe to exist in the shadows is false.

Unfortunately, that is no longer true.

# DEADFREEZE
By Anthony Giangregorio

THIS IS WHAT HELL WOULD BE LIKE IF IT FROZE OVER!

When an experimental serum for hypothermia goes horribly wrong, a small research station in the middle of Antarctica becomes overrun with an army of the frozen dead.

Now a small group of survivors must battle the arctic weather and a horde of frozen zombies as they make their way across the frozen plains of Antarctica to a neighboring research station.

What they don't realize is that they are being hunted by an entity whose sole reason for existing is vengeance; and it will find them wherever they run.

# DEADFALL
By Anthony Giangregorio

It's Halloween in the small suburban town of Wakefield, Mass.

While parents take their children trick or treating and others throw costume parties, a swarm of meteorites enter the earth's atmosphere and crash to earth.

Inside are small parasitic worms, no larger than maggots.

The worms quickly infect the corpses at a local cemetery and so begins the rise of the undead.

The walking dead soon get the upper hand, with no one believing the truth.

That the dead now walk.

Will a small group of survivors live through the zombie apocalypse?

Or will they, too, succumb to the Deadfall.

SEE HOW IT ALL BEGAN IN THE NEW DOUBLE-SIZED EDITION!
# DEADWATER: EXPANDED EDITION
By Anthony Giangregorio

Through a series of tragic mishaps, a small town's water supply is contaminated with a deadly bacterium that transforms the town's population into flesh eating ghouls.

Without warning, Henry Watson finds himself thrown into a living hell where the living dead walk and want nothing more than to feed on the living.

Now Henry's trying to escape the undead town before he becomes the next victim.

With the military on one side, shooting civilians on sight, and a horde of bloodthirsty zombies on the other, Henry must try to battle his way to freedom. With a small group of survivors, including a beautiful secretary and a wise-cracking janitor to aid him, the ragtag group will do their best to stay alive and escape the city codenamed: **Deadwater.**

# REVOLUTION OF THE DEAD
By Anthony Giangregorio
## THE DEAD SHALL RISE AGAIN!

Five years ago, a deadly plague wiped out 97% of the world's population, America suffering tragically. Bodies were everywhere, far too many to bury or burn. But then, through a miracle of medical science, a way is found to reanimate the dead.

With the manpower of the United States depleted, and the remaining survivors not wanting to give up their internet and fast food restaurants, the undead are conscripted as slave labor.

Now they cut the grass, pick up the trash, and walk the dogs of the surviving humans.

But whether alive or dead, no race wants to be controlled, and sooner or later the dead will fight back, wanting the freedom they enjoyed in life.

The revolution has begun!

And when it's over, the dead will rule the land, and the remaining humans will become the slaves...or worse.

# DEAD END: A ZOMBIE NOVEL
By Anthony Giangregorio
## THE DEAD WALK!

Newspapers everywhere proclaim the dead have returned to feast on the living!

A small group of survivors hole up in a cellar, afraid to brave the masses of animated corpses, but when food runs out, they have no choice but to venture out into a world gone mad.

What they will discover, however, is that the fall of civilization has brought out the worst in their fellow man.

Cannibals, psychotic preachers and rapists are just some of the atrocities they must face.

In a world turned upside down, it is life that has hit a Dead End.

# DEAD RAGE
By Anthony Giangregorio

An unknown virus spreads across the globe, turning ordinary people into bloodthirsty, ravenous killers.

Only a small percentage of the population is immune and soon become prey to the infected.

Amongst the infected comes a man, stricken by the virus, yet still retaining his grasp on reality. His need to destroy the *normals* becomes an obsession and he raises an army of killers to seek out and kill all who aren't *changed* like himself. A few survivors gather together on the outskirts of Chicago and find themselves running for their lives as the specter of death looms over all.

The Dead Rage virus will find you, no matter where you hide.

Also available as The Rage Plague by Permuted Press.

## DEAD WORLDS: Undead Stories
## A Zombie Anthology
### Edited by Anthony Giangregorio

Welcome to the world of the dead, where the laws of nature have been twisted, reality changed.

The Dead Walk!

Filled with established and promising new authors for the next generation of corpses, this anthology will leave you gasping for air as you go from one terror-filled story to another.

Like the decomposing meat of a freshly rotting carcass, this book will leave you breathless.
Don't say we didn't warn you.

# DARK PLACES
### By Anthony Giangregorio

A cave-in inside the Boston subway unleashes something that should have stayed buried forever
Three boys sneak out to a haunted junkyard after dark and find more than they gambled on.
In a world where everyone over twelve has died from a mysterious illness, one young boy tries to carry on.
A mysterious man in black tries his hand at a game of chance at a local carnival, to interesting results.
God, Allah, and Buddha play a friendly game of poker with the fate of the Earth resting in the balance.
Ever have one of those days where everything that can go wrong, does? Well, so did Byron, and no one should have a day like this!
Thad had an imaginary friend named Charlie when he was a child. Charlie would make him do bad things. Now Thad is all grown up and guess who's coming for a visit?
These and other short stories, all filled with frozen moments of dread and wonder, will keep you captivated long into the night.
Just be sure to watch out when you turn off the light!

# DEAD MOURNING: A Zombie Horror Story
By Anthony Giangregorio

Carl Jenkins was having a run of bad luck. Fresh out of jail, his probation tenuous, he'd lost every job he'd taken since being released. So now was his last chance, only one more job to prevent him from going back to prison. Assigned to work in a funeral home, he accidentally loses a shipment of embalming fluid. With nothing to lose, he substitutes it with a batch of chemicals from a nearby factory.

The results don't go as planned, though. While his screw-up goes unnoticed, his machinations revive the cadavers in the funeral home, unleashing an evil on the world that it has not seen before.

Not wanting to become a snack for the rampaging dead, he flees the city, joining up with other survivors. An old, dilapidated zoo becomes their haven, while the dead wait outside the walls, hungry and patient.

But Carl is optimistic, after all, he's still alive, right? Perhaps his luck has changed and help will arrive to save them all?

Unfortunately, unknown to him and the other survivors, a serial killer has fallen into their group, trapped inside the zoo with them.

With the undead army clamoring outside the walls and a murderer within, it'll be a miracle if any of them live to see the next sunrise.

On second thought, maybe Carl would've been better off if he'd just gone back to jail.

# THE MONSTER UNDER THE BED
By Anthony Giangregorio

Rupert was just one of many monsters that inhabit the human world, scaring children before bed. Only Rupert wanted to play with the children he was forced to scare.

When Rupert meets Timmy, an instant friendship is born. Running away from his abusive step-father, Timmy leaves home, embarking on a journey that leads him to New York City.

On his way, Timmy will realize that the true monsters are other adults who are just waiting to take advantage of a small boy, all alone in the big city.

Can Rupert save him?

Or will Timmy just become another statistic.

# SOULEATER
By Anthony Giangregorio

Twenty years ago, Jason Lawson witnessed the brutal death of his father by something only seen in nightmares, something so horrible he'd blocked it from his mind.

Now twenty years later the creature is back, this time for his son.

Jason won't let that happen.

He'll travel to the demon's world, struggling every second to rescue his son from its clutches.

But what he doesn't know is that the portal will only be open for a finite time and if he doesn't return with his son before it closes, then he'll be trapped in the demon's dimension forever.

# LIVING DEAD PRESS

Where the Dead Walk

www.livingdeadpress.com

Lightning Source UK Ltd.
Milton Keynes UK
02 March 2010

150835UK00001B/220/P